CAPTAIN JUSTICE

CAPTAIN
JUSTICE

Anthony Forrest

📖 HILL AND WANG · NEW YORK
A division of Farrar, Straus and Giroux

Library of Congress Cataloging in Publication Data
Forrest, Anthony.
Captain Justice.
1. Napoleon I, Emperor of the French, 1769–1821—
Proposed invasion of England, 1793–1805—Fiction.
I. Title.
PR6056.0683C3   1981   823′.914   81-2808
AACR2

For Sebastian

CAPTAIN JUSTICE

PROLOGUE

IN THE DARKNESS there was no sound except the steady slap of the water against the dinghy. Justice shivered. Unless there was a wind soon, to carry him towards the line of undulating sand-dunes he could just see in the light of a low quarter-moon, it would mean another miserable night in the open, without a boat-cloak or even a shred of sail-cloth to cover him.

At best, he would be cold and hungry. There was the chance he would be carried out to sea again, with little hope of rescue unless a coasting smack or smuggler's lugger came up on him out of the night. A patrolling frigate would sail past or smash the dinghy to pieces before the lookouts could see him.

He reached for the piece of floorboard which he had been using as a paddle. It was almost useless, so clumsy to handle that he could scarcely keep the bow of the dinghy headed to-wards the shore. In any case, he was getting weaker; since dusk, he had failed to make any headway against the ebbing tide. As he looked forward, the white face of his companion stared back at him, and he felt a whim of ghoulish humour.

"Your turn to paddle, Mister Mate. It's time you earned your keep."

There was no answer. The man had been dead for three days.

Justice looked past the corpse's clown-face to the shoreline, grey above the white strip where the waves rolled slowly up the sand. Since early morning, when a fair wind from the west had brought him near to France before it dropped and left him drifting about three miles offshore, he had been able to pick out landmarks quite easily. There was the spire of the church at Camiers. The 24-pounder battery which guarded the north side of the Canche estuary must lie just out of sight behind the high crest of the dunes at the Pointe de Lornel. Its site was marked on the Admiralty charts he had been shown in London; and there, behind it, over a mile inland, would be the road from Etaples to Boulogne, running at the foot of the chalk hills which had glowed so warmly in the sunset. To the south of the wide estuary was the L'Anse à l'Avoine, with its great guns set in the dunes to protect the boats at Etaples, about three miles up the river, where the main road to Paris crossed the Canche; as he came in, he had caught a glimpse of their masts rising out of their safe anchorage.

Since he could see so much, it seemed astonishing that no one had spotted him. A small cavalry patrol had swept along the beach just before the evening light faded, throwing up golden spray as the horses cantered, splashing through the shallows. But the dinghy lay so low in the water, with the sun behind it, that it must have seemed no more than the curl of a wave beyond the sand-bars. And he had watched men working on the boats in the estuary, repairing rigging and hammering at the sides of small craft left stranded at crazy angles as the wide and shallow estuary had emptied. But no one caught sight of him, and nothing had come out of the narrow winding channel that afternoon. Now it was too late, for it was dark, and only a few lights glimmered across the leaden water. It all seemed so peaceful, so normal.

Yet this was France, in July 1804; the Iron Coast of France, fortified with heavy batteries and defended by the crack divisions which Napoleon had assembled for the invasion of England. How could a man land unobserved, make his way through the network of sentries, watch-towers, and army camps which lay across the coastal dunes and woodlands? The smugglers seemed to manage it, and other men tried it. But many of them had merely disappeared, or figured in the list of executions in the *Moniteur*. He shivered. Those others had at least landed with a hope of evading capture. His orders were different . . .

Aware that he was making no headway, he threw the piece of floorboard into the bottom of the boat. He could do nothing to stop it swinging round like a bit of flotsam, and his palms were so raw that he let them hang over the sides to feel the clean sting of the water. He looked again at the shore, judging the distance and wondering if he should swim for it, saving himself but losing the carefully prepared proof that he was a castaway.

It was past low water, and the strong tide that had to fill the marshy estuary up to Etaples was beginning to run—it ran fast, as he knew, for he had often sailed this channel as a boy, fishing down the Canche from Montreuil in quiet summer days before the revolution had burned through France. There, up the Canche, at Montreuil, was the other lovely stream they called the Course, tumbling through its wooded valley from one mill-race to the next; and there again, above the village of Recques, was Valcourt, the graceful old house in which his mother had grown up, in which he had spent boyhood holidays, in which his sister had lived after she married his cousin Luc—Philippe Luc de Valcourt, about whom nothing had been heard since he went back to France two years before and declared for Bonaparte.

It was an odd way to be coming home, John Valcourt Justice thought, for he had always felt that way about the place which gave him his middle name. A second home—the source of the tangled inheritance that made him think like an Englishman and feel like a Frenchman.

He was coming back to France, and it was ironic that his best hope of safety lay in being openly and obviously English. A spy who wanted to be caught.

At the time, when Hatherley had suggested it in the security of a Whitehall office, this back-to-front scheme had sounded clever—clever enough, at any rate, to make him willing to try it. A mile or so off the coast of France, it was far less convincing. Like the notion of bringing Albert, as he had christened the dead man, who lolled awkwardly at the other end of the dinghy.

At first, he had thought it an ingenious idea to carry over the corpse of a smuggler, whistled up out of the marshland night by his servant, the resourceful Fred Scorcher. A body, Scorcher said, would add strongly to the story that Justice would tell—a story learnt so thoroughly that Justice was coming to feel that it had really happened. A sudden squall in the wake of the north-easterly that had recently ripped down the Straits, a smack dismasted on a fishing trip, three men drowned, the dying Albert helped into the dinghy, which, without oars or a stitch of sail, had been slowly carried towards France. But now he was wondering why any Frenchman should believe him. He was tired, thirsty, hungry—and if he was carried out to sea, he would be dead within a day or so.

There was a lift of wind, rippling the water and bringing the sweet smell of death from Albert's body. Within a few minutes, it freshened, driving the dinghy along the face of the dunes and towards the place where a long sand-bar pressed the channel close to the north shore of the estuary.

Less than a hundred yards away, the thin moonlight showed two dark shapes silhouetted against the beach, and Justice instinctively dropped to the floorboards before he remembered that it was his purpose to be seen. Upright again, he saw that the shadows were simply buoys left almost grounded at the bottom of the tide.

He was soon close enough to the shore to see the dark line of grass that ran along the top of the dunes and to hear the water slapping on the sand. He could tell that the beach sloped so gradually that even on the rising tide he was going to find it hard to pull the dinghy high enough to be sure it was not carried out on the ebb.

The dinghy touched, brushed over the sand, came free, swung broadside, and stopped. As he stepped out, he thought he was on a quicksand, for the sand was over his ankle before he could get a footing. He pulled at the dinghy. It was stuck. He tugged again. No good. He was not able to drag the dinghy and its grisly passenger up the long beach over the yielding sand.

Then he was going to have to carry Albert.

He came up to the corpse from the side and put his arms round its stocky shape. But he could neither lift nor twist the body out of the place where it had become wedged as the stiffness of death wore off.

He rolled the dinghy backwards and forwards to loosen the corpse, then crudely tipped Albert out. Sweating and panting, despite the freshness of the night, he had dragged the body some way up the beach before he looked back. The dinghy had been lifted by the incoming tide and was beginning to drift away. He left Albert, splashed after the boat, and pushed it through the lapping water to the point where he had dropped the body. On such a wide beach, where the water could still run in for another hundred yards or so, he was attempting the impossible. If he spent his energies dragging Albert up to the dunes, he would lose the boat, for it lacked any kind of anchor. But if he pushed and pulled the dinghy out of reach of the waves, Albert would be left in the water.

It was also getting more difficult to see, as the moon set behind the dunes on the south side of the Canche. There was little chance now of his being noticed. Certainly not before dawn—and it would take the better part of the short summer night to work Albert and the dinghy up the beach a few yards at a time, as the rising water helped him.

Dragging first one, then the other, and shaking with weariness, he finally got them both up to the soft light sand and the irregular line of crisp dry seaweed which told him that he was at last beyond the reach of the tide. Several times he thought of calling for help, and changed his mind. There was too much risk of being shot or cut down by a sabre in the dark before he could explain himself.

He guessed it was well past midnight when he at last threw himself on the sand in the lee of the dinghy, leaving Albert laid out about a dozen yards away and downwind. Sleep was the safest thing. Every muscle ached as if it had never known a bed, and he would need all his wits about him next day. And sleep would make his story more plausible. No one had ever heard of a spy who went straight to sleep on arrival.

Justice had scarcely time to smile at that sardonic yet comforting thought before he was asleep; and it was the first thing that came into his mind when he woke, cold and stiff, with the dawn pale in the sky.

He could just make out a large figure bending over Albert's body. And then he heard the man grunt. *"Mort,"* he said, and turned the corpse over with his foot before he came on towards Justice.

7

🕮 1 🕮

TEN DAYS BEFORE, John Justice had been playing cricket on the green at Appledore, where the crack of bat on ball echoed from the wall of the church like a pistol shot, scattering the doves that strutted round the edge of the cut grass.

Sitting on a bench under a plum tree, the scorer notched the runs with a horn-handled sailor's knife that cut deep into the edge of a willow-stick. "That makes it forty," he announced with slow satisfaction to no one in particular and to the world in general, which on this warm afternoon in July consisted of the Men of Appledore who were not yet at bat and those of their supporters not at the beer tent.

"Captain's not giving you much time for a drop, then, Fred." The voice came from back in the long grass, in the deep shade, and several men chuckled. Fred Scorcher's quart of ale had become a byword that summer of 1804, ever since he had come back from the war with a slow-healing wound in his leg and taken to scoring because he could no longer run. When the play was slow, he took short and frequent swigs at the pot, but when the runs flowed easily, the strong ale, which had the bitter taste of the local hops, was left untasted.

A shortish, leathery man with a shock of grey-flecked curly hair and bright eyes that gave him the look of an impish schoolboy, Fred Scorcher had spent his life on the sea or at its edges, for he was a Marsh Man; not a Man of Kent, nor a Kentish Man, but a true Man of the Marsh, who could make his living as a sheepherder if he had to, but would far rather make it as a sailor, a fisherman, or by the hard ways of the smugglers—the real rulers, once darkness fell, of that tract of soggy pasture and lonely coastline which so conveniently faced out across the Channel to France. Even before Scorcher was wounded and left with a limp that would never be right, he had a stiff but rolling gait.

9

One Marsh Man could recognise another, people said, simply by the cut of his shoulders in a sea mist or the way he walked up a beach on a moonless night with a brandy keg on his shoulder. They were fathers and sons, cousins and uncles, and they were all men of fierce loyalties, bred in wind-cut villages on the fringe of the sand and the shingle; but Scorcher had a special loyalty to the man at the wicket. He had been the Captain's man long before Justice had pulled him off a stone jetty in Brittany, where he lay with his thigh ripped by a cutlass, and got him away half-drowned in a pitching longboat, but now there was no man for him but the Captain.

"Two more." Scorcher notched the runs with satisfaction. The Men of Appledore had been set to make ninety-four by the Men of Rye, and they looked like getting them easily by the time the shadow on the sundial which served Appledore church as a clock crept round to five. Unless . . . Fred Scorcher cocked a seaman's eye at the fluffy white clouds which were building up into thunderheads above the hills beyond the marshland.

As his weather-eye dropped back to the pitch, he saw a movement by the railed triangle next to the church which served as the village pound. The stranger tying his horse to the rail was a travel-dusty man, whose black coat and breeches had a tired but gentlemanly look about them. Always quick to make up his mind, Scorcher summed up the stranger as a lawyer's clerk. To him the type spelled trouble, for the people of the Marsh had a poor opinion of anyone who earned a living from the assize courts.

The Rye bowler got through the four balls of another over before the newcomer made his way round the green to the group scattered about the scorer's bench. Scorcher heard him as he came up, for he was whistling a hymn tune through his teeth as if it were a sleepwalker's march, while he slapped his hand on his leather wallet to keep time with himself. Close by, Scorcher decided as he turned to say good-day, he looked more like a wandering preacher than a clerk. As the thought stirred in his mind, the man's reply to his greeting came in a genteel whine which clinched the matter.

"I mark you," Scorcher said in a sudden reply, surprising himself by this feat of memory. "Off Brest. Christmas, years back. You come off Lord Gambier's 74 an' guv us all a paper for the good of our souls." He notched another run, and glanced at his cronies. "Warn't too popular," he said, courting a laugh. "The people reckoned that a spoonful o' figgy pudding all round were better for Christmas, nor a paper they couldn't read, like."

Scorcher got the laugh he was looking for, but the man was not to be drawn.

"My name is Eli Dunning," he said portentously, and without being asked, as Scorcher looked back at the pitch where Justice had just sent the ball skimming to startle the doves. "I have a message," he added dolefully, as if he brought news of Judgement Day itself and was not to be put off by lesser matters.

Dunning opened his wallet, took out a heavily-sealed letter, turned it to inspect both address and seal, cocked a sceptical eyebrow at Scorcher, and began to put the letter back in his wallet.

Scorcher laid down his whittling knife and held out his hand.

"It is for a Mr Justice." Now Dunning leaned forward and spoke in a confidential tone. "They told me at the house to find him here."

"Not here but there." Scorcher nodded out across the grass, and wondered what was in the paper. Nothing official, he guessed, and felt disappointed. A messenger from the Admiralty would have something neat and urgent about him.

Yet it was clear to Scorcher that the messenger could not be a bill-server either. He was a shade more respectable than that, and anyway, the Captain seldom wagered. Nor had he ever been one to run debts he couldn't pay. Scorcher pointed his tally-stick at the batsman who was standing at the nearer wicket, looking anxiously at the leaden sky over the Marsh, the slanting columns of rain already visible to seaward. "That's your man, mister," he said. Sandy-haired, trim, Justice still had the fresh stance of a youth at that distance, and Scorcher decided that Dunning was wondering whether he was looking at the son when he had been sent to find the father.

"There'll be more prayers than prize-money today," Scorcher said, as a cloud covered the sun and heavy drops began to plop on the sheltering leaves.

Five minutes, eight runs. Ten minutes, four more. The Rye total was within reach. Then, with a sudden surge, the storm broke, sending the players scattering to avoid a drenching.

"Captain, sir!" Scorcher called to Justice, running past him towards the beer tent. Dunning got up grudgingly, as if it ill-befitted a man of sober principle to be teased, delayed, and soaked, all for a game of cricket.

As Justice came across, Dunning could take stock of the man for whom he had ridden all day from London. Though Justice seemed slight enough at a distance, the first impression gave way to a sense of hidden strength, for the muscles showed through the pale blue shirt which now clung wetly to his body; and the rain which darkened his fair hair and streaked across his leanly handsome face was forming glistening pearls of water on his whiskered cheeks and drawing attention to his deepset eyes. At twenty-eight, they were already etched with crow's-feet, and for all their glint of humour they had a distant quality about them.

Fred Scorcher simply inclined his head towards Dunning and stood back. Even if Justice was on half-pay and lacking a ship, Fred knew his place. Whatever close talk there might be between master and man at Hook Manor, when there was no one by, a captain's servant could make a quarter-deck out of a patch of grass when he had to. Dunning seemed about to say something, then he too remained silent and handed over the letter with a jerky little bow.

Justice broke the seals. The raindrops falling from his face blurred some of the ink-written words, and with a gesture born of filthy nights at sea he gave the letter to Scorcher while he reached to use his silk stock as a towel. The stock, Dunning noticed, was no mere touch of fashion. It served to cover a zigzag scar that ran perilously near the throat.

Justice caught Dunning's eye and carefully buttoned his shirt to the neck before he gave Scorcher the wet stock and took back the letter. In those moments Scorcher had tried to glimpse the contents, but he was a slow reader at best, and as he covered the page with his hand to protect it from the rain, he had only made out a printed heading and a few scrawled lines below it. Reluctantly, he passed the paper back. He had served Justice long enough, at sea and on shore, to know his master's business almost as well as his master knew it himself; there was not much room for secrecy in the cramped quarters of a man-of-war, and back here in Appledore—well, in Fred Scorcher's opinion, three generations at Hook Manor had almost made the Justices into Marsh people, for all that they were gentry.

After Justice had read the letter a second time, as if it might contain some meaning that had escaped him, he turned to Dunning. "Tell Mr . . ." Justice hesitated. "Tell your employer that I shall be pleased to wait upon him at noon on Monday." He paused. "And that—that I have no other pressing engagements."

"Begging pardon, Captain," Fred began as Dunning gave another of his jerky bows, so grudging that he seemed to be rusty, and walked away to his horse without a word. "He was near with me when I asked him, but I'm sure I marked that man before . . ."

"No," Justice said.

"When I was on *Hesperus* . . ."

"No." This time there was an edge to Justice's voice.

". . . or maybe when we was on *Hind,* Captain Cochrane . . ."

"No." Justice cut in sharply, and then eased the denial into a smile. "No, you notched a wrong score there, Fred."

That quick change of mood was one of the things about Justice that Scorcher always found bewildering. "One minute stiff as a boarding-pike," he had often said over a pot at the Woolpack, "and then he goes at a joke or a bottle like the next man." It all came, Scorcher thought, from being half-a-French, although that was not something said before mess-mates.

"If I'm to be in London by Monday noon," Justice said cheerfully, as he tossed over the shapely bat that Scorcher himself had honed from a carefully chosen piece of Marsh willow, "then we'll best be getting to the house."

He looked straight at Scorcher, who had glanced at him expectantly. "No," he said, guessing the unspoken question. "I go alone." Scorcher bit back his words. He would know soon enough what the dusty man from London had wanted. Tucking bat and tally-sticks under his arm like a bundle of captured swords, he stumped off behind Justice along the track which led past the church towards the rise of ground where the dull red brick of Hook Manor gleamed through the trees.

JOHN JUSTICE SAT, a brandy by his elbow, by the fireside, where a few logs of applewood burnt sweetly, for the evenings had been very chilly for July. From the kitchen, beyond the fireplace, there drifted the hum of conversation between the cook and Mrs Roundly.

High above him in the roof he could hear the sound of swallows. It was still only early evening, and they had begun to sing again as the storm passed over. Hook Manor was a hall-house, its roof a great vault of high-pitched beams, meeting with the precision of rigging at the apex. Perhaps it had been the shipshape feel of the place that had drawn his grandfather to it, Justice thought. The great beams had come from old ships' timbers. Indeed, the bastion of land where the house stood had been, in ancient times, the sea coast. For in those days the Romney Marsh itself had lain beneath the sea. A line drawn from New Romney to Appledore would once have been the tip of England.

Justice poured himself another modest measure from the decanter—which was always kept half-full, neither more nor less, by Scorcher. Discreetly, Justice never asked where the rare, almost unobtainable French spirit came from.

Then he picked up the letter again, and again tried to guess what lay behind it.

THE BOARD OF BEACONS, BELLS, BUOYS
&
MERCANTILE MESSENGERS

Friday 13th July 1804   Richmond Terrace
My dear Mr Justice
    Pray could you favour me with a call about noon on Monday on a matter of importance to the Board? I presume that will be sufficient notice to set your affairs in order.

Most faithfully your servant
George Lilly
Chairman and Commissioner

The letter was, he thought, characteristically brief and to the point—and, equally characteristically, told him nothing. George Lilly was the kind of man to whom everybody told things, and who in turn told nothing to anybody.

14

And the Board of Beacons, Bells, Buoys & Mercantile Messengers? Probably, Justice decided, one of those lesser bodies which spun in orbit round the all-powerful Board of Admiralty. An organisation providing sinecures for the well-placed, and generally getting in the way of honest sailors.

Yet an affair of that kind would not be Lilly's mark: his old acquaintance was too formidable a man to be concerned with trifles. As Member of Parliament for Launceston, Lilly had achieved a reputation as a debater and a master of the business of the House of Commons. Nowadays he sat on the Board of Admiralty, no less: his influence extended beyond Whitehall to the Royal Exchange in the City, where the costs and profits of war were giving power to a new breed of bankers and merchants. He was said to be welcome at Windsor when the King was in his right mind. More than any man in England, it was whispered, he had the ear of Pitt. Recently, during the brief, uncertain Peace of Amiens, Pitt had gone to the political wilderness, and Lilly with him. Now England was again at war with France, and Pitt was back in the saddle.

And Lilly with him: or so it was safe to guess. For there was no doubt that a nod from Lilly could make or mar a man's career in a service where promotion depended as much on the interest a man could muster in high places as on his merit as an officer or his bravery in battle.

Interest was something he had good reason to appreciate, Justice thought, as he watched the dry apple-logs spit against the iron fire-back. In return for an old kindness from Justice's grandfather, when Lilly was making his own start from humble beginnings, the great man had twice come forward as his patron.

The first time was in the dreadful summer of '97, when Justice was still a lieutenant, and fair-minded enough to speak out at a court-martial against the vile conditions which had driven the seamen at Spithead and the Nore to mutiny. He said no more than others said—no more than the hard truths that Admiral Jervis had told the Admiralty after he had won his famous victory at St Vincent with disaffected crews and rotten-bottomed ships; but Justice said it in public, and with the Thames left undefended when the mutineers took control of the fleet, it was a time of harsh judgements and broken careers. Thanks only to Lilly, who had taken his part, he had been posted off to the West Indies. Within the year, luck had so far run his way that he had earned enough prize-money to keep him comfortable for life—and, more to the point for an ambitious officer, been made post-captain before he was twenty-five.

And then, with his foot on the ladder of the captain's list that would lead to an admiral's flag if he lived long enough, Justice was in trouble again, and a different kind of mutiny was the cause.

At Antigua in 1798 he had been touched by the scandal caused by Thomas Pitt, the second Lord Camelford, who was heir to the fortune that "Diamond Pitt" had made in the East India trade. Camelford quarrelled with an officer on a neighbouring frigate and shot him dead for disobeying an order, and though a court-martial had found for Camelford, many people said the wild young lord was simply a murderer, acquitted because he was wealthy and kin to two prime ministers. Justice had served with Camelford, and knew that his uncontrollable temper verged on insanity, but he thought Camelford was in the right and that for once the gossips did him wrong. An argument with a Whiggish superior, some unwise words, and Justice found himself on his way home to England. His commanding admiral evidently preferred officers who kept such opinions to themselves. When Justice reached London, moreover, it was clear that my Lords of Admiralty had little use for a young officer with a reputation for awkwardness. With Pitt himself out of office, and no one wanting to support a man who had championed the prime minister's rake-hell cousin, the best that Lilly could do was to get Justice command of a sloop working out of Jersey on the unpopular business of running arms and supplies across to the royalist rebels in Brittany.

The memories of that time came back to Justice as he sat by the fire: muffled oars by night, the processions of swarthy, silent men moving the small barrels of powder across the heather. And one memory that was with him for life, the savage pike-cut at his throat that had almost killed him.

There had followed weeks of pain and fever in Jersey, convalescence at Hook, and silence at the Admiralty. He had written to their Lordships asking for a command. When he was better, he had gone up to London and hung about the drab waiting-room overlooking Horse Guards Parade, where there was always a cluster of disconsolate half-pay officers hoping for someone to notice them. He had spoken to friends, sent messages to influential acquaintances. But no one wanted his services, and he felt his pride ebb as the war went on without him.

But he still had enough pride left to know that he could not ask Lilly to help him for a third time. He had thought of it, more than once. He had even written two letters, and torn them up, reaching for the brandy-glass in disgust at a system that let good men rot on the beach while toadies walked the quarter-deck of so many of the King's ships.

And now, miraculously, Lilly had sent for him. As he looked at the letter for the tenth time, wondering what the Board of Beacons, Bells, Buoys & Mercantile Messengers might be, and feeling cheerful for the first time in weeks, he knew that he would do whatever Lilly wanted. Without question. Better to command a miserable little despatch cutter in a North Sea winter than to mope uselessly at his own fireside.

AFTER SUPPER he came back and wrote letters at the rosewood desk which had been part of his French mother's dowry. "Set your affairs in order," Lilly had said. Well, that was soon done. Lilly knew well enough that a sailor was like a snail, carrying his home, or maybe his troubles, on his back.

He wrote two letters. The first was to old Strang, the manager at Marsh's bank in Mayfair, giving instructions for monthly payments to Mrs Roundly so that she had ready money to settle with the tradesmen, to pay the cook, the housemaid, the gardener, and the groom—to see, in short, that life at Hook Manor went on with the steady rhythm of the country.

And this time, as Justice told Strang in his letter, there would have to be provision for Fred Scorcher, who had become a regular part of the household since they had both come back wounded from Brittany—and had lately taken to calling himself "the Captain's *wally de chamb*." The French phrase was a joke between them, at the expense of a foppish frigate captain who had given himself and his servant fancier airs than suited the rough life of a man-of-war, for no one could be less like a valet than Scorcher. It was a comfort to Justice, with Bonaparte's army camped on cliffs so close that you could see them across the Channel like a dark line, to know that the people at Hook could count on Scorcher.

The second letter was to Bristow Burgery, the secretary of the Tenterden Thespians, who so loved theatricals that for years he had been the life and soul of the town's little company of amateurs and to whose encouragement Justice owed his own passion for the theatre. Now he had to disappoint him. For the production of *The Recruiting Officer,* which Burgery had planned for the full-moon nights of August, Justice wrote, the company would have to enlist someone else in the title role of Farquhar's comedy. In these days, he knew Burgery would understand if he offered no excuse beyond urgent business.

Upstairs, he could hear Mrs Roundly packing his box. The familiar noise brought back memories of going back to school, with Mrs Roundly at the door in her white apron to wave him off, after she had tucked a packet of her cakes into the back of the carrier's cart.

Mrs Roundly had meant a great deal to him in the lonely years of boyhood. He had been nine when his father died of a fever, caught at Cape Castle on the way to India. His mother's death, four years later, had touched him more deeply; he had watched her pine away, doing her best to hide the grief that killed her, and he had tried—all so inadequately, for what could a boy of twelve do?—to take the places left vacant by a dead father and a brother serving in the navy. And when he was left alone it had been the comfortable, kindly housekeeper who had been the light of home, always there to say a goodbye or a welcome. Earlier today, when he and Scorcher had come back from the cricket field drenched to the skin, Mrs Roundly had scolded them both as if they were errant schoolboys, not grown sailors.

"There you are, Master John," she would say when the box was ready. "You just take care of yourself, now." The words had been the same for what seemed like a lifetime of farewells. To Mrs Roundly he had always been "Master John," but as he rose up through the ranks, she had been a Tartar with anyone who failed to give him his due. To everyone in Appledore he had to be "the young Captain," as his grandfather, whom Mrs Roundly had served as a girl when he first bought Hook with an unexpected flush of prize-money, was always "the old Captain." It was a matter of pride with her that everything at Hook was kept "just as the old Captain would have it."

Justice rose and went to the window, looking at the orchard, olive-grey in the light of the early moon. What would the old Captain have thought now, he wondered, when the house might soon be in the line of battle, with French grenadiers coming up the slope from the Marsh and skirmishing through the apple trees the old man had planted in his last summer? 1781. That was the year his father had come back from America, part of the army Cornwallis surrendered at Yorktown. Justice had been five. It was the only time he could remember the three generations being together, and he could still recall the excitement while the labourers dug the holes and set up the young trees.

He turned back to the fireside and poured another brandy. Well, it would not be the first time that the old house had seen violence. People in the village said that once, long ago, Appledore had been half-burned by French pirates coming from the sea, and that when the fighting was over, the surviving Frenchmen had been hanged on the gibbet that once stood beside the Manor. He could just remember his father showing him initials cut into a beam in one of the attics, saying they had been scratched by the condemned men.

Meanwhile, there was the question of Fred Scorcher. The picture of dejection since he had learnt the messenger was not from the Admiralty, Fred had stumped about the house glumly, muttering dark phrases. Several times during the evening he had peered in, ostensibly to see if there was anything the Captain needed. "Do 'ee expect to be gone long?" he enquired absently, poking up the fire unnecessarily for the fourth time.

"It may be."

Scorcher tried again. "Is it to be a command, then?"

"If I knew, I daresay I shouldn't tell. But I don't know, Fred. A summons to present myself in London, that's all. And that, mind you, goes no further. I want no whispering of my business round the taverns of Rye."

Scorcher looked pained. "You ought to know a secret's safer with me than at forty fathoms. Anyway, I har'nt been down Mermaid Street these six weeks."

But he knew how Fred felt. The next day, when he waited

for the hour to come round when he would need to leave for the coach, he deliberately spent time with him, looking at jobs that might be done about the place while he was gone—improvements to the apple store, stakes for a new fence, shingles for the barn.

Through the summer afternoon they talked gently of days past, of Scorcher's mysterious brothers, who came and went about the Marsh like shadows, and of the long line of Justice forebears stretching to the days when they had been ferrymen at Appleford on the Thames. Justice's own grandfather had been taken by the similarity of names when he had been looking for a house himself, and had settled at Appledore, convenient for the ships in the Downs off Dover. Hammering stakes for the fence, Justice had spoken too, though hesitantly, of the subject he seldom mentioned—his mother's family in France, and the house at Valcourt from which he took his middle name, and where he had spent his holidays as a boy, when there was no war, and the summer days were long with fishing and swimming, and learning to ride.

Then it was time to go, with the sun tipping longer shadows across the sheep-cropped grass. The groom had harnessed the gig, but Justice had decided to drive himself over to the Woolpack. He could hear in the distance the peal of Tenterden church-bells, announcing evening service. He would be in the town before the bells stopped, and, if the coach left on time, be gone before the vicar finished his sermon.

He waved to Mrs Roundly standing by the tiled porch. Speaking briskly, for he disliked long partings, he went over the arrangements for Scorcher to collect the gig next day. Then he looked at the long low house for the last time.

"Scorcher. If the French should come . . ."

"Sir?"

Justice spoke from a deep impulse more than from thought. "Burn the house."

"Sir?"

"Burn it. I'll have no toasts to Boney drunk in my house."

Then he flipped the reins, the wheels crunched as the mare pulled the gig round on the gravel drive, and he was gone.

ᗒ2ᗕ

I᛭ ᴡᴀꜱ ʟᴏɴɢ past midnight when the coach swayed up the Strand into the yard of the Golden Ball at Charing Cross, and the streets almost deserted as Justice and the ticket-porter he had hired to carry his box walked round to the Tavistock, a small hotel in Covent Garden known for its naval connection. It took several minutes for his impatient knocks to rouse a grumpy night-porter. Even then, the man needed to hear the clink of shillings before he conceded that he might find Justice a small room overlooking the piazza.

He slept fitfully for a few hours, and then roused himself to find the sun shining brightly and the open window letting in a cascade of sounds from the market below—the whinnying of ponies and the clatter of hooves and wheels on the cobble-stones, the oaths of men handling heavy sacks, and the shouts of marketmen crying up the morning prices. Now, as he lay on the bed, he saw the top of a pile of baskets pass the window, like a tottering pagoda, on the head of an unseen porter.

It was not the market noise that had woken him, however, but a discreet tapping. "Indy, sir. Shaving water, sir."

"Come." The crisp single word that ship captains used had become a habit.

The door opened to admit a dark and cheerful face known to a generation of the Tavistock's naval patrons. Many years before, the frigate *Indefatigable* had come across a sinking Arab slave dhow off Mauritius, and the only survivor had been a small boy, who was named after the ship because no one could understand a word he uttered. He had become a kind of mascot, and then the captain's servant, until his master gave up his commission and found Indy a shore job at the Tavistock. After his long service at sea and his years at the hotel, he was said to be able to put a name to the face of every captain and lieutenant in the navy.

"Water gone cold, Mr Justice, sir. I bring more." Indy put down the steaming jug and brought in Justice's boots. Spattered with mud the night before, they gleamed like ebony now. Justice dimly recalled ordering hot water for seven-thirty and realised that for once he had overslept.

"What time is it?" he asked, anxious that the morning might have slipped right away.

"Past nine, sir." Indy paused at the door, and looked at the full-dress uniform which lay unpacked from Justice's box. "Admiralty, sir?"

"No," he said, regretfully.

When Justice went down to the dining-room for his gammon and eggs, it was empty except for two midshipmen, filling in time before they took coach to Portsmouth. Their gossip was of the sloop they were to join before it left to rendezvous with the squadrons tramping up and down the waters outside Brest. Their enthusiastic talk was like his own at sixteen, going off with his cousin Thomas Justice to serve on the frigate in which his brother Matthew was the first lieutenant.

The fresh boyish voices stilled as the youths noticed him. "Pray continue, gentlemen," he said with a smile, but they seemed abashed. He caught a glimpse of himself in one of the mirrors which ran along the wall opposite the windows. To them, he thought, a captain in full fig would be an awesome sight, certainly enough to embarrass their chatter about their prospects.

He took another glance in the mirror and decided that he looked a credit to the service.

WITH ONLY AN HOUR to kill before he was due at Whitehall, less than half a mile away, Justice sauntered slowly through the crowd that always seemed to block the Strand. Whenever he came to London from the country, or from the sea, its streets reminded him of a fair, as smart carriages and loaded waggons eased their way through a press of strollers, hurrying messengers, women selling ribbons and other finery from trays, flower-girls, an organ-grinder with a parrot, a butcher's assistant with a clutch of chickens over his shoulder, a ballad-seller . . . On impulse, Justice offered a penny as the man whined "Help an old sailor, capt'n" and thrust some cheaply printed slips in front of him. He took one at random and the first lines of the song caught his eye.

> *Yes, afraid of the French we will be when the moon*
> *Shines as clear and as bright as the sun does at noon*

When the stars in their places no longer will stay
But turn into marbles, and boys with them play . . .

Stirring stuff, he thought, but what if Boney's cavalry swept up the Dover road and into London as they had ridden triumphantly into every other capital of Europe? People might then find themselves singing a different tune. He stuffed the song-sheet into his pocket with impatience. War, when it came to it, was much more bloody and boring than you would ever guess from such romantic bluster.

By the time he turned into Whitehall, he had fallen back into the cross-grained mood which had afflicted him all summer. Even if war was a brutal business, at least it was *his* business; the sooner he was back at it, the better. He passed the end of Downing Street and turned left into Richmond Terrace, a fine row of nine houses in stone and brick which ran towards the river.

Like the lawyers' chambers in the Temple, the houses did not have front doors, only passage entries, with the names of the occupants neatly painted on the wall at the foot of the stairway. Mercury House was in the centre, with columns running up to the fine classical pediment, and on the ground floor was the office of the Commissioners of Crown Lands. Above it, still imposing, was a division of the Tax and Exchequer Department—Justice recalled that Lilly had first made his reputation in that branch of the public service. Then the stair narrowed and the balustrade turned from polished mahogany into cast iron. At the next landing, a painted sign modestly announced that the Society for the Distribution of Improving Tracts for Seamen conducted its affairs within. Through the open door he saw the sombre figure of Eli Dunning, who noticed Justice as he hesitated. "Good morning, Mr Justice," he said, rather loudly and pedantically. "You'll find Mr Lilly upstairs at the Board, sir," he said almost reverently, and rolled his eyes upwards. "Went up only a moment ago."

At the top of the next flight, Justice found a white door marked only by a neat brass plate. When he knocked, the door was opened by a clerk, a slight, soapy-looking man who addressed Justice as if he were forgiving him for something, and showed him into a small ante-room furnished with a small table, two wheelback chairs, a bookshelf holding a set of the leather-bound sea-atlases which his grandfather would have called "Neptunes," and a few prints. One of them, Justice noticed, portrayed a small boat against the background of a tropical coast. Looking at it more closely, he saw that it was not a print but a well-executed water-colour.

"All my own work." There was a hint of irony in the quiet voice which came from behind him. He had not heard the door open. *"Infernal,* Captain Mackenzie, bomb-ketch, Leeward Islands, 1758. Now that, Mr Justice, was the year I was made midshipman, four wars and more ago."

As Justice heard the familiar naval form of identification, he turned to see a trim man for all his sixty years and thinning hair, and remembered that George Lilly had begun life as an orphan, taken to sea in kindness by a family friend. They had that much in common, at least, he thought; an unspoken bond that held them as they stood for a moment face to face. Then Lilly led the way into his office.

It was a small, bright room, perched high enough to catch the breeze of the Thames and avoid the stench and noise of the mews called Scotland Yard which lay behind Mercury House. Through the windows, across the wide right-handed turn of the river at Blackfriars, Justice saw the dome of St Paul's gleam like a great half-moon above the spires of the City churches. The room was sparsely furnished, with a pair of comfortable chairs by the window, a fair-sized rosewood table covered by maps and charts, and a glass-fronted bookcase filled with red-tied files. For decoration there were only two Dutch sea-scapes on the white walls, and a blue-and-carmine Persian carpet on the polished wood-block floor.

"Fine quarters, sir." Justice meant the compliment. Lilly's office reminded him of the clean-lined but attractive cabin that ran across the stern of a ship of the line.

"They serve the Board's purposes." Lilly spoke cryptically.

"And the floor below? I saw Mr Dunning . . ."

"A slight connection." Lilly smiled gently. "Our concern is with this kingdom, not the one to come. More especially, its safety." He gestured towards the chairs by the window. "Walls have ears and doors have keyholes, Mr Justice. Even here. What I have to say is best kept between us and the heavens. Meanwhile, you are fit again, sir?"

Justice had expected to be received with fusty formality, or

24

kept waiting an hour or two: in the time since he had last seen Lilly, he had cooled his heels too often outside too many doors of jacks-in-office. "Thank you, yes."

"I gathered so. I heard of your prowess at the game of cricket."

"In the absence of a more useful occupation . . ." Justice broke off, aware that the words might sound in some way ungrateful.

Lilly gave him an appraising look. "Well, it may be you will shortly find one. Your friends in Kent may soon find themselves engaged in a somewhat sharper conflict than bat and ball."

"You think Boney will come, then?"

"It is not yet certain, but I think it likely." Lilly spoke with dry precision. "Our reports tell us that Bonaparte has fifty thousand men massed on what he is pleased to call the Iron Coast. He has hardly put them there for nothing." He rose and went across to the table. "If you would be so good," he said, unrolling a sea chart, and inviting Justice to hold down one end.

Justice did so, then sat down, somewhat puzzled. Presumably, Lilly had not brought him up from Kent to discuss the higher strategy of naval warfare?

But if Lilly was conscious of mystifying his visitor, he did not show it. "You will be familiar with these waters," he said, and Justice realised he was looking at the Pas de Calais and the English Channel. "So too is Bonaparte—from what we hear, from hours of staring out towards the cliffs of Dover. For he must cross that narrow stretch of sea before he can fall upon us, and cross it quickly."

"Difficult." Justice did not envy the French captains who would have to guard Bonaparte's unwieldy transports and barges as they crept slowly across the Channel.

"As you say. But not impossible."

"Then Old Jervie—" He corrected himself: "Then Earl St Vincent—" It was scarcely three months since the old admiral had told the House of Lords: "They may come, but they will not come by sea." That defiant epigram had set the ears of England ringing.

"Fine words for a debate, Mr Justice," said Lilly dryly, "and they may comfort our fellow-countrymen. They have a more hollow sound to those of us who know that there are circumstances in which it may be easier for Bonaparte to sail against England than for us to stop him."

Justice glanced at Lilly's earnest face. The gesture must have revealed his surprise at such plain speaking, for Lilly went on: "Yes, Mr Justice, I will be frank with you. We feel secure, we may seem secure, but in fact we are in great danger. Our army, and even more our navy, was much reduced while Mr Pitt was out of office. No doubt we are making an effort now to repair the damage done in those months, and no doubt the soldiers will put up a good fight if they have to." His tone betrayed his scepticism, as he leaned over the chart and traced a line from the Thames to Hastings. "But there is more than one hundred miles of coast facing France, and we cannot hold it all in strength. If Bonaparte can once get his veterans ashore, and bring in cavalry and cannon, he could strike for London with every hope of success." Lilly paused. "Now see," he said, and stabbed a finger at Boulogne.

Justice had already noticed that the chart was ringed with circles that radiated from Boulogne and cut across the English coastline. On each circle, two sets of numbers had been pencilled.

"Those are simply guesses," Lilly said, anticipating the question. "The first figure gives the number of tides for which Bonaparte is left unmolested. The second is the estimate of the numbers he could then get to sea. And since he must keep his flotilla together as best he can, the circles show the daily range of his slowest ships in a four-knot wind from the east. Anything more would scatter his transports and sink his barges."

Justice had been doing sums in his head. "He needs at least three days," he said.

"And would of course like more. But that could be enough."

"And that is our margin of safety?"

"Or danger. It depends." Lilly lifted his hand and let the chart roll up with a snap that gave emphasis to his point. "Bonaparte can send Villeneuve out of Brest to fight a sea-battle which may make him master of the Channel. Or Villeneuve may go off on a wild chase across the Atlantic, with Cornwallis lured in pursuit, while Admiral Bruix drives off the small squadron we have blockading Boulogne and starts to ferry the troops across. Or Bonaparte may find some different combi-

26

nation. Anything will do, in fact, that gives him command of the Straits for only a few days when the moon, the tides, and the wind are right for him."

"But that is a matter of luck," Justice said. "You assume that every fact favours him."

"And so it might," Lilly replied. "So it might. That is precisely the risk. And it is greater, perhaps, than you realise. The navy is overstretched—blockade, patrols, transports, convoys. Many of our ships are worn out by years at sea, their rigging rotten, spars and timbers strained. We have first-rates off Ushant which would burst their seams if they fired a full broadside."

Why was he being told so much, Justice wondered. Lilly was talking more as if he were in the Board of Admiralty than addressing a relatively junior—and mystified—captain. No wonder, if such a man was pessimistic, that Mr Pitt was talking of packing the King and his family off to Worcester and that the rich were arranging to have their valuables moved out of town by Mr Pickford. In a quiet room in the heart of London, no more than a hundred miles from Bonaparte's armada, this man had made him feel desperately uneasy—not with the shiver of personal fear, but with the cold anxiety of danger beyond anyone's control.

"If they sail, then . . ." Justice had never really come to terms with that thought. Like most people, he had shared old Jervie's bluff confidence that the navy could always give Bonaparte's admirals a hiding.

"Precisely. So they must be stopped from sailing. By Admiral Keith's squadron, if possible. We scarcely have enough ships to cover the main threat from the Boulogne flotilla. And if Keith cannot stop them, others must."

"Others?" Justice was usually quick to catch the drift of any line of talk, but he still could not guess what Lilly wanted from him. Yet there was something purposeful in his approach: somehow, he sensed, he was being led link by link along a chain of logic which in the end would bind him.

"That, I hope, is where you can help us, Mr Justice."

"What I am about to tell you"—Lilly sat back, putting his hands together—"is, I need hardly add, for your ears only.

And before I go any further, I should make my own position clear. I am not speaking as a member of the Board of Admiralty, nor do I address you as a sea-officer in His Majesty's Navy. At the end of this conversation, I cannot give you orders. Nor can you afterwards make any claim on me—whether you accept or decline my proposal, whether you succeed or fail in what I may ask." He stopped, then added: "All the same, it is not a personal favour, but an errand on which the safety of this country may well depend."

Lilly got up and walked about the room as if making up his mind how to proceed. Then he turned back to Justice.

"I must go back a year or so," he said, "to the months after the so-called Peace of Amiens, when it seemed to me and some of my friends that the true interest of this country was abandoned by Mr Addington, that there was no peace, but only another truce in the war that France has waged against England on and off all through my lifetime. We were convinced that we must prepare to fight again, if necessary for another five years, even ten, and that we must use our minds and our money to that end. I speak in the plural, Mr Justice, for, although there were not many of us, there were enough—men without office, certainly, but men with resolve, with influence, with courage."

As Lilly spoke more forcefully, Justice saw a hard glint in his eyes and a touch of colour on his sallow cheek. "We became a band of gentlemen, leagued together for liberty as much as any band of bog Irishmen, the liberty which free-born Englishmen have had to defend in turn against Bourbon kings, Jacobin agitators, and the upstart Corsican. I will not speak of our work in detail. You may guess if I tell you that we could be found here in the City of London, in banking houses in Frankfurt, Geneva, and Milan, in the shipping offices of Genoa and Bordeaux and Hamburg. Where we could hear, we listened. Where we could act, we acted."

The rhetoric was impressive. It was not hard to understand how Lilly could hold and sway the House of Commons. "And this Board?" Justice asked.

"That came later, after Mr Pitt had returned to office. He thought we should find an innocuous and acceptable name for those parts of His Majesty's business which were far from innocuous and scarcely acceptable—at least to ageing admirals and dotard generals who still suppose war to be like a game of chess. For Bonaparte there are no rules, no limits, except those he can turn to his own advantage. Remember that, Mr Justice. You may greatly need to remember it."

"And the Board?" Justice said again.

"It already existed," Lilly replied. "Moribund, with a Fellow from a Cambridge college, of all things, comfortably drawing an income for doing nothing as its chairman. His uncle had been a Lord of the Treasury when the appointment last fell vacant." Lilly gave another of his rare wan smiles. "Now it serves a different convenience. Our beacons are a message of hope, our bells sound a tocsin, our messengers speak of strange things."

"What does the Board need of me?" Was he, after all, only to become some kind of confidential courier? If so, the end seemed hardly to justify such elaborate preparation.

"To solve a puzzle," Lilly said. "A man has disappeared. A man named Matthew Fielding."

"And you want me to find him?"

"It is not quite so straightforward as that." Lilly got up and strolled about for a moment, apparently lost in the prospect of the river down to Blackfriars. "I believe you are acquainted with the gentlemen of Lloyd's of London?"

"The underwriters?" Justice was astonished not so much by his companion's change of tack as that Lilly should know of his own contacts with Lloyd's, the great centre of marine insurance at the Royal Exchange. A few months back, when he had been worried about his future, he had seriously considered putting his knowledge of the sea to business use by becoming an underwriter himself and joining the syndicate of his old friend Edward Holland.

"They were among those who supported the Board's enterprise from the start," said Lilly. "Apart from their incomparable sources of information—there is little that goes on in the ports of the world and on the high seas that does not come to their attention—they were able to be helpful to our cause in a particular way. If a risk goes down, in peace or war, the underwriters pay their claims in the currency of the owner. Matthew Fielding is the Lloyd's man who pays these claims in Paris."

Lilly caught his own error and shrugged his shoulders. "Perhaps I should say that he *was* their agent, and ours as well. A draft from Amsterdam, a letter of credit from Geneva, gold taken in by an American ship—there were many ways in which the funds reached Fielding to settle the insurance claims; and the money was always more than he needed. That provided the margin to pay for what we wanted, to corrupt an official here, to support the enemies of Bonaparte there, to keep couriers alive and give them shelter. During the peace, and the early months of war, Fielding had done well, especially round Bordeaux, where there are old ties and sympathies with England, and in the Pas de Calais, where we have reason to think he had established an excellent network. For obvious reasons, Fielding gave us no details of how he worked, or with whom he worked. All we had were the results. Then, quite suddenly, things went wrong. You know the word *ratissage?*"

"A combing-out." The word came back from childhood, from hearing the beaters use it when he had gone out with the shooting-parties in the woods at Valcourt.

"Precisely. This goes back to that damned Cadoudal affair."

Justice nodded. It had been during the previous winter that the Breton leader, Cadoudal, had made an attempt to abduct Bonaparte that had ended in disaster.

"Since then, there has been such a combing-out in northern France that anyone who might be suspected has gone to earth," Lilly went on. "That is why Admiral Keith is driven to send one man after another ashore on the beaches round the Channel ports. The agents on whom the Admiralty depended for news of Bonaparte's preparations to invade us have all been seized or silenced. Or else they send such obvious falsehoods that they must have sold themselves to save their skins. We have lost the thread that led from Paris to Boulogne. What is worse, we have lost Fielding."

"When did that happen?"

"Some months ago, we think. News travels slowly and uncertainly." Lilly gave a wan smile. "More than half this tale, I fear, is like trying to steer a cutter through a fog on the Goodwin Sands without a compass or a chart. We lost him, what is more, when he had recently been sent a very large sum of money. Five thousand pounds, to be exact."

Justice was staggered. The sum was enough to buy and arm a ship of the line. "He was arrested?"

"In a queer sense, you could say so." Lilly drummed his fingers on the rosewood table. "In May last year, you will recall, Bonaparte found an excuse to detain all the Englishmen caught living or travelling in France when the war began again."

Justice thought back a year, remembering the rush to France when the Peace of Amiens made private visits possible again for the first time. He would have gone himself, indeed, if he had returned to England in time. But he knew that many had gone to Paris—aristocrats for whom it had been a second home, merchants who wanted to buy and sell again in France, young men making the Grand Tour, fashionable ladies eager to see the remarkable new Paris styles, companies of actors, musicians, artists, and, to England's shame, or so it seemed to Justice, those who had gone merely to gape at Bonaparte, or even to feast morbid eyes on the square where the guillotine had thrown its bloody shadow.

"And your man Fielding was one of them?"

"Yes, but not immediately. Like others who were useful to French trade, he was allowed to keep his office open for some time. Bonaparte is not a man to throw away money, especially English gold, and a good many French bottoms were insured at Lloyd's. Then, some time in March, so far as we can make out, Fielding was detained. We think at Blois, on his way back from Bordeaux. He was taken to Paris, where we lost sight of him for a while. Then we learnt he had been sent two hundred miles to the east to Verdun. That is where most of the *détenus* have been held—hundreds of them. From all accounts, it has become almost an English country town. According to our information, Fielding was in some kind of trouble. He was last seen being marched away under escort, and is rumoured to be dead."

"In Verdun?" Justice asked.

"We do not know. I have told you all we do know, except for one thing. His friends at Lloyd's have—since we last heard from him—received one brief communication. A short, obscure letter, written—perhaps under duress, for it contained some unlikely phrases—from Bordeaux. Probably it was given to an American captain, for it came in from Gibraltar. That letter is in the hands of your friend Mr Holland, who can perhaps make more of it than I can."

31

Justice let the question pass of how Lilly knew of his acquaintance with Edward Holland. Clearly, the Mercantile Messengers moved swiftly.

"You believe this letter contains a cypher?"

"If so, it is none known to the Board, where we have some use for such things," said Lilly dryly. "I am sure of only one thing. It would have been too dangerous for Fielding to tell us what he had in mind, and equally dangerous for us to ask. In this strange trade of ours, Mr Justice, one lives by hints and half-truths. But Fielding was a trustworthy and ingenious man, who would not have asked for so large a sum without a definite purpose. I believe that purpose was to hinder or prevent Bonaparte's descent upon our shores later this year. He had planned some enterprise—we don't know what. We need to find out." Lilly was a man of precise speech, but now his tone was oddly gentle. "We need someone to go to France. A brave man, a resourceful man, a man who speaks French like a native. I can think of no one better suited to such a mission than yourself."

"The mission would be—to go to Verdun?"

"To go to Verdun and find Fielding." The sentences came coldly, like an order. "Or what happened to him; that is one thing. For another, to find the money. For another again, to discover how Fielding planned to use it. Finally and most difficult"—Lilly paused—"to put Fielding's plan, whatever it was, into action."

For a few seconds the silence of understanding lay between them. For the last ten minutes Justice had been so intrigued by Lilly's story that he had been scarcely aware of the precise point to which it had been leading. Yet the alternatives . . . The loss of Lilly's favour, not to mention a slow death by rural vegetation. There was something that weighed with him besides—France, he thought suddenly, with a thrill that was half-fear, half-excitement. That beloved country that had baffled and enchanted him since his childhood.

"What I have spoken of"—Lilly continued quietly—"is a vital matter, a dangerous matter, and you may wish to think it over. Should you prove unable to help me, this conversation will be regarded solely as a confidential matter between two men of honour. In the meanwhile, time presses, and I should have to ask you—"

"You have your answer now," Justice said impulsively. "I'll go. Yes, I'll go to Verdun."

"I thought you would," Lilly said softly. "We shall take a glass of Madeira to seal our understanding." He rose and went to a door opening into an inner room. "Mr Hatherley, if you please."

The man thus addressed brought in glasses and decanter so promptly that it was clear Lilly had expected a positive answer. Justice had thought to see a neat clerk, or another sombre figure like Dunning, but Hatherley was a very different sort. Tall, so that he had to stoop in the doorway, burly as well, with a face that looked more crafty than clever, Hatherley was dressed in a style that bordered on the flashy—a high-collared canary coat, a dark green stock, black trousers, and high boots. He would have seemed more in place at a race-meeting, Justice thought, or placing a bet at a prize-fight, than in Lilly's company. Yet Lilly made no attempt to explain him beyond a formal introduction.

"Mr Hatherley is privy to the matters we have been discussing," he said, then turned back to the tall man. "Mr Justice will go to Verdun; he will be in to see you shortly."

"That is good news, sir." Hatherley gave Justice an inquisitive, appraising glance, then withdrew, apparently in no way over-awed by Lilly.

"Hatherley will look after certain practical matters for you. Your employment by the Board will be without pay, though you will find us more generous than the Admiralty about necessary disbursements." He paused, then added: "If you succeed, you can expect no public thanks. If you fail, your name will simply appear in the *Naval Chronicle* as lost at sea."

Justice nodded wryly and Lilly, perhaps sensing that his manner as well as his words had become both formal and forbidding, began to speak of personal matters: of Justice's family and the new mansion in Hampshire that Mr James Wyatt had lately built him. "We'll have a shooting week at Cuffwells in November, when you're back in England and Boney's beat," said Lilly, now in a euphoric mood.

Then the carriage clock on the mantelpiece struck twelve, and he put his glass down. "I have to go over to the Admiralty," he said. "If you step into the other office, Hatherley awaits you. In case I do not see you again—tomorrow I must be in Portsmouth—I wish you Godspeed. I have said to you everything but one thing." He came and stood close to Justice, speaking slowly and with unusually quiet force. "Fielding was a man of character and intelligence. Whatever he had planned, it would have been something clever, practical, and effective. That was the kind of man he was."

Justice caught the past tense but made no comment.

"Also the kind of man I believe you are. I wish you well." Lilly held out his hand. Then he was gone, his footsteps echoing briskly down the stone stairs.

⪻ 3 ⪼

TWO HOURS LATER Justice was sitting in a Thames wherry going down to London Bridge, admiring the skill with which the one-handed wherryman threaded his way through the clutter of barges and small craft on this stretch of the river. With his good left arm the man controlled the boat, making use of the current to cope with the long bend round past Somerset House round to Blackfriars; and with the other, capped by a hook which locked into an ingenious socket on the end of the oar, he kept up a regular swing which drove the boat along quite steadily. His right hand, he lost no time in telling Justice, had been taken off by a splinter at the siege of Calvi, and he had come to find the hook a useful tool, as well as a weapon against river thieves, who would call a boat at night only to rob the boatman. "Thinks twice, three times, they does," he said with a chuckle. "No point in being 'ooked like a fish for a few coppers, is there, cap'n?"

The man's cheerful manner was infectious, and welcome after the ominous talk with Lilly and the subsequent discussion of ways and means with his assistant. Hatherley had had a file of papers ready. "You will find little that the Commissioner has not already told you," Hatherley had said, as if he had been a fly on the wall throughout their conversation, "but you had better read it."

"As to your travelling arrangements—" Hatherley had sounded as casual as if he had been looking up the times of the

Plymouth stage-coach. Justice supposed that the plan would be for him to travel under an assumed name, but Hatherley had raised a bushy eyebrow. "No, sir. You travel as yourself. That will be safest. And will fit the arrangements we have made to land you. You live at Rye, or thereabouts, I fancy?"

"Thereabouts."

"As I thought. So your tale hangs together." Hatherley's precise, genteel tone overlaid what Justice guessed was originally the sharp and nasal accent of a Cockney. It occurred to him that the man was extracting a bonus of pleasure from giving instructions, or something like them, to a captain. "What we propose, sir, is a fishing-trip. Your story will be that you set off from Rye in a smack. That there was a mishap off Dungeness, in which your smack was dismasted. You had then taken to your dinghy, and found yourself drifting towards France. On arrival there, you will allow yourself to be arrested. Things will then take a natural course. As a British civilian prisoner, you will be taken to Verdun."

"And the dismasted smack?"

"There you must allow us to indulge our fancy, Mr Justice." Hatherley had given him a pale smile. "There will be no dismasted smack. You will be towed for a time down-Channel, to make you look more windswept. Which may be a touch uncomfortable, but will add, shall we say, a likely look to it."

An Admiralty courier, it seemed, was already riding for Dover; and would that night rouse out Lieutenant Hood, commanding the cutter *Adder*, with puzzling instructions to carry a dinghy to a rendezvous at Rye Harbour. "With a fresh northeasterly like this," Hatherley had said, looking out at the Whitehall weathercocks, "Hood should have no difficulty in meeting you. The problem may be waiting for a wind for France."

Hatherley's assurance had astonished and delighted Justice, who had long ago come to the seagoing man's opinion that Whitehall was all sloth and muddle; but so much had been left unsaid in their brief talk, so many questions left unasked, that he had been relieved when Hatherley had asked him to come back next day, saying there would be work to do before he took the afternoon coach down to Kent.

He lay back in the warm sunlight, as the boat passed close to Blackfriars Stairs, crowded with young women in pink and strawberry-coloured bonnets. The boatman grinned as Justice eyed them. When the sun glinted on the braid at his shoulders, one of them waved, and he waved back. There was nothing like a summer day in London to stir the senses.

"Been away long, cap'n?" Safely out of the navy, the boatman could afford to be familiar, and Justice smiled back. Thames watermen were known for their chirpy independence. As if they had woken him from a disagreeable dream, the girls and the boatmen had suddenly made the world real again.

WHENEVER JUSTICE had been to Lloyd's to call on Edward Holland, he had been fascinated by the old-fashioned style in which the underwriters did a business in which tens of thousands of pounds turned on a moment's decision.

"Confidence," Holland had said the first time he had taken him around the market. "Confidence is everything in this business, my dear John. Confidence that a man will stick to a bargain, and meet his obligations—even if he has to ruin himself to pay. Confidence that a man speaks honestly, whether it's about a cargo he wants you to underwrite or about some item of news he sends you from Philadelphia or Hamburg. Of course, we have our rogues, like anybody else. But a Lloyd's man is generally a true man."

Was that the case with Fielding? Justice remembered his friend's words as he went into Lloyd's and looked round for one of the red-robed waiters who still presided at the doors, carried messages, or inscribed in flowing calligraphy the latest additions to the sombre pages of the Loss Book. A foxy-faced man caught his look and came forward.

"Is Mr Holland in the Rooms?"

"I've not seen him since this morning, sir. I'll enquire."

Justice peered after the man as he disappeared into the crush of the Underwriting Room, where a stream of brokers swirled round the underwriters, who sat at what were still called boxes—small, partitioned tables that recalled the market's coffee-house beginnings. It was a world so busy, so cluttered with quill pens, and atlases, and reams of paper, that he wondered how Holland could bear to have left the freshness of the sea—except, of course, that he had left it to marry Kitty. That was the difference, and a good enough reason too, Justice decided.

While he was waiting, he noticed a display-case by the waiter's desk. Evidently, it contained some sort of commemorative medals.

Looking closer, he saw they were not medals but coins from the *Lutine*, a bullion-ship which had gone down in the sandbanks of the Zuyder Zee, it must now be five years back. The loss had meant some knitted brows in the market at the time, for the cargo had been worth a king's ransom in Spanish *pistoles* and gold *louis*. Now, according to a neatly-engrossed card in the display-case, part of the bullion had been salvaged and—since Lloyd's had paid up on the loss—become the property of underwriters. A further selection of *Lutine* coins, said the notice, was in the possession of the Committee and could be seen on application. The obverse side of the coin was also shown, stamped with the motto "Fidentia" and the Lloyd's symbol of an anchor.

Justice studied the display-case with a mixture of interest and unease. A sailor was always intrigued by anything brought from the sea-bed. He was still looking at the coins when the foxy-faced man came back: Mr Holland, it seemed, had gone to the Baltic Exchange about a claim on some fur shipments, but was soon expected back. "If you'd care to leave word, sir, I'll put it in Mr Holland's hand." The waiter ushered Justice across to the tall desk in the lobby and offered him paper and a quill pen, newly sharpened.

"Thank you." Justice stood for a moment, uncertain how to phrase the note. Then he wrote briefly, in the careful round hand that he found so useful for writing aboard ship, when he, the pen, and the paper might all be moving in different directions.

Dear Edward,
    I am in London briefly and desire your advice on a business matter. If you could spare an hour this evening, a message will find me at the Tavistock.

He glanced over the note, sanded it, scribbled John Justice, the day, and the time at the bottom; and while he ran his eye over the throng inside the Rooms in the last hope of seeing Holland, he absent-mindedly—and out of an old habit of passing signals back to the officer of the watch—handed the paper to the waiter. He was some way along Cheapside before he realised that he had not sealed the paper. But by then there was no point in turning back. In any case, there was nothing in the letter of any importance.

He left the Royal Exchange and began to wander slowly westwards, then decided to improve the hour by browsing for a while in the booksellers' shops in Paternoster Row. After twenty minutes of searching, he found what he was seeking: a book on the topography of eastern France. And for good measure, a book on the work of the Marquis de Vauban, the great builder of fortresses who had designed the Citadel at Verdun.

When he came out of the bookshop, he made his way west again, up Fleet Street and along to St Martin's—the navy's own church, he remembered, whose bells were always the first to ring the news of a victory at sea. And then he turned back to Covent Garden, past Coutts' Bank at the corner of the Strand, with its sign of three crowns glinting in the sunshine. It seemed to be a place for banks. Here was Tellson's, there Brown's, and across the street he noticed the triangle of three small birds above the entrance to Swift's. Looking at the banks, he stopped short. What the devil, he suddenly thought, did a man do for money if he ran up on an enemy beach as a castaway? Lilly had been airily promising about the Board's generosity over disbursements, but had it occurred to Lilly that a man might need a goodly sum of money to get himself to Verdun and stay there—to say nothing of somehow making his way home again?

Certainly, his own bank would not be helpful. Marsh's, the naval bank in Mayfair, were sticklers for tradition. His mind went back to a conversation a few months earlier with the manager, who had been complaining that some of the rival banks—Tellson's and Swift's had been singled out for the old man's protests—still did business at their Paris branches. "Damned unpatriotic, sir! It would never do for Marsh's!"

But even if it had done for Marsh's, a Paris bank would be no use in Verdun. Perhaps Hatherley had made some arrangements. At any rate, he would raise the matter in the morning.

When he got back to the Tavistock, his room was as he had left it, except for a sealed paper with the Lloyd's crest on the table. He picked it up, stretched himself on the bed, then broke the seal.

My dear John,

Kitty will be furious if you do not sup with us at Church Row and stay. The groom will take your horse, and I will drive you back to town at a spanking pace in the morning. My new rig goes like an albatross over the waves.

Edward

The letter, easy, impetuous, was just like Edward. It was also typical of his friend's informality that, instead of living in town, Holland chose to live in the agreeable line of houses that ran to the church at the top of Hampstead Hill, with the country at his door and the winds about him. Ever since they had met as midshipmen, Justice had felt that Edward Holland was as near to him as a brother.

But Edward had taken the lead, even with Kitty Rawlings. There had been a time, Justice thought, when she might have let him take her hand, as well as the modest fortune she had brought back from the West Indies when the fever had carried off both her parents in the same week. A shared voyage so often ended at the altar. But then he had been less of a catch, with his naval career in the shadow of the Camelford affair.

And so, of course, when he had introduced her to Edward—well, it had been inevitable. They were married within three months, and he had borne the pang of being Edward's best man. After that, he had been glad to be away, to see her only rarely. There was no longer the dull pain now, only the sense of might-have-been that had never entirely left him.

But if he let that kind of day-dreaming go on, he would be in a catnap, and late at Hampstead. He kicked off his boots, shouting to Indy as he began to pull at his buttons with one hand and to unwind his neckcloth with the other. "Indy! The boots, hot water, and a horse in fifteen minutes!"

His spirits rising at the thought of going to Kitty's, he did not at first observe that Indy, when he came with the hot water, seemed slightly troubled. But Indy seemed hesitant to go, so he asked if anything was the matter.

"No, sir. Hope not, sir. When you out, man bring letter."

"That's right, Indy. It was expected, and I have it."

Indy still seemed troubled. "You was out, sir, me too. Boy downstairs tell him your room. I come in—go upstairs. Man

39

pass me on staircase. I come in here—table drawer open, chest too."

Indy's speech always had a breathless quality, as if he had learnt English in a hurry, at a time when definite and indefinite articles were in short supply. When upset, he spoke still more in spasms.

"Did you get a sight of him, Indy?"

"Lean man, sir, cussed-looking. Sharp face like dog, sir."

"I shouldn't worry." He gave Indy a smile of reassurance. Holland would have given the same Lloyd's waiter his answer to deliver, he would bet a guinea. In which case had the man been hoping to improve the occasion with a little pilfering when Indy had surprised him on the staircase? Well, he would have found nothing—Justice was not a man for knick-knacks.

It was only when he was on the way to Hampstead that it struck him that the foxy-faced waiter might have had some other interest in him. A French agent at Lloyd's seemed hardly likely. Then a man of Hatherley's set to watch him? For a moment he felt uneasy, a world of shadows round him.

Then he spurred the horse up the steep dusty lane of Haverstock Hill, as if the fresh wind in his face would blow away the shadows.

"AND STILL NO Mrs Justice?" With her ash-silver hair, fine features, mock-astonished china-blue eyes, a skin that had stayed clear despite the West Indian sun, and a teasing smile, Kitty Holland, sitting at her dinner table, was as enticing as he had ever seen her.

"No. Not a sign of a sail." It had become an old joke between the three of them.

"Stay a day or two, John," she said, more seriously. "Hook must be a dull place, even if you do break the hearts of all the aspiring actresses in Kent with your play-acting. Besides, there's someone I particularly want you to meet. Rich, naturally, my dear, richer than I ever was, and quite the prettiest widow in London."

Justice was never quite sure whether Kitty's matchmaking was serious, or some kind of game, but each time he saw her she had some new prospect in mind for him. Especially widows.

It was odd, he thought, that she never invited any of them to make a fourth at dinner.

"Stay," Kitty said again, "and you may squire me to Covent Garden tomorrow night, while Edward eats himself into a stupor at the Fishmonger's Hall. Oh, those City dinners! No? I withdraw in dudgeon. There!" She rose, pouted, smiled at both men, and was gone.

Holland poured another glass of claret and raised it in a silent toast. "I'm afraid Kitty won't rest until she's got you safely married, John."

"Looking at you," Justice smiled, "it seems an enviable state."

"No complaints." Holland's brisk, spare manner of speaking, Justice guessed, stemmed from his way of doing business: an underwriter at his box was always rapping a quick acceptance or refusal of the risks brought him by a stream of brokers. "You'll take a glass of port?"

"Thank you."

Holland put the decanter down, and Justice looked at it with sudden interest. Round the neck of the decanter was a string of gold coins like those he had studied in the display-case outside the Royal Exchange Room. *Louis, pistoles, reales,* each with the obverse symbol of an anchor. "A presentation?"

"A damned expensive one, since my syndicate went down for £2,000 on the *Lutine* cargo. The committee of Lloyd's had them engraved like that for the leading underwriters, and a few others in the market. I treat them as a reminder not to write bullion risks in future." Holland smiled wryly, sipped his port, and sat back. "Well, John, how can I help you?"

"It's a somewhat delicate affair—" Justice hesitated.

"It might help if I tell you I met George Lilly the other day at lunch at Nathan Rothschild's. Some of us in the City like to keep in touch in a general way, you know, with how things are going." For a moment he seemed to be about to say more, then he broke off. "Lilly dropped me a half-hint you might be in some business for him. Something, he suggested, touching on Matthew Fielding."

"Yes. Fielding. Did you know him well?"

"We met—three times perhaps, and corresponded occasionally on matters of business."

"What do you know about him?"

"What do you want to know?"

"Anything you can tell me. Age, appearance, habits. As I say, anything at all, for I never heard of him before this morning."

"Age? Something close to fifty, I should say. Appearance? Lightly-built, about your own size. He gave me the impression that he liked to be taken for ten years younger. His wife died some years ago. Habits? I've been told that he enjoyed himself, and from all accounts, Paris has lately become a place where it's possible to enjoy oneself again."

"Cards? Women? Wine?"

Holland laughed. "Not cards, I fancy. As to women, well—a good-looking man, a widower in Paris . . ."

He gave Justice an appraising look. "You'd get on with him," he went on. "He's a whimsical fellow, jokey; likes the play, too, as you do, and he's bookish. Never met such a chap for quotations."

"What exactly does he do for Lloyd's?"

Holland took a draught of port and passed it. "Strictly speaking, he doesn't work for us. He's an agent in the shipping business. If a merchant in France wants to send a cargo from Marseilles or Bordeaux, Fielding would find a vessel for him. He's been particularly useful to the French, in these hard times of blockade, because he had an excellent connection with the neutrals—Americans, Swedes, Russians." Holland raised the decanter, but Justice shook his head. "Like all shipping agents, Fielding would expect to place the insurance and get a commission on it. That was how he came to deal with Lloyd's in the first place."

"Long ago?"

"Twenty years, perhaps. Before the revolution, certainly. It was a well-established firm and Fielding managed to survive one way and another. As things got worse, oddly enough, there was more for him to do—the more the French had difficulty finding bottoms to carry their goods, the more they needed people like Fielding. And all the time French merchants and shippers went on insuring with Lloyd's. The beggars may have been at war with us, but they knew where to lay off their risks. Fielding began to send more business to us, often through somewhat devious channels, and he also had to pay out whenever claims fell due. If there's a claim on the underwriter, it has to be paid in the country where the risk arose."

"And this still goes on?"

"Less so." Holland frowned. "Officially, it's now illegal to trade with the enemy. That's been the state of things since last year—officially. And if you asked me to underwrite a French ship, I'm damned if I would, but the same can't be said of everyone. The man in the next box to mine, for instance, has a very profitable line in writing Bordeaux vintners. Ask him once and he'll tell you the Bordeaux people are our best friends in France, and the trade in claret keeps them friendly— such a trade that even Bonaparte has to tolerate it. Ask him twice, and he'll tell you the shippers are old customers and he doesn't want to lose them. Ask him the third time, when he's had some of the claret that he likes, and he'll confess it's a pretty safe and profitable business."

"Coming back to Fielding . . ."

"You're right." Holland grinned, got up, and went to his desk beside the window. "I've been digressing. What you must see is this: I daresay Lilly hinted at it." He took a paper from the desk, then handed it to Justice. "It was the last word Fielding sent before he was arrested. Or perhaps it was sent afterwards, smuggled out by a friendly hand, or a bribed gendarme. Anyway, it eventually reached the man I just mentioned, who deals with Bordeaux cargoes, and he gave it to me. Frankly, if I didn't have reason to suspect that Fielding was trying to say something important, I should say he was drunk when he wrote it. Drunk or ill. Or had his head turned at last by living cheek by jowl with all those Frenchies."

Justice ignored the characteristic gibe, unfolded the paper, and read the scrawled writing.

Pray take Note of Special Perils attending Stowage of New Wine in Old Barrels. M. Georges of Paris to be Informed of the Arrival. The Race is to the Swift.

Greetings in the name of Liberty, Equality and Fraternity.

There was no date and no superscription. But the paper was stamped with a seal, a symbol of an anchor, intertwined with the initials "M" and "F."

"Well, you said he was a man for whimsies!" Justice remarked. "It reads like a parlour game. Consequences."

"Consequences, indeed. And damned serious ones, no doubt,

if we could understand the game. But we can't. Or at least I can't."

"Is nothing clear to you in the letter?"

"In one sense, everything is clear," Holland replied, almost with irritation. "That's what makes it so confusing. In form it is like an instruction to the market, or at least part of such an instruction, for normally one would begin with the name of the ship, its cargo, its destination, the amount of risk carried, and the premium. All we have here is a scatter of oddities. I presume it relates to some shipment from Bordeaux, because that's where Fielding had just been, and there's that odd reference to wine barrels. But what? Where? I'm baffled, John, absolutely baffled."

"Special Perils?" Justice picked out the phrases. "A warning, surely?"

Holland looked doubtful. "I don't see why. Perils is a common word in the insurance market. It covers anything that can go wrong—fire, shipwreck, takings at sea, pirates, barratry of the master . . . every kind of misadventure." Holland paused. "And when he speaks of an Arrival, that means the voyage is safely ended—that the underwriter's obligation is completed. But he hardly makes it easy for us. Is M. Georges a surname or a Christian name? There must be a thousand men with that surname in Paris, and ten times as many who were baptised with it. And of course the race is to the swift. Whoever doubted it? But what race? To where?"

The words must contain a cypher. Justice knew something of codes: in Brittany he had seen the Chouan resistance leaders sending messages whose sense depended on counting words, or initials, or exchanging words for numbers. He was certain that the key to Fielding's message lay in the words themselves, in the peculiarly proverbial phrases.

"No sympathetic ink?" he asked, knowing what the answer would be.

"No secret inks, it seems."

"And Liberty, Equality and Fraternity?" Of all the odd words in the letter, those were the oddest. The principles of the French Revolution were hardly likely to appeal to the gentlemen of Lloyd's.

"Some raised eyebrows there," Holland replied. "The letter was passed round a bit, you know, before it reached me. I first

44

learnt about it when I picked up a snatch of broker's gossip, and I smartly made it my business to lay my hands on it. It seemed a bit late for Fielding to be ranting like a Jacobin—just when Bonaparte is making himself the Emperor Napoleon." He paused. "But anyway, there's Fielding for you. Memorise the letter if you will, and give it back to me in the morning."

More than once in the course of the evening, Justice had wondered whether his friend was also involved in the affairs of Lilly's mysterious Board, and the last sentence sounded almost like an official instruction. But before he could say anything, Holland lifted the branch of candles. "It is late, John," he said more warmly. "I fear Kitty will not have waited. But let us go up and see."

The warm flickering light of the candles threw Justice's reflection on the window-panes. For a moment, by a trick of vision, Justice saw himself standing alone, as if a curtain had come down behind him and hidden the room, giving the impression that another man was looking at him, from the other side of a stretch of water.

"BY THE WAY," Justice said next morning as he and Holland sat at breakfast. "Those waiters of yours at Lloyd's—"

"Yes?" Holland appeared more interested in his gammon and egg.

"Where do you find them?"

"To be honest, I don't really know. Some are old sailors—you see the odd chap without an arm or an eye. I suppose we find a place for a fellow if someone speaks for him. Why?"

"Only that—the man who brought your letter to the Tavistock." Justice ran over Indy's tale of the encounter on the stairway, and he saw that Holland was listening intently, though he appeared to make light of it when he answered.

"I doubt whether you'll find French spies at Lloyd's, though you never can tell." Holland poured himself a cup of coffee. "But I'll ask about him." He dropped the matter so sharply that Justice was content to gossip about more agreeable topics as they finished their breakfast.

"Like old times," Holland said, as he drove Justice down into London. And as he dropped him at the New Oxford Road, he leaned over the side of the gig to shake hands. "Good luck,

John," he said. "I won't ask where you're going, but I suspect you'll need all the luck in the world." With a flourish of his whip, and a nod, he turned off to the City.

It was less than a twenty-minute walk to Richmond Terrace, where Justice found that Hatherley was before him, with two other men, who were never introduced. One of them was very knowledgeable about the chart of Boulogne which lay on the table before them, about the movement of vessels in and out of the port, and the attempts that Admiral Keith's squadron made to harass them.

"We've no idea what you'll need to know," Hatherley said, as they went over tide tables and soundings. "The devil is that we don't want to tell you more than you need to know."

It was that sense of caution, Justice decided, that made Hatherley's other assistant speak so briefly, and rather obscurely, about clockwork fuses, and a new infernal machine which could be exploded under water, and something he called a plunging-boat, which was at that moment being given sea-trials in the Solent.

"Fielding may have had something similar in mind," Hatherley said after the two men had left them, "but we've no notion what it was." He was clearly a man of few words. "What else?" He appeared to be addressing the question to himself as much as to Justice.

"Money," Justice said. "Safe places to stay. Means of return."

His experience in Brittany had taught him that life depended on such practicalities.

"Money's a problem," Hatherley conceded. "A castaway can't go ashore with a pocketful of guineas." He gave Justice a sharp look. "But a gentleman can always borrow, can't he? . . . Safe places, now." Hatherley pursed his lips as he continued. "There's none left that we dare suggest, Mr Justice. As Mr Lilly said, after the *ratissage* . . . As for getting you back, well . . ." His habit of leaving sentences unfinished was disconcerting, and it made what he said afterwards sound grudging. "Captain Sidney Smith is at the French coast off and on, and his friends may have an eye for you, as for any officer that escapes."

He was rolling up the chart as he spoke, as though that part of the morning's business was finished. "There are always the smugglers, too, as you may know." His tone made Justice wonder whether Eli Dunning had made enquiries about the Men of the Marsh before he rode into Appledore. "And you speak French, Mr Lilly tells me, like—like a—" For once he seemed at a loss for a word.

"A Frenchman," Justice said plainly, amused at Hatherley's embarrassment.

"Quite." The conversation was clearly over, and Justice rose to leave. Hatherley also stood, but he put out a hand to detain Justice for a moment, and he gave a friendlier smile. "One thing more, Mr Justice," he said. "We want something better than a pair of ears or a pair of eyes. We can buy those easily enough, if that's all we ask, and still know nothing about Matthew Fielding. My word, sir, if we're going to discover what he's been at, and finish it, what we need is a person of quality." Hatherley gave a deprecating cough as he came to speak so directly, and Justice realised that it was a kind of professional shyness that had made him appear so curt. "That's what Mr Lilly told me when he first mentioned you, sir. That you were a gentleman who could whistle up Old Nick to help him. Put Mr Justice on a sinking schooner in a slack tide, barely a puff to push him, Mr Lilly said, and he'll still come spanking up to Portsmouth Point as if he had the Trades behind him."

It was the first time that Justice had seen any life in Hatherley's face, and he was so surprised that he said nothing as they walked together to the door.

Hatherley held out his hand. "It's a fine compliment, that, sir, for Mr Lilly's not a man for singing anyone's praises."

"Except the Lord's," Justice said facetiously, and then felt sheepish as he thought of the pious Eli Dunning on the floor below, packing tracts for seamen, and probably putting rods in pickle for the enemies of Mr Lilly and Mr Pitt.

"As you say, sir." Hatherley was not a man for a joke, and his face was expressionless again.

Nor, thought Justice, as he turned out of Richmond Terrace, hurrying to fetch his bag from the Tavistock and catch the afternoon coach from the Golden Ball, was Hatherley a man who would take failure lightly. His last words had made it quite clear that Justice was expected to succeed against the odds, and that he had been chosen for this desperate and puzzling mission because Lilly was prepared to gamble on him.

On the coach, trundling down the Dover Road beyond Rochester, he watched the moon breaking through patches of heavy cloud, making pools of broken light in the orchards and glinting off a farm-house window or a duck-pond. What he had promised to do was to go into the darkness without any light at all, and to search without knowing what he sought, or where to look for it, or what he would do if he found what had happened to Fielding, or any trace of what Fielding had intended to do. The more he thought about it, the more he felt that Lilly was very like an admiral, asking the impossible, and making out that it was simple if a man obeyed orders and used his wits.

It was blowing hard as the coach came to Ashford, and the ostler at the King's Head turned him out into a cold drizzling dawn.

BY SATURDAY, the north-easterly had at last begun to blow itself out, though there was a sound of smacking sail-cloth and sighing marshgrass round Rye Harbour as Justice and Scorcher spent the day making ready, and waiting for the cutter to stand in close to the mouth of the Rother.

The disconsolate Scorcher was full of foreboding as they worked, predicting that Justice would soon be regretting his absence, and that no good would come of setting off on a fool's errand with a corpse in a rudderless dinghy. But Justice himself felt relieved. Wherever this journey was going to end, it was at least beginning in a familiar way, with the creak of timber, and the smell of salt, and the eager sound of water rippling past a boat's planking.

⚓ 4 ⚓

JUSTICE FOUND it so difficult to scramble up the steep and slithering dune that the fisherman had to dump his lobster-pots on the spiky grass and lean over to pull him up. Filthy, stiff, and famished, he looked like a castaway, and felt like one. The man plainly took him at face value, for, after a flurry of questions in French, which Justice parried with shakes of the head, he was apparently content to make do with signs, and offer a friendly arm.

So far so good, Justice thought, and a little farther on might be even better, for the fisherman had raised his elbow as though he were drinking from a bottle, then pointed up the rough track that ran towards Etaples. Such a fraternal welcome was better than being treated as a spy, but Justice was puzzled by it. In some odd way, the man had not seemed greatly surprised to find him lying on the beach.

Now the sky was brightening fast, and from the low ridge on which they were walking, Justice could see rows of huts and tents stretching away through the sand-hills. There were soldiers stirring everywhere, and guards every hundred yards or so along the edge of the track, some hunched moodily over the embers of a watch-fire, others staring out towards the lines of boats along the estuary. The first man they came to looked lazily at them. "Another?"

The fisherman nodded. "Poor devil, from the wrecks," he said. "And one more body back there on the beach."

Justice groaned and leaned more heavily on the fisherman's shoulder, and he was relieved to see that once they had passed the first sentinel, the others waved them on. If he was going to play a part, he had better do it properly. And so, limping, hobbling, and stumbling against his helper, he kept going until he could see the church tower rising above the roofs of Etaples.

That would be Saint-Eustache—he had forgotten the name until he saw it on the map that Hatherley had shown him. Near the church there was an inn. The Lion d'Or? No, that had been in Montreuil. The Auberge des Voyageurs, that was it, where the Paris coach from Boulogne made its first change of horses. He could remember standing there as a boy, watching the ostlers hurrying in and out of the stable yard.

The thought of the inn made him feel even hungrier. Would it be too dangerous to walk in and order a meal before he gave himself up? He was still turning the idea over in his mind when he realised that the fisherman had left the track and that they were heading for a clump of wind-blown trees on the edge of the dunes.

"*Attendez.*" The man tried again to make him understand, making a waiting motion with his hands, and then pretending to eat. *Manger,*" he said.

Justice smiled and nodded, eager for the man to leave him.

It was ironic to find a helper here, when he least needed one. There was no means of knowing whether the fisherman was simply a good sort, or whether he had taken him for a man on the run—a deserter, perhaps, or even an English agent. So · many of the people along this coast had good reason to resent Bonaparte and his army—taxes, quartermasters with an eye for a horse or a sack of corn, a son taken off to die for *la gloire* when he was needed to man the family fishing boat. So many, too, had old ties with England. How often had Fred Scorcher told Justice, with a knowing look, that any man from Rye could find friends along the French coast?

He watched the fisherman go off through the dunes, and gave him a few minutes to get clear. There was no point in dragging the good-natured man into trouble. Then Justice set off himself, back to the track that led to Etaples, and on through a scattering of houses to the square.

There were a few people about, but none of them paid any attention as he walked past the church, past the inn, still catering to the carriage trade as the Auberge des Voyageurs, past a row of shuttered shops: he supposed he looked like another farm-hand or a fisherman, off to a day's work, and that he might have trudged all the way to Boulogne without being challenged. It was all too easy, surprisingly easy.

If he wanted to be arrested, he would have to give himself up. And better the gendarmes than some army officer suffering from spy-fever and a desire to cure it by a hurried court-martial.

Justice stopped outside the low, yellow-painted building where the tricolour flag drooped over the entrance, and hammered at the door. The gendarmes apparently slept well in Etaples, for there was no answer. He tried the handle, and the door creaked back. The dark hall was empty, but as he went in, a sleepy-looking man in a half-buttoned uniform came stumbling out of a room on the right.

"*Eh, alors, alors. Taisez-vous, donc.*" The man was annoyed and flustered.

Justice stood his ground as the gendarme came up to him. "I am English," he said. "*Anglais.* I have been ship-wrecked . . ."

"*Les Anglais? Merde alors!*" Justice could not finish his sentence as the man backed away in bewilderment, shouting. "Raoul! Raoul! *Au secours.*"

It took Justice a moment to grasp what was happening. Either the drowsy fellow took him for a watchman, bringing news of an English attack on Etaples, or he had mistaken him for one of the attackers. In either case, he was likely to get shot before he could explain himself, for a second and equally bemused gendarme was coming out of the room, clutching a musket.

The situation would have been comic if it had not been so full of risks.

Justice stared at the two men, judging how they would react if he started to raise his hands above his head in a gesture of surrender, and deciding that any sudden movement of that kind might startle the man with the gun. He took the simplest course. He gave a gasping cry, let his knees buckle, and fell down as if he were in a fainting fit.

He could hear the two men chattering as they dragged him into the guard-room and splashed water on his face, and they sounded more worried that he had caught them napping than by the fact that he was English. For a few moments he was afraid that they might simply put a musket-ball through him to avoid an awkward explanation when their sergeant came on duty, but as they recovered their nerve, they became quite agreeable, half-lifting him into a cell and bringing him a platter of bread and goat's cheese before they shut him up.

One of them must have gone to fetch the sergeant, for before long a ruddy-faced self-important man came and shouted abusive questions through the metal grill on the door. Was he a lousy English spy? Of course he was. Where the hell did he think he was going? Boulogne? A coarse guffaw. He'd be lucky to live long enough to get there.

Justice was almost provoked into swearing back at him, but he kept repeating his story of shipwreck, eked out with a few words of French, until the man finally caught the drift of it and walked away down the passage, muttering darkly.

He was gone for about two hours, possibly to consult some superior, and while Justice waited, he wondered how the French handled such matters, and whether Hatherley was right in assuming that he would eventually be taken to the naval headquarters. That depended on the sergeant's state of mind, and Justice had very little confidence in that after several attempts to insist that he was a half-pay officer. *"Demi-solde. Demi-solde,"* he had shouted at the gendarme, but the man had simply given an oafish grin and resumed his ranting about spies and traitors.

Then, in the distance, he heard voices. Had the sergeant brought back a magistrate, or a file of soldiers? As Justice peered sideways through the grill, he saw the sergeant talking to another gendarme, who had a pair of hand-irons and a length of chain dangling from his belt, and he could just catch snatches of conversation.

The newcomer, he gathered, had stopped at the inn for breakfast, on his way back to Boulogne after taking a prisoner to Montreuil. And the gendarme at Etaples would be delighted, it appeared, if he would take the English *espion* to Boulogne. Justice could not make out from the tone of the conversation whether the local sergeant was trying to save himself a walk of twenty miles, or whether he simply wanted to get Justice off his hands, with no questions asked. Whatever his motive, he soon persuaded the sergeant from Boulogne to oblige him. Within minutes, Justice was dragged out into the square and prodded onto the road that led up the coast.

Justice found it odd to have a sense of satisfaction at this turn of events, for a five-hour march in manacles was no joke, but at least the sergeant was taking him where he wanted to go, and his spirits rose as they tramped on through the warm summer day. It was afternoon when they came over the hill above Pont de Briques, and Justice saw the familiar shape of the Haute-Ville at Boulogne, locked behind its ramparts, with the long hill running down to the huddle of houses and sheds along the quayside on the river Liane.

As they approached the town in the clear afternoon light, he saw that the hills on either side of the valley were covered by military encampments. There were soldiers everywhere—groups of men marching, drilling, their uniforms patches of blue against the green hillsides; officers clattering about on fine horses, gesturing and shouting orders; knots of sailors on the riverside, farriers at work on forges set up in the open air, men hauling on ropes, carrying bundles, loading drays; piles of barrels and boxes; and a slow-moving press of waggons, carriages, even cannons being hauled towards the Arsenal. All brought here, he thought grimly, for one simple and deadly purpose—to throw fifty thousand armed men onto the quiet beaches of Kent and Sussex.

Then the valley was opening out before them, and Justice almost gave a low whistle as he saw the invasion flotilla itself. Stone quays had been built on both sides of the river. On the south side of the Liane, a large basin had been cut out to hold hundreds of the smaller boats on which Napoleon proposed to ferry his invasion army. As they came past the Arsenal wall, Justice could see row upon row of brigs, sloops, gunboats, *prames* to carry cavalry, and barges to transport infantry. He guessed that he was looking at about five hundred craft.

It was a sight calculated to strike terror to a landsman: for a moment his mind went back to England, and for the first time he felt a shiver of fear for his country. These preparations seemed so professional, confident, and efficient compared to the improvised defences he had seen men building across the road from Dover to London.

And yet that one quick glance at a scene which Lilly's Admiralty friends would have given a small fortune to hear described in detail had revealed, to his sailor's eye, a flaw in the French preparations. *There were too many craft.* For all the costly improvements, the harbour was clumsy and cramped: those boats could never put to sea on the same tide, the same day, or even the same week. They would have to be worked out along the narrow mouth of the Liane, assembled behind the line of guard ships he could see protecting the entrance . . .

"Have a good look, English spy," the sergeant shouted in a voice loud enough to make people turn and stare. "You won't be seeing them again, that's certain."

"Where's he going?" a woman called out from a window.

"To sleep with the Widow!" The gendarme made a chopping motion across the back of Justice's neck, and was so taken by the grisly joke that he guffawed, spat, and repeated it.

"Makes me jealous, I'm sure," the woman cackled. "See they cut him off at the right end, won't you?"

Suddenly he recalled something Hatherley had said on that last morning at Richmond Terrace. "A plausible tale would be the worst of all things, Mr Justice. For the French, they say, are lovers of logic, and a sensible spy would be ready with a convincing account of himself. The more improbable your tale, the safer." Hatherley had looked at him with sly approval. "They tell me you have a taste for play-acting, sir. It could serve you well."

Now the moment had come, surely, for directly ahead of him was a long wall, pierced with embrasures for heavy cannon which pointed out across the harbour entrance, and he judged by the number of officers passing in and out by the guardhouse that it must be the naval headquarters. All self-importance to cover his uncertainty, the gendarme went off to report, leaving Justice in the care of two marine sentries.

"Why am I being treated in this way?" Justice adopted the haughty tone that should suggest the affronted English milord. "Why am I chained like an animal? Take me to the commandant at once."

The men did not show any sign of understanding. *"Espion,"* one said in a sour voice, sending him sprawling with a kick, and then prodding him to his feet again with the point of a bayonet. Justice was still dusting himself when a sergeant came over, shouting and waving his arms at the marines.

"Aux cachots," he cried. *"Allez aux souterrains."* Before Justice had a chance to repeat his protest, he found himself being dragged backwards across the barrack square. Then down a slimy stone stairway to a damp corridor, where a pool of dim grey light revealed a line of cell-doors. As the guards pulled back the bolts, a chorus of obscene yells and shouts came from behind the other cell-doors.

"Welcome," one of the marines said with sour sarcasm, pushing Justice through the narrow doorway with such force that he collapsed onto a heap of straw that was soggy with stale urine. Choking at the assault on his nostrils, he heard the bolts slide back, and staggered up.

At least he could see the light of day. There was a small barred window, barely a foot square, through which he could just hear the sounds of the town. But at the moment there was one thing he needed more than food or liberty. He lay down on the loathsome palliasse and closed his eyes. Sleep, he thought as he drifted off, was the only luxury in a prison.

A long time later, or so it seemed, he heard the boots of the guards stumping back along the stone corridor. The bolts were pulled back, the door opened, and a marine poked him with a musket.

54

"*Marchez!*" he said angrily, as if he had been put to a great deal of trouble for nothing. But this time, Justice noticed as he limped along the corridor, there was no abuse, no violence. Someone somewhere up there in the fading light of day had had a change of mind.

PINIONED THOUGH HE WAS, and blinded by the evening sunlight, Justice was grateful for the refreshing breeze as he was marched across the parade ground to a pump where the guards made him strip before they sluiced him down with water. When he had dried himself on a strip of sail-cloth, he felt more like a human being: he held his head up as the marines escorted him to a two-storied building with smart sentries at the door, through a lobby where gold-braided officers drew back as he passed, up a flight of stone stairs, and into a small lobby. Past an open door, he could see into a larger room where a thin grey-headed man in uniform sat reading at a desk.

"*Ah. Le prisonnier anglais,*" he said as he looked up. "*Vous parlez francqis . . . monsieur?*" The pause was nicely judged, and Justice acknowledged it by a slight bow before he shook his head.

"*Très peu . . . monsieur le capitaine.*" Formal courtesies were a better beginning than his uncouth treatment so far.

"That is unfortunate, for my English is not distinguished. Still, my assistant understands it well enough."

Justice looked round the pleasant white-painted room. Seated by the window, and silhouetted in the fading light, was a short plump figure whose appearance startled him before he realised that the man must have cultivated his resemblance to Bonaparte, even to the lick of hair across his forehead.

"I am Captain Saint-Haouen," the thin man went on in a now-to-business tone. "I am responsible to Admiral Bruix for the safety of the port, to keep it safe from spies, *saboteurs*, all the *mauvais sujets* . . . I think you say troublemakers, eh?" He rose and walked round his desk to stand close to Justice and look him over. "From gentlemen like yourself, perhaps?" He left the harsher implication hanging. For all his diffidence, Justice noted, he spoke English with some precision; from his name, he guessed, Saint-Haouen would be one of the aristocratic officers in the navy who had survived the revolution, then been restored to favour when Napoleon had made himself First Consul.

"I must protest against the brutal manner in which I have been treated." Justice decided that it was time to take the initiative.

Saint-Haouen went back to his seat behind the desk and took up the paper he had been reading. "The gendarme tells an odd story," he said, ignoring Justice's complaint. "Perhaps the man is not very sensible, perhaps he drinks a little too much, perhaps he does not understand what you say at Etaples. Perhaps I do not understand myself. Perhaps this, perhaps that. So perhaps you would begin again from the beginning."

It was the first chance Justice had been given to tell his rehearsed story coherently, and he heard the pen of the clerk busily scratching notes. Saint-Haouen let him speak without interruption until he described his walk into Etaples.

"Let me go back . . . Captain . . ." He looked at the scrawl on the paper. "Captain *Justice*." As he used the French pronunciation, he looked out under his heavy eyebrows.

"The name of the boat that sank under you, Mr Justice?" Saint-Haouen had neatly emphasised the point about his rank and moved on, though Justice saw copies of the *Naval Chronicle* on a table by the wall and knew that his statements would be checked as soon as he left the room. Probably the papers had found their way from England on the same smuggling luggers which carried the *Moniteur* from France to Hatherley in Richmond Terrace.

"It was a smack," he replied. "The *Emily*, out of Rye." The homey girl's name sounded ridiculous in these formal surroundings. "It was not a naval vessel—a fishing boat."

Saint-Haouen looked puzzled. "An officer, fishing?"

"I am on half-pay," Justice said. "I have had no command since I was wounded last winter in a running fight in the Channel. I live near Rye, and a fishing boat is one way to keep one's hand in . . ."

"At sailing in coastal waters." Saint-Haouen almost mumbled an end to the sentence, and let its implications pass unstated. "You have had bad luck for an experienced sailor, no? Dismasted, wrecked, only two hours after you sailed." Saint-Haouen rose. "But I forget my manners, Captain Justice. I think you will be hungry. May I ask Fayol to bring you some food, some wine? A Chambertin, maybe? We keep a stock of it here, for the Emperor prefers that to all the other wines of France."

Justice bowed his agreement. Was Saint-Haouen simply playing with him? His doubts increased after Fayol had left the room, for the man suddenly spoke casually, as if to an ordinary acquaintance. "Tell me," he said in a confidential tone. "Is Justice a common name in England? Do please be seated."

"Not particularly common. Why do you ask?"

The commandant shrugged. "A coincidence, no doubt. But I happen to come from this part of France, not far from Abbeville. Some acquaintances of my family lived at a house called Valcourt."

Justice remained impassive, but he inwardly cursed. Of all the officers who might have interrogated him, he had drawn a man who knew his family.

"One of them married an Englishman," the commandant went on, "and his name I think was Justice."

There was a moment's pause. Then Justice shook his head. "No, Monsieur. I am no relation." He remembered with gratitude that his French middle name had never been printed in official publications or the *Naval Chronicle*. A shrewd man like this would easily make the dangerous connection.

"Pardon." Saint-Haouen appeared satisfied. "It was possible—" He broke off as Fayol came back with a carafe of wine, a loaf, some cold chicken, and two hard-boiled eggs, setting the tray down with a disapproving slap that made the glass and carafe rattle.

Saint-Haouen waited until his assistant was back at his desk, then he walked across to the window. "On a clear night," he said musingly, "if you stand on the cliff-top, you can sometimes see lights from Dover. It makes it seem a very short journey."

Justice said nothing.

"But a very difficult one—for us, and also for you, Mr Justice, now you are here in Boulogne." The line of thought led him to the obvious question and he swung round to put it. "And what do you now expect?"

"To be exchanged, naturally. And as soon as possible."

"Naturally, but unfortunately that is not possible." Saint-Haouen spoke more crisply. "You were not taken in an action, you were not wearing a uniform, you were not armed, you have no papers; and now you say you have no command, and that you are a half-pay officer. I think we should have a hard time persuading my Lords of Admiralty"—he gave a slight, satirical bow in the general direction of England—"to accept you—even if we were willing to let you go after what you have seen." He waved his hand languidly at the forest of masts that could still be seen through the window in the last gleam of the sunset. "It is a better view, is it not, than your English lookouts will ever get from the topmast of a frigate rolling about, three miles off the coast?"

Hatherley had judged well. Whatever else the French might do, they would not send him back.

"I have a right to exchange." Better to insist on it, now he knew there was no chance of being taken to Morlaix and rowed out under a flag of truce to a blockading English frigate.

"And we have a right to shoot you." Saint-Haouen's tone was icy. "Or to send you to the galleys, or let you rot below here. There is no evidence to support your story."

"You can search for my dinghy, and the dead man I brought ashore with me."

"Your dinghy has been found. Also the body of your companion."

Justice nodded, relieved. At least his story had been corroborated. "May I ask that he be given Christian burial?"

"Naturally. We are not savages, monsieur." Saint-Haouen gave a thin smile. "As to yourself, let me put our position more precisely. Over a year ago, the Emperor decided that all Englishmen must be treated as prisoners. Anyone fortunate enough to come to *la belle France* must stay here. Which leads, perhaps, to a certain paradox. If a Mr Justice is an officer in the British navy he can be exchanged with a French officer, be allowed to go home, and fight once more against us. But if this Mr Justice is not a serving officer, he may not go home to England, just in case he should afterwards become an active officer in the navy, in the army, the fencibles, the militia—the militia is especially what the Emperor had in mind—and then fight against us when we come to England, next week, next month . . ."

Justice made a gesture of impatience. "I can go free if I can convince you that I am a sea officer who intends to fight against you as soon as the rules of war permit. If I merely wish to go back peacefully to my own house, I must stay here as a prisoner. This is ridiculous."

"Perhaps you would prefer a court-martial to decide that you are a spy?" Saint-Haouen spoke languidly, but his voice was cold. "I regret that until it is clear what you really are, Mr Justice, we must assume that you are not what you seem." Now the French logic was being neatly turned against him.

The interview had ended badly.

"I am sorry," Saint-Haouen added with ironic politeness, "that I cannot offer you a more comfortable lodging. We are a little pressed for space here in Boulogne. If you would be so good—" He gave the smallest of nods as the marines seized Justice by the arms.

He was almost through the door when he heard Saint-Haouen speak to his assistant. "It is now your affair, Fayol."

He was still wondering whether he had been intended to hear the words as he was hustled back across the darkened parade ground.

How LONG HE LAY in the stinking prison he never knew at the time—only that days faded to night, and then to dreary dawn again as the sun woke him through his slit of window. One week, two weeks . . . three weeks . . . His food consisted of stale bread, and a pale swill which on one day of the week— perhaps Sundays, he thought—was flavoured with a lump of hard meat or cured fish.

Worse than the boredom were the bouts of questioning. Twice a day, and sometimes at night, he was fetched from his cell and taken to a bare stone room upstairs, where he was forced to stand facing the wall and answer the same questions again and again. There was no violence, apart from the rough handling he received from the guards, but the repetition made him want to scream, to say something fresh to break the tedium. How big had his boat been? Where had they been when the squall had hit them? What colour had the boat been painted? How much drinking water was there in the dinghy?

Once, exhausted by the questioning, he had fallen to the floor in a deep sleep, and been left there till morning, so that the first he knew of the dawn was a succession of crashes from above his head, mingling with a troubled dream in which George Lilly was rolling cannon-balls down the stairs at Richmond Terrace. Then he was awake and knew he was listening to guns at sea, and the heavier crunch of French 32-pounders in answer. No more than a mile away, possibly less. Admiral Keith's inshore squadron must be close to the sand-bars at the mouth of the Liane.

Just before the firing died away, Justice heard the distant snap of muskets, and he tried to picture what was happening out there in the early mist. An attack on the line of guard-ships? A cutting-out operation? An attempt to capture some small convoy seeking to sneak in along the coast? Whatever it was had obviously failed to make any impression on the strong defences, for he heard the gun-crews cheering, and when the guards came for him they went through a grinning dumb-show to rub in how easily the English had been driven off, then dragged him out of his cell with more ferocity than usual.

Next morning he was awakened by the sliding of the bolts: Fayol must be coming for the interrogation earlier than usual.

But it was not Fayol. It was the guards, marching him out of the *souterrains* and to the pump, where he was sluiced with water.

Then was he to see Saint-Haouen again? At first it seemed so, for he was marched briskly past the smart sentries. But instead of going to the commandant's office, the guard turned off into a small ante-room looking onto the courtyard, where a line of soldiers stood fingering their muskets with an obvious uneasiness.

Even so, it took Justice a minute to realise what was going to happen. First he saw a cart arrive with a load of men in ordinary clothes. Their hands were tied and they were blindfolded. Then, casually yet precisely, guards tied each man to a post. From somewhere, as if in a nightmare, he heard a staccato order. A puff of smoke from the muskets of the line of marksmen, and he heard the crack of the volley. The smoke cleared, revealing the figures slumped and hanging from the posts, except for one whose legs still kicked with involuntary movement, until the officer in charge ceremoniously walked across, took aim, and fired his pistol into the drooping body.

Justice felt anger and disgust. Death in the smoke and sweat of battle was one thing. The grisly ritual of calculated execution was another.

"One regrets the necessities of war." The silky voice came from beside him. He turned to see Saint-Haouen.

"Fire-raisers, landed yesterday from the English squadron and caught with incendiary materials. They have no protection under the laws of war, as you know. They are like spies."

At that moment Justice wished he could have faced the Frenchman sword in hand, even if he had been cut down himself. But he kept his temper under control as he watched the bodies being pitched into the cart. He was not going to give Saint-Haouen the satisfaction of seeing how the scene had affected him.

"You have no news for me?"

"Regrettably not. The guard was premature in bringing you here."

Justice ignored the excuse. There was no doubt that Saint-Haouen had fetched him to see the shooting. An object lesson like that might well make a man change his tale.

FAYOL DID NOT come again after this macabre exhibition, and Justice began to wonder whether there had been a change of plans. Perhaps there was a paper in Saint-Haouen's office waiting for the signature that would send him to face a firing-squad on one of these misty mornings. Perhaps they were expecting some word from Paris. Perhaps he was being left to rot because no one could decide what to do with him.

He remembered the wretched Carter, first lieutenant of the *Columbine*, who had spent a year in the *cachots* at Toulon, half-starved, and more than half-mad with frustration because he had stumbled on Boney's plan to sail for Egypt and there was no way that he could smuggle a message out to one of Nelson's patrolling frigates. Justice was in a similar plight, with Boney himself only a couple of miles away in his headquarters at Pont de Briques, making ready to throw his army across the Channel when the autumn winds and tides were right. By now, as the weeks rolled into September, Lilly must be thinking him a failure—or worse, for in London they would only know that he had disappeared without trace, just like Matthew Fielding.

Sometimes, when his mind was searching for an occupation in the lonely hours of the night, he thought about Fielding, wondering whether the French had finished him, or whether he lay cooped up in some other foul dungeon, struggling to keep hope flickering in the monotonous misery of a prisoner's life. For Fielding, after all, had been a commercial man, whose life of comfort could scarcely have fitted him for a career as a confidential agent, where death or degradation sat daily at his elbow. And yet, Justice realised, Fielding must long ago have learnt to accept the loneliness of his task, to manage without having anyone to whom he could confidently turn. "Trust nobody," Hatherley had said. That was a very difficult maxim for a seagoing officer who had been trained unquestionably to accept what his superiors said and to count on his comrades-in-arms.

Every day Justice asked the guard if there was news of his fate, and every day he got the same surly answer. *"Rien du tout!"* Then he woke one morning from his sweaty, restless sleep to find a sergeant standing over him, and he thought that Fayol had sent for him again. But this time he was marched out to the parade ground and back to the pump. As he dried himself, he noticed that one of the marines had impaled his filthy clothes on a bayonet and was carrying the bundle to a slow-burning pile of rubbish. He was about to point irritably to his nakedness when a sergeant came up with fresh garments over his arm, as well as a mirror, razor, and a bowl of soapy water.

This *service de valet* astonished Justice, all the more because nothing was said. It could be preparation for a court-martial, though it seemed unlikely that the French would waste either clothes or time on a doomed spy. Or Saint-Haouen might have had second thoughts about exchanging him. That would be an ironic anticlimax, and he wondered what Hatherley would say if he heard that Justice was back in England with nothing accomplished, and half the summer wasted. His feelings of frustration were so strong that he growled at the orderly who came to fetch him to Saint-Haouen's office.

As he waited in the ante-room, peering through the door in the hope of seeing something that might tell him his fate, he noticed that Saint-Haouen had another visitor, who was on the point of leaving by the corridor entrance, so that Justice could not see his face. He was a stocky man in a coat that looked like but not quite like a naval uniform. A port official, Justice guessed. The French had a passion for dressing everyone, even humble employees, in blue and braid and buttons.

The door closed, and Saint-Haouen went back to his desk, ringing a bell for Justice to enter. He was as coldly agreeable as before. "We have been considering your case," he said, as if Justice had been waiting comfortably in a tavern while the officials tried to make up their minds what to do with him. "There were, as you will appreciate, some odd aspects of your story, and I had to refer to Paris."

Justice saw no point in complaining about his treatment: even if Saint-Haouen did not mention it, he knew perfectly well what had happened and he clearly proposed to ignore it.

"I will be frank with you," Saint-Haouen went on in his dry fashion. "When you first came into this room, I had written down four questions on the gendarme's report." He tapped the paper before him and held up his little finger. "One. Were you who you said you were? A half-pay officer in the British navy?" He picked up the post-captain's list from his desk. "The answer to that is here."

Saint-Haouen raised a second finger. "Two. What brought you to France?" He looked hard at Justice. "Shall we agree that it was an accident?"

Justice felt so relieved that his improbable story had been accepted that his feeling must have shown in his face, and he was about to speak when Saint-Haouen forestalled him by raising a third finger. "I am prepared to believe you because I have a satisfactory answer to my third question. On both sides of the Canche estuary there are many soldiers. Yet you land at the Pointe de Lornel, sleep on the beach, and calmly announce your arrival to the gendarmes. How could that happen?" Saint-Haouen spread his hands. "That was an easy question. A few days before you came ashore, General Bonaparte was here to inspect the army and the flotilla. There was a sudden storm from the north-east. Several gunboats and sloops had to cut and run for it, chased down the coast to Etaples by your frigate *Leda* and some smaller vessels. Unfortunately, your frigate sank some of our ships. More than two hundred men were thrown into the sea, drowned, or washed ashore dead and half-dead. When the guards were questioned, they said that they took you for one more survivor from the wrecks."

"From the wrecks." The fisherman's words. And the storm would have helped Saint-Haouen to believe his tale about a squall on the English coast on the same day.

"Lastly," said Saint-Haouen, raising his forefinger. "Were you missed in England?" He fixed his eyes on Justice. "We have certain arrangements for learning what happens on the other side of *La Manche*. There's no secret in that. The contraband trade has advantages for people on both sides of this small stretch of water that separates our countries. What do we learn? That in Folkestone, in Hythe, in Rye, there are *affiches*, *placards*, which say that a fishing boat is lost with a Mr Justice on board, and that his friends offer a reward for news of him."

"I hope you will claim it." Justice spoke casually, realising that Saint-Haouen expected him to be impressed by the ease with which the French got news out of England. "Unless you mean to let me go home?"

"Regrettably not." Saint-Haouen made an apologetic gesture. "You will recall our first talk, when you spoke of the paradox of your situation—whether we were to regard you as an officer or a private gentleman. It seems that the Minister in Paris is also baffled, and his answer is a judgement of Solomon. As an officer you *could* be sent to Verdun as a prisoner. As an ordinary citizen you *would* be sent there as a *détenu*. Thus, if you are sent to Verdun, there will be no need to solve this legal riddle. In short, it has been decided to send you to Verdun.

"In your situation," Saint-Haouen continued, "it will be wise to resist any temptation to escape. You will therefore give your parole to Colonel Manaluz, who is expecting you. He will also provide the necessary *fiche*, with all your personal particulars, and arrange for an escort."

Justice nodded. "There is another matter," he said in a tone which had an aggrieved ring to it. "How am I to manage in Verdun?"

"For money?" Saint-Haouen's reaction was so similar to the way Hatherley had responded to the same question that Justice had a fleeting impression that everything was somehow arranged for him, as it might be in a good hotel by a courier specially engaged for the purpose, but he had shaken it off before Saint-Haouen finished his answer. "The house of Havart and Ruis in Rotterdam is accustomed to handling remittances for the English in Verdun, I believe," he said. "Fayol will do what is necessary—provided that your bank or your friends will give you credit."

"Certainly." Justice sounded confident, but he felt uneasy when Saint-Haouen began to indicate the scale of his expenses.

"Fayol will advance a hundred gold *louis.* Two months from now, when you should be in funds at Verdun, you will repay that amount, with twenty-five *louis* added for interest."

Saint-Haouen waited a moment, half-expecting a protest at this money-lender's rate, and then he added, with the air of a man casually mentioning the customary *pourboire* for the servant: "And you will, naturally, pay another ten *louis* for the clothes that Fayol obtained for you."

"Naturally," Justice said icily, remembering how often the French used the word, and how many shades of meaning they could give it. The whole exorbitant transaction was a means for Saint-Haouen and Fayol to put some gold in their own pockets—their small share of the stream of golden guineas that Bonaparte must be extracting from the *détenus.* Justice began to see what the French had gained from the detention of so many Englishmen of wealth and rank—most of them too old, or too young, or too sick, or too indifferent ever to take arms against them. "I presume," he said sarcastically, "that I am not required to provide the new Empress with a set of pearls for her coronation."

"No." Saint-Haouen kept a straight face, though there was a flicker of a smile round his eyes. "It would be appreciated, perhaps, but I think, Mr Justice, that it would make no difference to your peculiar situation."

"TO YOUR RIGHT, M'sieu, you see the Château de Pont de Briques, named after the Roman bridge across the Liane. Also the Emperor's headquarters." The earnest sergeant who had been sent to accompany Justice was clearly anxious to talk. From the moment the post-chaise rolled out of Boulogne, he had kept up a flow of information.

Justice glanced at the turreted square mansion, which he re-membered seeing on his way from Etaples. With its windows shuttered against the sun, and a set of motionless sentries on the gravel drive, it looked more like a model than the place where the Corsican Ogre sat, hatching his plans to attack and conquer England.

"You speak very good English." He made it a perfunctory compliment.

"That is very kind. I am glad of the opportunity to practise. I have the honour of being one of the interpreters who will go with the army to England, and explain everything to every-body." It occurred to Justice that the man threatened to van-quish the English by boring them to death; but there was no one to share the joke. "What matters is the honour."

"Quite." One word was enough to make Sergeant Franz Rit-ter bristle with pleasure. Although he was German by birth, the son of a Protestant minister in Baden, he lost no chance to demonstrate his Bonapartist fervour.

Or to instruct Justice in topography, history, politics, and German *lieder*—though his harsh voice made a mockery of the gentle music. While he droned on, Justice dozed, trying to re-store his jaded faculties, resentful when he was prodded awake to see a canal under construction, peasants harvesting, a church of merit, a town hall, or a château standing back from the road. The countryside looked rich in the golden colours of late sum-mer.

Two hours on from Boulogne they were running past some banks of osier, and Justice saw that they were coming to the place near Montreuil where the Course ran into the Canche. When he was a boy, coming to Valcourt, he always watched for the bridge, knowing that the road to Recques would turn off to the left and that within a half hour he would catch his first sight of the long grey house among the trees on the hillside.

Ritter must have caught some idea of his mood. *"Ce paysage vous intéresse, m'sieu?"*

It was done so naturally that Justice was almost taken una-wares, and he just managed to turn the beginnings of a French answer into an inarticulate grunt. "Huh?" he said, seeming puzzled.

"Excuse me." If Ritter had set a trap, he skilfully covered its failure. "You find this country interesting?"

Justice had already learned from this brief exchange that he could never relax, never trust himself; in half a sentence he could have given away the fact that he spoke French, that he knew where he was, perhaps the connection with Valcourt. "A man who comes from a dungeon finds everything fresh and pleasant," he said blandly.

"Evidently." Ritter was silent long enough for Justice to slip back into sleep, with his last sensible thought being the worry that he might trip into self-betrayal.

BY THE FIFTH DAY, as the post-chaise rolled over ill-made roads, and the weather got warmer, Justice found sleep the best defence against a slip of the tongue that might reveal too much, as well as a means of escape from Ritter's rasping chatter. Most of the time they had been travelling to the south-east, skirting the Belgian border, but Justice woke to find they were running south through a range of high wooded hills that sloped to a river.

"*Mort Homme,*" Ritter said, pointing to the highest of them.

Dead Man's Hill. The stark name came at Justice like an omen, and it stayed with him as they came out of the valley and saw a town in front of them, circled by impressive walls, and dominated by the twin towers of a cathedral and the bulk of a great fortification.

The chaise ran for a mile or two along the edge of the wide, slow-moving river, crossed it by a bridge, and came to a stop in front of a fortified gateway.

"Welcome to Verdun," Ritter said formally. And while Justice looked about him he heard the sergeant explaining that this was the Porte Chaussée, that it was a copy of the Bastille, which had been destroyed by the heroic people of Paris, that . . . this . . . that . . .

Ritter was certainly well informed. Perhaps he was too well informed. From the moment that Justice had walked into Saint-Haouen's room five days earlier, he had felt that he was walking into a trap.

But at least he had reached Verdun.

5

Ritter climbed down from the post-chaise and spoke to the sentry at the gatehouse. Meanwhile, Justice gazed round, remembering the book on Vauban's architecture he had bought in London. It was not hard to see why the town, perched on its wall of rock, had been chosen as France's strongest eastern bastion. Surrounded by the broad stream of the Meuse and by the massive walls, the whole town was virtually a fortress, and its only entrance was this fortified gatehouse, the Porte Chaussée. The warren of small streets round the base of the hill would be the Lower Town, the poorer quarter. Above it, he remembered from the book, was the Haute-Ville, and above that was poised the Citadel—said to be able to accommodate several thousand soldiers and the whole population in case of an invasion.

Then Ritter returned, and they were through the gate, the horses picking their way slowly along the narrow streets.

"For a garrison town," observed Justice, "there seem to be remarkably few soldiers."

The sergeant shrugged. "Most of the *détenus* are civilians. They would not know how to escape if they wanted to. As to the officers, they have given their parole. General Bonaparte's ideas, you understand, are humane and yet effective."

By now the post-chaise was more than half-way up the steep hill, passing the cathedral. To Justice's astonishment, the people in the streets—most of them evidently English—had a look of being at home and far from persecuted. At the top of the hill, Ritter pointed out the green square called the Roche, so filled with people that it seemed to Justice's astonished eyes as if the style of a fashionable resort in England had been imposed on the seedy military town. In the town itself, the streets and shops sparkled with elegance: here was a London boot-maker, who had opened a branch to cater to wealthy clients in Verdun, there a tea-room; here gentlemen with powdered wigs and gold-knobbed canes, there ladies in sedan chairs in a blaze of silks and satins, or walking on the arms of officers or with lady's maids in attendance. There were even small children scampering on the green of the Roche, under the watchful eye of governesses.

Ritter studied Justice's surprise with smug amusement. "You

see, they are content and comfortable. You agree, in France things are ordered not so badly?"

Justice let the observation pass, and for once the sergeant did not press it, for they were now crossing the deep dry ditch which divided the Roche from the Citadel itself. "You will have the honour, very likely, of meeting General Wirion himself," Ritter said in an awed tone.

"General Wirion?"

"The commandant. He is a general in the gendarmerie." Justice nodded. It sounded as if the man would be some jumped-up bully grown to power in the revolution.

The post-chaise came to a halt beside the guard-room at the entrance. Ritter took Justice inside and left him to be guarded by a sentry while he bustled off, clutching the wad of papers he had brought from Boulogne. A few minutes later he came back, with his usual air of being on urgent business. "I am told the General will see you now. The orderly will take you. As for me, I have been given leave." He bowed correctly. "It has been a pleasure to be M. le capitaine's companion. I wish you well."

Justice could not quite bring himself to echo the sentiment.

"We shall meet again. Perhaps when we come to England with the Emperor."

"Long before that, I hope," Justice said with exaggerated politeness.

"Thank you." Ritter gave a stiff nod of thanks. Irony, Justice had soon discovered, was lost on him.

RITTER'S DESCRIPTION had led Justice to expect a formidable man—a cavalry commander perhaps, with splendid whiskers and imposing bearing. But when he looked at the man in charge of the Verdun prisoners, he almost burst out laughing.

The desk at which Wirion sat was certainly *formidable* in the French sense. Like the rest of the furniture and pictures in the room, it was probably part of the loot which Bonaparte's soldiers had carried off from castles and country houses all over Europe. But the man himself was almost comic—small, with spiky hair, protruding nose, and small moustache. The effect of caricature was heightened by his costume, for he seemed to be peering over the top of a high-collared coat with gilt froggings and such heavy epaulettes that Justice wondered whether it was the official uniform of a general of gendarmes or whether Wirion's tailor had made it specially to satisfy his client's self-importance.

"Captain Justice." Wirion grunted reflectively, and looked more closely at the paper in his hand: it was the *fiche* on which Justice's personal details had been entered at Boulogne. "The paper is in order," Wirion said as if to himself, and put it in a folder. Then he fixed his dark eyes suspiciously on Justice. "I have been expecting you," he remarked in such an accusing tone that Justice felt he was being reprimanded for late arrival, like an errant schoolboy.

Or did the simple phrase carry another meaning—again, as before at Boulogne, he had the odd feeling of taking part in a play whose plot had already been decided.

Wirion was still rooting through his other papers. "Most troublesome—irregular—letters from Boulogne—from Paris—uncertain status . . . However, it is not my business to decide such things. But it is my business to keep you here at Verdun. Whether you will be comfortable here is another question, which only you can answer."

It seemed to Justice that this was a set speech delivered to every new arrival. Unfortunately, Wirion seemed to need to make it at close quarters, for he got up and came round the desk, so that Justice was uncomfortably aware of the general's personal odour, in which stale tobacco, wine, and garlic were merely additional spices.

"Do I make myself clear, Captain?" Wirion's voice was now wheedling. "Personally, I would wish to see you make yourself at home in Verdun. Things are not so bad, considering that England makes war on us when all that the Emperor desires is peace; it is not difficult to pass the time agreeably here, if you have the means . . ."

Justice edged himself back on his chair with a feeling of distaste: the words were all too clear a hint of bribery and sneaking blackmail.

"If you do not have the means, or do not like the little rules I am obliged to impose, or if you make trouble, try to escape—well then, things are not so easy." Wirion screwed up his eyes and for a moment seemed about to stand on tiptoe to gain an extra inch of authority. "Then you know, there is always Bitche, where the *souterrains* are said to be unpleasant."

Justice breathed out sharply. Bitche and Sarrelibre were the two penal fortresses, a few days' foot-march from Verdun, where parole-breakers and would-be escapees were taken. He had first heard the names grimly whispered at Richmond Terrace; it was possible, Hatherley had said, that Fielding had been sent to one or another of them. And Bitche had been a favourite topic of the knowledgeable Ritter. A yellow lion of a fortress, he had said, crouched on the hills above the German frontier.

"Such places," went on Wirion, "are reserved for *mauvais sujets*—of which I am sure you are not one, Captain Justice."

"Thank you for your confidence, m'sieu." Since he could not kick the odious little general's teeth in, he might as well seem to wallow in self-abasement: his ability to move freely about Verdun would depend on Wirion's favour. "As to money, I have adequate means for a few months."

"That is very good." Satisfied that Justice could pay for his privileges, Wirion raised a finger. "One thing more. Your *parole d'honneur* must be confirmed."

Justice had thought a good deal about that promise not to escape. Even with so much at stake, he could not flout the strict British code of honour, with its unvarying insistence that an officer could not break his pledged word. "At best, you would be socially ruined if you broke your parole," Hatherley had told him. "At worst, you could be returned to the French. Of course, if you are under restraint . . . One key turned in a lock, one hand laid on you, would be enough."

Justice saw that he had no option. "I confirm it."

"Very well. In that case, you may live in the town. I grant you permission, for the usual fee." Wirion was certainly a man for direct dealing. "And you may have permission to go up to five kilometres from the town, if you leave your *carte d'identité* at the gate. There will be a fee for the permission, naturally."

"Naturally." There was something so degrading in the cool assumption that corruption was a normal thing between a jailor and his prisoners that Justice could not conceal his sarcasm; he was glad when Wirion said brusquely that he would be lodged with a M. Hahn, at 17, rue de Jemappes, and sent an orderly to escort him.

"Very good lodgings," the orderly remarked as he led Justice to a small house just off the street that led down steeply from

71

the cathedral into the Lower Town. "A friend of the general, you will see."

After that discouraging information, Justice was ready to be fleeced again, and M. Hahn did not disappoint him. The first room he was shown was an attic, with a bed, a chest, and a chair, and no fireplace: it looked as though the bailiffs had just left. Hahn, a small and cadaverous man with a tremor that made him seem even shiftier, asked a price that would have kept Justice in comfort at the Tavistock, with all his meals and wine; added that a superior room might be had on the second floor at twice the price; and, when Justice did not seem disposed to bargain too hard, stipulated for meals and laundry *en plus*.

Wirion, no doubt, was taking his commission on each transaction.

THE PORK CHOP was gristly, the carafe of red wine too acid, the cheese dry: M. Hahn evidently began as he meant to go on. Yet Justice was hungry enough to eat what Hahn's sullen serving-maid had set in front of him. There was only one other person in the dining-room—a small, thin man in his early fifties, who was finishing his dinner. "I fear M. Hahn's establishment is not for gourmets," he said, observing Justice's struggle with the pork chop.

Justice smiled; his fellow-guest sounded as if he spoke from experience. "You've been here long?"

"Since last winter. I had a piece of work to do in Paris, and by misfortune I arrived the week the English were detained there. And you?"

"I arrived today from Boulogne."

His fellow-guest was sufficiently discreet, or sufficiently English, not to pursue that line of conversation. But when he got up to go he offered Justice his hand. "My name, by the way, is Hunt. Nathaniel Hunt. By profession, portrait painter."

Justice in turn introduced himself and went on to ask what the town had to offer in the way of entertainment.

"It depends where your interests lie. There are gambling-houses, inns, and taverns. Balbi's, near the cathedral, is the favoured place, though I believe you must be a member. Or there's the theatre, if you have a mind for it. They say Mr Moon and his players are very droll."

"A gambling-house. A theatre. And a racecourse, I presume?" Justice was astonished at the style of life. The painter nodded agreeably.

"We English seem to make ourselves at home," he said. "But I am no authority on these matters, I fear, for I am generally too busy."

"Yours is a highly agreeable and, I hope, a profitable profession."

"I can't complain," said the painter placidly. "Work is always preferable to the pursuit of pleasure, which most of our fellows here are condemned to. As to profit—well, I'm lucky to have a waiting list of subjects. Mine's a trade which thrives on those with time, vanity, and money, and there are plenty of them in Verdun."

When Hunt had gone upstairs, Justice selected a cane from a set which Hahn kept in the hallway, and set off for the Place du Roche, wondering what the painter would make of a trade where the pursuit of pleasure was so woven with the pursuit of danger. It was well past seven o'clock, and in the fading violet light Justice noticed that many people were carrying the lanterns which Ritter had told him were obligatory for civilian *détenus:* not being bound by the officer's code of parole, they were required to carry this sign of their status, on pain of losing their privileges and being shut up in the Citadel at night.

As chattering groups pushed past him, their yellow lamps swinging and bobbing, the women laughing eagerly and leaving a trace of perfume in the air as they passed, Justice felt his spirits rising. In this provincial town, which had once offered nothing but the grubby pleasures required by a garrison, it appeared that a man could now find anything that money could buy. The quiet little painter had been right. With the arrival of the English prisoners, many of them with ample funds on call, Verdun had become a town given up to their amusements.

Yet it was still a small town, where gossip would run fast, and Justice guessed that he might find a trace of Fielding more simply than had seemed possible in London. Fielding would have had lodgings, made friends, dined out perhaps; and people would have noticed when he disappeared. The difficulty, of

73

course, was that Justice could not directly ask what he needed to know, going about Verdun like an attorney's clerk collecting evidence for a trial.

The first direct question, put to the wrong person or passed on by an informer, could only too easily give him away. He would have to come to the matter slantwise, on a tack across the wind, hoping to get a sight of his quarry without revealing his own heading, praying that luck would be with him and that the answers would come quickly. For time pressed—pressed desperately, he had decided as he took a last glance at Bonaparte's flotilla on his way out of Boulogne. There were too many ships and soldiers there for an Englishman's comfort.

But where to begin—a gaming-room or the theatre? He would meet casual acquaintances in both places, and his eye was caught by a theatrical bill that could have come from a wall in Tunbridge Wells. "Mr Montague Moon's Company," it ran, "Present Mr Holcroft's Tragi-Comedy, *The Road to Ruin*, widely acclaimed Last Season and now Repeated by Popular Request & Subscription." But the performance, Justice noted, had begun at seven, and as he had never cared for the fashionable habit of going late to the play, he concluded that Mr Moon would have to wait for his patronage.

It had better be a gaming-room. Even if Holland was right that Fielding's tastes did not run in that direction, it was easy to meet people in such a place and pick up the gossip of the town; and Nathaniel Hunt had said that a man called Balbi kept a set of rooms up near the cathedral.

Justice turned in that direction. He found his way easily enough by keeping an eye on the towers, catching the moonlight above the rooftops, until he came to a solid, double-fronted stone house, with a lamp on a bracket over a painted sign. Justice looked closer. There was no name, only two crisp sentences. "This Bank is kept for the English. The French are forbidden to play at it."

"M'sieu is English?" The doorman's question underlined the point, and when Justice nodded, the man immediately demanded a membership fee of five *louis*. "It is the commandant's rule," he said, and from his tone Justice suspected that a large part of the fee might also be the commandant's commission. "And one must also sign each time one comes in," the doorman added, pointing to an open book on the table in the hallway.

Presumably, General Wirion liked to have an idea how much business M. Balbi might be doing.

There was a small room on the right, where a few women sat on sociables, with men standing beside them as if they were at a private party. Beyond, through a folding door, Justice could see a couple of groups playing cards, and from somewhere else in the house he could hear the even, high-pitched call of a croupier controlling a game. At this hour in the evening, it all seemed most decorous.

"Isn't it John Justice?"

The unexpected sound of his name made Justice turn sharply before he checked himself with the uneasy thought that he might have given himself away; and he was relieved to feel a friendly grip on his arm and to see a half-remembered face. There were bound to be people at Verdun who would recognise him, and the sooner he could claim an acquaintance or two, the easier it would be to make his story seem plausible. The presence of friends always vouched for a man.

"Pullen," he said, reaching back over three years for a name. "You had the *Sophie*. In Jersey."

"Not a place to boast about here," Pullen said cautiously in a low voice, and as he turned Justice towards a quiet corner of the room, he looked about, to make sure that no one could overhear them. "There are people in this house who would catch a whisper and run to turn it into gold—or a favour."

"Informers?" Narks were common enough in English gaming-houses, and Justice saw no reason why things should be different in France.

"And worse. Anything from tale-bearing to intrigue. You watch what you say in Verdun if you're wise, Justice. Even among our own countrymen."

The warning was direct, and it was enough to deter Justice from pressing Pullen with reminiscences and questions. The young man clearly had something on his mind; as they talked, he kept looking quizzically at Justice, as though he was on the verge of a confidence; and then, taking his own advice to heart, he changed his tone, putting the conventional questions that would be asked of any new arrival, and listening politely while Justice went over his tale of shipwreck and capture.

"Oh, God," Pullen broke in suddenly. "The club bore."

Justice made way for a military-looking man in his late thirties, well-built, with a hearty manner that suited his figure.

"Who's your friend, Pullen?" the newcomer asked bluffly, and went on to introduce himself before Pullen had a chance to reply. "Giles Lovell," he said, giving a short bow before he held out his hand. "Formerly Major Lovell, 72nd Foot."

Justice took Lovell's hand as Pullen completed the round of introductions. "May I present Captain Justice, who has recently joined us?" The formal phrase made Justice realise that Lovell was accompanied, and that his broad shoulders had hidden his elegant female companion, standing a pace or two behind him.

"Sorry," Lovell said offhandedly. "Madame Lamotte." He took the woman by the arm to bring her forward. "Madame Lucienne."

Justice caught this subtle shift in the use of her name as he looked at her, and saw that she coloured slightly at the snub. "I am delighted, madame," taking her hand with the politest of bows. It appeared that the raffish major was a boor as well as a bore.

Madame Lamotte certainly made an odd pair with her escort. Lovell, puce-complexioned and heavily whiskered, looked like a country squire out for the night in London, while she could have been on her way to a ball in Berkeley Square, with half the town waiting to dance attendance on her. She was small, strikingly beautiful, with a dash of auburn in the dark hair which framed her oval face, and set off the brown eyes which rested steadily on his own.

"This is indeed alarming." She spoke with a flicker of smiling self-mockery that Justice found engaging, and softened the flirtatious style of her words.

"Alarming, madame?"

"To be surrounded by my country's enemies."

"Who are your country's captives, madame, and your own." Justice noticed that she had gently disengaged herself from Lovell's arm as he spoke. "Englishmen will never yield to Bonaparte, but they are instantly conquered by the beauty of a Frenchwoman."

She turned to Pullen, speaking clearly in English with an accent that Justice found hard to place. "Your friend turns a pretty compliment, lieutenant. One might almost take Captain Justice for a Frenchman himself."

It was a risky moment. Pullen was probably unaware that

Justice had a French mother, but he certainly knew too much for comfort about the work that Justice had been doing along the coasts of Normandy and Brittany; and even if he guarded his tongue, he could easily let slip the fact that Justice spoke French as easily as any man who had spent much of his boyhood on an estate in Picardy.

Pullen, however, was no fool. He gave the impression that he had scarcely heard the exchange between Justice and Lucienne, and that his attention had been caught by some movement in the inner room. "If you will excuse me," he said. He caught Justice's eye as he nodded politely, and Justice realised that it was discretion rather than boredom which prompted his departure.

"Of course." Justice would not have chosen Lovell's company: his companion looked far more congenial. Yet he had to say something as they continued to stand with him. "Have you been long in Verdun?" The trite opening would do as well as any.

"Too long." Lovell spoke with feeling. "Too damn long. Came here at the start, after a spell at Lille." Lovell appeared to be a little uneasy, as if he might give something away if he explained too much, and he turned the question back on Justice. "And you?"

"Just got here. Wrecked on a fishing trip, of all things, and blown ashore in France. Wretched business."

"Should you not be sent home, then, or exchanged?"

"My idea, exactly. Can't wait to get out of the place." Justice spoke lightly, hoping that he sounded like an agreeable but not very intelligent officer. Lord knows, there were enough of them in the service to make the part seem convincing. "Can't persuade the Frenchies. Some muddle in Paris, I say. So I'll try to make the best of things here while they're making up their minds."

"It's all right if you've got the money," Lovell said meaningfully. "And a miserable, cold, and hungry life if you haven't." As he spoke, Justice was aware that the major was looking at him cagily, sizing him up for some undisclosed purpose.

"I am sure the captain will be comfortable here." Lucienne Lamotte held out her hand in a way that implied an invitation rather than a dismissal. "He seems to be quite at home already."

"Promised at Creange's Club." Lovell broke in before Justice could answer Lucienne. "Only place for a gentleman who likes to play high. Happy to propose you."

Justice was surprised to see Lucienne slip away before Lovell had finished his sentence, and then, as he watched the major leave, he saw that Lucienne had joined a couple near the window and had gone off with them to another room. It had not occurred to him until that moment that she might be employed by Balbi. And that if she was, she might have known Fielding.

But he could do nothing about that possibility now. And in any case it would be wiser to wait until he saw how the wind lay in that quarter—with her, and with Lovell as well. All he could do for the moment would be to take a look at the members' book in the hall to see whether Fielding had actually been to the place, and how often.

He stood at the table, casually flicking the pages. It would be the normal thing for a newcomer who knew nobody in the place, and he tried not to show too much interest in the scrawled signatures; gamblers, it was clear, were not much given to copperplate writing. There was nothing in February, or in March, but he found what he was looking for early in April. *Matthew Fielding.* His pulse quickened. Seeing the name, written more clearly than most, almost as though Fielding had expected someone to come looking for it, he felt for the first time that he was seeking a real man—a man who had walked through Balbi's door only a matter of weeks before. It was Fielding's hand all right; the same hand that had scribbled the hurried note he had read in Holland's dining-room. And as he turned the pages on through April, he saw Fielding had come there often, every two or three days in fact. The last entry was on the 22nd of May.

So Fielding had certainly been in Verdun until the last week of May, as Lilly had suspected. It was not much to learn, but it was a beginning; and there might be more to be learned if he went back into the inner room and used his eyes and ears.

LIKE ALL MEN who live by the sea or by war, Justice had a streak of the gambler in him: an ability to reckon odds, and take chances against them, was one condition of survival. Yet he had no taste for *rouge-et-noir*, or for any form of cards, or for anything that gave the false excitement of winning a few gold coins on a wager.

He came up to a table where four men were playing what, so far as he could tell, was a variant of euchre. Others were standing about behind the players. One, who kept slightly apart, was a small, bristling-bearded Frenchman whose eyes continually flitted from one face to another, and back again to the piles of counters stacked on the table, and Justice was aware that his own arrival had been noted. This must be the *patron*, M. Balbi.

The players all appeared to be English. One was a pale, puffy-faced man who looked the worse for drink and was nonetheless respectfully addressed by his companions as "m'lord." If he was typical of the English aristocrats who had been swept up into Verdun, Justice thought, no wonder Bonaparte believed that England was ripe for the taking.

The deals went round: three cards, then two. Then the bidding in the quaint terms of euchre—"eldest hand," "order it up," "march." Justice looked closely, trying to discover how the hands were played. After a while he sensed that his interest had attracted the attention of a dark-featured man with a sardonic expression on his face, somewhat older than himself though of much the same build. The man was looking at him so intently that Justice twice avoided his eye, at the same time wondering if this might be some acquaintance he had forgotten. He nodded casually a couple of times, and then moved away to watch another table.

He had been watching for a minute or two when he heard a voice beside him, so soft that at first he did not realise someone was speaking to him. Then, again, came the strident whisper. "M'sieu." There was a tug at his sleeve, and Justice turned to see the small, bearded man at his elbow. "My name is Balbi. I do not know yours, m'sieu, but I must ask you to come outside." Justice, puzzled by the request, followed him into an ante-room. He saw that the *patron* was perspiring.

"Justice. Captain Justice." He might as well use the title.

"So, Captain Justice." Balbi paused, looking ill at ease. "I have an unpleasant duty. It may be a mistake, no doubt, but I cannot say nothing."

Justice was bewildered. "What is the matter?"

"It is signals, m'sieu. You were seen by one of my assistants."

"Signals?" repeated Justice, genuinely mystified.

"To the milord. To Lord Brantbridge, at the table." He pointed through the open door to the table, where the aristocratic gamester lay sprawled and yawning across the cards. "Twice, after the deal, you nodded, and made other gestures during the play."

Justice felt a flush of anger, but he controlled himself. "I assure you, m'sieu," he replied coldly, "I know next to nothing of cards. But if I did wish to pass a signal, I could think of better ways of doing it. And I have never met Lord Brantbridge before. I only arrived in Verdun today."

Balbi was taken aback. "In that case . . ." he began.

"In that case, sir, I expect an apology or—" Justice felt that he too could wring some advantage from this game of unfinished sentences, and he noticed that several men now stood at the doorway watching the altercation. Unless the matter was settled at once, he could drift into a situation where he would have to make a challenge. He had no idea what rules of etiquette applied in a prison-town like Verdun, but he was certain that the last thing he wanted was to run the risk of a duel.

"There was a mistake, m'sieu." Balbi stammered with anxiety.

"Thank you." The exchange had been quiet, but people had stopped talking to look at Balbi spluttering at a stranger. Once the thrill of a scandal was snatched away, however, the players went back to their gaming.

Justice thought it best to stand his ground for a while. He stopped a waiter carrying a tray of champagne and took a glass, sipping the chilled wine slowly as he looked about and tried to make sense of the incident. Had Balbi's mistake been genuine, or was there someone in the gaming-rooms who wished Justice no good—who had caught his name, perhaps, when Pullen introduced him to Lovell and Madame Lamotte, or had seen him skimming through the members' book, or simply thought he was helping Brantbridge to cheat? He could ask the questions, but he had no means of discovering the answers. But he doubted whether it had anything to do with Fielding. No one could possibly have known that he was coming, or why he was there.

Justice finished his champagne and went to the door. He was relieved that no one seemed interested in him any more: even the doorman was casual, nodding him out into the night with a mumbled courtesy.

Outside, it was cooler, the streets quiet, and much darker, as the summer afterglow had faded and the lantern-carrying strollers had gone home. There was no one in sight as he went up the hill towards the Roche, except a beggar huddled in the porch of the cathedral, with a bowl beside the stump of his leg.

Justice believed that any man who had smelt gun-powder owed something to another, and he never passed a wounded beggar. He had nothing less than a franc, really too large for the purpose, but he leant over to drop it into the bowl.

"Merci, m'sieu, votre santé." The cripple had just given a cringe of gratitude when Justice heard the scuff of a foot, the rustle of a coat, and then felt a swinging brutal blow on the side of his head that seemed to rip his body with pain. He felt himself begin to fall to the ground, half-heard the beggar's surprised cry, and then seemed to be tumbling endlessly through dark clouds lit by streaks of coloured lightning.

He was unconscious before he hit the cobbles.

⚜ 6 ⚜

JUSTICE LAY in a large room with an ornate ceiling whose mouldings dipped and swayed each time he opened his eyes to look at them, and after a few minutes he felt himself dropping back into a nauseous blackness while a far-away voice put questions he lacked the strength to answer.

When he woke again, he found himself lying face downwards, with a pair of competent hands probing the muscles at the base of his neck.

"He'll do well enough. You can turn him over. But gently, now." The words were spoken in a soft Irish brogue, and as the strong arms of a serving-man helped Justice to roll over and sit up, he saw that the speaker was a large, thickset man in a light wig, who was just taking his place in a chair beside the couch. For one moment he wondered whether his mind was still wandering, for on the Irishman's shoulder there was perched a neat, gray-faced monkey.

"That's a poor welcome to Verdun for you, Captain Justice." The Irishman's tone was so cordial, and Justice was still so confused, that he watched the servant go out of the room before he realised that he had been addressed by name.

By then it would have been churlish to ask how the stranger knew him, and he waited for the big man to settle himself in the chair.

"You'll not mind the little fellow?" As the man spoke, he gave the little ape some kind of signal that sent it scurrying across the room to fetch a bunch of grapes.

"No." Justice had no objection to monkeys. Many seamen who had served in the tropics kept them as pets on board ship. But there was something about the way this creature fetched and carried for his master that disturbed him.

The man beside him sensed his reaction. "The little fellow does no harm with his tricks," he said reassuringly. "All the same, if he bothers you—" He made a short noise with his tongue and the monkey hopped back to his shoulder. "Animals have gratitude, you know, sir. I brought him from the medical faculty at the Sorbonne. If I hadn't, he'd have been dead fur and bone long ago. And I believe he knows it."

"You seem to make a habit of helping those in trouble."

"I try my best." As the Irishman told him a long anecdote about the monkey, Justice tried to piece together what had happened to him, and to guess where he was. He remembered the sudden blow; half-heard voices; a lamp-lit room; a violent spasm of retching. And now it was daylight, with the sun falling warm on him through a window.

The room gave onto another, reached by a short flight of steps, where the furniture was pushed back to the walls, leaving the way clear to a staircase beyond. This odd arrangement gave Justice an idea and he looked at his host, whose eyes gazed unwaveringly in a beam of sunlight; and then he saw the walking-cane close to hand. The man must be blind, or as near it as made no matter.

"I should be sorry to think of an Englishman spending his first night in Verdun lying like a sack of Galway potatoes in a merchant's doorway." The soft speech had an attractive turn to it.

"Was I unconscious long?" Justice was eager to know what had happened to him, but the Irishman was taking his time, in the way of his countrymen. "Long enough. An hour, perhaps."

He would be in his late forties, Justice guessed, with firm but melancholy features; and his well-cut dark coat, silk cravat, and the elegant gold cap on his cane all suggested the worldly comforts of a professional man—a lawyer, perhaps.

"As long as that!" It was no wonder his head felt as if he had been half-brained by a falling spar.

"You'd lain there for a moment, the beggar said, when my man came up and saw you. He fetched help from Balbi's, where the doorman remembered you. He brought a chair and he and my man carried you back here. 'Twas as well they did, for if you laid there in the gutter, you'd have been stripped of your purse and silks as easily as a peasant takes an egg from under a chicken. This town's full of evil ways, and picking a stranger's pocket is reckoned to be fair game."

"It's the same in London," Justice said. "One's always likely to be attacked near a gaming-house." Though he thought it wise to make light of the affair, he could not help wondering whether there had been more to it than that—whether someone was already interested in what he was doing in Verdun.

"Now, can you answer me this, precisely? Can you recall what happened just before the blow fell?"

"I remember feeling in my pocket for a coin to give to the beggar, and then I heard a noise behind me. After that, the blow fell."

"That's good news indeed." The Irishman sat back, evidently relieved. "The head is the most precious piece of mechanism the Good Lord gives us. If there is immediate recollection of what passed before a blow, it means there is no serious damage to the cerebral tissue."

"Then you are some sort of doctor, sir?"

His host seemed amused. "There are those who would say that was a fair description. My name is Declan O'Moira, sometime graduate of Trinity College, Dublin. Do you know the City of the Four Courts?"

Justice shook his head. A softer tone had come into the man's voice.

"It's not among the grand places of the world like London or Paris. Yet for a gracious queen of cities, a little past her prime, you might travel Europe and find only Vienna that might match it. I practised a while in Merrion Square, and specialised a little, until last year. That was when the world began going dark about me. I happened to know a clever fellow in Paris, by the name of Marc Marsan. His work on lenses was ahead of everything in Europe, and I came across to see him. That was at the end of last year. I only had two treatments from him before they started rounding up the foreigners in Paris. Then the darkness closed in completely."

"That was a hard blow of fate."

"In one way, perhaps. But not entirely. I happen to believe there's a kindly destiny that shapes us," continued O'Moira gravely. "If I was not to serve my countrymen as a physician, then perhaps I was picked out to do some other kind of service. I have good friends in France, despite the terrible times this unhappy country has known of late; thanks to them, and in a little measure to my humble skills, I've been able to ease the way for a few poor souls in Verdun."

"So your loss has been a gain for others. And for me—"

"I like to think so." The Irishman stopped Justice's expression of thanks with a gesture. "But I must not tire you. Talk's the besetting sin of any Dublin man, and I'm no exception. I've a short call to make, and I'll leave you to lie back a little. The brain needs a good rest after a shock like that."

Justice nodded. His head still ached, and it had been an effort to talk. Soon after the doctor had carefully felt his way out of the room, he was asleep.

He had no idea how long he slept, but when he woke, his head was clearer and he found that he could stand without more than a passing wave of dizziness and nausea. As soon as he could trust his legs, he made his way to the window.

He was looking down into a narrow street from a room that seemed to be part of a gate or bridge across it, and for a moment he wondered whether he had been taken into the guardhouse at the Porte Chaussée; but that dismal fancy was chased away by the sight of a small garden, with a conservatory full of dark grapes, that ran across the wall below him. It was obviously the doctor's private house, built into one of the medieval walls of the town.

The room was stuffy and the garden looked inviting. In a cautious fashion, like a drunk going below decks, Justice made his way down a narrow staircase. At the bottom was a glass door, which seemed to lead into the conservatory. He turned the handle, but the door did not budge. He tried again, pushing at the door. There was no give in it. Someone must have shot the bolts on the other side, and left him a prisoner.

He had already turned to look for a chair or some other object with which he could smash a way through the glass, when he heard a door close, the tap of a cane, and the quick patter of the monkey's feet. O'Moira was back in the house, and it would be best to meet him coolly.

The Irishman heard him in the passage. "Up and about, I'm glad to hear," he said, lowering himself onto an upright chair. "Sure, it's a warm morning for a man that's used to the mists of Dublin." He cocked his head at Justice. "Will you be feeling like a little dinner soon?"

"My appetite's worse than my head, now." Justice laughed.

"And a turn in the conservatory till my man's ready to serve it? I've sweet-scented flowers there that'll freshen your spirits." As O'Moira came to the door, Justice watched to see whether he unlocked it. At the first turn of the handle, O'Moira grunted, and Justice felt his suspicions rise again.

"Give it a pull, there's a good fellow," O'Moira said. "The damn thing's always sticking, and I'll wager your arm is stronger than mine."

At the first tug, the door came open with a jerk, and Justice chided himself for being so foolish. Still feeling the effects of the blow on the head, he had been trying to open the door the wrong way. And he was so taken aback by his own stupidity that the doctor was half-way through his praise of the grapes when he caught the thread of the sentence. "Colmar country . . . finest early grapes in France . . . don't leave them on the vine too long . . . or fail to prune them . . . go rotten, like some poor souls in this hothouse town, devil take the place."

Justice tried one of the lush clusters the doctor had picked. "They are magnificent," he said admiringly.

"You're feeling better, I gather," O'Moira said sympathetically.

"I am. And would like to ask how I may repay your kindness."

"You embarrass me," O'Moira replied, rather forcefully. "I don't care to count the cost of such things. But if you will, you can help me to the theatre this evening. I have a pair of tickets for Moon's piece and the picnic supper afterwards, and a friend is always better company than one's manservant."

THERE WAS A French theatre in the lower part of the town, Justice learned from Dr O'Moira as they walked slowly across the Roche and down a flight of steps at the side of the looming Citadel. Montague Moon and his company, however, had the use of a hall which had once been the church of Saint-Amand and was now at the disposal of the English *détenus* for their theatricals, balls, and assemblies.

For the next two hours Justice had good reason to regret his impulsive acceptance of the doctor's invitation. His head was sore, his back ached, the seats were hard wooden pews, the hall was smoke-filled and stuffy, and it was hard to hear what the actors said. The stage was small and they huddled at the back of it, apparently afraid of their costumes catching fire on the oil flares that served as footlights. And the play was a wretched piece of melodrama, which Justice had thought poor stuff when he had seen Munden in the lead part at Covent Garden—and Montague Moon, for all his silvery good looks and sonorous delivery, was certainly no one to match against Munden.

But none of these things could diminish the thrill of pleasure which Justice always felt as he entered this world of make-believe. He was in a much more cheerful mood when the curtain finally came down and he and O'Moira worked their way through the press of people to reach backstage, where the players were preparing supper in the old vestry that served as a green-room.

Moon was mellifluous and gracious. His daughter, Effie, a sweet-faced girl, gave Justice a hurried smile as she tried to set pies and platters on a large table, hindered by other members of the company, who seemed more eager to eat than to remove the carmine, pomatum, and vermilion from their faces; and while they waited they talked in the hectic manner of their profession about the performance. Justice enjoyed passing from one chatterbox to another, until he found himself talking to a middle-aged actress who was introduced by O'Moira as Mrs Williams.

"And what do you think of life in Verdun?" Justice asked this fragile-looking lady.

"Lud, sir, it is almost my second home." The actress had apparently taken on the vocabulary and quaint inflexions of a character in one of Sheridan's comedies. "And you, sir?"

"Oh, I am newly come to town. Involuntarily, like all the rest."

"Egad, but these are dreadful days." Mrs Williams gave an affected shudder. "I told Monty Moon 'twas folly to come scudding over to this country as if the world was his lobster, but no, he would not be gainsaid, and like a loyal fool I followed. And, in truth, it is no worse than playing Chatham or Winchester for a twelvemonth."

"Loyalty is the best of qualities." Justice sought safety in a platitude.

"But it is wasted on some." With this cryptic remark, Mrs Williams sat down at the long table, now stocked with plates of *pâté*, game pies, and long-necked decanters of white Alsatian wine, and made room for Justice on the bench beside her. Effie Moon, who had thrown Justice several encouraging glances, was beyond reach of hand or conversation, at the far end of the table, and her father sat on one side of her, with O'Moira on the other. The doctor was apparently accepted as one of the family party.

While Mrs Williams talked to her neighbour, Justice encouraged a shy and gentle young man on his left to say that he was Etienne Mandin, the stage manager, and that he came from Paris.

"Working for an English company? In a prison fortress?"

"It is necessary for the stage manager to speak French to instruct the stage-hands," Etienne said simply. "Mr Moon had the kindness to engage me in Paris. I am happy with the work. I make one or two good friends in the company. When they are sent here, I do not wish to leave them. And my wages are still paid, after all." He shrugged his shoulders, and gestured towards the table. "One eats, too."

"I would hardly say that." A lugubrious character actor with a rounded Yorkshire accent leaned across the table to speak to Justice. "It is all very well for bucks and blades and their fine ladies, but if you're an actor, sir, it's hard times, scratching for a guinea wherever you can find it." He looked up and down the table, and lowered his voice to a stage whisper. "There's some as aren't too particular about it, eh, Etienne?"

Justice felt the French youth stiffen beside him, and knew that some indecipherable gibe had struck home—that there had been a hint in the Yorkshireman's words that echoed Pullen's warning the night before. Life in Verdun might appear to be agreeable, but there were hidden stresses wherever one went—even here, in a green-room alive with the jollity that always seized actors after the play.

Etienne said nothing, but an affected-looking youth who sat next to him picked up the Yorkshireman's remark. "The worst of it are the dreadful rules and regulations. That man Wirion. *So* vulgar. A butcher, they say. Quite dreadful. And those *appels*. Twice a day one has to *humiliate* oneself by standing in a line to report to some tedious, rancid-smelling sergeant. And to carry lanterns at night, like so many glow-worms. And to stay in one's lodgings, and heaven knows what else."

"You should play the part of a man for once, then, and escape," the lugubrious Yorkshireman cut in sarcastically.

"What, and get sent to some absolutely hideous dungeon in that awful place at Bitche! Which is well-named, I fancy." The young man tittered, and then turned away so sharply that Justice guessed that he had caught a disapproving grimace from Mrs Williams.

"Are many sent there?" He put the question to Etienne, hoping to draw him out again.

"Those who annoy General Wirion." Etienne spoke like someone who wanted to change the subject. "Enough to make people afraid of him. Enough to make them pay him—one way or another."

There was clearly no more to be learned from Etienne while he was nettled by the teasing of the Yorkshireman, and Justice turned back to Mrs Williams.

She so claimed Justice's attention with a chronicle of complaints that he did not notice that Major Lovell and Madame Lamotte had joined the party, until he saw Moon ushering the fascinating lady to a place he had made between himself and the blind doctor. At Balbi's, Justice recalled, she had seemed almost showily provocative. Now there was a cool chaste look to her high-cut green satin dress, and a firm set to her face.

88

"It is rare, indeed," Moon boomed as he waved Lovell to a seat and fawned over Lucienne, "very rare, I may say, for we poor mountebanks to have the honour of entertaining Beauty and Valour at our humble table. You know us all, I think."

"I think not." Dr O'Moira had been quietly feeding tidbits to the monkey as it squatted on his left arm. "Madame Lamotte has not met Captain Justice, I believe."

Justice met her gaze across the table. "Indeed, I had the pleasure only last night," she said warmly. "I think I was among the first to welcome him to Verdun."

"And Major Lovell?" The doctor, of course, had missed Lovell's gesture of greeting. Yet there was a curious pitch to his voice. It made Justice feel that O'Moira was somehow drawing special attention to his presence—or possibly to Lovell: but he could not be sure, and in any case he had no idea what might be implied by the Irishman's stress on the formalities.

"Old friends. Old friends." Lovell spoke so thickly that it was obvious that he had been carousing at Balbi's before coming on to the theatrical party; and once he had reached for a decanter of wine, he seemed content to drink and drowse his way through the rest of the evening.

The chatter had died away as O'Moira set his monkey to its parlour tricks. Actors will always give another entertainer a chance, and the grey-furred creature had been well trained to serve his blind master. O'Moira dropped his napkin. The monkey retrieved it and then, with the fussy care of a valet, tucked it in the doctor's neck-band. O'Moira whispered a command. The monkey scuttled along the edge of the table, fingering into Lovell's coat and producing a silver watch—a trick that evidently irritated Lovell, for he roused himself and snatched angrily at the watch while the actors laughed and applauded.

"I need an apple," O'Moira said loudly, as though to distract the company from Lovell's gaucherie. The monkey lolloped over the empty pie dishes and used platters to a fruit bowl, picked an apple, and carried it back: rummaging into O'Moira's pocket, it produced a bone-handled scalpel, with which it peeled the apple and cut it into small pieces for its master's pleasure.

Justice caught Etienne's eye. "I should be nervous if that creature lived in my house," the young Frenchman said. "A pickpocket. A murderer, even. Who knows?"

89

"The doctor seems to have it under control," Justice said lightly.

"He is a good man." Etienne paused as if he intended to say more. "He is very kind." It struck Justice that the stage manager was a nervous young man who might well need the help of a doctor; he had once known a lieutenant with the same edgy quality, who had been frightened to face his creditors and had yet gone bravely to his death in a desperate act of courage. He wondered what O'Moira had done to earn Etienne's gratitude.

While the monkey had been at its tricks, Montague Moon had seized his chance to move closer to Lucienne Lamotte, and Justice noticed that his left hand had slipped under the table.

Mrs Williams had also caught the movement. "We shall soon see the rising of the Moon," she murmured acidly.

"I beg your pardon?"

"The rising of the Moon." She repeated the words in a way which left no doubt that the lewd meaning was intended. "But he will not, I fancy, manage to shine through *that* window . . ."

"Is there a M. Lamotte?"

"There was." Etienne caught the question. "A Captain Lamotte, to be precise. It is said that he was killed at Hohenlinden. After that, Madame apparently lived in Hamburg for a time, in Paris, in Metz, too; and then here in Verdun."

"She has means, then?"

"Not at all. You see, she is employed at Balbi's—she is one of the ladies of the room. You know how it is—they make a set at *trente-et-un* or *loto*, they encourage idiots with more money than sense, they tell Balbi who is gambling too much or drinking too little."

"I see." Though Justice nodded, he was puzzled. Lucienne Lamotte did not seem the kind of woman who would make her living like that: it would be easier to see Lovell helping to fleece unwary gamblers. Yet he had seen her at Balbi's, apparently working in partnership with the bibulous major, and he could not avoid the thought that the pair of them might have had something to do with the attack on him.

There might, indeed, be some connection with Fielding. If she worked in the gaming-room, she was bound to have met Fielding, and she might even have known him quite well. For

Holland had said that while Fielding was no gamester he did have an eye for a pretty woman, and it could have been the charms of Lucienne Lamotte which had drawn him to Balbi's.

Perhaps Fielding had even confided in her. Justice caught his hopes running on unjustifiably with his fancy, and he realised that he had been staring so hard at Lucienne that she had coloured as she had done when Lovell snubbed her. She was certainly not a brazen professional.

It was Lovell himself who provided the distraction that enabled Justice to smile and look away, for the major had risen to propose a toast to Pitt. By the time he had done urging confusion to England's enemies, and the glasses had been emptied, the lugubrious actor from Yorkshire had set up a cry for Moon to recite.

"Give us Tom Campbell," he shouted, and the others took up the chant. "Tom Campbell. Tom Campbell."

Moon needed little urging to deliver the poet's latest patriotic ode. Striking a heroic attitude, he began:

> *The meteor flag of England*
> *Shall yet terrific burn . . .*

and before he came to the final lines most of the company were chanting in unison with him.

"There'll be trouble soon," Mrs Williams muttered to Justice. "I've told Monty that he's going too far. These Frenchies don't like to be teased, don't you know."

"Surely a poem or two won't harm them," Justice said.

"Lud, it's not the poem but the play," Mrs Williams said in such a downcast voice that Justice could tell that she was genuinely anxious.

"*The Tars of Old England.* That's the stuff to give 'em!" The Yorkshireman had picked up her remark, and as he spoke he thumped the table so hard that the glasses rattled. "Moon's right. A mean fellow, by God, but an Englishman all the same. Be damned to that snot-nosed hedgehog Wirion, I say."

Justice caught the drift of his exclamation. *The Tars* was a crude, rumbustious piece of ribaldry by Tobias Smollett, which the Tenterden Thespians had once done as a Christmas entertainment; and Justice, the only member of the company with a passable French accent, had played the part of Captain Champignon, the ludicrous naval officer who was the butt of the farce's laughter. Nothing could be better calculated to taunt the objectionable commandant of Verdun and to rouse the spirits of his prisoners.

"Here?" he asked with some astonishment.

"Here, indeed." The Yorkshireman's heavy face broke into a schoolboy's grin. "And this week as ever is we'll do it, whether Wirion and some of his English lickspittles like it or not."

"They'll put Moon in Bitche for it." Mrs Williams wailed so piteously that she forgot her mannered speech and the hidden Welsh vowels came through. "It'll be the end of the whole company, I tell you."

"It is not wise, I think." Etienne, too, was clearly afraid of the consequences.

"Wise or not, Moon's the man to do it when he's asked by a lady, especially when it's for the first masked ball in Verdun."

But before Justice could ask what the Yorkshireman meant, he saw the monkey scurrying along with a note between its forepaws. It stopped, sniffed, and jumped onto Justice's shoulder as he wondered how O'Moira had so quickly trained the creature to recognise him. The paper was covered in the looping scrawl of a blind man's script. "Shall we go? D. O'M."

"At my age, a man's evenings are measured in short candles," O'Moira said as Justice went over to him. "Will you have the kindness to accompany me to my home?"

BY THE TIME that Justice and O'Moira made their farewells and emerged from the hall, the stream of Englishmen and townspeople in the narrow, winding streets had thinned to a trickle. Justice remembered with a touch of anxiety that *détenus* were subject to a curfew, but the matter was lightly disposed of by O'Moira.

"As a medical man, I have a *laissez-passer*. If we are stopped, I shall say I had to see a patient, and that you are seeing me home. I doubt we shall have trouble—I am tolerably well-known in the town."

"Not least, so I have been hearing, for your kindness," said Justice as he took the doctor's arm along a steeply-mounting cobbled street.

"Well, an old teacher of mine at Trinity used to say that an ounce of understanding was better medicine than any potion," rejoined O'Moira.

"I sensed you had given more than an ounce to that young man, the stage manager."

"Ah, Etienne. Poor Etienne has his troubles." He tapped with his stick what Justice sensed to be a tutting rhythm. "How is your own health? No headache?"

"No. And I followed your advice about the wine. Only two modest glasses."

"Our friend Moon made up for you," chuckled O'Moira. "Even though you're better, I suggest you stay at my house tonight. You can go back to M. Hahn's tomorrow."

By now the cobbled streets around the Place du Châtel had cease to echo. The night was warm but muggy. Mist covered the moon and shrouded the Citadel, from which a solitary light gleamed through the darkness. There was something reminiscent of Mermaid Street at Rye about the steep cobbled lanes of the curious hill-town. Justice began to regard its little, enclosed world of ivy-covered walls and narrow cul-de-sacs with interest, almost with affection.

But his mood was to be suddenly broken. They were just ascending the slope to O'Moira's house when Justice was aware of a military tread behind them. He turned to see two gendarmes in uniform, accompanied by a long-nosed, hungry-looking man in plain clothes.

"Is that Dr O'Moira? We have just been to your house." It occurred to Justice that, since the civilian did not identify himself, his voice must be familiar to the blind man. "I would be obliged if you could spare me a word in private."

"Well, I suppose so, though it's late." O'Moira did not seem pleased. "Captain Justice was kindly seeing me home. Are you acquainted? This is M. Charvet."

"I heard of Captain Justice's arrival." The Frenchman gave Justice a searching look; the use of the third person seemed to convey a subtle insult. "If you would be so good as to withdraw over here a little, Doctor."

O'Moira went across the side-street with him, and for a few moments Justice heard the sound of muffled, then more heated, voices. Then their talk became softer again. Justice tried in vain to listen, then became aware of a cloaked girl striding purposefully uphill. It was Lucienne.

"Is there some trouble?" she asked, stopping beside Justice.

"An argument with M. Charvet."

"Oh." She raised an eyebrow, as if such things were not uncommon.

By now Charvet and the gendarmes had moved off, and O'Moira came over to where they were standing on the other pavement. "So much for the land of liberty," he said. "Is that not Lucienne? I thought I caught a whiff of a perfume that reminded me of the sweet soft flowers of County Wicklow. So I'm in luck: to exchange Charvet's company for yours."

"What was the matter?"

"Oh, nothing, nothing. Is Lovell not seeing you home?"

"He had business."

"At this hour?"

"With M. Balbi."

"Ah." O'Moira took a firm step forward, as if to change the subject. "Well, then, you have found yourself two trusty escorts. Your lodgings are by the Citadel, or I'm mistaken?" He took her firmly by the arm, so that Justice was emboldened to take the other. "Moon was in good patriotic vein tonight, did you not think so?"

"He was indeed." Lucienne smiled, looking up at Justice as if to recall the actor-manager's amorous attempts, which could not have been noticed by the doctor. "Is this your first visit to France, monsieur?"

Justice nodded. "Yes."

"And do you like it?"

"I am beginning to feel at home. Climbing the hill just now, it struck me this town is rather like a place near to where I live in England. Which made me think a little: that one may like a place, or love it, without needing to bang a drum about it. Or wishing to plant one's own flag in other lands, where you may be less than welcome. I wonder if we may live to see a day when patriotism means affection for one's country, not the conquest of others."

"That would be a day worth seeing indeed," put in O'Moira. "I take it you were thinking of Bonaparte's ambitions?"

"I suppose so."

"Ah, but then sometimes the boot is on the other foot. An Englishman may proclaim his sturdy independence: but an

Irishman or a Yankee might sing a different song, not quite so much in England's favour."

Justice had the grace to feel embarrassed. From the Irishman's viewpoint, England's sturdy will to independence would ring a little hollow.

"Then perhaps it is at least good that you can speak of it," said Lucienne with a smile. "French, Irish, English. And we have not come to blows about it."

"One day the world's problems may be disposed of thus." O'Moira tapped his stick on the ground as if in approbation. "But it will not come tomorrow, or the next day. This is your street, Lucienne, is it not?"

"Yes." She stopped beside a small house with an iron railing. They were almost at the summit of the town: somewhere in the silence of the mist, Justice could hear the click of soldiers' muskets and a muffled command from the Citadel gate. "Thank you for accompanying me, messieurs."

"It would be an odd fellow who failed in such a duty." As O'Moira kissed her hand, she turned to Justice. "Good-night, Captain."

"Good-night. I have enjoyed our conversation."

"I am sure it will not be the last," she said, and closed the door.

"SHE IS A WOMAN of some character, despite all appearances," O'Moira said firmly as Justice took his arm again and they retraced their steps towards the Place du Châtel. "Do you not think so?"

"Indeed yes." Justice was unusually silent. He was used to beautiful girls, aristocratic girls, flirtatious girls—and if he was honest, that was how he tended to classify them. Lucienne was something different: then was hers the quality of France, which he had for so long been missing?

He let it go, and changed the subject. "What was the matter down there?"

"With Charvet, you mean? The fellow's a creature of Wirion's, and always making trouble," said O'Moira irritably. "It seems a damned young fellow—a servant of Sir Jerome Franklin's—missed his *appel*. A *détenu* may only do so if he has a doctor's certificate, and the young man happens to be my patient. They wanted to know had I given him a certificate. Of course I said that I had done so."

"Will you be in trouble if they find out you did not?"

"Oh, my back is broad. The young man will be called to the Citadel tomorrow morning, and a few more francs will find their way to Wirion's pocket."

"What's Wirion's history?" asked Justice as they turned into the Place du Châtel. "Was he a soldier?"

"I'd say he's been no closer to the sound of gunfire than Killarney is from Howth. He was the son of a pork-dealer from Picardy; that's the *on dit*. He made himself useful to Bonaparte in some way, and was rewarded by being made a general of gendarmes. All the same, of the two scoundrels, I prefer him to Charvet. He's coarse, and crude, and sly, and greedy, but at least he makes no bones about it. That Charvet fellow has a creeping-caterpillar feel about him; he wears righteousness on his sleeve, like an Antrim Protestant."

"But is not righteous, do you mean?"

"Well, they say he hangs about a certain English lady, who is not unkind to him, in return for favours. But that's gossip." O'Moira broke off. "Of which there is enough in this town without my adding to it. Come now, we'll not let the fellow spoil our evening."

"Since you were abstemious at supper, we might try a glass of cognac," he said, when Justice had guided him indoors and lit the oil-lamp. "I've a good bottle or so I brought from Paris, and 'tis a better sedative than anything our chemist friends brew at their burners. You'll find it in the decanter on the sideboard—the glasses in the cupboard."

Justice poured them both a measure, then noticed something. There was little in the way of decoration on the handsome cedar sideboard. Two plain candlesticks, and between them a gold coin in a plush-lined box.

Justice quietly reached for the box, lifted the coin, and turned it over. It was the twin of the coins that Holland had shown him in Hampstead. A *louis d'or*, with the reverse skimmed to take the engraving of an anchor and the single word "*Fidentia*."

A *Lutine* coin. A Lloyd's coin. Fielding's coin, for sure.

"You have found something that interests you?" O'Moira was

staring at the wall with the patient expectancy of the blind, but he had sharp ears.

"The coin intrigues me," Justice said, passing it to O'Moira.

"I'm sure it would," the doctor remarked as he fingered it, "for it's an odd thing in itself, to see a coin altered in that way."

As O'Moira spoke, Justice wondered whether he had any idea of the coin's history, and felt tempted to prompt him; and then, thinking better of it, let the Irishman run on.

"And it's part of an odd story, too, I'm afraid." O'Moira paused. "I've often thought there was more to it than I knew, but never mind that, for it's none of my business, I suppose." He waited for Justice to sit by him and then, laying a story-teller's hand on his arm, began the tale.

"There was an Englishman brought to Verdun a few months back, you see—a decent fellow, about my age, who had been in the commercial side of things. I often met him in the Bishop's Club, where we would have a game of chess, or a crack or two about books, for he was a man with literary tastes, you know. And while he was as restless as most men are when they first come here, I thought he was settling down and beginning to make the best of things. I'd become quite accustomed to his company, and I was dreadfully sorry when he got into trouble."

"Trouble?" Justice hoped one flat-spoken word would not betray his interest.

"Trouble about cards, it seems. And it was to be the death of him." O'Moira paused for effect. "One night there was some kind of scuffle at Balbi's, the gendarmes came, and my friend was carried off to the Citadel."

Justice remembered how Balbi had tried to pick a quarrel with him, and how his angry denial of cheating had been followed by the savage and treacherous blow as he left the gaming room. Was there a connection between the quarrel and the blow? Had the lucky arrival of O'Moira's servant saved him from the same fate as Fielding?

"That could not have been a serious matter," he said as coolly as possible.

"Not at first. But it seems he insulted that pompous fool, Wirion, and got sent off to the punishment cells at Bitche. Six days' march, they say, and a damp cold dungeon when you get there."

"And died there? In the fortress?"

"No. Trying to get out of it. I'm told that he fell forty feet down a sheer wall into the ditch, though that's only gossip. You can never be sure about things like that."

"How did you hear about all this?" Justice had the feeling that O'Moira was testing him out, wondering whether to confide in him. So many of those he had met at Verdun seemed to be on the verge of confidences and yet reluctant to trust him. Perhaps O'Moira had put the coin on the sideboard as some kind of signal.

"From Fielding's landlady. Madame Cartier, in the rue des Prêtres."

All the time O'Moira had been speaking, Justice was waiting for him to mention Fielding by name. But when he did speak directly of Fielding, it came as a shock, and he let the doctor run on to be sure he did not betray himself by some unwitting response.

"It appears that the poor fellow wanted me to have the coin as a memento. At least, that's what he told Madame Cartier—she was to bring it to me if anything happened to him. That's why I said it was an odd story. After all, I was only a casual friend."

But the coin was important, Justice said to himself. It was like Fielding's flamboyant signature in the members' book at Balbi's. It was there to be seen, by anyone who came after him.

It was probably there to be used in some way, as well, though Justice had no idea what Fielding could have had in mind. Perhaps it showed that O'Moira could be trusted—that he might know Fielding's secret and was waiting for Justice to show that he also knew the meaning of this special coin. Was that where all this talk was leading?

Or was it a sign that Fielding was not really dead? A coin dredged up from the *Lutine* wreck could well serve as a clever man's hint of survival.

Justice rose, deciding that the less he showed an interest in the coin the better. "It's a cautionary tale," he said portentously.

"It is, and all." O'Moira held out the coin between thumb and finger. "If you would oblige me . . ."

"Of course." Justice fumbled as he took the gleaming gold-piece, knocking it down and sending in clinking across the polished floor.

"I'm sorry," he exclaimed, going down on his knees and scrabbling towards the wainscot, so that the noise covered the swift movement with which he picked up the coin and pocketed it. "Terribly careless of me." He had to lie so crudely that he could only hope he sounded convincing. "It's slipped between two boards."

"No matter," O'Moira said easily. "My man can look in the morning. There's no need to fuss."

He was treating the matter so lightly that Justice concluded that the coin could mean nothing more to him than a casual and curious souvenir. All the same, it had to be taken. As soon as Justice had seen Fielding's token, he had been sure that it would sometime serve his turn; and although he felt a qualm at deceiving the blind man, he could not afford to be squeamish—or to leave the coin resting on O'Moira's sideboard when it could be kept easily to hand in his own pocket.

And he was only running a modest risk, he assured himself as he bade the doctor good-night and made his way to bed. It was most unlikely that the kindly O'Moira would suspect that Justice had deceived him, or that he would have his man tear up the whole floor next day simply to find the missing coin.

Next day. There was mist lying over the town as Justice looked across to the towers of the cathedral. Next day, in a small street near those towers, he would find Madame Cartier and talk openly for the first time about a man called Fielding.

ᐊ 7 ᐅ

DURING THE NIGHT there was a storm. When Justice woke, feeling himself again, the air was fresh and the cobbles of the lane that ran under his window were still glistening with the rain. O'Moira's servant brought him coffee and a croissant, saying the doctor was busy with a patient, and Justice saw, with a twinge of nostalgia for Scorcher's services, that his clothes had been brushed and laid out neatly for the first time since he left Hook.

A few minutes later he was on his way to find the rue des Prêtres, crossing the top of the rue Mazel, the busy thoroughfare where so many shops had been opened for the benefit of the English that, according to O'Moira, everyone called it Bond Street; finding his way past the front of the cathedral, giving Balbi's mansion a thoughtful look on the way, and then following the instructions of a old flower-seller who sent him into a maze of steep passages.

Justice stopped at the first door and asked for Madame Cartier. Just there, he was told, and as he went up to the door of a narrow shuttered house, which looked as though it had been forced between its neighbours as an afterthought, a greying wispy woman came out with a bucket of slops and threw it into the runnel that drained down the lane.

"Je cherche Madame Cartier," Justice said in halting French.

"C'est moi, m'sieu'," the woman said, with a slow smile. "I can understand if you speak English. Please." She gestured towards her house, and led Justice into a small and musty parlour."M'sieu?"

"I'm told you might have lodgings to let."

"I'm sorry. The house is *complet.*" She looked closely at Justice, leaving the next move to him.

He tried again. "I heard you had lately lost a lodger . . ." His voice tailed away as he caught the glint of suspicion in her eyes.

"One goes. One comes. I can find ten lodgers in a day if I wish." Madame Cartier gave nothing away. "Where does M'sieu stay now?"

"At M. Hahn's."

She gave a wry grimace that was comment enough, and picked up her pail.

Justice saw that he would soon find himself in the street again, and none the wiser, unless he took his chance. "It was Mr Fielding's room I was asking about."

Madame Cartier put the pail back on the floor as if the gesture was a sign that she was willing to parley, though she said nothing. From all he had seen in Verdun, Justice decided, she was wise to be cautious.

"We had friends in common," he said. "In London. They would be glad to have news of him."

"Do you know he is dead?" Now she spoke frankly, and when Justice nodded, she went on with her tale. "Or so they said.

100

The gendarmes came one day to tell me, and to say that he was a *mauvais sujet.*"

"Is that what you thought?" Justice guessed from her tone that she was no admirer of the commandant and his lackeys.

"Come." She trustingly took his hand and showed him through to a small kitchen. "There," she said, pointing above her little stove to an image of the Virgin, with two burnt candle-ends before it, and a vase with a bunch of withered wild flowers. "That is what I thought of M. Fielding."

Justice was puzzled, and she saw it. "Whenever M. Fielding could get a pass, he would go out to the country . . . walking . . . walking . . . it seems he was always walking, and often he would bring me a few flowers. He was a kind man, and he knew I liked them."

"And those?" Once more, Justice had the odd sense that Fielding had deliberately left a sign behind him.

"*Des orchis.* The last time he came back, he brought those—from somewhere near Houdainville, he said. As . . . as . . ." She searched for the English word. "As a *souvenir* . . ."

"A remembrance," Justice guessed, and saw her eyes light up.

"That was his word," she said. "So I remember. I keep his flowers here, and each time I light a candle I pray for him. He was a fine man."

"I think so, too." Justice spoke simply and softly. "And you have nothing else?"

"His friends here had everything—it is the custom. After the gendarmes were finished, of course. They came twice. Pigs! They root through everything, asking questions. That Charvet, I can tell you! He even takes up the boards on the floor. For what, I ask. Mind your own business, he says." Madame Cartier was so angry that she was speaking in little bursts. "And then? Nothing. Naturally. What could they find?"

Justice wished he knew what Wirion's men had been seeking. "But his friends?" he asked. He recalled the naval custom of selling off a dead man's kit at the mainmast. It was one way officers eked out their clothes on a long commission. "Were his clothes sold?"

Madame Cartier screwed up her eyes. "I can't say their names," she said after a moment. "I think some poor *détenus* had the clothes. A coat here, you know, a pair of boots there."

"The doctor had a coin," Justice said to encourage her, and for a moment he wondered what effect he would have on the woman if he produced it from his pocket. Even the mention of it sent a shadow of caution across her face. "Mr Fielding left it for him, I believe."

She was clearly relieved by this assurance. "Some days before the gendarmes took him," she said quietly. "And I hid it from them. Look." She took down the image of the Virgin in its wooden frame, turned it over, and showed Justice how it slid back to reveal a small recess that might once have held a religous relic, or perhaps a lock of hair from a dead child. "And then the red-faced Englishman . . . the Major, M. Fielding called him . . . took it to the doctor."

Then Lovell had known Fielding well enough to do the last services for him, had been aware that he was a friend of O'Moira, seen the *Lutine* coin. "And there was nothing else?"

"Only the books—the old ones and the new ones, which he took for the other English to read, he said."

"Old ones. New ones." Justice tried to keep the interest out of his voice.

"Yes," Madame Cartier said straightforwardly. "The ones that came a few days after M. Fielding was sent to . . . to Bitche." The way she hesitated over the dreaded name showed how much the place was feared. "Four or five books, in a parcel from Paris. I think M. Fielding was waiting for them. He had been several times to the post-house. But I don't know. He said nothing to me."

Madame Cartier clearly had nothing to add. Justice had already thanked her and was on his way to the door when she ducked into her front parlour and brought out a slip of paper. "There was only this," she said apologetically, as if she wished she had done more to help.

Justice felt his hopes rise as he guessed it might be a message from Fielding himself, and then he saw that the slip of paper was merely an invoice.

"It came afterwards," Madame Cartier said.

Justice looked more closely at the angular script. Matthew Fielding, Esq., it appeared, had owed the Verdun *Argus* five francs for the insertion of an advertisement on 23 May.

A bunch of wild orchids, a missing parcel of books, and a bill for five francs. They were all apparently trivial things, like the signature at Balbi's and the gift of the *Lutine* coin to O'Moira. Yet, put together in the right combination, they must be important—vitally important if Fielding had taken so much trouble to hide his secret when he felt that Wirion and Charvet were closing in on him.

As Justice walked up the hill towards the cathedral, he reflected on the odd turn events had taken. Lilly had called him away from a sailor's life, where a man worked at the puzzles set by wind and water, and sent him across France to read the mind of a man of very different experience.

Could he do it? And, what's more, could he do it in time? Whatever scheme Fielding had devised to disrupt Bonaparte's invasion plans, he would have expected to act in the late summer or early autumn, at the moment when the threat was greatest.

He nodded to a lounging group of English people that he passed along the way. The *détenus* had all the time in the world to waste. And he had none.

As Justice neared his lodgings, he half-expected to find one of Wirion's gendarmes hanging about in the street. After all he had heard from O'Moira and Madame Cartier, he was now convinced that Verdun was full of spies and informers. But there was no one about, and he went into the house. He noticed that the door of the parlour was open and he could see Nathaniel Hunt sorting through a portfolio of sketches.

The painter turned at the sound of his step and greeted him. "I'm glad to see that you've recovered," he said with a note of genuine relief in his voice. "I had heard you were hurt in a scuffle. Which can be a bad thing in this town."

It occurred to Justice that Hunt might be hinting at Fielding's fate. "You thought I might have been arrested as a troublemaker—sent to Bitche, perhaps?"

Hunt refused the gambit with a non-committal shrug. "It's happened to others," he said. "One can't be too careful. Life here seems calm on the surface. But below there are deep currents that can suddenly drag a man down."

Everyone said the same thing, Justice noted. "Dr O'Moira was kindness itself," he said, turning the conversation.

"He has that reputation. Unlike his colleague, Dr Madan . . ."

"And he . . ." Justice saw that Hunt needed encouraging.

"They say he sells false certificates for those who wish to avoid the *appels*—and that Wirion takes his share of the fees, as usual. Nothing happens in this town without the commandant's knowledge, you know; it's bribes and blackmail all the time." Hunt made a sour face. "Even a painter must pay his due. I painted his wife's portrait a few months ago. That *poissarde!*" He spoke with contempt. "I'm told she worked her way up from the fishmarket in Les Halles to keeping a sporting house in the rue Saint-Honoré. Paris was well rid of her. All the time I was painting her, she was telling lewd stories, tippling, cursing at the servants. You never saw such a woman."

"They sound a real pair," Justice said, toying with a couple of copies of the *Argus* which lay on the table. He turned up one paper in a casual way and saw that it was published by Lewis Goldsmith from 21, rue Montgaud.

"But I shall lose the day talking," Hunt said cheerfully, "and there's a river scene south of the town I thought to dab at. Which way do you go?" He picked up a satchel of paints and a light easel.

"Merely to stroll. I have scarcely seen the town. I will go some way with you if you can wait while I change my line."

Hunt chattered easily as they crossed the Roche, picking out people with the sharp eye of a painter.

Justice noticed that Hunt seemed on good terms with everyone he greeted, and said so.

"I think I've no enemies," Hunt said. "I make myself agreeable, and there's good company here if you look for it." He nodded generally at the parade of men and women taking the air in the brilliant sunshine. "Here's a man who made the Grand Tour and measured the dome of St Peter's," he said. "There's a squire who knows all about the rotation of crops and Bakewell's sheep. That vacuous-looking ninny could recite you the whole racing calendar, and this sobersides coming towards us is a Cantab who has the *Gradus ad Parnassum* at his finger ends." Hunt stopped and wagged a finger. "I tell you, Mr Justice, there's no bet you can make, classical or political, commercial or military, but you'll find someone in Verdun who can settle it."

The little man had clearly come to terms with his life in Verdun, Justice decided, as Hunt went off with a genial farewell.

He found the rue Montgaud without difficulty, though he had first to listen to a tirade against Goldsmith and his newspaper from a naval officer whom he had asked to direct him. Number 21 was the largest house in the short street, with a plate announcing the *Argus* just below the grill in the door.

Moments after he rapped the knocker, a yawning youth peered out of the grillwork.

"Is Mr Goldsmith at home?"

"Il dort." The youth was about to slam the little shutter, when Justice stayed it with a finger.

"I wish to see some old copies of the paper."

"De quelle date?"

Justice was annoyed by this foolish quizzing, but he saw no point in picking a quarrel, which could only draw attention to his enquiry; and for the same reason he was vague in his answer. "Early June, late May perhaps," he said as the youth grudgingly swung back the door. "The guest-list for a ball," he added vaguely, following the young man through to a large room where a confusion of papers, quills, and boxes of type was dominated by a large hand-printing press.

"Voilà!" The word and a wave were enough, for the side of the room was untidily stacked with bundles of the *Argus;* and as Goldsmith's uncouth assistant slumped on a stool to watch him, Justice started to scan the flimsy pages.

There was not much of interest—ludicrous reports of British defeats at sea, vainglorious praise of Bonaparte, toadying references to Wirion and his wife; but Justice took time to work through several issues, and to pause as he went, before he turned to the advertisements in the copy he wanted. A lady was offering a reward for a string of pearls lost near the Roche on the previous Sunday. Regimentals were made to measure for gentlemen by M. Houzelle in the rue Mazel. Sir Jerome Franklin, Bart., wished it to be known that he no longer held himself responsible for his wife's debts . . .

Then Justice came upon the words which could only have been written by Fielding.

Gentleman, who recently proposed the formation of a literary circle to meet at the Bishop's Club Library, and to study the doctrines of Liberty, Equality and Fraternity as evinced by Dean Swift in *Gulliver's Travels,* regrets that the project must be postponed until October, owing to his sudden indisposition.

Liberty. Equality. Fraternity. That was certainly Fielding. Dean Swift. *The Race is to the Swift,* Fielding had written in the scribbled note that had come to Edward Holland. And here he was again, sending much the same message at the moment he knew that his enemies were closing in on him. That ominous phrase "sudden indisposition" could only have one meaning.

Justice read the message again to memorise it as he casually dropped the paper back on the pile and took up another. As he did so, another point struck home to him. *The project must be postponed until October.* Fielding must have known the date when Bonaparte planned to sail for England. October. That had been Lilly's guess as well.

And October was scarcely more than two weeks away.

IT TOOK JUSTICE only a few minutes to find the Bishop's Club. Most of the clubs formed by the *détenus* were in houses on the south side of the Roche, and he had noted them as he walked along with Hunt that morning—Creange's, where Lovell said the bucks played for high stakes; the Carron, the Cod, and Taylor's. But the staid club favoured by the more respectable members of the English society was in part of the former bishop's palace, from which it took its name.

The entrance hall was imposing, with squares of black-and-white marble on the floor, and a good deal of faded gilding among the plaster moulds on the walls and ceiling. Justice passed a couple of men collecting message-notes from a rack: club members, he knew from long experience of testy men, never liked answering questions. And the elderly lady who sat knitting at a table at the foot of the stairs looked to be an equally forbidding *concierge.*

"Can you direct me to the library?" Justice realised that he was probably expecting too much. But Fielding had mentioned the library, and Lovell had told Madame Cartier that he was taking Fielding's books for other English people to read. There was a chance . . .

"Upstairs, m'sieu." She let Justice start up the steps before she gave a shrill bark of satisfaction. "But it is closed, m'sieu. Until the librarian returns."

She obliged Justice to ask the obvious question, and took pleasure in her vague answer. "At three, perhaps. And then, possibly, at four? The library is not my affair."

With such equivocation to irritate him, and a growing hunger to remind him that he had eaten nothing since the snack brought him by O'Moira's servant that morning, Justice paced restlessly about for a few minutes before he strolled into the card-room. It was clearly not used for play before whist began with afternoon tea, and there were only two or three men dozing on sofas or in the deep chairs pushed back to get the light from the windows.

Justice walked slowly round the room, trying to identify the biblical scenes painted on the walls, and deciding that the artist must have had more experience of painting pagan gods than Jewish prophets.

"Damn my eyes, it's John Justice." The voice from the armchair on his left was peremptory, as befitted its owner. The third Lord Chiltington was a man of considerable possessions and indifferent temper. In Justice's opinion, he had done nothing to deserve his handsome house in Sussex, or its cedar-shaded cricket ground, where Justice had once hit fifty against the famous Men of Hambledon, or the fine collection of Dutch sea-paintings which the first Lord Chiltington—who had been an Admiral of the Blue—had hung round the dining hall. Above all, Justice had decided, his lordship did not deserve the lovely Caro Chiltington, with flaming hair and olive skin, who had made the evening of that cricket match memorable by an unexpected and unsought intimacy on the terrace after supper.

That was one reason for remembering Caroline Chiltington well. Another was her friendship with Kitty Holland, who had taken the part of the handsome but low-born girl when the manner of her marriage to Chiltington had made her the talk of London.

Suddenly there was Chiltington, looking more like a tired tortoise than ever. Justice had not heard that the Chiltingtons were detained in France. Kitty had merely said that they were travelling in Italy. They must have been taken on a captured merchant ship.

"Sit ye down, Captain," Chiltington growled. "Take something?" Justice saw that he had a half-empty glass beside him. His irritability was said to be due to his intemperate affection for port, but Justice knew that he was not choosy. Any wine would do, as long as there was plenty of it.

"New here, ain't ye?" Chiltington said as Justice declined a drink and drew up a chair beside him. He was a man of few words, and he did not seem surprised by Justice's sudden appearance in Verdun. "Tiresome business. But things ain't so bad as they might be. Better than all that damn travelling—Greek bugs, Italian fleas, boiled donkey-drops for dinner. At least you can get a clean bed and a decent meal here."

"You're still a prisoner," Justice remarked.

"Not so you'd notice it," Chiltington said complacently. "As long as you keep your nose clean. That Wirion's quite a decent chap, when it comes to it. Thief-taker and all that, of course, but he knows his place with the quality."

"Is her ladyship in Verdun?" Justice preferred to talk about Caro than to hear Wirion's praises sung by an Englishman.

"They tell me so. Hardly see her." The sour joke was typical of Chiltington's humour. "Social life, and all that, y'know." He raised himself in his chair. "Been in England lately?" he asked, as if he were simply meeting another traveller in a foreign hostelry.

"This summer," Justice said vaguely; there was nothing to be gained by arousing Chiltington's interest in him. The man could too easily blurt out something about him that Wirion or Charvet would give much to hear. "Country's pretty resolute."

"Resolute?" Chiltington looked bewildered. "Oh, I take you. Boney. But it won't come to that. And if it does, we'll be better off here until it's over."

His nonchalant smugness infuriated Justice. Chiltington was like so many rich stay-at-homes who were content to let pressed men go through the horrors of a sea-fight to keep the country safe for them—and then call for the rope and the cat-o'-nine-tails when the seamen complained at their hard lot. He stood up, keeping a check on his tongue. "My respects to Lady Chiltington," he said with a stiff bow, relieved that Chiltington made no attempt to detain him. He was beginning to see what the Yorkshire actor had meant when he talked about Wirion's English lickspittles.

The *concierge* nodded as he walked back into the lobby, and

Justice ran lightly up the stairs to find the library on the first floor. There was no one in the book-lined room except an old man in rusty black, with orange stockings, who was writing at a table by the window that opened onto the cloister.

"I'm sorry to disturb you." Justice was not sure whether the librarian was some survivor from the past or an English scholar who had been carried off to Verdun and found a congenial task.

"Pray do not apologise," the ancient said agreeably, in the accents of an Oxford Fellow. "You are my first visitor today. In fact, I get out of the habit of expecting anyone." He gave a benign smile. "I understand that there are other attractions besides books in Verdun."

"A pity, when you have such a magnificent collection." Justice looked at the shelves with genuine admiration.

"What you see, sir, is the private library of the last bishop. I fear a mob chased the poor man out with only a shirt to his back. It was lucky they did not burn his books as well." He took Justice over to some shelves close to the window. "Now we have a small number of English books over here . . ."

"If I may browse without disturbing you," Justice said, letting the old man return to his studies, and quickly running his eye over the English titles. There were small volumes of Maria Edgeworth, Defoe, Sterne, Richardson, Smollett, presumably donated by *détenus* who had brought them to Verdun in their baggage. A large set of Gibbon's *Decline and Fall;* a few books of history and travel; a good deal of Shakespeare, some Milton and Dryden; a scattering of philosophical works. Could any of these have come from Fielding's lodging? Justice opened a few at random to look at the book-plates and signatures, but there was no sign of Fielding's name.

He looked for Jonathan Swift, and found two titles. *A Tale of a Tub* was there; and *The Drapier's Letters.* But nothing else.

He had no choice. He went back to the librarian.

"Do you have *Gulliver's Travels,* by any chance?" he asked; and he had to wait anxiously while the librarian burrowed in a pile of books underneath his table.

"Yes, yes," he said, "I thought so. A fine copy. Quite new."

As Justice reached out his hand for the book, the man drew back. "To be frank, sir, I am not sure if I can let you have it." He craned his head to look under the table again. "Those books, you see, were the property of a gentleman who came to an untimely end."

"Then he has no need of them." Justice regretted the impatient remark as soon as he made it, but the man's indecision teased him.

"A friend of his brought them," the old man said reflectively, "so perhaps . . ."

Justice changed his tack. "Could it be bought in Verdun?"

"Oh, no." The question distracted the librarian. "This must have come from Paris." He opened the cover and peered at the first page, but Justice, looking over his shoulder, could see nothing on it. "It should have a bookseller's label there," he said like a reproving scholar who had found a mistake in a text, "but it seems to have lost it. Pity." He handed the book to Justice. "I have not entered it," he said, "but if you care to look at it here."

"I was simply seeking a reference," Justice replied, and went over to sit by a pile of books on another table.

The volume was new, as the librarian had noticed. But as soon as Justice picked it up, he observed one peculiarity. The pages were all cut, although Fielding had been arrested before the book arrived at Verdun.

Could this be some kind of code, like words pricked with a pin or an unusual crease on a page? If it was, Justice knew that he had no chance of deciphering it without the key. Or had the pages been cut by someone who had looked at the book after Lovell had collected it from Fielding's lodging? Lovell himself might have glanced at it, though he was hardly a reading man; or it could have been opened up by the librarian or a member of the club; or Charvet could have tracked it down. There was no means of knowing.

Justice looked more closely at the binding. It was possible that someone had in fact tampered with the end-papers: if they had been steamed off, the bookseller's label could easily have come unstuck in the process. There was only one way to find out. Justice looked across to the librarian, drowsing over his task, and slipped *Gulliver's Travels* into his pocket. Then, taking a book from the pile which looked similar to the volume of Swift in size and binding, he went back to the old man. "Don't disturb yourself," he murmured politely, bending over to conceal the fact that he was returning a fine copy of Plato's *Republic*. "I can put it back."

The old man had opened one eye and gone back into his doze before Justice was out of the room.

IN THE LATE afternoon the sun was still warm, and Justice sat on an empty bench at the side of the Roche, thinking about the Swift novel and trying to guess at its secret.

He had taken the book back to his room, ready to steam off the end-papers or split the binding. As soon as he had looked at it closely, however, he had seen that no one had interfered with it. The volume was as clean as the day it had come from the press. There was only a faint wrinkle on the paper inside the front cover to suggest that the librarian had been right in thinking the book had lost the bookseller's label; and whoever had cut the pages had done it very carefully, with a sharp knife.

That was all. Justice was so baffled that he had even speculated about the editor's name and the date on the title page. But what could he make of the fact that John Nichols had published this edition in 1801? Nothing.

Finally, in the hope that the name of the book might have had some meaning for Fielding, or that some turn of this nautical tale might have a bearing on the movement of Bonaparte's ships, Justice had started to read Swift's allegory for the first time since he was a lad. That, too, had failed him. He might have been reading *Don Quixote*, for all the help the text was to him.

He sat there, frustrated, so absorbed in his thoughts that he scarcely heard the step behind him before he felt a clap on his shoulder. "It looks as though you'll need more than a penny for your thoughts, Captain." Before Justice could put Swift's novel back in his pocket, Lovell had swung himself down beside him. It was better to leave the book where it was, rather than make a furtive attempt to conceal it.

"I'm already weary of this place," Justice said with a ring of truth in his voice.

Lovell gave him a sharp glance. "You sound like young Pullen, poor devil."

Justice turned to him with such evident surprise that Lovell could tell he was the bearer of bad news. "You've not heard? He made a bolt for it last night. Must have been about the time we were at supper with Moon and his people. He and a young Scotsman hid themselves in the cathedral after the evening service, worked their way out through the organ loft and over the wall of the cloister. At least, that's the story I heard at Creange's a while ago."

"And were caught?" Justice now understood why Pullen had been cordial but cryptically evasive when he met him at Balbi's: with escape on his mind, he did not want to compromise himself—or drag anyone else into it.

"Worse luck, yes. They must have been shopped." Lovell smacked his palms together. "Gendarmes waiting for them. Clapped them straight into the Citadel, and they say that Wirion had packed them off to Bitche before it was light this morning."

"Do many try?" Justice needed to know.

"Not too many. Usually the younger chaps, sailors like you. Some of the older officers are sweating on an exchange, you know. And most of the civilians haven't got the nerve—or the puff, when it comes to it!" Lovell gave a coarse laugh. "It can be a soft life, as I said to you when we met at Balbi's the other night, if you've got money and the right kind of company in bed. There's one they call the German Princess. That's a royal treat, I promise you."

For a moment Justice thought Lovell was about to give him a graphic account of this courtesan's charms, but the major came back to his point. "I've thought of it, and decided that it's no good to go it alone. You need company, for one thing. Someone who can speak a bit of French—or German, if you're to get over the Rhine. For another, you need some ready money. Damn peasants won't take a note of hand like gentlemen do." Lovell pulled at his sideburns, as if judging how far to go. "Had it fixed once," he said, "and then it all fell through."

Justice was sure that Lovell was hinting, trying him out. He could think of several reasons why the man might be anxious to get away from Verdun—gambling debts, an irate husband, the risk of a duel, perhaps a desire to get back to his regiment, for he had probably been a good soldier in his time; but there were only two obvious reasons why Lovell should try to draw a newcomer into an escape plot. Either he was a decoy, full of patriotic bluster to conceal the fact that he was earning his keep from Wirion as well as Balbi. Or he had a doubtful reputation, and no one except a new arrival was likely to trust him. That could explain why he had raised the subject before Justice had been long enough in town to hear what people said about him.

The more Justice thought about these two possibilities, the more it seemed odd that, according to Madame Cartier, Lovell had known Fielding well enough to dispose of his effects. Was it an escape plan with Fielding that had been fixed and fallen through?

"How would you go?" He decided that it was best to let Lovell do the talking.

"You can see the lie of the land quite easily." Lovell began to trace a crude map in the dust with the point of his cane. "The Citadel, here, lies like a great six-pointed star at the west end of the town, with a small canal running in from the Meuse and passing along the foot of the walls on the south side. Where we were the other night, with the actors: the hall backs onto the water just by the postern gate. On the north side, where we are now, there's no water, and the walls are sheer."

Justice got up and sauntered over to look down from the rampart. "Almost vertical, and sixty feet of smooth masonry," he said as he took his place again besides Lovell.

"Difficult," Lovell agreed. "But if you did get down with a rope, and across the ditch, you've pretty empty country close at hand. Mostly forest, where you can hide easily."

"And just as easily get lost." Any sailor on the run, Justice felt, would rather be out in the open, where he could guide himself by the stars.

"Those are all the hard ways," Lovell conceded. "That's how you would have to go if you were billeted in one of the barracks in the Citadel, or if you were in the guard-room or one of the cells. It would be easier through the town. Out through the Porte Chaussée, in fact."

"The main gate? Breaking your parole?" It was something Justice was ready to do in an extremity, to finish Fielding's work, and let Lilly argue the case with the Board of Transport when and if he got home. But the cool way in which Lovell was suggesting that means of escape must be either a provocation or the desperate idea of a man who was facing ruin.

"It wouldn't matter if they were already after you," Lovell said darkly. "If you had the thief-taker's men on your tail." He sensed that he had gone too far, and tried to recover with a piece of bravado. "Don't shrug off a man's help too quickly, Justice," he remarked as he rose to go. "You may come to need it."

As the dusk came on, Justice realised that he had worked up an appetite that was robust enough to face whatever supper M. Hahn's cook would produce, and as he walked back to his lodging, he came up with Nathaniel Hunt.

"You've had a long day," he ventured agreeably.

"A long walk," Hunt replied. "I was at the limit of our liberty, by the great bend the Meuse makes as it comes towards the town. It is quiet there. Few of our countrymen care to walk five kilometres each way for a little solitude, and the soft lap of water among the reeds."

"May I see what you have done today?"

It was clearly the wrong question, for the painter hitched his portfolio more tightly under his arm, and seemed put out. "I believe an artist should only share his secret with his brush until his work is done." Hunt spoke with some asperity. "In any case, I have to sell most of what I do. I have little left to show."

"Of course." Justice wondered what nerve of pride he had unwittingly touched. Or was there a hint of secrecy in Hunt's defensiveness? "That's quite understandable," he said, to put the painter at his ease.

"I don't mean to be unfriendly." Hunt was bothered by his momentary discourtesy. "It's kind of you to ask, most kind." Yet he still seemed uneasy. "At supper—" he said, and broke off. "Yes, we shall meet at supper."

They were already by the staircase at Hahn's when Hunt paused to let Justice go ahead. The move left Justice in no doubt that the painter was afraid that he might follow him into his room, or at least see through the open door.

In this town of secrets, Justice reminded himself, even the gentle painter had something to hide.

8

JUSTICE LAY AWAKE for much of the night, worrying at the clues which Fielding had trailed behind him as he went into the darkness, and failing at each attempt to make a sensible pattern of them.

He had the coin—and though he could not begin to guess why Fielding had left it to Dr O'Moira, he was sure that it must be some kind of recognition signal, like the secret numbers which men-o'-war ran up on meeting another vessel at sea. He had the book as well, and that must be another signal. Fielding had obviously been waiting for it to arrive from Paris, and Justice suspected that it might be something to do with the lost money, or even the sailing date for Bonaparte's invasion fleet. It must have come from someone who was party to Fielding's secret, and if he could trace who had sent it, or divine what purpose it was meant to serve, he knew that he would be close to discovering that secret for himself.

But he could make no better sense of the peculiar advertisement in the *Argus* than he had made of the letter which had reached Holland in London. He felt like Gulliver in Lilliput, tied by a thousand small threads and unable to make a move. Then he dozed into a restless dream, waking to hear a patrol pass down the street, and the sound of a distant trumpet from some camp outside the town.

Outside the town. The idea of the countryside set his thoughts running in a fresh direction. If he put himself in Fielding's place, he could imagine waiting in Verdun, as patiently as possible, for a sign that his plans were coming to the point of action and that his helpers were ready for him to join them, or at least to tell them exactly where and when to strike. Justice knew what it was like to hang about for weeks on end, hoping that the next sail would bring the news that would send the ship's drummers beating to quarters.

Yet, while Fielding had filled in time at Verdun, pretending to be no more than another bored *détenu*, he would certainly have been preparing to get away at a moment's notice. He would have had the means of escape to hand. That might explain Lovell's interest.

Money. Lovell had mentioned money more than once. Clothing, perhaps. And papers. Could Fielding have persuaded Hunt to forge a passport for him? The artist was clever enough to do it.

Justice sat up with a jerk. Of course. Fielding must have made a cache of such things as he needed. And if there was a cache, it might even contain some indication of his plans.

He was always walking, Madame Cartier had said. Walking . . . walking . . . bringing back bunches of flowers for his landlady, so that she came to expect them. *The last time he came back, he brought these—from somewhere near Houdainville, he said. As a souvenir.*

A bunch of withered wild orchids.

HE WAS DRESSED, all but his boots, when Hunt knocked at the door of his room, smiling agreeably as though to efface the memory of his brusqueness the night before, and holding out a folded paper. "It just came by messenger," the painter said. "M. Hahn was most impressed."

Justice could not make out what Hunt meant until he turned the paper and saw the embossed coronet.

It was from Lady Chiltington. A formal invitation to a ball the next night, which made sense of the Yorkshire actor's remark about a masquerade and a play—and Moon being unable to refuse a lady. That impressionable gentleman would have done anything Caro Chiltington wanted of him.

There was a message in her own hand, too, scrawled along the top of the paper. "Delighted you are in Verdun. Come to see me."

"Shall I keep the porter?" Hunt had stayed at the door.

"Thank you. I'll scribble an answer when I've got my boots on."

Justice had just despatched his reply when Hunt joined him at the street door. "You are going to the country again?" Justice asked.

"Later, perhaps. I must first get my pass."

"Then I will come with you." Justice realised that it would be easier to get over the formalities if he went with someone who knew how to handle Wirion's underlings. "A bribe?"

"It depends if the sergeant is hungry." Hunt's sarcasm told

Justice that he need not expect much difficulty—a few francs would probably be enough to buy a pass for the day.

"I thought of going towards Houdainville," Justice said as they walked together towards the guard-office in the Citadel. He had decided that he could trust Hunt, and that he had better ask fairly directly for what he wanted. Yet he noticed Hunt gave him a sharp look when he mentioned the name of the hamlet.

"That's near the place where I was sketching yesterday." Hunt spoke so deliberately that it seemed he might mean more than he said. "It lies just above the great bend in the Meuse. But the village itself is outside the range of our liberty. And, in any case, there is nothing notable to see there. Just a few cottages, and a small church."

"I am less interested in buildings than in flowers." Justice was aware that his remark came oddly from a sailor, and he thought of softening it by talking about the hedgerow and water plants that abounded on Romney Marsh; but the idea came and went as he appreciated that he would get more from Hunt by plain dealing than by a more devious approach. "In wild orchids, as a matter of fact, though the season's past."

For the second time in the same conversation, Justice could tell that Hunt was on the verge of putting a question, and that once again something had held him back. Was it simply uncertainty—the possibility that Justice was an innocent who was stumbling upon some secret? Or was it fear that he had caught glinting in the painter's eyes and stiffening the small muscles of his face?

Yet the little man gave him a cool and frank response. "I've only noticed them in one place," he remarked, as from one amateur botanist to another. "Close to where I was painting, in fact. On a kind of island—it's more of a promontory, really, now the river's low at the end of the summer; and there's a wood that was full of them towards the end of May."

Hunt's answer told Justice exactly what he wanted to know, and as soon as they reached the head of the line of *détenus* waiting for their day passes to the countryside, he excused himself.

"*Bonjour, M. le capitaine!*" The greeting broke in on his thoughts so abruptly as he walked down to the Porte Chaussée that Justice was taken aback to find himself facing a young French officer in uniform—a blue tunic, with two rows of gilt buttons, a fine pair of epaulettes, cocked hat, white breeches. The officer was Etienne Mandin, and he was accompanied by three other actors from Moon's company carrying odds and ends of costume. "You've been promoted, I see," said Justice.

Etienne appeared to be enjoying his charade. "From stage manager to *capitaine* at one leap. I am to play Champignon tomorrow, and I have been to borrow a uniform from a friend." He gave a pirouette for effect. "Not bad, *hein*? It's his father's coat from the army, as a matter of fact, but who cares? It's only a play." He gave a nervous laugh, and then looked more serious. "Perhaps it will not be so funny later. The commandant . . ." As he broke off with a doubtful gesture, Justice remembered how Mrs Williams had been afraid of Wirion's reaction.

ALTHOUGH THE TRACK which ran southwards along the Meuse was clearly used as a tow-path for boats going upstream, for Justice could see many hoofmarks in the softer ground by the edge of the water, there was no traffic and few people about. A couple of Englishmen introduced themselves, and strolled with him part of the way, but they soon turned back when they realised that Justice was bent on a vigorous walk; and by the time Justice had gone two miles from the town, he was quite alone.

Or so it seemed, for there was no one in sight whenever a turn in the stream gave him a chance to look back along the track, and he could hear nothing but the calling of birds and the sound of the breeze in the drying leaves of the forest. And yet he had the sense that someone was following him—so acutely, indeed, that at one point he slipped into the undergrowth and waited to see if he was overtaken. No one came up. It was either his imagination, stimulated by so much evidence of intrigue and surveillance in Verdun, or he was being watched by someone who knew his business. Could it be Charvet, or another of Wirion's agents?

He had walked for more than an hour, he judged, before he saw the neck of land that Hunt had described: a swampy depression showed where the water cut it off when the river was high, and there was a rickety bridge of planks set on the

118

stumps of logs leading across into the trees. Through the wood, as he crossed, Justice could see a small and ramshackle building, a little more than a hut and less than a barn, which might be used by reed-cutters to store the osiers that grew all through the low-lying ground by the river.

As he came up to it, cautiously peering through the doorway, he saw that he was right. There was a crude ladder up to a makeshift loft, which appeared to be stacked with bundles of reeds, and there were more of them piled against the walls of the hut. There was no sign of life, except for the swallows which had nested under the thatch.

Justice looked around the hut as well as he could in the shafts of light where the sun filtered between the rough boards. There was a patch of blackened earth where someone had made a cooking fire; a coil of threadbare rope; a long wooden handle from a mattock or a pick; a few pieces of sacking that might have been used by reed-cutters working in the rain. He sat uncomfortably on a large bundle of reeds and concluded that he had come on a fool's errand. If he had guessed right, then he would surely have found some trace of Fielding.

He sat so still that a swallow dipped through the entrance and into a corner of the hut, squirming into some nest that Justice could not see in the shadow. He had just decided that he must burrow among the heaps of reed, in case Fielding had hidden something beneath them, when the bird flew out again and its movement gave him the flickering of an idea.

It was easier to reach up and touch the nest than to see it, and as Justice put up his hand, it brushed against something that felt like a bunch of dead grass. He grasped, and it came away in his fingers. Withered wild orchids, just like those which Madame Cartier had shown him.

He reached again. They had been tucked into the entrance hole of an old nest, where the mud and straw had been broken away to enlarge it.

So his guess had been right. No one would have pushed those flowers into that hole but Fielding.

He probed beyond and behind the nest, feeling the touch of metal, lifting down a box. As he did so, he sensed a movement in the doorway, a change in the light, and swung quickly to avoid being taken by surprise.

It was nothing but the same swallow swooping in and out

119

again. But as he stood in the door, with the box in his hands, he caught a flash of light in the reeds. It might have been sun on a patch of water, or an empty bottle bobbing and twisting as it drifted down the river. It could also have been someone watching him through a glass.

Justice stepped back into the shelter of the hut and opened the box. On the top was an official-looking card, complete except for the name of the bearer, and carrying a personal description in such general terms that he felt it would have fitted him as well as Fielding. Under the *fiche* was a *rouleau* of gold coins, which would be more than enough to get a man to Paris, or to the coast. Nothing more.

As he closed the box and pushed it back, he felt it knock against something on the ledge where it had been hidden. Fetching two bundles of reeds to serve as makeshift steps, Justice stretched in to find another box, and the moment his fingers closed on it, he knew what it was. A travelling pistol. Small, but deadly at close range; with a powder flask, percussion caps, lead balls, wads, and ramrod. He lifted the pistol and balanced it in his hand, tried the action, and was about to fire one of the percussion caps as a test when he realised that the sharp crack could well carry to any watcher in the reeds. He carefully put back the boxes.

Fielding had been ready to run for it. That much was now certain. But to where? And to what end? Justice felt his satisfaction ebb, and then a fresh question came to him. Where would Fielding have left an answer? Surely not here in a remote hut, where it could easily be missed. It would be somewhere in Verdun. Somewhere it could be seen. Somewhere it could be understood by anyone who had seen his letter or his advertisement.

When I see it, Justice said to himself, I am bound to know.

It was well into the afternoon when Justice got back to Verdun and found his way to the Impasse Lepic, where the Chiltingtons lived in a handsome house at the end of the cul-de-sac.

"What name, sir?" Justice felt a twinge of homesickness as the footman spoke in the honest coppery accent of Sussex, and he saw the man pause as he gave it. Presumably the Chiltingtons had their own servants travelling with them, and the footman might even have remembered that far-away cricket match.

"I will see if her ladyship is at home."

While Justice waited, he walked across the hall to look at the portrait that was the only decoration on the bare white walls. It was Caro in a black velvet dress. Prettified a touch, he thought, and wished that the painter had brought out the wilder side of her. If Kitty Holland was a very English rose, from a sheltered garden, Caroline Chiltington was a child of nature—or, more precisely, of a publican in Hackney.

She had begun life as Hannah Pratt, he had heard from friends. Before she was fifteen, her mother had taken five pounds to place her in a dubious establishment in the Vale of Health on Hampstead Heath; it was known as the Temple of Hygiene, and among the other pleasures it had offered young bucks and blades with money was a series of classical panoramas in which the naked Hannah played the part of Venus.

Within three years, Hannah had become the mistress of a young rake named Lord Archie Graham, and changed her name to Caroline Lefranc. Not that she spoke a word of French, it was said, but Lord Archie thought the change stylish for the few months he kept her before the drunken deal in which he exchanged her for his gambling debts to Lord Chiltington.

Caro accepted the bargain, and stuck to it, though once she was installed at Chiltington Place she held out for her own terms, barring the bedroom door to his lordship until he agreed to take her down to the parish church and make her Lady Chiltington. She had always looked virginal, and the gossips said that since her marriage she had surprisingly kept her virtue.

Flirtations, Justice thought ruefully, but no more.

Then the footman was back and showing him into a drawingroom where Caroline sat on a long red ottoman. Facing her, in an upright chair, was a man with his back to the door. As Caroline greeted him with a cry of pleasure, the man rose and turned to make his stiff bow. It was Charvet. And if the man had been there long, he could not have followed Justice out to Houdainville and back.

121

"John. Dear John. As soon as Chiltington told me . . ." She stopped to give a perfunctory wave to Charvet. "But I forget. *Vous connaissez M. Charvet? M. le Capitaine Justice.*" Caro broke into French, and sufficiently well-spoken French to surprise him.

"*Oui, madame.*" Charvet was already replying. "*Je le connais, mais . . .*"

"*Pardon, m'sieu.*" Justice pronounced the words clumsily. "I regret I speak no French . . ."

"But you do, John, I remember . . ." Before she caught herself in mid-sentence, Justice saw his pretences crumbling and the prospect of a long walk to Bitche before him. Or worse. "No. Of course, how stupid. I am always confusing you with Harry Courtenay."

It was a quick recovery. She would have made a good actress, Justice thought, as he walked swiftly across to kiss her outstretched hand, and felt her give his fingers a covert squeeze as he lifted it to his lips. She had taken the point at once.

"Milady would speak very good French if she would honour us more with her company." Charvet was obviously reluctant to leave the subject, though it was impossible for Justice to tell whether his suspicions had been aroused by the exchange. "His lordship is on excellent terms with the commandant."

"So I believe." Justice spoke coldly. He was recalling what Dr O'Moira had said about Charvet and a certain English lady. It could be Caro he meant. These innocent eyes and frank manner concealed a sharp instinct for survival.

"He's waiting for Chiltington," Caro said so dismissively that Justice could feel the edge of her contempt for the French police agent. "He's always hanging round the place." She gave Charvet a patronising smile to cover the coming insult. "It makes me uneasy, John. I've had bum bailiffs in the house too often in my time . . ."

Her chatter saved Justice and Charvet the trouble of making polite conversation, and before she had finished, the footman returned to say that his lordship was now at home to M. Charvet.

"Ugh," Caro said as soon as he was gone. "What can I say, John, except that the creature disgusts me and that you are more than ever welcome in his place." She moved her feet to make room at the end of the ottoman, and gave a free-running laugh. "Here, Jack my boy," she said. "Etiquette be damned. While his lordship and M. Charvet are fawning all over each other, you shall bring me news of London, and Kitty."

"First you must tell me about your masquerade," he said. "And the play."

"Oh. The ball. That was my dear husband's idea. A compliment to General Wirion and his wife." She gave her easy laugh again. "John. The devil knows I'm no snob. Can't afford to be, with my origins. But that woman . . ." She gave Justice a wicked look. "So I am giving the ball as Chiltington asks. And Mr Moon and his friends will give their play—as I ask."

"They say there will be trouble." Justice saw that she had no fear of the consequences.

"So much the better. Because I am bored to death, John. Bloody, bloody bored." She looked him straight in the face. "You've no idea how the sight of you cheers me, John Justice. When you came in, I was on the point of telling that French pot-licker what I thought of him—in the kind of language Madame Wirion uses when she's cross."

Justice stood up and walked to the window. This was no time to revive that lost moment of intimacy with Caroline Chiltington, whatever the temptation and the opportunity. But she mistook the reason for his move. "Did I say something wrong just now? About the play?" She shook her head. "No. It was earlier. When I said that you spoke French. Only I was so sure I remembered Kitty saying you had a French mother . . ."

"She died when I was a boy," Justice said quickly. Caro might be trustworthy, but she had never been noted for her discretion. It would be safer and more pleasant to talk of Kitty and her husband.

They chatted busily about the Hollands for ten minutes or more, and Justice was beginning to hope that Caro herself might make the connection between Edward's work at Lloyd's and Fielding—whom she had surely known. She was not the kind of woman to let an attractive and agreeable man pass her door unregarded. But his momentary stiffness of manner had affected her, and she kept to pleasantries; and their talk had begun to flag when the footman came back to say that his lordship would be glad of her ladyship's company.

"So it is, John. Until tomorrow." She rose to go with him into the entrance hall on her way to Chiltington's study, and there they stopped in front of the portrait. "Do you like it?"

"Seen beside the original, it pales a little," Justice said with gallantry and truth. "Was it painted here?"

"Yes, a few months ago. By a nice little fellow called Hunt."

"I know him," said Justice. "We share the rigours of M. Hahn's lodging-house."

"I met him through a mutual acquaintance who'd already commissioned a portrait from him and liked his work." She gave a gentle sigh. "Poor Mat Fielding," she murmured. "Such an unnecessary death."

Justice thought it wise to ignore the reference to Fielding in a house where Charvet was a welcome visitor; for the moment he was more interested in the fact that Hunt had known Fielding, and known him quite well—well enough, perhaps, to explain why he was so reluctant to let Justice see the work he kept in his room.

Caro was still chattering on as Justice pressed her hand, now anxious to get away.

"Come again, John," she said, aware that the footman was within earshot. "Come again when there's nothing on your mind, my dear, and we can laugh together."

As the door closed and Justice went down the narrow street, there was indeed something on his mind. Nathaniel Hunt was probably the only man in Verdun who could tell him what he needed to know.

❧9❧

JUSTICE FOUND it hard to contain his impatience as he sauntered back to his lodging-house, conscious that he would attract attention if he pushed his way too hurriedly through the busy lanes.

But as soon as he was in the house, he ran quickly up the stair to Hunt's room and knocked. All was quiet. He knocked again, and tried the handle. It would be embarrassing if Hunt came up as he entered the room, or if the painter were merely dozing on his bed. Yet it would be no more than a breach of manners, and Justice was in no mood for niceties.

To his surprise, the handle turned, and Justice eased the door open to look into the room. It all appeared to be in order. The bed neatly made in the corner by the window. A set of portfolios lying against the wall. A clothes-press. A few drawings on the table.

Justice slipped through the door and closed it behind him. In the middle of the room, where the best light fell on it, there was a half-finished painting on a studio easel. The subject was a dark-skinned woman in a low-cut dress, with an Indian shawl thrown over her shoulders. He had never seen her, and he surmised that she must be a creole, probably the kept woman of one of the richer *détenus*, and of no interest to him. There could be no connection between Fielding and a picture on which the paint was not yet dry.

Could Hunt have kept the portrait that Fielding commissioned? Justice was beginning to have doubts. Why should he have done so, unless it was finished after Fielding disappeared?

There were a few canvases stacked behind the easel. Two of them were blank. A third carried a charcoal cartoon. Another showed a haughty-looking man in front of a statue of Apollo. As Justice saw the name "Elgin" scribbled on the back, with the words "Send to England," he thought this might be the cryptic message from Fielding for which he was searching. Then he recalled that Dr O'Moira had mentioned that among the travellers detained at Verdun was a lord with a passion for the relics of antiquity.

Two more of the canvases were clean. There was nothing that could have had anything to do with Fielding.

Disappointed, anxious to be out of the room before Hunt caught him prying, Justice turned back towards the door. What he saw was the last thing he expected.

There, on the back wall, where no one who glanced casually through the door could see it, was a full-length portrait of a young woman in a simple white dress, clasping a bunch of wild flowers. Justice took in the fact that they were orchids before he realised that the woman was Lucienne Lamotte.

He stared at the painting for a moment before he went over to the wall and reversed it to see if anything was written on the canvas. It was blank.

If this was Fielding's last message, it was even more obscure than the others. For Lucienne was blindfolded by a slip of muslin round her eyes.

And behind her there was a formal background of the kind that painters often supplied to indicate the vocation of a client—a set of Roman columns for a statesman, a battle scene for a soldier, and so on . . .

In this picture Hunt had painted a small Greek temple on a cliff, with three ships at anchor below it, and a storm brewing on the horizon. Over Lucienne's head, three birds that looked like swallows were perched on branches of blossom that dipped into the scene—two birds above a third, so that they almost formed a neat triangle.

But what did it all mean? A woman who could not see, holding a posy of orchids. A distant temple. Three ships. Three birds.

It was baffling. It was worse than baffling. It was more frustrating than the familiar tease of sailing under sealed orders. But he knew that if he could somehow read the riddle the painting would be as good as a set of written instructions. Damn this clever fellow Fielding!

Justice brooded on the puzzle. Could Fielding have said anything at all that might explain the peculiar combination of images? Or had he simply found an excuse for inserting the details he wanted—a classical allegory, no doubt, or a suitable myth. Justice thought of the hours he had spent groaning over Greek and Latin texts as a schoolboy and he marvelled at the odd set of chances that made him wish to remember them in an artist's room in Verdun.

There were only two people who would know: Hunt and Lucienne; and he had to ask them, whatever the risk of giving himself away.

At the foot of the stairs he saw M. Hahn sitting in the little ante-room that served him as a parlour and an office.

"Have you seen Mr Hunt?"

"Not since this morning, m'sieu, when you left together. He should be back by dark." Hahn looked out into the hall at the row of lanterns belonging to the *détenus* in the house. "His lamp is still there, you see. Is there a message?"

"No," Justice said casually. "I'll take my supper alone, then."

126

If Hunt had not returned by the time he finished, he would go to find Lucienne at Balbi's.

Justice felt a shiver of worry about the painter. He might know more about Fielding than he realised. More than was safe for the friend of a man who had died in Bitche.

As JUSTICE LEFT the house to go up to Balbi's, he ran into Etienne for the second time that day.

The rehearsal for *The Tars* had been tiring, it was clear, for the young Frenchman was somewhat dispirited. "Mr Moon is not satisfied," he said wearily. "He makes me try again and again, until I have no humour left in me."

"He's right, you know." Justice was genuinely sympathetic because he had once discovered for himself that farce was terribly exhausting. "One of the great English actors said that comedy is a serious business."

"This part is not agreeable to me." Etienne ignored what Justice had said and went on with his complaints. "I was foolish to accept it. After all, it is difficult for a Frenchman to play this foolish Captain Champignon. There are no such people in France."

"Of course not," Justice said hastily before Etienne started to give him a lecture on the glories of the French navy. "In any case, it's a hard part for anyone . . ."

His interest cheered Etienne into a smile. "If I might ask," he began shyly as they came to the corner where their ways parted. "We rehearse again tomorrow. Would you care to come? I am sure Mr Moon would be delighted."

"If I can. I'm not sure about tomorrow." As he answered, it occurred to Justice that these were the truest words he had spoken since he arrived in Verdun.

Everything was in a state of uncertainty. He did not know what he would say to Hunt or Lucienne when he found them. He was not even sure what best to do from one moment to the next. Watching Etienne walk away into the gloom, he had noticed that he was almost opposite the Bishop's Club, and it had struck him that he might find the painter in the dining-room.

But there were only a couple of old men sitting over their claret and cheese. The rest of the club was pretty well deserted, too, and though Justice could hear a lively argument coming from the billiard-room, he knew that it was useless to look there for Hunt. The painter was no man for such raucous company.

He was about to leave when he heard Lovell's thick voice and he looked round to see the major and two other officers pawing and pushing each other as men do in their cups.

"Coming to Balbi's, Justice?" Lovell was speaking loudly to make himself heard over the aimless quarrel of his companions. "You never know, you might have a run of luck." He leaned closer and lowered his voice. "Or some other kind of run, eh?"

Justice was not certain whether Lovell was hinting at pleasures other than gambling which might be found at Balbi's, or whether this was another clumsy hint at the possibilities of escape.

"Have you seen my friend Hunt?" he asked in a cold voice.

"No idea. Don't care for painters m'self. Still, every man to his tastes, what?" It was hard to say whether Lovell's tipsy vulgarity was genuine. Justice had the feeling that the major was actually in full command of himself, and that this bucolic manner was merely a way of shepherding the two officers towards Balbi's gaming tables.

"You've not seen him at all today?"

"Been at Creange's since noon. Then here."

Justice thought Lovell was a little quick to insist that he had been in Verdun all day.

"And now on to Balbi's." A pleasantry was the simplest reply.

"Where else?" Lovell was clearly anxious to lead his two captives to the gaming-house while wine kept them in the mood, and Justice let him go ahead.

He did not want Lovell at his heels when he spoke to Lucienne.

WHEN JUSTICE ARRIVED at Balbi's, he found the house packed as if for a gala evening; the whole *demi-monde* of Verdun was there, and it was difficult to circulate through the press of rich and rakish Englishmen with their attendant ladies. Justice was beginning to despair of talking to Lucienne, when he saw her rise from a table as a party broke up at the end of a game of *loto*.

She came over to him with a smile. "I was afraid you had deserted us."

"That's not so easy, you know. Between the growls of General Wirion's watch-dogs and the charms . . ."

She did not let him finish the compliment. "Will you play?"

"I had hoped to talk to you." Justice did not feel in the mood for any kind of gambling.

"Not now," Lucienne said, glancing across the room. "When we are busy . . ." She caught something serious in the way Justice had spoken. "Is it important?"

"It could be." Justice looked her steadily in the eye. "I wanted to talk about your portrait."

The expression on her face sharpened from amiability to concern, but she said nothing.

"The painting by Mr Hunt." Justice was uncomfortably aware that Lovell might intrude at any moment, and that he must quickly come to his point. "It was commissioned, I believe, by a gentleman in whom I have a certain interest. A Mr Fielding."

Lucienne did not reply at once. Justice felt that she was weighing one chance against another before she came to a decision. "As you please," she said slowly, "though we cannot speak here. Wait for me a little after midnight. When it is quieter, I will tell Balbi I am unwell and must go home."

Justice filled in two restless hours watching the gamblers, chatting casually to other unattached men, and venturing an occasional coin on the green cloth of the roulette table; but he was afraid that if he loitered too long it would be evident that he was waiting for someone, and he went outside to walk the streets until it was time to meet Lucienne. Even at that hour, there were a few people about, and Justice wondered whether one or more of the shadowy figures he passed were Wirion's men keeping watch—on him, perhaps, or anyone who took it into his head to be abroad at this time of night.

After he had heard a clock strike twelve, he waited for a few minutes in the shadows opposite Balbi's rooms until Lucienne appeared, laughing, with a man and a woman who left her at the door.

Justice came up quietly and took her arm, feeling that the use of Fielding's name had made a bond between them. Lucienne apparently felt much the same, for she began speaking of Fielding directly. "He was a friend of yours?"

"A friend of friends, rather." Justice was reluctant to say more than was necessary. If she had any knowledge of Fielding's clandestine interests, the phrase would be enough to prompt her. "Did you know him well?"

"It was sometime in March that I met him," she said slowly as she led off towards the Roche, apparently seeking a place where they could talk without being overheard. "He came into Balbi's one night. He was alone, and after a while he asked me to drink with him. He spoke good French, and we talked for an hour or so. He told me about his loneliness since his wife died, about his work, the usual things . . ." She stopped and turned so that the starlight fell on her face and Justice could see the firm beauty of her features. "What was this business called? I forget."

"Lloyd's." Though Justice kept his answer as casual as the question, he had an idea that she was testing him.

"Lloyd's. That was it." She nodded. "Such things are not part of my life, you know." She walked on a few paces. "I think it was difficult for him in Paris, when the war started again. All the same, his work must have been useful to the government, for he was allowed to go on with it for almost a year after the other English were detained." Justice felt her give a slight shrug of the shoulders. "He said it was something to do with ships and money."

The more she spoke, the more he was impressed by the ease of her English, and intrigued by her subtle shifts of accent and emphasis. They had come to the Roche, and Justice paused by the bench where he had talked with Lovell on the previous afternoon. "Would you like to sit awhile?"

She hesitated before she agreed. "It's an odd thing," she said as she took her seat. "I usually saw him at Balbi's, and then he would walk home with me after the rooms had closed. When the nights got warmer, we sometimes walked on the Roche." She spoke pensively. "One night we sat just here, like you and me, and he told me he had conceived an affection for me."

Justice waited a moment before he put his question. "Was it returned?"

"Affection, yes. Nothing more."

He thought he had given offence and diverted her when she was on the verge of a deeper confidence, but when she continued, she spoke even more intimately.

"Let me tell you a little of myself, since you ask such questions. I was brought up by a father who was loving—but stern. A man who demanded much of himself and of me, for you must know that these have been hard years in France for men of principle. To survive, we had to make many changes . . . in our names, in the places where we lived, in our friends."

"You had no home?" Justice was beginning to see that she was a woman of some birth and education, and he wondered what strange roads she had travelled before she came to Balbi's.

"Not after my mother died. I was eight, and then we went away from France, for years. That was when I learned to speak German and English, you see, thinking I might become a governess in Hamburg, or with some travelling English family, perhaps."

"Were you with your father?"

"From time to time. And with his brother, who cared for me. But then my uncle was taken, and only a few days later he died on the scaffold." Lucienne put her hands to her face. "I can see it still, in the dark," she said in a low voice. "And whenever I think of it, I hate the people who killed him."

It was a story that might have been told a thousand times in France during the Terror. Justice laid a gentle hand on Lucienne's shoulder, and she put up her own to touch it.

"All my life it has been the same," she went on. "Running away. Hiding. Pretending. New faces. New places. Then I was married. Just for two years. But there is no peace for a soldier's wife. One trails after the army, or one waits endlessly for news." She paused. "Bad news. When my husband was killed, I had no means of living. I stayed with his parents in Metz for a little while. Then I came here because a friend of mine was working for Balbi . . . But I did not know . . . you can imagine what such a life is for a woman."

"And then Fielding made you an offer?" Justice guessed where this long explanation was leading. Kept women were so common in Verdun, Hunt had told him, that they were even accepted socially.

Lucienne stood up and walked to look over the edge of the rampart. When Justice joined her, she spoke as though she had come to a decision. "Yes," she said frankly. "I was not his *bonne amie*, Mr Justice, if that is what you mean. But I would have gone away with him. I think I would go with anyone who would take me away from this cursed place."

"Gone away with him?" Justice was so surprised that he echoed her phrase.

"Oh, yes. He was intending to escape, you see."

Could Fielding really have told her what he proposed to do? Justice could scarcely believe that he would have been so indiscreet. Was it simply an affair of the heart, as she had suggested?

"And where were you going?" He asked as lightly as possible, fearing that too much interest might be resented.

But she had apparently decided to trust him. "First to Paris. I think to get money. Then to Rouen, he said. To get a passage to America. He talked of going away to start a new life in Philadelphia."

Anything was possible. Fielding might have been planning to use Lilly's money and abscond across the Atlantic, taking Lucienne with him. It was much more likely that he had devised that story to mislead her or anyone else who might have got wind of his preparations—Lovell, for instance: such care would fit better with the concealed messages that Fielding had left behind him. But unless Lucienne was embroidering a fragment of conversation with Fielding for some purpose of her own, it did seem that he had been of a mind to take her with him when he left Verdun.

It was at this moment that it occurred to Justice that he might be quite mistaken about Lucienne. As they sat in the dark, more like furtive lovers than a couple talking about a dead man, he had been questioning her as if she were quite ignorant of Fielding's secrets. But suppose she had been in his confidence—one of his agents, indeed, who had come to Verdun to help him?

That could explain why she appeared to be both wary and confiding. Why a woman of her kind, seemingly so respectable, should have taken employment among Balbi's ladies of the room, where she could hear so much revealing gossip and meet so many people. And why only part of her story made sense.

If she had worked with Fielding, she would be as anxious as Justice himself to avoid giving anything away before she knew who Justice was, or why he had come to Verdun.

These thoughts crowded in so fast that Justice stood silent for a minute or two, staring out into the darkness that lay across the countryside, with only an occasional light to break it.

"Why did you not go?"

"Because he had to wait. He said everything was ready but he still had to wait."

Lucienne's simple reply was unexpected, and the more convincing for it. "Wait for what?" Justice himself now had an idea of the answer, but he had to hear what Lucienne thought.

"I don't know. It might have been a message. I think he was hoping for a message of some kind."

Madame Cartier, Justice recalled, had the same impression. In his last days in Verdun, she said, Fielding had gone several times to the post-house to see if his package of books had come.

The arrival of *Gulliver's Travels* had been a signal. And it had come too late.

"If he had gone two days earlier, all would have been well," Lucienne said, as if she had read his thoughts. "Perhaps he was being watched. Perhaps it was one of Wirion's tricks to get money. But one night at Balbi's he was accused of cheating. There was some kind of trouble—I don't know exactly because I was at home in bed with *la grippe*. The gendarmes were there at once, and Fielding was taken off to the Citadel." She sounded angry, and sad as well. "I expect you know the rest."

"More or less," Justice said. "Dr O'Moira told me the gist of it the other night. It seems I was lucky to escape the same sort of trap."

Lucienne was about to speak when Justice gripped her arm. He had just seen the outline of two gendarmes cross the lamp outside the guardhouse on the Roche. "I think I should take you home," he said. "It is very late."

They had only gone a few paces before Justice came back to his first question. "I asked about your portrait."

"So you did," she said. "It was a kind of joke, in fact. One day when I was with Mr Fielding we met Mr Hunt, who was complaining that he had to paint Madame Wirion. He is *gallant*, in his way, and he said he would not be objecting if he was going to paint me."

"Then it was his idea." Justice was disappointed. The painting was merely an elaborate compliment.

"Oh, no. Mr Fielding laughed. 'Do it, Hunt,' he said. Those were his actual words. 'Double the fee if you can do it in two sittings.' 'Done,' said Mr Hunt."

"And that was all that was said?"

"Except the jesting about my scarf. It blew across my face, as the wind caught it, and Mr Fielding gave me an odd look. 'Iphigenia, Hunt,' he said. 'To the life, by God. Paint her that way.'"

Before Justice could say anything, she stopped and put out her hand. "Here is my house. You know, you remind me a little of Mr Fielding," she said as a servant came to the door with a candle. "I hope you may be luckier."

As the door closed behind her, Justice turned homeward, excited by the knowledge he had gained. He knew now how Hunt had come to paint Lucienne's portrait in that classical pose. But he was no nearer understanding why, or what Fielding had meant by it.

The lodging-house was shut when Justice returned, and the servant he roused to admit him was full of sleep and ill humour. Had M. Hunt returned? Justice had to put the question twice before he got an answer. "No," the man grunted. And when Justice asked where he was, the man rounded on him: "What do you take me for, a gendarme?"

Justice had to be content with that surly answer, though it did nothing to allay his impatience and uneasiness.

There would be no help from Hunt that night.

⊷ 10 ⊷

HAHN STOPPED JUSTICE in the hall as he came down next morning. "You were asking for M. Hunt," he said in a flat voice which made Justice uneasy. "I am afraid that I did not hear until last night when the gendarme came . . ."

"Has something happened to him?"

"No. What should be wrong?" Hahn was puzzled by the interruption and looked curiously at Justice. "He was working at a house in the country, it appears, and had permission to stay out of Verdun for the night. They sent a message from the guardhouse. It is the custom."

Justice thought it a little peculiar that Hunt had said nothing about his plans when they had gone to get their passes. While there was no particular reason why the painter should have done so, it was nonetheless annoying. From what Hahn said, it was unlikely that Hunt would be back in Verdun before late afternoon; and Justice knew that he would spend the intervening hours in an agony of frustration.

Then he recalled Etienne's invitation. It would at least be diverting to watch Montague Moon rehearsing the nautical farce, and it crossed his mind that Caro Chiltington might go down to the Saint-Amand hall to make sure that everything was well in hand for her ball that night.

The workmen were certainly busy when he got there, carrying in tables, putting up bunting, stacking flowers round the entrance, but there was no sign of Caro herself—or of any of the actors on the stage. Rather than squeeze his way through the confusion, Justice walked round the side of the hall, where it ran along the canal bank, to look for an entrance at the rear.

There was a door, with a gendarme dozing in a chair propped up against a sunlit wall. Justice had now learned enough about the way General Wirion managed things to guess that there would be a fee for the gendarme's attendance, whether he was there to prevent the *détenus* running away or to keep the citizens of Verdun out of a private entertainment.

The man took no notice as Justice squeezed past him and found himself in a long corridor which ran behind and beneath the stage. He stepped over rolls of painted canvas laid along the floor—backdrops, he decided as he looked at the scribbled labels: Castle, Roman Columns, Shipwreck . . . That was one they would be using tonight, he was sure. Then he came to the green-room, where the actors had given their supper party, and beyond it he saw two doors, presumably leading to dressing-rooms, for there was a buzz of conversation from them both.

In the men's room Etienne and two of the other actors were busy dressing. "You are a little early for us," Etienne said nervously, taking up Champignon's coat and slipping it on over his shirt and breeches. "But dress rehearsals never begin on time, you know."

"In this company we're always late. I think Moon's the only actor who could miss his own benefit." The gloomy Yorkshireman was evidently cast against nature as one of the Jolly Tars, for he was trying the effect of Powdered Blue on his forearm to give the impression of a tattoo. "Can't leave well alone, can't Moon. He's had half a dozen new ideas since yesterday."

"What's he doing?" Justice always felt relaxed when he smelt the peculiar aroma of fusty clothes and grease-paint that hung around every dressing-room he had known.

"He's written in a whole new scene, with himself as Neptune." The Yorkshireman sounded more than a little jealous. "He rises from the waters, wearing the Union Jack, and then recites one of his patriotic poems. That man . . ."

"He is cross," Etienne said, jerking his thumb at the Yorkshireman. "M. Moon will not let him recite the new poem that Dr O'Moira wrote for the play."

"And sure 'tis a fine poem and all," the Yorkshireman said in a mock brogue, putting one foot on a chair and striking an attitude. " 'In the dungeon of Bitche a poor captive of Erin . . .' That's a good start now. 'Lamented his fate as he lay on the straw . . .' Well, if he's a Paddy he'll be used to it." He broke off and slumped so dejectedly on the floor that Justice saw that he had the makings of a good comic.

"What's the objection? It sounds like a good prologue." Though Justice was encouraging, he could see that Moon might well baulk at a set of verses that began with a reference to Bitche.

"It's not the words but the tune, damnit." The actor raised his arms in imitation of Moon's florid style and broke into song. " 'What patriot is there here who'll dare to sing the notes of *Erin go bragh!*' And after all the trouble the good doctor's taken for the occasion. Sure, 'tis a crying shame."

Justice suspected that the Yorkshireman was as fond of Dutch courage as of Irish balladry and that he might well mutiny against Moon's command once he started prancing about on the stage. Well, *The Tars* was the sort of piece where anything could happen and no one would greatly notice or mind if it did. It was just the romp for a party.

For the next hour, indeed, he let himself forget about the real war, and Bonaparte, and Fielding, and he sat out front enjoying himself while Effie Moon played the part of an English beauty, captured by French privateers, defying the seductive ardours of Captain Champignon. Poor Etienne was continually interrupted by Moon leaping onto the stage to suggest new bits of business likely to make the Frenchman seem laughable, or to attract patriotic applause from the English audience; and Justice understood why he had been so upset by the previous rehearsals that he would cheerfully throw up his role and go back to being stage manager.

There were a number of onlookers scattered about the hall, and at the end of the first act Justice felt someone tap him on the shoulder. "Hahn said I should find you here." Lovell was subdued this morning, and as Justice turned to look at him, he caught a flash of a very different man behind the flabby features: for all his dissipation, there was a kind of animal strength in him.

From these first words Justice concluded that the major must have brought bad news of Hunt, but Lovell simply nodded at the actors relaxing on the stage. "How are they doing, d'you think?"

"Well enough," Justice said with a grin. "As long as Moon doesn't turn it into a new play before the morning's over. Are you coming tonight?"

"Probably," Lovell said as he came to sit beside him. "Though I haven't got a mask yet. Classical, ain't it?" He gave a grunting laugh. "They'll know who it is if I come as Bacchus, I suppose." He stopped and gave Justice a sharp look. "Fact is, I'm in trouble."

"A duel?" Given the way Lovell lived, Justice thought, that was always likely.

"No such luck. I could cope with an outraged husband. No, trouble at Balbi's. One of those fellows you saw last night. Started a row and I backed him up."

"What's wrong with that?" Justice had seen for himself how easily one could cross the disagreeable little man who ran the gaming-rooms.

"Balbi's wrong with it." Lovell spoke so wretchedly that Justice could tell he really was in deep water. "That damned Italian holds too much of my paper. A word from him to Wirion

. . ." Lovell did not need to finish the sentence. Verdun was a bad place in which to owe money, especially to the commandant's flunkeys.

"I've only a little cash," Justice began, expecting Lovell to touch him for money, or to produce a bill for him to sign.

"Thanks all the same," Lovell said gruffly. "It's too late for that." He glanced about him. "I thought you and I might run for it."

Justice was not altogether surprised by the suggestion after the hints that Lovell had dropped when they talked on the Roche, and he realised that he had to judge his reaction carefully. It would be just as foolish to show too much interest as to reject Lovell's proposal out of hand. "Just like that?" A tone of astonishment was best.

"Just like that. Tonight." Lovell settled forward to speak persuasively. "Look. With this masquerade, the town will be full of people in all sorts of costumes. The gendarmes won't know who anybody is or where they are going, and I should guess that any of them who are near the hall will have found their way to a bottle or two in the course of the evening."

"That's likely." Justice saw where Lovell's argument was leading.

"And there's Moon's play, too." Lovell looked at the portly actor, who was busy trying an effect with makeshift Union Jacks in the ship's rigging on the stage. "The place will be in an uproar before it's half over. And with Wirion here . . ."

"How would you go?" When Justice put the question, he got a crafty look from Lovell. The major might be a boor, and a trickster in the gaming-rooms, but he was no fool.

"We'll come to that if you say you'll try it," Lovell said cautiously. "But it would need two of us. That's why I'm asking you. One goes as a Frenchie; the other a prisoner under escort, as himself. That's the beauty of it."

"Through the Porte Chaussée?"

"That's the sort of thing," Lovell said evasively. "Just till we get clear. Then we can go on together or separate as we decide."

Although it was possible that Lovell really intended to escape, his plan was clearly made up on the spur of the moment. In any case, Justice suspected the kind of trap into which young Pullen and his friend had fallen. Lovell had made too

138

much of a set at him in the past few days. "It's short notice," he said, temporising.

"All the better." Lovell talked in a cocksure way, but Justice had the impression that he was very agitated. He stood up. "You'll find me at Creange's," he said. "I'll hole up there till it's dark."

As Justice settled to watch the actors begin again, Lovell slipped out to the end of the row. He hesitated and came back. "I should take your chance, Justice, if I were in your shoes. You might not get another."

Watching Lovell walk away to the door, Justice wondered whether he had made a similar proposition to Fielding.

Or given him a similar warning.

In the course of the day, Justice thought a good deal about Lovell's words. There could be no question of escaping with the major, even if he trusted him, for Justice felt that he was as far away as ever from discovering Fielding's plans. Until he had some idea where to go and what to do, he would have to stay in Verdun and run whatever risks that involved.

That much was certain. But he had a sense that events were closing in on him—the same sense, he guessed, that had made Fielding so apprehensive in the days before he was arrested and carted off to Bitche. He might even be forced to seek safety in flight before the pieces of Fielding's puzzle fell into place. Whatever lay ahead that night, he would face it better for a few hours of sleep. That was his habit at sea, if he expected an action, and it would serve as well in the fortress town of Verdun.

Before he went into the lodging-house he saw that Hunt's window was still closed, and the servant shook her head when he asked if the painter had returned.

"But there is a package for M'sieu." The girl went to fetch it, and while Justice waited in the parlour, two figures passed close enough to darken the room for a moment. It might have been no more than a trick of imagination, yet Justice had the impression that they were Charvet and one of his gendarmes, and they appeared so close upon Lovell's warning that he felt quite uncomfortable.

"The man said he came from Milady Chiltington, m'sieu."

The servant held out a box, neatly wrapped and tied in ribbon.

When Justice got to his room, he opened the box. It contained a gilded *papier-mâché* mask, and a headpiece with a pair of wings attached.

Mercury. The messenger of the gods. Caro must have hit upon this disguise by accident. There was no way that she could have heard of Lilly's secret Board and the Mercantile Messengers who served it.

Except from Fielding.

And that unlikely thought was still distracting Justice as he fell asleep.

HE WOKE thinking he heard someone stirring below and wondering whether it was Lovell come for an answer. It was dark, and he heard eight o'clock chime from the cathedral tower as he roused himself to dress for the masquerade. He lit a candle, and then thought of Hunt. Going down a floor, he knocked. There was no sound from the room. The whole house, indeed, seemed unnaturally quiet.

Justice tried the handle as he had done the day before, and it turned as easily, letting the door creak back. It was clear that Hunt had returned. In the flickering candlelight, Justice could see his satchel of paints on the table and his portable easel propped against it.

He looked round the room again, and lifted the candle to the portrait of Lucienne, taking in the details—the little temple, the ships, the birds, the bunch of wild orchids—and, after their conversation on the Roche, appreciating how well Hunt had caught her temperament. There was pride, dignity, and courage as well in the way she carried herself.

He thought of scribbling a note for Hunt, and as he put the candle on the table to look for a crayon and a piece of paper, the yellow light glinted on something across the room. It was a foot in a silver-buckled shoe, sticking out below the curtain which concealed a small recess for hanging clothes.

Justice ripped back the curtain. Hunt's body, still supple from life, had been bundled in so clumsily that he appeared to be crouching in the corner. When Justice gently turned the dead man over, he could see why he was in such a curious posture. Both hands were clutching at his belly, where blood

140

had run freely onto his clothes. And beside him, as if he had pulled it out in his last agony, was a long bone-handled knife which Justice had seen on the table last time he had been in the room.

Justice realised with bitter anger that someone had killed Hunt while he was sleeping in the room above. Within the hour, probably, for the blood on his hands was not yet dry. Had Hunt been killed because he knew too much? Or to provide an excuse for silencing Justice—for sending him to the guillotine rather than to the *souterrains* of Bitche?

Justice had scarcely posed the questions before he had an answer. There were boots on the stair outside, giving him enough warning to turn and meet the gendarme who burst into the room waving a heavy pistol. He had been trapped, after all. But not by Lovell. By Charvet, for the man was one of those he had seen patrolling with the police agent. By Charvet, who might be on the man's heels, or in the street outside.

"*Voilà! Voilà!*" Justice shouted urgently, pointing at the huddled figure of Hunt on the floor. The French phrase was enough to confuse the gendarme as he paused to see what was happening, and that moment of indecision gave Justice his chance.

He swept Hunt's satchel of paints off the table and flung it in the man's face. In the same quick movement he chopped savagely at the hand which gripped the pistol, sending the weapon clattering to the floor, and then swung sideways to let the man lunge past him. Justice was accustomed to fighting at close quarters, but the gendarme was no novice. Instead of going after the pistol, he checked, grabbed at Justice, and pulled him into an arm-breaking grip that must have been used on a generation of drunkards and deserters.

As his arms were forced up behind him, Justice knew that one would break unless he found a way out of that agonising wrestler's hold. He tried to get a better foothold as they staggered, locked together, found his heel kicking against Hunt's body, and realised that the back of the dead painter would give him the leverage he needed. He let the gendarme push at him, bent his knees as he fell backwards, and felt the man's arms come loose as he toppled over.

Justice scrambled free, kicking at the gendarme's knees,

hearing him swear with the pain, seeing, with horror, the glint of steel which told him that the man had fallen where the knife came easily to hand, realising that it was no longer a question of arrest but of life and death.

The pistol was no use, even if he could find it quickly. The fall would have knocked the priming out of the pan. He moved backwards slowly, feeling behind him for the chair, fearing that Charvet could be standing in the doorway, waiting for the cold ring of a gun-barrel on his neck. Yet they must be alone in the room, for the gendarme was taking his time, coming forward with the knife thrust out in the Italian style, making sure that he was not tricked again. Then, as he came at Justice in a rush, he slipped. The blood that had oozed from Hunt's body when Justice pulled it out of the recess, and when both men fell on it, had formed a pool where the gendarme could not see it in the shadow; and as he lunged over the corpse, his boot skidded and he fell heavily on his face.

Justice was on his back at once, and as he pulled at the man's hair to force back his head, he felt a shuddering gasp. His opponent was more badly winded than he had expected. There was another gasp. The gendarme arched his back as if he were trying to throw Justice off it, and dropped back to the floor. Justice could tell he was dead before he rolled him over and saw the knife skewered through his neck. In trying to keep hold of the weapon as he fell, the gendarme had impaled himself on it.

The first thing that came into Justice's mind as he stood panting, looking down at the two bodies, was Lovell's warning. Unable to explain how Hunt had died, and equally unable to defend himself against a charge of murdering the gendarme, he had to get out of Verdun at once. And he thought of Lucienne's words, too. "I hope you will be luckier than Fielding." Had Lovell and Lucienne both known that he was in danger?

The temptation to run for it was strong, yet he knew that panic simply addled a man's mind, and that he would need all his wits about him if he was to get safely clear of the town that night. And then, in the calm mood that always came over him after a fight, he realised that there was a last thing he must do. He took the candle over to Lucienne's portrait again and looked above her head.

Two birds on the upper branch, and one below. It was a

simple pattern. And Justice remembered where he had seen it before. It was in London, on the day when he had first gone to Richmond Terrace, and seen the signs of the private banks near Charing Cross. He remembered, too, old Strang at his own bank, his words as exact as though he counted them like money. *Some of the private banks still do business in Paris, so they say, sir.*

At last he saw the point of Fielding's whimsical puns—hadn't Holland said he was a bookish man?

The Race is to the Swift. Gulliver's Travels.

Swifts. The birds were swifts, not swallows. The emblem under which Swift's bank did its business. And so the book must be more than a signal. It must be something that could be taken to Swift's branch in Paris and turned into money. Fielding's money—Lilly's missing five thousand pounds.

Justice was sure that there was more to Fielding's cleverly concealed messages than that, but at least he knew now where he must go immediately and what he must do there. He must get to Paris and Inform M. Georges of the Arrival.

Justice looked down at Hunt's body. There were different ways of dying for one's country, he thought as he closed and locked the door, and those who died in the dark sometimes deserved the greatest honour.

⊰ 11 ⊱

JUSTICE WASHED the blood from his hands, stripped, put on the clean clothes he had ready, made sure he had Fielding's *Lutine* coin in an inner pocket, swung his cloak over his shoulders, and picked up his mask.

Whatever happened, he would not be coming back to Hahn's lodging-house, and he looked round the room for the last time as he went to the window-shelf to take the copy of *Gulliver's Travels*. There had been nowhere else to hide it, and he had hoped that anyone who searched through his few possessions would not notice it tucked in between a couple of travellers' tales he had borrowed from the wretched Hunt.

The book was gone.

There was no time to look for it, and no point. Justice was sure that it had been taken deliberately, and that certainty made him even more eager to get away before Charvet came pounding at the door to find his gendarme.

He dare not risk the street, for it was bound to be watched once the trap was set to catch him. But on the day he arrived he had noticed that there was another way to leave the house. Below Hunt's room there was a half-landing with a door to the closet. Within the closet there was a second door, with a few steps down to the yard, and he had seen the night-soil men using it when they came up the lane at the rear to collect the ordure.

As soon as he was in the lane, and wearing his mask, he felt reasonably safe. In the dark, no one was likely to recognise him before he reached the hall. Then he would have to take his chance of escape.

There would be plenty there to see him go, Justice thought while he elbowed his way through the press of people at the entrance—half the town, it appeared, had turned out to watch the English make a carnival for themselves, as if they were the masters of Verdun and not its prisoners. There were link-men with flaring torches by the door, the orange flames catching on a glittering mask here, an extravagant costume there; and from within the hall there came the hubbub of a crowd settling itself for the farce.

First the play, then the dancing, and so there were only a few lanterns to show Justice the gods and goddesses, the pashas, Indian princesses, harlequins, and dairymaids who were milling about, greeting each other and trying to find seats. He caught a glimpse of Caro, dressed as Diana the Huntress, complete with bow and arrows, and he assumed from the crush around her that close by were Wirion and his wife. There were a few women in the flimsy dresses which had come into fashion as France recovered from the puritanical mood of the revolution, men in regimentals with the narrowest of masks, others in full costume and quite unrecognisable, and quite a number dressed like himself, in decent plain clothes. Caro was not one to leave a man out because he was too poor a prisoner to afford a fancy dress.

It made little difference to Justice, who scarcely knew anyone in Verdun. A few yards away, a broad back bobbed, half-turned, and Justice caught the mask of Bacchus quick enough to be able to avoid facing Lovell. All the time, he was easing his way forward, hoping he might see Etienne, for the absurd Captain Champignon did not come on until well into the first act; and as he apologised for treading on a man's toes, someone spoke to him directly.

"Mr Justice, is it not?" A black velvet mask was no disguise on O'Moira's high-domed forehead, and in any case the monkey sat gibbering on his arm. "I am at an advantage here, for faces are always masked to me." The doctor's fingers reached out to touch Justice's mask and run up to the pair of wings. "If I may . . ." O'Moira's gesture was natural in the circumstances, yet it made Justice uneasy. The Irishman could simply be eager to know how to find Justice again in this throng. But with two men lying dead only a few hundred yards away, Justice did not feel in a trusting mood. It would be safer if even his friends were unable to pick him out.

"Mercury," O'Moira said. "And you appear to be living up to your role, Mr Justice. I have the impression you are in a hurry. Pray do not let me detain the celestial messenger when he is on a mission. We shall meet when the play is over, no doubt."

"I was looking for Etienne Mandin." O'Moira's flowery speech was an irritant to Justice when he was so pressed for time.

"He was talking with Madame Lamotte a few moments ago." O'Moira was about to sit down. "I can't say where exactly, as you will understand. Somewhere near the stage. The poor youth was quite consumed with anxiety. I think Moon has pressed him too hard in his first real part."

Moon himself had twice peeped through the curtain while O'Moira was speaking, and Justice could tell that the play was soon to begin. He was about to pass through the door which led backstage when someone grasped his arm. It was Lucienne, wearing the plain white dress in which Hunt had painted her, though tonight she wore an ordinary mask in place of the circlet of muslin.

"You come as Iphigenia, then," Justice said, remembering Fielding's comparison and wishing he could remember his classics well enough to place it.

Lucienne brushed the remark aside, and Justice saw that she was very agitated. "There are gendarmes at the door asking for you," she said, speaking low. "I do not know what they want, but Charvet himself is with them. I heard Major Lovell talking to them, and I think he guessed you were in danger. He said you had not arrived."

Justice had an impulse to tell her what he was about to do. If she had helped Fielding, she had a right to know. He dismissed the thought as it came. If she had really helped Fielding, she would understand afterwards why he had gone without a word.

And there was no time to say more. At the back of the hall there was some kind of commotion. That would be Charvet and his men, unpopular enough for any robust Englishmen present to obstruct them if they appeared to be on duty. A few yards away, in front of the stage, Justice saw Caro sitting next to her husband, who was turning in his seat to see the cause of the commotion and then glancing back anxiously at Wirion.

"Delay Charvet if you can," Justice said, pressing the hand that Lucienne had laid on his arm. "Bless you and keep you." It was the nearest he could come to a farewell as he slipped through the door.

MOON HAD at last sent up the curtain, to a roar of cheers, and he was launched into his patriotic prologue when Justice passed by the stairs that led up to the stage. In the wings on the other side he could see Effie Moon chatting to a couple of the Jolly Tars while she waited for her first cue; and where the passage led to the green-room he bumped into the burly Yorkshireman, who stared at him uncomprehendingly until Justice whipped off the gold mask and said "Good luck" as the actor squeezed by.

"We'll need it," he answered, rolling his eyes upward in a look of helplessness. "Yon Etienne's back there quaking like t'jelly. Moon's fair clobbered him." He appeared to have lapsed into his native accent as soon as he put on his tarpaulin hat and pea-jacket.

Thinking that the Yorkshireman had nodded at the first of the dressing-room doors, Justice pushed it open and was greeted by a wild cry. "Lawks a mercy!" Mrs Williams in her smalls, half-dressed for the part of a dowager in the last act, was a gaunt and unattractive figure; and her appearance was not improved by the simpering grimace she made when she saw Justice.

"Wrong room," he said brusquely, afraid that she would scream again or else involve him in a rigmarole of explanation.

Her first shriek, however, had brought Etienne to the next door. He, too, was getting ready, and as he stood in the doorway with make-up smeared on only one cheek, visibly trembling with stage fright, Justice saw past him to the officer's coat hung on a peg.

He pushed Etienne back into the room, and was astonished when the youth grasped at him imploringly. "Please do it. Say you'll do it."

"Give me that uniform!" Justice had been prepared to stun the young Frenchman, or truss him with rope, or stuff him into a clothing hamper, but he had not expected Etienne to greet him as a last-minute and heaven-sent understudy for the part of Champignon.

Etienne needed no encouragement. His hands were shaking as he helped Justice into the gold-buttoned coat, handed over a sword and a cocked hat, passed a pair of buckled shoes, which Justice tucked into a capacious pocket before he replaced his cloak.

"Keep out of Moon's sight, that's all," Justice said sharply.

He had intended to walk out through the hall as soon as he had secured the uniform, pretending that his swaggering appearance was merely a piece of comic business, and then make for the Porte Chaussée. From what Lovell had said, he assumed that it would be pretty easy to bluff one's way out on a Saturday night—especially dressed as an officer and speaking French as well as anyone in Verdun. But Charvet's arrival had ruined that plan.

He would have to go out by the back door of the hall, on the canal bank, where the gendarme had been on guard that morning.

Leaving Etienne to recover his nerve, as he slumped onto a chair, Justice walked cautiously along the corridor behind the stage where the backdrops lay rolled.

The same gendarme was there, only now he sat inside the door, scowling as Moon finished leading the audience in a rousing chorus of "Hearts of Oak" and came off with a roar of cheers to reward him. Justice had only a moment to note the bizarre combination of seaweed and Union Jacks in which Moon was dressed before the old actor spoke as commandingly as Neptune himself.

"Mr Mandin, sir." It was too late for Justice to draw back before Moon caught sight of the cocked hat and brass buttons. "Up in your place, sir." Moon was in full voice and temper. "No more snivelling."

Justice looked from Moon to the gendarme, saw there was no way of getting to the door without a fuss or a fight, and ran quickly back along the corridor. He recalled that there had been a window in the dressing-room where he had left Etienne.

Moon was so close as they came to the door that he pushed his way in before Justice could close it, and the lamp-glow was strong enough to show him Justice in uniform and Etienne standing up with surprise as they burst in on him.

"In heaven's name!" he cried. "What are you about, sir?"

Justice had already seen that there were bars on the windows and little hope of forcing them. He faced Moon. "England's business, Mr Moon! With your help."

Moon stood stupefied, and Justice realised that all this must seem like a practical joke, with a parody of patriotic lines from the play. He put his hand to Moon's shoulder. "I am in earnest, Mr Moon. Deadly earnest. If I am not out of here directly, I am a dead man."

It was an appeal Moon could not reject, though he clearly did not understand what Justice was talking about. "I am at your service, sir. And my country's." He spoke with florid bewilderment, clutching nervously at a trail of seaweed from his costume that had caught on the door handle.

"Then stop Charvet coming through here." Justice turned the actor into the passage and gave him a push towards the door that led in from the body of the hall. "Any way you can. For as long as you can."

Behind his back, Etienne slipped out without saying anything and ran towards the gendarme, who had been sufficiently intrigued by the fuss to start towards the dressing-rooms. Justice saw that he was now trapped on the other side of the stage, between the gendarme and the threat from Charvet, and he realised that the only way he could reach the door that opened onto the canal bank would be to cross the boards in full view of the audience. He felt as he always did when a boarding-party went over the side and everything seemed to be happening at once—and yet very slowly.

Moon had his back to the door at the end of the passage and was beckoning the burly Yorkshireman to help him. Etienne was at the other end of the passage, arguing, yes, arguing with the gendarme, not encouraging him. Ahead of him, on the stage itself, Effie Moon was pacing up and down, improvising a song while she waited for Etienne's overdue entrance.

Then Justice was out on the stage, to a round of ironic booing, and a shout from Charvet, who was standing just beyond the row of flaring lamps at the front of the stage and trying to climb up on it. Effie ran towards him with a startled cry, and he caught her in a close embrace which evoked cheers and whistles from the crowd. "I'm in trouble," Justice said forcefully, swinging her round. "Play up to me."

As he spoke, she gave another little scream and pointed at the gendarme, who had pushed Etienne aside and lumbered out from the wings. "Faint in his arms," Justice said, disengaging himself. "And hang on to him."

Effie slapped his face, screamed again, and, to the delight of an audience which was in the mood for patriotic farce, fell upon the gendarme with such energy that the man staggered back and instinctively took hold of her.

Charvet was almost over the footlights, with one of his men scrambling close beside him, and Justice reached for the sword which Etienne had so recently buckled to his waist-belt. As it came out of the scabbard, he could tell by the weight that it was only a wooden property sword and that it would not even serve as a baton. Charvet would scarcely feel a crack on the head from that thin stick. Throwing it down with a gesture of disgust which brought a new round of laughter and cheers, he looked for another weapon.

There was nothing else on the stage but a ship's capstan. Guessing that it would be made of wood and canvas, Justice snatched it up, and holding it before him like a clumsy broom, he swept at Charvet and his helper just as they were getting to their feet. Caught off-balance, they tumbled back off the platform into the hall, where the cheers and jeers had turned into pandemonium.

When Charvet had clambered up on the stage, it was clear to those who recognised him that there was more to this interruption than knockabout clowning, and when he fell, several of the younger *détenus* rushed forward—ostensibly to help him to his feet, but actually to make things as difficult for him as they could. They could tell that there was trouble, even if they had no idea what it was about.

Justice took a quick look round the stage. Effie was still clinging to the gendarme, and a couple of the Jolly Tars had come forward to put their arms round the man on the pretence of supporting him.

Montague Moon, Justice thought grimly, would not be the only person to pay tomorrow for helping the King's business tonight, and he felt a surge of gratitude to the actors—and to Etienne as well, whatever had prompted the young Frenchman to obstruct the gendarme. This performance of *The Tars* had turned out to be far more than a piece of comic bravado.

For the sake of the company and the audience of *détenus,* he could not resist a final touch. He looked straight at Wirion, sitting convulsed with rage a few yards below him, and removed his cocked hat for a formal bow.

He could hear the crowd in the hall shout and stamp as he ran off, jumping the steps in one leap, tugging at the door, feeling the air fresh on his face after the fug in the hall.

Unless the actors took more risks for him than he had any right to expect, he had two or three minutes' start on Charvet. No more.

THE CANAL WAS his only chance. He had seen the possibilities that morning when he had walked behind the hall before the rehearsal. It looked like the easiest way to get out of Verdun. It could also look like the easiest way out of this world for an English officer who had apparently gone berserk, killed two men, and behaved like a madman at Lady Chiltington's entertainment.

There were a few houses standing along the bank, squeezed between the water and the town wall, and behind one of them he had noticed a small rowing-boat, upside down on a strip of grass. It was probably there in case anyone fell into the canal at that point, for a little farther down, the stream dropped over a weir on its way back to the main channel of the Meuse. If he

150

was right, there would be a pair of oars close by, or underneath. If he was wrong, he would have to swim and push it.

He looked back at the hall. The noise had increased. Moon and his company must be keeping Charvet busy, but the seconds were ticking away. Stumbling in the dark, tripping at a wood-pile, he found the dinghy, lifted it, felt underneath. No oars. With a curse he tipped it over to slide it into the water, and heard a clatter. A pair of oars were tucked under the rear thwart.

He had pulled away under the bridge before he saw a flicker of lanterns on the water, and heard shouting. Charvet had found his way out too late.

He was soon rowing vigorously past the stretch of waste land they called the Digue, where soldiers drilled and the poorer prisoners spent the day wandering disconsolately. It had a bad reputation at night, he had been told, and it seemed sensible to get well past it before he ran the boat up on the far bank.

Throw one oar into the water. Count ten. Pitch the other after it. Count ten again. Throw in the cocked hat, travelling cloak, the pair of shoes he had stuffed into a pocket. Turn the boat upside down and give it a shove into the current. If Charvet had men watching the bridge, the signs of an upset boat would be far more convincing if they drifted down haphazardly, or fetched up at different places along the width of the weir.

Drowned. That would be the entry in Wirion's register.

For more than a mile, Justice ran as fast as he dared in the dark, keeping close to the gleam of water on the canal, hoping he would not put a foot in a rabbit hole or run into a farm full of barking dogs. For the next mile, he trotted. He could tell that he was already swinging towards the Meuse because the lights of Verdun were now lying on his left instead of behind him.

In less than an hour he reached the place where the canal cut away from the river, and he was back on the tow-path on which he had walked to Fielding's hiding place.

It was an eerie walk. The country, so vividly alive by day, always seemed deader than the sea by night; and the occasional screech of an owl and the splash of a rat plunging into the water merely added to the effect. Justice was glad that he was

not superstitious. It was bad enough to feel as lonely and uncertain of what lay ahead as he had felt when he first drifted
into that beach near Etaples.

He picked his way over the planks to the promontory, coming up quietly to the reed-cutters' hut, listening for any sound
that might suggest a trap. He had nearly been caught once that
day, and Hunt's fate was a savage warning against carelessness.

Once inside, he made a rough bed from two bundles of
reeds, pulling the uniform coat over him with a wish that he
could have kept his cloak to serve as a blanket. The hut might
not be a very safe place to spend the night, but it was better
than pushing on in the darkness, without a map or any idea
how to reach Paris. That was tomorrow's problem. He was
asleep before he had time to worry about it.

❦ 12 ❧

As JUSTICE WOKE, he imagined that he was back in a shepherd's
lean-to on Romney Marsh, for the reeds in the hut smelt like
the osier-swamps between Appledore and Brenzett. But the
neighing of a horse reminded him where he was, and he
tensed: Charvet might still have men out searching for him.

Then he relaxed, recalling the hoofprints on the tow-path.
Somewhere nearby, a barge must be going up the Meuse.

"I thought I would find you here." The words came from
the shadows.

"What the devil!" Justice scrambled up from the floor.

"Easy now." It was Lovell's voice, with a sharp edge to it.

Now Justice could see him more distinctly. The major had
certainly left Verdun comfortably, and in style, for he was
dressed in travelling clothes—hat, cloak, breeches, and boots.
He could only have managed it, Justice guessed, if Charvet had
helped him.

"What do you want?" he asked, though he felt he knew the
answer. He had been trapped, like Pullen and Fielding before
him.

"To go with you. To share your luck."

"That's impossible." Justice was puzzled. That was not the reply of a man who had a pair of gendarmes waiting outside. He took a step forward.

"Easy," Lovell said again. "Nothing's impossible while I have this in my hand." Justice saw the glint of light on a gun-barrel. "With this I can send you into eternity, Captain Justice. Or back to Verdun, for Wirion to do the same."

Justice tested his balance, flexing his leg muscles, calculating whether Lovell was within reach. It was worth a try. A pistol ball was better than the guillotine.

"Before you move—" Lovell had anticipated him and lifted the gun. "Listen to me."

"I have no choice, it seems." Justice gave a resigned shrug. "What is it you want from me?"

"Money, to put it bluntly." Lovell gave one of his coarse laughs. "What I always want. And to get it I'll offer you a bargain. Your money for your life."

"I've no money," Justice said curtly. "If you wish to play the highwayman, go back to Hounslow Heath."

"I mean Fielding's money. You know where it is, I think. And how to get it."

Lovell spoke so familiarly that Justice wondered again how much he knew and how he knew it.

"You've come to the wrong place," Justice said evenly. "I never knew the man."

"What else could have brought you here?"

Justice was so taken aback by the question that it took him a moment to realise that Lovell was not referring to his secret mission to Verdun but to his presence in the hut, and before he could reply, Lovell fumbled in his pocket. "Here's the proof," he said. Justice expected him to produce the volume of *Gulliver's Travels,* and was astonished when he pulled out Fielding's box. "I found this when I followed you here," Lovell explained, obviously pleased with himself. He chuckled, and lifted the muzzle of the pistol. "This, too. Very useful." He tucked the box away carefully before he motioned Justice to move away and sit on a bundle of reeds.

"And now," he went on conversationally, as though he and Justice were on a stroll together, "Fielding's money. Give me your word that we'll go shares, or I turn you over to Charvet."

"I wouldn't give my word to a renegade." Justice spoke with contempt. "But that's neither here nor there, since I've nothing to bargain about."

The horse neighed again, and the sound made Lovell restless. "Come on, man. Make up your mind." He looked down to make sure the pistol was cocked. "Wirion will give much the same for you dead or alive. Especially after last night."

He suddenly stopped speaking. Justice was astonished to see him cross the hut to stand close inside the doorway, and then seize the cloaked figure that came in from the sunlight.

It was Lucienne. Carrying a basket, as if she were off to market.

Justice was still thinking that she must be the major's accomplice when he saw that Lovell had put his gun to the nape of her neck and that he had grasped her firmly by the arm. "A new stake on the table," Lovell said. "It's one that's more to my liking, too." He released Lucienne's arm and raised his hand to fondle her.

"Wirion's pig!" she cried, disregarding his pistol and turning so fiercely that Lovell stepped back half a pace, giving her room to slap his face and pull on his whiskers. "Spying on everyone at Balbi's, even on Balbi." She hit him again, while he tried to fend her off with his free arm. "Sponger. Decoy duck."

Lovell tried to keep his gun levelled, but Lucienne's angry attack distracted him. "I'll shoot," he half-screamed. "Get back! Get back!"

Justice doubted whether the man had the nerve to shoot Lucienne, and it was obvious that he would be unable to take steady aim while she belaboured him.

He was on his feet, running at Lovell, diving low, as Lucienne swung her basket under Lovell's elbow and knocked up the pistol. Her blow snapped the trigger shut. The flash was so close that it dazzled Justice, and he smelt the powder before he felt the ball cut a searing line across his forehead.

The force of the dive swept Lovell off his feet, and as the two men toppled onto the earth floor, Justice felt that he was fighting the gendarme all over again. For Lovell was a big man, too, and while he forced Justice down with one clenched fist, he was pounding him in the face with the other.

Justice caught a glimpse of Lucienne scrabbling for the pistol. "Leave it!" The shout was enough to make Lovell look over his shoulder, and the slight relaxation of pressure gave Justice the chance to bring his knee up into the major's groin. He heard Lovell gasp, but the man was not easily stopped, even though Justice was clawing at his neck, trying to find a grip which would give him leverage. It was Lovell who got to the throat first, squeezing at Justice's windpipe with his thumbs, cursing as Justice got the palm of a hand under his chin and forced it back.

And then Justice heard Lucienne shout, felt Lovell loose his hold, rolled clear with Lovell's cloak ripped off in his hand. He could scarcely see what he was doing as his own blood ran down into his eyes, but he could tell that Lovell was on his feet and reeling through the doorway, while Lucienne stood beside him with the long wooden pick-handle in her hand.

"I didn't hit hard enough," she said regretfully, as Justice took the wooden shaft from her hand and ran after Lovell.

It was a futile chase, for the major was already across the plank bridge and untying a horse from a tree. He saw Justice and shook his fist.

"Here." Lucienne came out of the hut with the pistol in her hand.

"It's no use," Justice said, watching Lovell ride away. "Even if it was loaded, it wouldn't reach that far." At least Lovell was riding away from Verdun: if he had been going to fetch Charvet, he would have gone in the other direction. All the same, he could easily set an ambush farther up the river.

"I owe you my life." Justice took Lucienne by the hand as they turned back to the hut.

"I could say the same." She looked steadily at him for a moment, and then they both laughed with relief.

"Why . . . what . . . where were you going . . . ?" There were so many questions that Justice could not decide which to ask first.

"Go and wash your face in the water," Lucienne broke in with a wave towards the river. "Then I can see who is talking to me."

WHEN JUSTICE came back, he saw that she was taking bread, cheese, and a jar of wine from her basket, and that she had torn a strip of cloth from her clothing to serve as a makeshift bandage. "That's better." She smiled as he entered the hut. "Sit and eat, and let me attend to your head."

She talked freely while she carefully wound the cloth over the shallow wound. "There was terrible trouble after you got away from the hall, you know. Wirion shouted at Lady Chiltington, at Dr O'Moira, at Mr Moon." She laughed a little. "The more he shouted, the more the *détenus* stamped their feet and sang your English songs." It was plain that she had enjoyed the commandant's embarrassment. "Then he cancelled the ball and sent everybody away."

"What will happen to Moon, Effie, Etienne?" Justice was genuinely concerned. "I couldn't have got away without them."

"Not very much, I think." Lucienne was surprisingly confident on the point. "There will be threats, fines, of course. But I suppose that Lady Chiltington will pay for them all, and Wirion knows that his lordship has deep pockets." Lucienne tucked in the end of the bandage. "There." She hesitated. "They will all blame you. And as you are dead . . . That's what Charvet said. He came back and told Wirion that you were carried over the weir."

"But you didn't take his word for it?"

"I did not believe that a captain in the English navy would drown so easily in a little French canal." Lucienne went to the door and glanced out. "That beast Lovell," she began, so that Justice thought she had seen the major returning, and then she paused. "He was waiting outside the hall for me. He took me to my lodging, and all the way . . . he had been drinking, as usual . . . he wanted . . ." She forced herself to the point. "He said that I should go to Paris with him, and that we should have money . . . Mr Fielding's money." She stopped and gave Justice a worried look. "He was sure that you had escaped. He told me that he would find you at this hut and force you to give him the money."

"He just tried." Justice gave a wry smile, and tapped his head.

"That *sot.*" Lucienne was contemptuous. "I told him you knew nothing of Mr Fielding's plans." She apparently felt that her last words gave a wrong impression. "For escape," she added. "With me."

"He knew that Fielding had money?" Justice still found it hard to understand how Lovell could be so sure of that.

"He boasted so much." It was not clear whether Lucienne was answering the question or running on with her own explanation. "And then . . ." She was evidently uneasy.

"Go on." Justice guessed what she was about to say.

"He . . . he . . . he said that you had killed Mr Hunt." The accusation came out in a rush. "Because he knew too much about Mr Fielding." She was using the same words which Justice had used to himself when he realised that Hunt might be in danger. "And that you had stabbed a gendarme, too." Lucienne was going on, while he tried to make sense of it all.

"I wonder how he knew," Justice said, half-aloud.

"I think Charvet told him when the gendarmes came to the hall." Lucienne took the question more literally than Justice had intended.

"I did not kill Hunt." Justice felt the assurance was necessary.

"I know. I was sure of that when that *potin* pushed his face in mine and swore you might also kill me. Ugh! What a filthy devil!" She came back from the door to sit beside him, and Justice could tell that she had something else on her mind by the change in her tone. "John." She spoke gently, addressing him by name for the first time. "Ever since you talked to me about Mr Fielding, I have been wondering what to say to you. How to help you, because I could tell that you were in danger. As he was." She put her hand gently to his face and ran it along the line of the bandage. "You see, I was right."

"It was lucky you came." Justice meant it.

"Not simply luck." She spoke with such assurance that Justice felt she knew far more about Lovell, and about Fielding, than she had been willing to disclose. "I left Verdun before he did—when he came up behind me on the track, I hid until he passed."

"But why did you come?" Justice was still waiting for an answer to his first question.

"I thought you might want this." She rummaged in her basket and brought out a package wrapped in a white garment, and as Justice unfolded it, he saw that it was a chemise.

"The guards would not look further," she said, catching his eye.

Inside was a book, and also a small box of the kind which normally contained playing-cards.

Justice saw before he opened the book that it was the missing volume of *Gulliver's Travels,* and he looked sharply at Lucienne. "Where did you get this?"

"From Lovell, last night."

"He gave it to you?" Justice was incredulous.

"Oh, no. He showed it to me. He said you could do nothing without it. I don't know what he meant, but . . ." Lucienne shrugged. "So I took it."

"He said nothing when he was here."

"Perhaps he had not missed it." The more Justice saw of Lucienne, the more he realised how different she was from other women he had known—even from Caro Chiltington, who had also learned about the world the hard way. "I took it from his coat pocket," she said coolly. "When he tried to embrace me."

"And this?" Justice was so relieved to recover Fielding's book that he opened the small box absent-mindedly. Inside, under some playing-cards, were two layers of gold coins.

"From Balbi's." There could be no doubt what she meant by the answer. "It was owed, anyway. And I knew we should need it."

Justice caught the word. *"We?"*

"Certainly. To get us to Paris."

"That's not possible," Justice said, hoping he spoke as firmly as she had done. "You have been kind . . . more than kind." He found himself at a loss over what to say. "But you must go now. You'll be missed . . ." For all her help, there could be no question of taking her, as she said Fielding had planned to take her with him.

"I have to come." She spoke as if that matter was beyond argument. "Where else can I go? With you gone, Lovell gone, that poor Mr Hunt—there will be such a *blague,* such a scandal."

"It is impossible," Justice tried to insist. "It will be dangerous . . ."

". . . And dangerous for me to go back to Verdun." Lucienne pointed to the coins, gleaming in the box.

At every turn she is before me, Justice thought. He went to the doorway, mulling over all she had said, while she stood silent. Through the trees he could see a farm-house close to the river, with a small barge tied up on the bank, and a man and a boy were talking to the farmer. From their gestures it seemed to Justice that they were discussing a large stack of hay-bales by the barn. Or chatting about the weather, for the farmer was pointing to a bank of grey clouds rolling up from the west.

"They will be taking the hay to Void." Lucienne was at his side.

"How far is that?"

"A day's walk up the river, perhaps a little less. The Paris coach from Metz passes that way." As she spoke, Justice wondered whether Lovell would take that coach—whether there was some hidden pattern behind everything that had happened in the last few hours. But if the barge could carry them to Void, to the coach . . . He realised that he had unwittingly accepted what Lucienne had proposed, and that moment she pressed her case again.

"You have no papers," she said. "I have. They describe me as a married woman, a *femme d'officier*. You can pass as my husband. Also you do not speak French. So, if you are wounded, and cannot speak . . ." For the second time she put her hand to his face.

Justice let the notion settle in his mind while he watched the farmer and the bargeman haggle. "How far from Void to Paris?" He was still calculating.

"Perhaps three days by coach. If the weather is good."

They could be in Void next day. And there was a daily coach, they could be in Paris on Thursday, Friday. Within the week, in any case, and before September turned into October.

"Why are you so anxious to go with me?" Justice was now sure that Lucienne had some stronger motive than she had told him when they talked about her hopes of running away to a new life with Fielding.

She waited a little before she answered. "If you know as much about Matthew Fielding as I believe you know," she said, as if she were not yet certain in her mind, "you will understand, and be patient." She reached in the top of her blouse and brought out a folded piece of paper. "This came the night you spoke to me on the Roche. It was in my room when I returned."

Justice opened the squill of paper and read a single scrawled sentence. *Ask for Martel at the Hôtel des Etrangers in Paris.* There was no signature, but there was a dab of wax with a seal on it. Justice did not need to look closely at the initials and the anchor to recognise the mark of Fielding's ring.

He stared at the paper, unbelievingly. If Fielding was still alive . . . if he had somehow got away from Bitche . . . if Lucienne . . . There were so many uncertainties. Could Fielding have changed sides and sought to cover his tracks by pretending to be dead? Such things happened. And in that case . . .

"You believe it came from him?"

"It looks like his writing. His ring, too." Lucienne seemed determined to say as little as possible, and Justice respected her reticence. He was no more willing to confide in her. If they were to travel to Paris, it would have to be a cautious partnership.

Until they found Fielding.

That must come before anything else.

Justice watched the men by the barge. They had begun to stack the bales in the shallow hold. In a couple of hours they would be finished and pulling on the canvas covers before the horse started tugging the craft upstream.

"All right," he said suddenly, aware that he had no choice. Without Lucienne, he would have no way of being sure that Martel really was Fielding. "We'll go together, as you say."

≈13≈

WHEN THE BARGEMAN and the boy finally got the covers on the bales, they went back into the farm-house. It was easy for Justice to scramble over the stern of the barge, out of sight of the farm, and to swing Lucienne up after him, but it was harder to find a hiding-place. The hay was packed tight, the long bales fitting close together, with the canvas lashed firmly over them.

Crouching low, Justice loosened one end of the rope, rolling back one end of the cover, and dragging at the first bale he could reach. It came away easily enough, and he tipped it over the side to drift away downstream. He was about to lift out another when Lucienne gave a low cry and pointed towards the farm. The bargeman was at the door, pausing, then walking a few paces from the house to answer a call of nature.

"Quick," Justice said while the man's back was turned. Lucienne slipped under the canvas and stretched flat where the first bale had been, pushing at the second to help Justice move it once the bargeman was back indoors. The difficulty, Justice saw as he climbed in beside her, was to make the rope fast from the inside. He managed to thread it through the metal eyes along the edge of the cover, and he was leaning out to make a dummy knot round the stanchion on the deck when he heard voices.

He could not risk the bargeman or the boy seeing a movement of the canvas. Better to leave the rope loose, keeping the canvas stretched against the edge of the hold with his hands. He heard the man's feet on the deck close by.

"Bertrand, tu es animal, alors! Tu as oublié le cordage."

Justice heard the boy squeal as the man cuffed him, and felt the canvas go taut as the boy tugged to fasten the knot.

"It's all right." He could hear Lucienne's breath coming in short gasps as the man and the boy moved away.

All the same, it was a long wait before they moved; and Justice was beginning to suspect that the man had noticed something when he heard him shout to the boy. *"En avant."* The boy must have been fetching and harnessing the horse, for immediately the tow-rope dragged and Justice felt the boat begin to slide through the water.

For a long time he lay quietly beside Lucienne. He could barely see her in the dark grey light that came through the thick canvas, and he did not dare to risk any word to her. They were too close to the bargeman, who stood in the wheel-house that provided him with a crude shelter against the weather.

Then he realised that the side of the cover would be out of sight from the wheel-house, and he worked at it with his fingers, forcing the edge up to make a small gap through which he could see.

Marshy banks, willows, a swirl of fields running back towards wooded hills. It was all very gentle—a Sunday afternoon in the country, with a horse and a boy trudging beside the lapping water, the bargeman half-asleep with the warmth and the wine, birds rising and dipping away from the reeds as the boat disturbed them.

He looked at Lucienne. The motion of the barge had lulled her into sleep. In the feeble light he could just make out the glow of her skin, the rise and fall of her breasts. Impulsively, gently, he put his hand on hers. She stirred, then latched fingers.

Trust nobody, Hatherley had said. Was there danger here? Or help? There was no means yet of knowing. There were only the sure signs that she had trusted him. With the book. With the money she must have stolen from Balbi's rooms. With Fielding's note. With her life at the moment she had rounded on Lovell in the hut . . . He was still running over these puzzling facts when he too fell asleep.

He woke as the boat stopped moving and the bargeman yelled at the boy to unharness the horse.

He lifted himself on an elbow to look through the peep-hole and saw that it was night; and he guessed that the bargeman was going ashore to the village, where a few lights glimmered in the windows. With another shout and a grunt as he swung himself over the side, the man was gone—and the boy as well.

It was safe now to loosen the canvas, though it was far from easy to work the knot free at arm's length, and as Justice threw back the cover, the cool air woke Lucienne.

"Where are we?" She came to her senses quickly enough to keep her voice low.

"I've no idea. Near some village. I think they've gone to the inn." Justice glanced down at Lucienne's face, glowing under the stars as he had seen it that night on the Roche, and let his eyes run down the line of her body as she lay on the hay, her skirt rucked up in sleep to reveal the curve of a thigh.

She straightened herself and moved to make room beside her. "John," she said softly, as he lay back and let her take his hand.

"It's strange to find oneself at rest like this," he said. "With danger all round us. Like a calm at the centre of a storm."

"Except . . ." She turned towards him so that their eyes were level and only inches apart. "Except that I am not exactly calm, John," she whispered.

He put a hand behind her head and drew her towards him, his mouth on hers, his fingers running down her back as her tongue darted at his lips with quick hints and insinuations. And the world fell away from them.

THEY HAD BEEN lying there for some time, rested, secure, when Justice heard a movement on the tow-path. He raised himself enough to peer out over the side. He could just make out the boy coming back, and he had stopped to move the tethered horse to a new patch of grass.

That gave Justice enough time to crawl onto the deck, though he had to leave the cover loose. Speed was essential. The houses were so close that people would be on the spot at once if the boy raised the alarm.

He came out from behind the wheel-house just as the boy saw the loose rope and sagging cover, closing his hand over the youth's mouth, winding him with a sharp blow to the ribs, stepping round the bent figure to crash a fist to the side of his head.

"Mon Dieu. You've killed him." Lucienne was at his side as Bertrand collapsed.

"I think not." Justice bent to feel the pulse at the boy's neck. "He'll wake up with a headache. That's all." He put his arms under Bertrand and dragged him to the edge of the hold. "There," he said, dropping the boy among the hay-bales. "We'll be in Void before he can explain how he got there."

It took longer than Justice expected. As they trudged on through the night, he realised that the barge had moved very slowly and that he had not made enough allowance for the loops in the river. They must have been ten miles short of Void when they left the barge, and it was farther still by the time they turned off the tow-path at every clutch of houses, breaking across the fields by dead reckoning and stumbling along the edge of the line of woods.

The sun had been up for a couple of hours when they tramped into Void, dusty, weary, and footsore, and found the post-house on the edge of the village. Two men, breakfasting while they waited for the coach, gave them a curious look that made Justice feel uneasy. Charvet could well have sent a description of him, or of Lovell, to all the post-houses near Verdun.

But a small mirror in the outhouse where he went to wash told him why the men had stared at him, and why Lucienne had quickly diverted their interest by saying that he had been injured. He looked more like a straggler from a battle than an officer travelling with his wife. There was dried blood on his bandage. His face was grimy and unshaven. And both Lovell's cloak and the blue uniform coat he had taken from Etienne were badly crumpled. Charvet himself would find it hard to recognise him.

Justice realised that Lucienne was right—that he would be a good deal safer travelling in Lucienne's company than if he had attempted to make the journey to Paris by himself, and been forced, all the time, to give explanations that could easily give his game away.

He grinned at his reflection. It would be safer. It would also be much more pleasant than he had imagined when he bolted from Verdun.

IT WAS A very warm afternoon, and the inside of the coach reminded Justice of the crowded little gunroom of the *Hesiod*, running down from Antigua in the torrid wake of a storm. It smelt just the same—stale wine, stale food, stale bodies, hot wood, and musty clothing; and the badly-sprung box swayed and groaned as if it were being dragged over waves instead of pot-holes.

He fancied he could hear sailors laughing on the deck above him, caught himself about to shout an order in English, and knew that he had been startled awake from a dream. Over his head, with only frame and leather between them, the coachman was telling a bawdy tale to the outside passengers.

Lucienne spoke quickly in French to cover his stifled words. "It's just the fever again," she said to the man opposite her, who appeared to be sitting at a curious angle as Justice squinted at him from below the bandage. He was still gathering his wits, and it was only when he saw that the two other passengers on the far seat were in the same odd posture that he understood that he was lying almost lengthways, with his head in Lucienne's lap.

As he stirred, she passed her hand over his cheek to sooth him, and the bristle of his beard was stiff against her soft palm. He let the sensual shiver run through his body. If one had a fever, well, it had better be convincing.

"Seventy hours to Paris," Lucienne had said before they boarded the coach. "You must seem very sick. How else can you sit there so long without saying anything?" She gave him a quizzical look that was somewhere between comedy and concern. "Otherwise? Someone speaks to you. Poof! He sees you can't speak a word of French. Poof, again! He says nothing. But at the next post-house . . ."

It was Lucienne, too, who had thought of the story about a gang of deserters who had attacked him as he came to collect her at Verdun, on his way from Cologne to his new appointment in Paris. Justice had listened in amazement as she rattled on to their travelling companions, spinning out a whole life for him which was far too convincing to have been invented on the spur of the moment.

"In the Army of the Rhine? Of course, m'sieu. For five years, under General Legrand. A grenadier, what else?"

As the questions and answers stitched Lucienne's tale together, Justice learned a good deal about Captain Lamotte and his family—how one brother had served under General Hoche in the Vendée, and was dead; how another went with Bonaparte to Egypt, and was a prisoner for three years; how his father, a lawyer in Auxerre, had been a deputy in the Convention during the heady days of the revolution; and much more besides. But it was all about the captain and nothing at all about Lucienne herself.

"To the Ministry of War in Paris? Yes, madame. Certainly, madame." The young sergeant was all politeness when a patrol of gendarmes stopped the coach as it rumbled over the cobbles into Saint-Dizier, and he had not bothered with more than a casual glance at Justice through the door.

Justice dozed through much of that afternoon, and it was quite dark when he finally woke, freshened at last, and saw that there was smoke everywhere, throat-catching smoke, swirling into the evening mist, and pierced by one line of fires after another, so that it seemed that the coach was passing through the bivouac of an army. For mile after mile, as they came up to Vitry-le-François, the peasants were burning off the autumn stubble, and the red glow made him think of his final cry to Scorcher. "Burn the house." Some week soon, if he failed, Scorcher would be throwing a blazing torch into the roof timbers at Hook, and watching the flames spring up in all the villages across the Marsh, as they were spreading here across the flat cornfields than ran to the Marne.

There was still mist next morning, lifting in gold and silver braids from the river, but Justice was in a more pacific mood. On such a morning, he felt, a man brought up along the banks of the Marne must be as content as he was when he looked across the Marsh on a fine May morning, when the apple trees were white and pink with blossom and the new lambs were running among them. The long years of war seemed very far away. "Perhaps," he said to himself, "perhaps one day I shall come back. Who knows?" And he turned to look at Lucienne beside him, smiling slightly as she slept, with her hand in his.

There was only one thing that nagged at him. At Vitry they had taken on a new passenger, a gross and noisy commissary from the barracks at Reims, with a snuff-stained shirt and a much-tippled flask of spirits, who ogled Lucienne with such grotesque lechery that Justice itched to throw him neck-and-crop into the nearest hedgerow. At one post-house, around midnight, the man had gone too far, and Justice had rounded on him with a torrent of stable-yard abuse. All the weeks of pretending he knew no French had proved too great a strain at last; and in his anger Justice came out with the obscenities he had learned from the grooms at Recques, who had taught him to ride like a gentleman and swear like a stable-boy.

He had so frightened the drunkard that the man had let the coach leave without him, and he had thoroughly surprised Lucienne. He caught her staring at him, wide-eyed, as he helped her back into the coach.

But she had said nothing, whatever she thought, until the coach stopped again in the middle of the night and they were alone for a moment. Then she spoke in French, as she took his hand. "What does it matter what language one speaks, if one speaks the truth?"

The truth. For the next few hours Justice had worried at the word, trying to discover what she could have meant by it, thinking what excuse he might make for concealing the fact that he spoke French as well as or better than she spoke English, exploring his own confused feelings about her.

The truth. The war broke truth into fragments, and when the pieces were put together again, they usually seemed quite unrecognisable.

He did not speak French again while they were on the coach. It was still safer to let Lucienne do all the talking, for he could too easily have made a simple mistake—the name of a general, the date of a battle, the price of wine, or any of the common-place things that a Frenchman would know at once.

It was a sensible decision, for the commissary's place was taken by a talkative dealer in champagnes, who was full of anecdotes about his business and equally curious about Lucienne and her sick husband. But even he fell silent after a while, as the last day turned to night and back to day again, and the passengers dozed, woke, lolled against each other, slept, and woke for the last time as the sun came up. Then there were more people about on the road, and carts moving even more slowly than the coach, ambling along with potatoes and cabbages and sacks of wheat. There were soldiers cantering in groups, and solitary well-dressed men riding on as if they had important business in the capital.

Soon after midday, the coach came out of a wood beside the Seine, and away along the curve of the river there was a line of carriages and pedestrians waiting to go through the *barrière*.

Lucienne gave a cry of genuine pleasure. "Look." She pointed at the towers of Notre Dame rising golden-brown in the sunlight. "Look. Paris. At last."

As THE COACH rolled into the city, Justice could scarcely believe that he was in the capital of the most powerful country in Europe. Its narrow streets ran rough and refuse-filled between unpainted houses, and there were few other vehicles threading their way through the crowds.

Even at the rue du Bouloi, where all the coaches coming into Paris stopped, there was nothing plying for hire, and Justice saw that other passengers were engaging porters or making off, bag in hand, through the throng of people who had come to greet or bid farewell to their friends. He was amused to see the champagne salesman embracing a dark and pretty girl. A traveller in champagne, he had told Lucienne somewhere along the road, was always welcome to take a guest to the Café Suchard, or to Frascati's . . .

Justice was about to draw Lucienne's attention to the couple when another figure caught his eye, and he pulled her behind a coach that had just rolled into the street.

"What is it?" She was taken aback by his sudden reaction.

"Over there. By the steps of the church." He had seen the

burly man quite distinctly. Even without his whiskers, there was no mistaking Lovell. "Be careful you are not seen."

Lucienne pulled her hood over her face and peeped round the rear of the coach. "What should I see?" she asked, glancing round, aware that they were now speaking French as easily as they had spoken English in Verdun. "I thought it must be Charvet, you were so surprised."

Justice had already made up his mind. Unless she saw Lovell, he would say nothing. "I thought so, too," he answered as casually as he could, when she drew back, shaking her head in bewilderment. "I must have been wrong if you can't see him."

All the same, as Justice led her away in the other direction, doing his best to make sure they were not followed, he could not shake off a bleak feeling of uncertainty. Once before, in Verdun, he had suspected that Lovell and Lucienne might be conspiring to deceive him, and the sight of the major lurking near the coach-stand had revived that suspicion.

Justice was so absorbed that he let Lucienne lead him through the streets, which were little more than a maze of lanes, some of them so full of beggars, barefoot children, and girls hawking themselves for a few sous that it seemed to him that neither the revolution nor Bonaparte had done these pitiable people much good. Lucienne also appeared to have something on her mind. She stopped a couple of times to ask her way, but when Justice asked how far they had yet to go, she shook her head and hurried on.

"There." Like everything else in Paris, so far as Justice could judge from what he had seen on the walk from the rue du Bouloi, the place was shabby and there was reason to doubt the fading sign which proclaimed that it offered every comfort to the traveller. But it was close to the Bourse, which Lucienne had pointed out as they passed it, and it would therefore be convenient to provincials or foreigners whose affairs took them to the money-market. Somewhere here, Justice surmised, Fielding would have had his office, somewhere close enough for him to know this *quartier* well, to come back to it if he was on the run . . .

The entrance hall was dark, with heavy furniture making it more sombre, and the clerk was cast in the same gloomy mould. "For two persons?" he asked with a glance at Lucienne, as Justice enquired for a room, and then shook his head.

"But for *M. le capitaine*—" Lucienne spoke almost as though she were reminding him of a reservation.

This time the clerk looked at Justice with a very doubtful expression. "At this time of year, after the harvest, you understand . . ." His voice trailed off without making any explanation, except a mumble about *négociants*.

"We were to ask for M. Martel." If that card had to be played, Justice decided, it was better to play it boldly.

Once again the clerk shook his head, and he turned doubtfully to scan a row of pigeon-holes behind him. "We have no one of that name," he said, but he stretched out a hand to lift a key off a hook. "On the third floor." His expression did not change as he passed the key to Justice. "On the right."

At the top of the second flight of stairs, Justice told Lucienne to wait. If there was a trap, it would be better to enter the room alone. And if the man who called himself Martel was inside— well, Lucienne could join them soon enough.

As Justice tried the handle, he recalled how he had twice entered Hunt's room and twice been astonished by what he found. But this room was empty, except for a plain wooden bed and a cupboard and a washstand, and a rush mat on the floor, and there was no view beyond a tangle of chimney-pots.

Lucienne had come up behind him and closed the door. For the first time since they had arrived in Paris, she smiled at him. "I think you are disappointed," she said, consolingly. "All day you have been waiting for this moment. I could tell." She walked slowly towards him and looked him full in the face. "Since you cursed that *pochard* you have been angry—at yourself, at me. Perhaps he will come, now we are here. Or there will be a message." She put her hand to Justice's cheek as she had done on the coach. "Meanwhile, we must be patient." She moved past him to stand by the bed. "Come, Jean." As she used his name in French, he felt oddly touched. "Kiss me now, before we go to dinner, and I shall know that we are friends once more."

THE DINNER was in keeping with the style of the hotel—heavy, unappealing, served by a gloomy waiter, and complemented by a sour red wine. Yet Lucienne had recovered her natural liveliness, as if she had been relieved to discover that there was no message waiting from Martel, or Fielding, or anyone else, and that she and Justice were still alone together; and by the end of the meal Justice noticed one or two of the other diners glancing admiringly at her and even enviously at him.

Neither Lucienne nor Justice said anything about the mystery which both united and divided them. They talked, instead, of trivial things, of childhood memories, and of incidents on the journey from Void which their self-imposed silence had prevented them discussing along the way. The nearest they came to a confidence was Lucienne's enquiring statement, "You are half-French, I think," and even then she seemed content with a smile for an answer.

They were on the way out of the dining-room when Justice saw a broad-backed man talking to the clerk. He stopped, tensed, and in the same second decided that he was becoming obsessed by Lovell. This man, turning to face him with a pleasant smile, was about his own size and age, sandy-haired and tanned by the sun; and he was dressed in fine broadcloths and a pair of good boots that were clearly not of French cut.

"I beg your pardon, sir. Do you by chance speak English?" Justice had met enough Yankee skippers to recognise the Boston twang.

"A little." Justice watched Lucienne go up the stairs while he walked the man out of earshot of the clerk. No. This could not be Fielding. This man was too young. In any case, Lucienne would have known him.

And the man's first words revealed what he wanted. "I was asking the clerk how one entertains oneself in Paris. But he has no more English than I have French."

"There's everything a man wants, they say, from opera to the usual vices." The enquiry poignantly reminded Justice of his first conversation with Hunt, on the night he arrived in Verdun.

"After three months at sea . . ." The American obviously thought that sufficient answer.

"You are a sea-captain?" Justice wondered again whether there might be more to this meeting than met the eye. And even if there was no connection at all between this man and Fielding, an American ship could be very useful if he wanted to leave France in a hurry.

"A venturing owner, sir, from Salem in Massachusetts, if you've heard of the town." The American motioned Justice to a seat at the far end of the hallway.

"And what brings you to Paris?" Justice felt he had to go on to see where the conversation led.

"I had fetched a cargo of furs from Petersburg."

Justice nodded. The Americans had made much of that trade since the Russian Emperor had seized all the British vessels in his ports some time ago. Lloyd's, Edward Holland had once complained to him over a brandy, had paid up on a series of swingeing claims.

"Grounded off Terschelling in a storm," the American ran on. "Had to put into Flushing for repairs. The shipyard said it would take the best part of three weeks. So I thought I'd treat myself to a first sight of Paris."

"If I were you, I'd try the Palais-Royal." For a moment Justice thought the man was about to ask for his company for the night, and he offered the only advice he knew. He had never seen that set of notorious shops and restaurants and pleasure-houses, but every Englishman who visited Paris during the short-lived peace had come back with tales of its liveliness and lechery. "Anyone will direct you," he said as he rose.

"Captain Cobb." The American paused at the door and bowed. "At your service, sir. At any time."

THE ROOM was in darkness when Justice opened the door, but he saw Lucienne silhouetted against the window. When she heard him, she turned and came towards him. "You must hold me, Jean, and say nothing, for tonight I belong only to you."

Justice folded his arms about her and felt her move within them so that his hands cradled her breasts and felt the nipples hard between his fingers. She gave a deep sigh, and as her buttocks worked against him, her hands slipped up behind her to work at the buckle and belt of his breeches.

"Oh, Jean." Her voice was warm and full. "I am a woman again, and we have a bed and not a bumpkin's hay-pile."

She was ungirdled, and in her shift, before he was stripped, throwing her clothes loosely upon a chair. Then he stooped and ran his hands upwards, lifting and touching at the same

171

time, until she stood naked as a statue, lit so faintly in the blue gleam from the window that he barely saw the circles that capped her breasts as he bent to kiss them.

"So you speak French, my dear one," she whispered in the softest of voices as he lifted her to the bed and lay beside her. "Can you make French love, too?"

She drew herself up on her knees to lean over him, so that she could swing her nipples slowly across his lips, teasing him, and then her mouth began to murmur its own language as it searched down his body to take his quivering flesh.

"Oh, my pasha!" she cried, as her legs forked his bandaged head, and his tongue sought her. "Oh, my Turk!" And then her tongue was silent again, as it darted and explored and caressed him.

It was the first time that a woman had taken Justice in this way, and the sweetness was there for the sharing when it was over, and they kissed again, and his strength returned to bear her up as the shivering came and went in long ripples through her body.

"Oh, Jean. Oh, Jean." He felt the slash of her fingers down his back as he clasped her, driving down, down, down . . .

She slept for a little time, murmuring half-words he could not catch, and when she woke she ran her fingers gently where her nails had cut. "I have given you a love-scar, Jean," she said very quietly. "So you will not forget me. There may never be another time." Then her fingers began to move more nimbly, rousing him again, and he felt her nipples rise as he took them in his mouth.

They lay silently for a long time, and then Justice put the thought that still lay unsettled between them. "Do you know why?" he asked in the darkness.

"Perhaps," she said, and let the question go past her as if it were no longer important whether they spoke French or English.

Justice put out a hand to touch her. In this bed, in this city he had never seen before, he felt that he had come back to some old and distantly remembered home.

❧ 14 ❧

THE SKY WAS blue beyond the window when Justice woke next morning, and he could hear distant cries and the sound of horses in the street below. The city, too, was awake again, and he had urgent business in it.

Lucienne slept on as he dressed, slipping the copy of *Gulliver's Travels* into one pocket, making sure he had Fielding's coin in another. It would be risky going about Paris in this rough-and-ready costume, without papers, but Lovell's cloak merely left a hint of a blue tunic and a gleam of buttons, and Justice had seen on the journey that his bloodied bandage attracted as much sympathy as it did curiosity. If he could get himself cleaned up at a barber's shop, send the lather boy for the makings of a breakfast, begin to get his bearings—well, that would do for a start to the day.

He was in the hallway when the door was flung back and Captain Cobb lurched in, so close to falling that he would have sprawled on the floor if Justice had not caught his arm. Clothes rumpled and dirty, reeking of brandy, he had so riotously made up for his three months at sea that Justice marvelled that he had found his way back to the hotel.

He was, in fact, speechless, and Justice had to ask the clerk for his room number. "Twenty. Second floor." The clerk handed over the key with such alacrity that he clearly hoped Justice would relieve him of the task of hauling the American up two flights of stairs.

Justice was willing to oblige. For one thing, there was the old fellowship between seafarers. One sailor should always be willing to put another to bed. For another, he was eager to take a closer look at Captain Cobb.

"Contrary to opinion," Fred Scorcher once said, "drunks and dead men carry worst." The American was a case in point, Justice thought, as he hoisted him up the narrow stairs and dumped him on his bed, snoring like a sick horse. But at least he was past struggling as Justice stripped off his coat and trousers, laying them carefully on one side, ready for use, before he slipped off the soft leather money-belt which was fastened round Cobb's waist.

To his amazement, it was still full of gold-pieces, and the folded travelling papers which certified the bearer was Jonathan Cobb, of Essex Street, Salem, in the Commonwealth of Massachusetts. There must be a special Providence that looked after Yankee skippers, Justice decided, as he hid the belt under the heap of clothes. This man had come out of the Palais-Royal, dead-drunk, without anyone laying a finger on him or his money, but he might not be so lucky with the clerk of this dingy hotel.

There was a barber less than thirty yards from the hotel, and Justice relaxed in the chair while the man scraped at his face, gossiping without saying anything, in the manner of barbers everywhere; and when he was shaved and pomaded, and the barber had found a fresh bandage for his head, he sat by the window, watching the world go by while he breakfasted on the small loaf and coffee that the barber's boy had fetched for him.

He asked the barber about the Bourse, and brought the talk round to banks and commercial houses. But the man shrugged his shoulders. "Clients, yes. Merchants. Travellers. Perhaps bankers." He waved a razor. "Don't ask me, *M. le capitaine,* if you want money. I'm a poor man. Go down the rue du Temple. That's where you'll find the money-lenders."

Justice was looking so closely at a man farther down the street, who appeared to be taking an interest in the Hôtel des Etrangers, that he did not react at once to what the barber said. Even the words did not quite come through to him. *Go down the rue du Temple.* There was simply an image of Lucienne in his mind's eye, with three birds on a branch, and three ships below a cliff on which a small Greek temple stood.

"Is it far?" He spoke absently, as he often did when too many impressions crowded in on him at once.

"Is what far, m'sieu?" The barber had not followed his leaping thought. "Oh, *pardon.* The rue du Temple? Quite close."

While the barber gave him directions, Justice saw the man who was standing in the shadow just beyond the hotel come out into the sunlight. Once again, unmistakably, it was Giles Lovell.

He beckoned the lather-boy and gave him a franc. It was as much as the boy was likely to see in a week, but he wanted to be sure of him. Justice pointed to Lovell, now making his way up the street, and held up another coin. "Come back and tell

174

me where he goes," he said, holding up another coin. "And a third when you take me to him."

As soon as the boy had followed Lovell out of sight, Justice set off himself, working his way through the alleys to a broader tree-lined street which looked like the mall of a country fair. There were stalls in it, selling sweetmeats and gee-gaws, a carousel turning slowly without any children on its brightly-painted animals; there were women with empty baskets for sale, and peasants butchering rabbits and hens in the gutter; and fair-people everywhere—jugglers, dwarfs, dusky Arab sword-swallowers, fortune-tellers, and half-naked dancers. But for the better-dressed men heading towards the Bourse, and groups of clerks scurrying into buildings farther down the street, nearer to the river, he would have doubted whether this was the kind of place in which to find a merchant bank.

Justice sauntered along like an idler with time to kill. He was so anxious to seem casual, indeed, that he almost missed the sign hanging from a bracket over his head. It was a metal circle with three birds inside it, exactly like the emblem he had seen at Charing Cross.

He stopped, putting his foot to the mud-scraper by the doorway, looking at the brass plate with the words "Swift's Bank" and the hours of business inscribed on it. This was where Fielding had sent him, as surely as if he had been following a chart.

He moved on, stared through a window at some clerks driving their quills at large ledgers, and crossed the street as a nearby clock struck eight. He had ample time to go back to the barber's shop before the bank opened at nine.

THE BOY was there and waiting for him, so breathless with excitement that Justice could not catch what he was saying, and the barber had to repeat it. "Place des Vosges," he said, jerking his thumb vaguely towards the eastern part of the city.

As the boy led him up one alley and down the next, Justice was glad he had someone to guide him. He knew that he was close to the crowded *faubourg* of Saint-Antoine, and he had no desire to get lost in that maze of slums, where the mob had gathered for the storming of the Bastille. It would be even worse, he guessed, than an accidental stroll through the stews of Seven Dials.

175

Suddenly, as they turned into a handsome arcaded square, the boy tugged at his arm. *"Voilà,"* he said, with a note of pride in his small voice, nodding across the square at a café with a few tables set under the arches. At one of them sat Lovell, a newspaper half-lifted in front of him and a glass of wine by his elbow.

Justice gave the boy his promised francs, with another to pay for a new errand; and as he watched him loiter round the square, coming up finally to the café where Lovell sat, he tried to guess why the major had first gone to the Hôtel des Etrangers and then moved on to the Place des Vosges. Had he also received a cryptic note with Fielding's seal on it? And what was he staring at so intently over the top of his paper?

The boy was now going from table to table, begging impertinently, and when he reached Lovell he was so persistent that the major irritably pushed him away. At the same time Justice edged cautiously round the arcade, so that he was quite close to the café when the boy knocked the glass of wine over Lovell's breeches. As Lovell stood up, with a curse and a blow, the boy snatched his hat from the table and ran off with it, ducking and weaving through the arches, drawing the irate major out of the square and into the nearby alleys.

The boy had done exactly what Justice wanted. While Lovell was chasing after his hat, Justice went over to the table and looked across to the corner. He could see three shops. He was sure that Lovell had been watching one of them, waiting for someone to arrive or leave. But which?

An instrument-maker's, the sun glinting on the brass in the window? Next door was a herbalist, or perhaps an apothecary, with large and colourful bottles on display. There was no obvious reason why either of them should interest Lovell. And from that distance Justice could make nothing of the third shop, for a youth in a green apron was taking down the shutters and it was impossible to see what was painted on them.

Justice took the chance that Lovell would come back and see him. Keeping close under the arcade, so that he could slip out of sight in a doorway, he arrived at the little shop as the youth lifted down the last of the shutters, and saw, in gilt letters on the glass, the proprietor's name and occupation.

Henri Duhamel. Librairie des Vosges.

A bookseller.

As Justice followed the youth inside, he recalled what the old librarian in Verdun had said when he looked at the copy of *Gulliver's Travels.*

It should have a bookseller's label there, but it seems to have lost it.

And only Lovell had handled that book between its arrival at Fielding's lodging and its delivery to the library. That was why he was watching the bookshop, waiting for Justice or anyone else he might recognise.

All the more reason for haste, Justice decided, moving farther into the shop. The assistant was already up on a ladder, dusting a shelf, but a stocky man of about sixty came forward from a desk at the rear, peering over his spectacles to see Justice against the light. "M'sieu wishes . . . ?"

"You are M. Duhamel?" Though Justice had only a moment to make up his mind, and everything might depend on what he said, Lovell's presence in the square convinced him that Fielding's package had come from this shop.

The man nodded. "At your service."

"I wish to sell a book," Justice began, "if you are interested."

"That depends." The bookseller looked curiously at Justice's bandaged head and travel-tired clothes.

"An English book."

"There is little demand these days," Duhamel said carefully. "The war, you know. But if M'sieu . . ." He stopped, inquiringly, as he caught sight of the gilt-buttoned tunic under the cloak.

"*Capitaine* . . ."

"If *M. le capitaine* has the book . . ."

Justice could tell that this halting introduction was making Duhamel suspicious and that he must come quickly to the point—even at the risk of betraying himself. "It is a book by Jonathan Swift."

Duhamel started to reply, checked himself, and then led Justice to the back of the shop. "And the name?"

"*Gulliver's Travels.*"

Duhamel controlled his expression admirably, but Justice caught a slight tremor in his voice. "May I see it?"

"Certainly."

Duhamel took the book and looked at the spine with a professional eye. "It is a fine copy," he said. "Where did you obtain it?"

"In Verdun," Justice answered firmly. He desperately wanted to watch the door for Lovell, but he was afraid of giving Duhamel the impression that he was uneasy. "I think you sent it there."

"What is that to me?" Duhamel was giving no ground at all. "I send many books to the English *détenus*." His disclaimer sounded so genuine that Justice was dismayed. Perhaps Duhamel was nothing more than he seemed, and the volume of Swift that he had sent to Verdun had no more significance than the other books in the parcel.

There was only one more thing that Justice could say. He glanced round to make sure that the assistant was at the other end of the shop, and spoke quietly. "You sent this copy to Matthew Fielding."

At last a phrase struck home. Though Duhamel made no comment, he turned to lead Justice through to a small parlour. "Why do you come here?" he asked after he had closed the door, speaking briskly, like a man with responsibilities.

"Because Fielding is dead," Justice answered. He could tell that he had to be equally sure of himself if he wanted to win the bookseller's confidence. "And I have taken his place."

Duhamel gazed at him steadily for almost a minute. "You do not speak like an Englishman," he said eventually, "but . . ." He looked at the book in his hand. "Do you know what this is?"

"I think it is a message," Justice said with more confidence than he felt, hoping that his guess was right. "When I leave here, I shall go to the bank. To ask for M. Georges."

"That would be wise." The bookseller nodded. "I am no more than a messenger, you understand. Even that is dangerous." For the first time he gave Justice an encouraging smile, but he stopped, as if baffled by the turn of the conversation. "What is it you want?"

"I need to find Fielding's friends," Justice said. "In Boulogne, especially."

He now had no hesitation about plain-speaking. Fielding had undoubtedly done all he could to cover his tracks, in Verdun and in Paris, but he must have left some means of reopening contact with the Boulogne *réseau* if anything went wrong.

It must be through Duhamel. If the bookseller was the go-between with Swift's bank, his shop was likely to serve a more general purpose as a clandestine post-office. What could be better than a business which was always sending and receiving packages?

Duhamel took his time to answer, and Justice had to curb his impatience. He saw a small perpetual calendar on the mantelpiece and felt he wanted to pick it up and shake it at Duhamel. In three days it would be October, and if the wind was right . . .

"I will do what I can, but the decision is not mine," Duhamel said, as if fearing to promise too much. "Where can I find you?"

"At the Hôtel des Etrangers."

"I will try to send word within the hour. If you hear nothing by then, it means I cannot help you."

As the bookseller finished speaking, he took Justice out through a kitchen, where a serving-girl was chopping vegetables, across a courtyard, and into an alley. "To the left," he said, "until you are well away from the Place des Vosges." He gripped Justice warmly with both hands. "And God go with you."

JUSTICE HAD only gone a few hundred yards when he noticed a tailor's, with ready-made jackets and cloaks hanging from a rack. A change of clothes, he decided, would make it harder for Lovell to pick him out in a crowd, and in any case it would suit his purpose better at the bank.

In ten minutes he emerged from the shop in a black coat that was a rough sort of fit, a round hat that covered the fast-healing scar on his head, and a riding-cloak that gave him quite a stylish air as he walked briskly down the rue du Temple and turned in between the imposing door-pillars of Swift's bank.

"I would like to see M. Georges," he said to a young clerk who was perched on a counting-house stool in the hallway.

"M. Edouard or M. Philippe, m'sieu?"

"M. Edouard." Justice assumed that the clerk would name the senior partner first.

"He does not come down until later, m'sieu."

"Then I will see M. Philippe." Justice could only hope the younger man also knew Fielding's business with the bank.

"If I may have your name?" The clerk waited politely.

"He would not know my name," Justice said, still wondering

179

how he should begin his tale this time. "Tell him I have an introduction. From Lloyd's of London." Justice saw the clerk give him a sharp look at the mention of Lloyd's. Even though the bank had long been an English outpost in Paris, and Justice could see engravings of London on the walls that reflected the old connection, it was still run by Frenchmen, whose country was at war with England.

It was a sobering thought that, on the strength of a scrap of paper and some shaky guesses, he was about to show these Frenchmen almost all the cards that Lilly had dealt to him that morning in Richmond Terrace.

"M. Philippe will see you." The clerk led him to a panelled office, where a young man rose to greet him.

"Good morning, m'sieu . . . ?"

"Walcot. From New Orleans." Something like his own middle name would do, Justice decided, and the fact that he came from Louisiana would explain why he spoke French.

"But an American?" M. Philippe seemed relieved as Justice nodded, as if something troubled him.

"In the shipping business. As a result, I have several friends at Lloyd's, and one of them . . ."

"The clerk mentioned that," M. Philippe said, offering Justice a seat.

"A Mr Holland, a Mr Edward Holland, learning that I was to come to Paris, entrusted me with a small commission." It was proving as difficult to bring this conversation round to his point, Justice felt, as it had been to discover how far he could trust Duhamel. "It is a matter of an insurance claim on some vessels travelling in wine from Bordeaux. I think the hulls and cargoes were insured at Lloyd's."

"Who made this claim?"

"The Paris agent, I understand, was a Mr Fielding."

"What is your business with it?" M. Philippe asked in such an uncertain voice that Justice wondered whether it was something more than the mention of Fielding's name that was upsetting him.

"I believe you hold the funds," Justice said, hoping to reassure the man by a calm reply, "and I have authority to receive them and to make the payment in place of Mr Fielding."

The young banker was staring at Justice as if he were looking at a ghost. "I think, m'sieu . . ." He pulled himself together.

"I think we had better discuss this matter with my father."

Without saying another word, M. Philippe led Justice back through the counting-house, up a winding stair, and into what was clearly a set of private apartments. He knocked on a door opposite the stair-head and went in directly, inviting Justice to follow him.

It was a comfortably and casually furnished room, with a pile of ledgers and other papers on a table; and by the window, reposing on a chaise-longue, sat a rumpled-looking old man who seemed to have been caught in a doze.

"M. Walcot from Louisiana," M. Philippe said formally. "My father, M. Edouard Georges."

Justice bowed and held out a restraining hand as the old man made an effort to rise.

"Always a pleasure . . . from America, you say . . ." M. Edouard spoke English with such an atrocious accent that Justice barely understood what he was trying to say, yet he had more than a touch of Englishness about him. Sitting there in the sunlight, he could have been an aged worthy in a London club: years of association with Swift's bank had left their mark on him.

"If M. Walcot will excuse me." The younger man, still visibly anxious, began to summarise what Justice had told him. The reference to Lloyd's and to Holland: the insurance claim: Fielding's name.

While he was speaking, Justice watched the old man's expression change from surprise to shrewd appraisal and then to caution. "Thank you, Philippe," he said politely but dismissively, and he waited until his son had left the room before he spoke again. "You have, of course, some credentials?" It was the obvious question, apparently innocent, and Justice was prepared for it.

"Nothing that says my name is Walcot." Justice saw that honesty would do more to win this man than any hints and half-truths. "Nothing that says you are to pay me five thousand pounds. Only this." He reached into his pocket for the copy of *Gulliver's Travels* and put it in the old man's hand.

"Am I to pay such a sum on such security?" M. Edouard spoke as though Justice were joking with him, but he kept the book in his hand.

"Would you prefer gold to paper?" Justice was disappointed

that the sight of Fielding's book had not been more persuasive, and it struck him that the old man might be waiting for some further proof.

"What banker would not?"

Justice felt in his breeches for the screw of rough paper in which he kept the *Lutine* coin.

"Does this convince you, m'sieu?" He saw the old man's eyes glitter as he twisted the coin to catch the sun. "Like the book, it came from Matthew Fielding."

The old man stood up, saying nothing, and walked slowly to a cabinet, reaching inside to release a hidden drawer. "Here," he said, turning with something bright in his palm. "You will find they are twins." He took Fielding's coin and laid it alongside the other, so that Justice could see the anchors and the single engraved word on both of them. *"Fidentia,"* he murmured, tracing the letters with his finger. "Yes, I shall trust you, M. Walcot, whoever you are, and wherever you come from."

Justice was about to speak when the old man stopped him. "And you must trust me, too. And be patient. Oh, yes, you shall have your money, never fear. But before we come to that, I have something serious to say."

The way he spoke made Justice both excited and uneasy. Was he about to say that Bonaparte had already sailed for England? Bankers often heard such things first, he knew.

"Did anyone else know that you were coming here?" Justice felt relieved by the simple question after such an ominous beginning. He shook his head. He had said nothing to Lucienne, and he was sure that Lovell had not followed him to the rue du Temple.

"Only . . . it is odd . . ." M. Edouard was finding it hard to break his news. "You have been anticipated," he said abruptly. "Early this morning, soon after the bank opened, two other people came to claim that money. A man who said his name was Fielding, and a young woman . . ."

"Fielding!" Justice was astounded. Had he really kept his rendezvous with Lucienne at the Hôtel des Etrangers? Or was this some new trick by Lovell to lay his hands on Fielding's money? "Fielding," he repeated, incredulously.

"I think not," M. Edouard said with sudden anger. "Our cashier was deceived, though I cannot blame the man. After all, the account is in sufficient credit. The client is a middle-aged Englishman, a little unwell it seems, for the young woman had to help him walk. And he had Fielding's papers to prove who he was."

"So he paid out the money! Over the counter?" Justice could not bear the thought that he had come too late.

"No. Not like that." M. Edouard was quick to pacify him. "Have you ever seen that sum in gold? It would take two men to lift it. All the same"—he paused, to go on regretfully—"the cashier did give a draft, payable at Boulogne five days from now . . ."

"At Boulogne!"

"Yes, at Ribault Frères, a discount-house of our acquaintance in the rue de Calais."

"Then the money is gone. Beyond recall."

"Gone, yes. But not beyond recall." M. Edouard was more cheerful once he had confessed to his employee's mistake. "The cashier, naturally, knew nothing of . . . of our special arrangements. As soon as my son heard of it, however, he told me. That is why we were both astonished when you arrived . . ."

"You concealed it well," Justice said admiringly.

"We are bankers." M. Edouard spoke with professional pride. "And as bankers we have means to deal with frauds." He held up a sealed paper. "See. This letter goes by fast post-cart tonight, so that Jacques Ribault will know how matters stand."

"A fraud," Justice said slowly. "How can you be so sure it was not Fielding?"

"Because Fielding never came near this bank." The old man was speaking more confidently now. "That was our agreement, during the last short peace, when we saw that there would soon be another war. It would be safer for both of us, though it was hard for old friends to part like that. And when money came for him . . ."

"From Switzerland," Justice interjected, and M. Edouard gave him a knowing look.

"Sometimes. Or from Hamburg, or Rotterdam. No matter how. Whenever it came, I sent him a message."

Justice leaned over to touch the copy of *Gulliver's Travels*. "Through the bookseller," he said, and saw that the old man was glad he avoided Duhamel's name. "And the reply?"

"By the same route. Telling us to send a draft here, to make cash available there. You understand how it is done."

"To Bordeaux." As Justice said the name, it was half a question.

"Perhaps." The banker grew cautious again. "To some shipyard, possibly. I am not sure I can remember."

Justice could tell the vagueness was deliberate and for safety's sake. He would get no more answers in that direction.

"I have lived in this house for many years." M. Edouard picked up his thought again as he glanced down into the crowded rue du Temple. "I have seen things I never thought to see, and things I wish I had never seen. I have seen a king and queen pass by in farm-carts to their deaths. I have seen a Corsican soldier of fortune climb over a million corpses to make himself emperor in their place. I have seen mobs go screaming down the street and victorious regiments march up it. And I have learned to live with the knowledge that no man in this street will trust another, and that no man knows where it all will end. In more victories? In glory? In ruin for France, I say." He gave Justice a sorrowful smile. "It is better not to remember anything too well—except one's business, and one's old loyalties, old friendships . . ."

"I believe Matthew Fielding is dead," Justice said gently.

"I guessed as much," the old man said. "Months back. When I sent the usual message and heard nothing." He picked up the book, and dropped it back into his lap. "Then, this morning . . . first the man who called himself Fielding . . . and when you came I was sure of it." He rose wearily and held out his hand. "I do not expect that we shall meet any more," he said wistfully, "but perhaps you will sometimes think of an old man who saw the saving of your country as the best means of saving France."

He moved to the fireplace to pull at a bell-rope. "You will have your own draft on Jacques Ribault before you go," he said, suddenly business-like. "My son will see to it."

At the door he shook hands for the second time. "But hurry," he said. "In God's name, hurry to Boulogne."

Justice was half-way up the rue du Temple, with the bank draft in his pocket, when he realised why the banker had kept Fielding's book and coin.

Paper and gold could serve as souvenirs as well as security.

184

IT WAS STILL only half-past nine when Justice got back to the Hôtel des Etrangers. There was no one in the hallway except a bleak-faced woman whom he took to be the *patronne*, and since she was watching a skivvy scrub the floor, Justice hurried past her without a word.

Lucienne had gone.

All the way back from the rue du Temple he had been hoping that he had been wrong—that it was some other woman, and not Lucienne, who had called at the bank an hour before.

Now there could be no doubt. He had been deceived. In the first surge of bitterness, he could not tell whether he was more angry with her or with himself. He only knew that there was no time to waste on casting balance-sheets of feeling.

The *patronne* was waiting at the foot of the stairs as he came down. "Madame has left," she said flatly, eyeing Justice to see how he reacted.

"Alone?"

"With a gentleman." She was getting a good deal of pleasure in eking out such news.

"What kind of gentleman?" The rigmarole was making Justice even angrier.

"I never saw him. The porter said he came in a *fiacre*. From the rue du Boilou, perhaps."

Or going to the rue du Boilou? Where the coach to Boulogne would start.

Justice realised that the woman was waiting for him to settle his account, and when he had paid her, she became a little more agreeable. "There was also a message," she said. "A servant came."

That would be Duhamel's kitchen-maid, for sure.

"She told Gaston," the *patronne* said, and Justice saw that she was uneasy. "I hope that was right, m'sieu?"

Justice was annoyed at missing the girl. "What was the message?"

"I have no idea, m'sieu. I will ask Gaston." She disappeared into her own quarters, and came back with a gangling youth.

"You have word for me."

The youth nodded and gave such a vacant grin that Justice feared that he had forgotten what he had been told. "Tissot," he said, apparently uncertain whether this was a word or a name.

"Go on."

"Tissot at the Chapeau Rouge." He delivered the phrase in a high-pitched tone, as if it were a line from a song. "Tissot at the Chapeau Rouge," he repeated. "Any Monday after six."

"That was all?"

"Should there be more? Madame seemed to be satisfied."

"Madame?"

"Yes," replied Gaston. "She was on the stairs as the girl spoke to me."

Justice stifled an oath, and as Gaston went back to the kitchen, he grimly wondered what Lucienne would make of that. If she was only interested in Fielding's money, it would be meaningless. Yet the message that the boy had delivered so casually might seal the fate of Bonaparte's invasion fleet.

If he could reach Boulogne in time.

He went up the stairs again. There was one more thing to do.

Cobb had not moved since he left him snoring on the bed, and his money-belt and papers still lay beside him on the chair. Justice smiled. Hatherley would have been proud to see a half-pay officer succeed where the cut-purses of the Palais-Royal had failed.

As he took the belt and papers, he hoped it was an omen.

❧ 15 ❧

JUST OUTSIDE MONTREUIL, the diligence lurched suddenly. There was a loud crack as it tilted back again, throwing the inside passengers into a heap, and then it dropped to a grinding halt. Past midnight, with Boulogne only a score of miles away, the coach had run into a deep rut and broken an axle. He would have to share a roadside bivouac with his drowsy and disconsolate travelling companions, unless he was prepared to walk on alone through the darkness, explaining himself to nervy sentinels who would think anyone speaking English was a spy.

"Too much sail swallows a failing wind," Scorcher had said one summer evening when Justice was trying to run down a French privateer before the light had faded; and the implied reproof came back to him as he fretted to be on his way.

"If we go on to Montreuil, we may find horses." It was the young naval lieutenant who had boarded the coach at Amiens and introduced himself as Jacques Valbonne.

"At this hour?" Justice sounded genuinely doubtful as he picked up Valbonne's suggestion. If horses could be found on Sunday night, the war must have greatly changed the little town on the hill above the Canche.

"Perhaps. From the garrison, of course." As they came up to the town gate, Valbonne was already calling for the sergeant of the guard, and generally making such a fuss that the men on watch must have thought that General Bonaparte himself was on his way.

"Soldiers will do nothing unless you shout at them," Valbonne cried derisively as the men on duty pulled themselves into some semblance of tidiness and order. "The lazy bastards eat all day and sleep all night if you give them half a chance."

And he was giving them no chance at all. Within fifteen minutes he had fetched an officer out of his bed, shown his papers, asked for two good horses, and got them, already saddled; asked for some wine and victuals and got those too; asked for the passwords of the night and got those as well; and they were mounted and away into the night while Justice was still wondering at the way the young man had carried off the whole thing by sheer cheek, just for the sake of making some landsmen jump.

Valbonne's energy had undoubtedly got Justice out of an awkward corner; and as the two men trotted from one picketline to the next, Justice saw how much trouble he had been saved by the lieutenant's uniform and his knowledge of the passwords. Every mile or so, it seemed, they came on a knot of men warming themselves by a fire and were greeted by the cry of "Lodi!"—and were waved on as Valbonne replied "Marengo!" Bonaparte, Justice noted, even used the daily passwords to remind his soldiers of his victories.

He rode behind and close to Valbonne, following him by the silhouette of his hat and cloak against the stars and the sparks that flew as his horse kicked up flints on the track.

What next? Ever since they had ridden out of Montreuil together, Justice had been trying to think of a good excuse for leaving Valbonne, and they were on the long chalk ridge above the valley of the Liane, with the lights of Boulogne winking at them five miles away, when his horse stumbled in a pot-hole, neighed, and settled the matter by stopping.

"What is it?" Valbonne wheeled round and came up with Justice.

"Lamed, I believe." Justice swung himself to the ground before Valbonne could steady his animal and dismount. "See." The word was meaningless in the dark, but it sounded convincing; and it was enough to stop Valbonne looking too closely.

"Will it go?"

"Cussed beast." Justice bent over a foreleg, running his hand down the shank. He hoped that was how a Yankee merchant swore. "Maybe it can walk a pace or two. But you go on. I'll manage. *Allez. Allez,* Lieutenant. I'll turn the horse in when I get there."

"Are you sure?" From his hesitant tone, Valbonne was clearly torn between courtesy and relief. "I am awaited, you understand. On official business."

"Of course."

But Valbonne was hardly out of sight before Justice heard him clattering back. "I forgot," he said. "Without me, you may have difficulty on the road. I shall warn the pickets to expect you." He laughed. "I would not wish to see my American friend arrested for stealing an army horse. Or even for spying!" He was still chuckling at his own joke as he waved his hand and cantered away.

The jest was too close to the bone for Justice to smile.

WITH THE EASTERN sky already brightening, it was foolish to go on. Boulogne would be full of military patrols, public busybodies, inquisitive innkeepers, informers, possibly a man or two who might recall his face from the prison yard or Saint-Haouen's ante-room.

There was nothing that Justice could do until it was time to seek out the man called Tissot at the Chapeau Rouge.

A farm. He would have to take his chance on that. And the square-walled building he could see against the streaky dawn, no more than a quarter of a mile away across the fields, would do for a start.

The farmer, grizzled, stocky, was lashing an ox to a cart with a crude web of ropes when Justice led his horse through the arched gateway, lapsing into the Picardy speech he had known since boyhood. He had, he said, no wish to take his horse into Boulogne where it might catch the eye of some quartermaster with a requisition order.

"You're right at that," the man said in a sour sort of way when he saw the colour of a gold-piece. "I know what they're like." He squinted up at Justice, judging his man. "Dare say you know as well as I do."

Justice let him run on, watching while he backed the ox under the single pole that ran as far as the animal's great horns.

"They'll take anything that can stand up," the farmer grunted, pulling the ropes tight with his vehemence. "If it's a cow, they'll eat it. If it's a horse, they'll ride it to death or pull the heart out of it dragging a cannon. It's all one to them. It never costs them a *sou*."

"You don't seem to like the army much," Justice said cautiously, sounding him out.

"Like 'em?" The man gave him another searching look, and spat as he jerked a finger upwards. "They took both my sons," he said. "Took 'em just like they was horses, or corn, or anything else they want. *La gloire! Merde*, I say. What's *la gloire* to a man who's left with only his own two hands to work the place?" He struck the ox as if the beast were a recruiting officer. "*Liberté*, they say. *Egalité*. Bloody *Fraternité*. Words, that's all. Lousy, bloody words. Words won't plough. Words won't sow. Words can't swing a scythe, can they?"

There was something in the fierce man's words that went on ringing in Justice's head.

THE INN where he hoped to find Tissot was one of several in a winding street off the quayside, and far too close for comfort to the squalid prison where Justice had rotted in July.

"Up there, beyond La Beurrière," a sailor said, giving him a sharp look and pointing past a large old tavern whose sign showed a woman churning butter. "You'll see it when you come to it, all right. There's a red cap on a pole over the door."

The Chapeau Rouge. The old Jacobin cap of liberty that everyone had worn in the heady days of the revolution. That would explain the sailor's odd reaction, Justice thought as he ducked in at the entrance. Dark, crowded, noisy with talk, stuffy with stale tobacco smoke, it wasn't the kind of place where a respectable man would normally turn for a meal or a bed. Just one simple room, with trestle tables, and the *patron* standing by a row of barrels at the back and keeping a close eye on the pot-boy.

There was an earthenware *cruchon* on the plank before him as soon as he sat down, and while he sipped the coarse wine, Justice looked carefully about him. If this was a trap . . . well, that steep narrow staircase, two small windows, and a low door would make a hurried exit almost impossible. It was the sort of drinking den where a press-gang would have an easy time.

And in case of trouble he would find few friends here; he could be sure of that. The rough-bearded men in the blue smocks that French fishermen and sailors wore, the pair of clerks or chandler's tellers in the corner, the little cluster of men in cheap uniforms who could be watchmen or minor officials in the port—these would all be Boney's men, waiting for the day when they could toast the invasion flotilla as it sailed out of the mouth of the Liane and set a course for the beaches of Kent.

Tissot was here, somewhere. But who was he? And what did he know? And what part was he supposed to play in Fielding's scheme of things? The questions had buzzed at Justice all the way from Paris.

A few things were clear, or seemed so.

The hints in Fielding's letter, and the traces he had left in Verdun, had led Justice to Swift's bank. At least he knew what had become of George Lilly's money, and even if that had been whisked away from him, he still had the draft for it folded safely into Captain Cobb's money-belt.

He had a good idea, too, why M. Edouard had dropped a hint that Fielding had paid a good deal of money to a shipyard in Bordeaux, most royalist of all the French seaports. The more he had thought of Fielding's original letter, and the more he had seen in Verdun of the way Fielding used simple but effective codes to conceal his meaning, the more certain he had become that the puzzling phrase "Special Perils attending Stowage of New Wine in Old Barrels" could have only one meaning.

The yard must have been constructing some special weapon which could be used against the flotilla in Boulogne, and possibly other harbours along the Channel coast. But he still had no idea what it could be, or how Fielding had proposed to get it to Boulogne and use it.

It was bound to be something of most innocent outward appearance, Justice decided. Otherwise, the French authorities would have been on to it at once. It was just as obvious that it must float—though for a wild moment Justice recalled seeing a balloon ascent in St James's Park and wondered whether Fielding had planned to launch balloons over Boulogne to drop fire or explosives on the huddled ships. And it was possible that Fielding had thought of some way of introducing the infernal machines that Lilly had mentioned right in among the brigs and barges.

But surely Lilly would have known if that had been the case.

He got that far, as he sat by the farmer's fire and tried to put his ideas together before he walked into Boulogne. Then his reasoning ran out, and there was only one question opening out of another, like the set of Chinese boxes which his grandfather once brought home from sea as a present for him.

In a few minutes, perhaps, he would have some answers.

If Tissot came.

It had already chimed six as he was walking along the crowded waterfront.

JUSTICE WAS unsure how to begin. This time he had nothing to serve as an introduction. In any case, he could not imagine waving a copy of *Gulliver's Travels* in this man's face, or holding out a *Lutine* coin in a drinking-shop where some of the customers might casually kill for that amount of gold.

He did not even have a password that he could trust. "The Race is to the Swift"? What would this innkeeper make of a *bourgeois* who came in muttering proverbs like that?

Perhaps he was making a problem out of nothing. Duhamel, after all, had simply told him to ask for Tissot, and the name must be a false one . . .

"You want something?" The *patron* cuffed the serving-boy out of earshot.

"Tissot?" One word was best.

The man gave him a hard look, then jerked his head towards the stair. "First floor, right."

Justice had his foot on the first tread before he realised that the man had been waiting for the question.

Justice looked back. The *patron* had apparently lost interest in him and begun a lively conversation with a long-armed seafarer.

He paused outside the door and listened. It was hard to tell with such a row coming up from below, yet the room seemed quiet enough. He knocked gently. There was no reply. He knocked again, lifted the latch, and went in.

"Stand still." The French command was incisive.

Across the small room, well-lit by a lantern on the table in front of him, sat a determined-looking man of about forty, in a blue uniform he wore with evident authority. And on the table, too, was a pistol. Cocked. Pointing at him.

Justice heard someone close the door behind him. So it was a trap. And the only way out was through a shuttered window behind the seated man.

"At last," the man said in a critical tone, as if Justice had been wasting his time. "I've been expecting you."

Justice looked more closely. He saw a strong face, with the etched lines of one who had spent his life between wind and water, and the stern eyes of a man who would take time to come to an opinion, and then stick to it. And a strong body as well, filling that close-fitting uniform with bone and muscle.

This must be Tissot. But if it was, why the trap? Why the unrelenting hostility in his expression?

"I do not know why you should expect me." Justice broke the pause. "But if your name is Tissot . . ."

"It will do for tonight, and tomorrow it will not matter."

Justice caught the threat in Tissot's voice as he tried to finish his sentence. "I have come . . ."

"I know exactly why you have come," Tissot said. "But what shall I call *you?*" He held up his left hand, folding down the fingers one by one. "Captain Lamotte, a dead grenadier who takes a journey to Paris? Captain Justice, a shipwrecked Englishman who has killed a man in Verdun and run away . . . Shall I go further back?"

Justice could not tell what was coming next. The man

seemed to know everything about him. But who could have told him all these things? Justice was so astonished that he could find nothing to say.

"Perhaps so." Tissot took his silence for assent. "And as our time is short . . ." It was another threat.

Tissot ticked away his forefinger. "One more part to play. Captain Philippe Luc de Valcourt, of the *service des renseignements*, or, to put it bluntly, an agent for M. Fouché, who controls all General Bonaparte's spies?" Suddenly his voice hardened. "And the man I have waited a year to meet. The man who has bettered himself by ruining his friends. The man who met Cadoudal on the beach at Biville and betrayed him again and again until he was taken. You are lucky, M. de Valcourt, that I did not kill you like a dog as you came through that door."

The last accusation was the most staggering blow of all. Luc! His own cousin. His sister's husband, who had left Valcourt after her death and gone no man knew where. Luc. Of whom things had been hinted in those sad letters from Mary during the few months of peace. And now . . .

"A spy for Fouché!" The words jerked out in his surprise, and the shock must have showed in his face, for Tissot looked sharply at him.

"As you say yourself." Tissot picked up the phrase as if it were a confession and he the judge. "After the *ratissage*, when they took Cadoudal, Fouché was bound to try a new game, to set an agent among us—someone we might trust, someone who might then betray us, too."

"That's nonsense!"

As Justice started forward in anger, Tissot dropped his hand to the butt of the pistol. "This gives me the right to finish what I have to say, I think."

Like anyone who had to command a ship in action, Justice had long ago learned to divide his mind, to watch and listen and plan and act at the same time; and he tried to sort out what Tissot was saying. A French agent. A royalist plot. Either he had blundered into a terrible misunderstanding, or he also had been betrayed.

"Go on."

"Thank you." Tissot gave a correct nod, though his voice was icy. "Of course, M. de Valcourt, you know your own story better than I do, for I know only what I have been told. But I find some pleasure in telling you that you will die knowing that you have failed. It will only be the same bitter truth that Georges Cadoudal faces as he looks at his executioners."

Tissot hesitated, as he mentioned the royalist conspirator again. "All these months, as I worked here as one of the harbour-masters, I have waited for a chance to avenge him," he said. "I could do nothing but wait. Yesterday I learned that you were on your way. Since then I have counted the hours."

"You are quite mistaken." Justice had to make the denial, though it sounded perfunctory. It would sound even less convincing to burst out with a claim that he was not his own cousin. There would be no hope of persuading Tissot to accept that coincidence. It would only seem like the last attempt at deception before an admission of guilt.

Yesterday! That meant that Tissot, as he had said, knew only what someone else had told him. Someone who must have come from Paris. Someone who had known where to find him.

"The mistake was your own," Tissot replied before Justice could do more than glimpse that his line of thought seemed to point again at Lucienne. "It was a clever idea, trying to pass yourself off as an English agent. Even though it has been done before, you apparently fumbled your way so convincingly that you might have come here and convinced me. But in fact you discovered nothing, except the name I use for this work and the place where you could find me, and tomorrow those will be changed." He looked at Justice without a trace of pity. "In any case, tomorrow morning you will be lying up an alley with your throat cut. And then we shall be quits, M. de Valcourt."

"A mistake . . ." If he could keep Tissot talking, Justice felt, he might find some way to convince him that another and even more deadly error was in the making. "Who told you this?"

"Fielding," Tissot said so tersely that the name jarred. "You thought he was dead. On the contrary, he is very much alive."

As Tissot said the words so calmly, Justice felt a wave of relief run through his tensed body. If M. Edouard had been wrong, if it was really Fielding who had reappeared in Paris and come on to Boulogne, it would be easy to find a path out of the maze, to persuade Tissot . . . unless . . . unless . . .

It was impossible. Fielding could not be alive, unless he had been deceived at every twist in the game that had been played at Verdun, unless Fielding himself had been Fouché's man from the start, a renegade setting up the whole affair to lure money and men from England, turning Justice's arrival to every possible account, telling a lie here, laying a false trail there, watching him, holding doors open for him, urging him on, setting Lucienne to deceive him.

It was a shattering conclusion. A traitor? And a faithless woman? In that case, there was no scheme to attack the flotilla in Boulogne harbour, or anything else that might hinder Bonaparte's plans. Only a deftly-spun web to catch Bonaparte's enemies, to make a triumph for the First Consul as he declared himself Emperor and launched his ships against the last nation to challenge his mastery of Europe.

"Fielding is here?" He had such a sudden and despairing sense of nearness to the man he had never seen that he might have been in the bare room with them. If Fielding was alive, and a renegade after all, both he and Tissot were in the greatest danger. Now. Tonight.

Tissot bent his head impatiently, eager to be done.

"And you have seen him?"

"Of course."

"And the woman?"

For the first time Justice caught a glimpse of something more than remorseless judgement in Tissot's face.

"That was the last thing I had to say. She asked me to give you a message."

Tissot stopped. "She said you would understand."

"Yes." Justice thought that there was nothing Lucienne could do which would touch his feelings now.

"Simply this. Tell him, she said, that in the end it does not matter whether one speaks French or English."

"She is right!" Justice knew that it was time to seize the initiative from Tissot. "It does not matter what language you speak—if you speak the truth." His words came so forcefully that they clearly had some effect. "And I say that your Fielding is an impostor, and that he lies."

"That is easily said." Tissot looked straight at him with narrowed eyes. "A man will say anything to gain a few minutes at the end. Even a long prayer, or a confession."

Justice thought he heard a footstep outside the door. "I could prove it," he said in a steady tone.

It was odd how a stray phrase could slip into your head at a moment of danger. He had just remembered a piece of advice that old Bristow Burgery had given him when he first took the lead part in a play. "Always keep them hanging on your words, dear boy," Burgery had insisted, "especially when you are going to do something surprising. They'll be watching for the wrong thing."

There was that sound again. Either a board was creaking or someone was standing there, listening. Was it the man who called himself Fielding?

"How?" So he had caught Tissot's interest and turned his mind from that hard obsession with revenge.

"With money."

Tissot stood up sharply, the flush rising in his cheeks. "Bribery will not save you," he broke out fiercely, taking a short step towards Justice.

"Nor would I expect it." Justice kept the same reasonable tone. "I said proof. I have brought the money you have been expecting from Paris—the English money—the five thousand English pounds the real Fielding never sent you. Because he was dead."

Something was wrong. Tissot seemed more bewildered than convinced. But all he said was "Show me."

Justice dropped his hand to pull away the flare of his coat and reach inside his shirt for the fastening of Captain Cobb's fine money-belt. He stopped as he saw Tissot look at the table.

"No." Everything depended on holding Tissot's attention now. "I have no weapon." He ripped his shirt open. "Only this." He was slipping the buckle before Tissot could react, and the long leather band with its little pouches was dangling in his fingers.

"See for yourself." Justice tossed the belt to Tissot, who grabbed at it involuntarily. In the same movement he lunged at the table, beating Tissot to the pistol by a clear yard, clutching him upright by one of the broad lapels on his uniform, and then holding him at arm's length while he levelled the pistol.

There was no fear in Tissot's eyes, only fury. "It was a trick, after all." An edge of disappointment in his words made Justice feel that the offer of the money had made some kind of impression. "I was a fool."

"Perhaps not." Justice had everything to gain by calming him. "But first call in the man outside the door."

As Tissot stayed sullenly quiet, Justice raised the pistol an inch higher, so that Tissot could see death down the steel tube.

"Call him." He was dealing with a stubborn man, and a strong one, and he dare not relax his grip to go over to the door himself.

But the door was already open, and the long-armed seaman whom Justice had seen talking to the landlord was coming at him with a knife before Tissot could say a word.

There was no point in clinging to Tissot. Justice had been in enough fights at close quarters to know the danger of that. Tissot had only to drop to the floor to pull him off-balance, while the second man struck at him. And there was no time to use Tissot as a hostage to stave off the attack.

It was easier to use him as a weapon. Before the door opened, Justice had been ready for such a move, and as the seaman burst in, he turned Tissot's own surprised reaction into the first inches of a swing which brought the harbour-master round as a shield against the sailor, who was hesitating as he saw the entangled bodies dark against the lantern light.

That flick of uncertainty was enough. While the man was looking for his mark, Justice let Tissot go in a staggering fall that stretched him on the floor and brought the sailor down with him, the knife skittering away as he lost his grip.

"Stay there." Justice had long ago learned that it was safer to watch two men on the ground. With a single-barrelled pistol there was always time to shoot one and club the other before he could scramble to his feet.

"*Alors.*" He needed a moment to catch his breath.

But there was no time to argue with Tissot. In any case, after such a scuffle, the man would be in no mood for reason. He had to do something dramatic. Fast. While he had an advantage that could be lost in a flash if another man came up the stair.

"It is a matter of trust," he said frankly to Tissot. "You put your trust in the man who says he is Fielding. I put my trust in this pistol. I suggest an exchange."

Tissot growled, as if he could not grasp what Justice meant.

"To put it simply," Justice went on, "I will give you a different kind of proof."

He moved to the table and stood by it. "There." He put the pistol down, though close to his hand. "There is my first promise."

It was a gamble. If it failed, he was finished. But at least Tissot had made no effort to profit by the gesture.

"He is fooling us." The long-armed sailor spoke for the first time, and Justice was surprised to hear the clear speech of an educated man.

"No, Pierre. Somehow I do not think so." Tissot looked up at Justice. "May I stand?" It sounded like half an answer.

"Of course. But only you. For the present."

As Tissot rose, he gave Justice another appraising glance. "And your second promise . . . ?"

"That you will find that I am indeed an Englishman, and that my honour rests on my word."

"And that is all?"

"No." As he spoke, Justice uncocked the pistol and turned it round so that Tissot could easily lay his hand on it. "There is this, too."

As Tissot was about to reach for the gun, Justice raised a cautionary finger. "On one condition."

Tissot lifted his eyebrows.

"That you take me to meet the man who says he is Fielding."

Tissot thought for a second. "He has papers, you know," as if he were warning Justice of a wager against the odds.

"They must be forgeries."

"And the woman speaks for him. The second man as well."

Tissot seemed to produce surprises like a clerk in an auction holding up one lot after another. The second man . . . it must be Lovell. But this was no time to bandy arguments with Tissot. He must take his chances as they came.

"Never mind." Justice made a show of confidence by walking away from the table towards the door, while Tissot went over to where the knife had fallen and picked it up.

Pierre got to his feet and put out a hand towards it.

Tissot shook his head. "Here," he said to Justice, laying it beside the pistol. "As you say. A fair exchange."

He waited until Justice had picked up the sharp, short-bladed knife, almost as if he was choosing weapons in a duel. Then he took the pistol, stuffed the money-belt into his pocket, and motioned towards the door.

As Justice obeyed, the seaman slipped through ahead of him, and stood on the landing. And Justice realised that Tissot had paused because he had something more to say. "I have agreed to nothing, you understand. Only your one condition."

Justice nodded.

"You see," Tissot added, "it is a very curious thing. There are two men in Boulogne tonight who say they are Englishmen. And both of them want to give me five thousand pounds." He gave a polite bow as Justice went out of the room and turned to follow the other man along a passage which led to the back of the inn.

Then Justice heard a click.

It was Tissot cocking the pistol again.

❧ 16 ❧

"This way." Pierre opened a door and led the way on to a narrow gallery that ran along the back of the inn, linking several buildings together before it pitched down some wooden steps into a yard. Like the men who ran the taverns and whorehouses of Portsmouth Point, Justice thought as he grasped the rail and followed Pierre, these harbourside innkeepers no doubt found it convenient to provide another way to enter or leave their premises. And what served for men with stolen or smuggled goods on their hands, or eager for a furtive roll with someone else's wife, would serve Tissot's clandestine purposes just as well.

As they crossed the yard and pushed along a crowded alley, Justice realised that Tissot was staying a pace or two away from him, as if he were minding his own business. He obviously had no intention of being seen with a man whose body might be found in a gutter before the next dawn.

It would be easy to run for it, then. The idea had no sooner come into Justice's head than he saw that the two men elbowing their way on either side of Tissot were keeping uncomfortably close. With Pierre ahead, and Tissot not far behind, this escort would see that he did not get far before there was a knife-blade in his ribs.

And where would he run if he could? Tissot was the one man in the world who mattered to him at this moment.

And no doubt Tissot knew it. This walk might even be some kind of trial. Philippe Luc de Valcourt would certainly make a break for it in these circumstances. A confidential agent from England would be forced to try his luck with the man he had come to find.

At least, Justice hoped that Tissot thought like that, but it was too dark to see any expression on his face as Pierre turned a corner, stopped, and waited for Tissot to come up past Justice and murmur a word to him. They were facing a row of high, clapboarded structures which, even in the poor light, seemed oddly familiar to Justice.

Then it came to him. They were net-houses, exactly like those which stood by the Rother bank at Rye, and the Rye fishermen called "herring-hangs," for it was there that they dried bloaters, made and mended their nets, and kept their lobster-pots, canvas, barrels of tar and long hanks of rope, blocks of rough salt for pickling. Places where people came and went all the time, at any hour, as the winds and tides served them. Places where one could hide anything. Even a body. With barrels and brine to hand, a man did not need to come out of there in one piece.

They were coming to the net-houses from the back, but Justice could guess how it would face onto the quayside, close to the water, each house with a blank boarded face reaching up to the small door under the pointed gable, where a man could stand on a platform and look out while nets, or sails, or anything else was being hauled up on the roof-beam that ran right through the building to form an anchorage for the lifting-tackle.

And the back, as he could see from the rise of the darkened windows, was divided in the same way as it would be in Rye. Four or five floors, each with a working-ledge giving on to the clear space where the nets could drop free from the roof to the ground, each with one or two small rooms which could be shut off and used as stores, or somewhere for the crew of a fishing-boat to doss down when they were not at sea. Such men, Justice knew from Fred Scorcher's chat about his acquaintances, lived quite as roughly as the between-decks people of a sloop or an inshore gunboat.

He was scarcely through the door which Pierre held open for him, trying to get some sense of his bearings in the gloom, smelling the timber and the pitch and the damp rope which made him long for the feel of a deck again, when his arms were seized and twisted behind him.

"After our last encounter . . ." It was Tissot himself who was running the length of rope round and between his wrists, chafing tight, knotting it with the deft touch of a man accustomed to handling lines in the dark. "To make sure . . ." As Tissot finished the second of his grunted sentences with a final tug, he ran his hand around Justice's waist-band until he came to the knife, which Justice had slipped in above his left hip, where he could get at it quickly.

So Tissot had fooled him. He had been stupid to give up the pistol in such a quixotic attempt to convince the man. The gesture had obviously made no impression on Tissot, who had merely pretended to accept his offer in order to get him to leave the inn without a struggle. Though, to be fair, Tissot had promised nothing—except a meeting with Fielding.

"Up the ladder." It was almost impossible to climb the narrow rungs with his arms secured behind him and Tissot hanging on to the trailing end of the rope. He could only dimly see his footing by the light of a guttering tallow candle which Pierre had lit on the floor above, turning the trapdoor into a yellow square over his head. "And again." The second floor. He fancied there was someone in the room where the rough door stood ajar, although it was in darkness, but Tissot was urging him on before he could look twice. "Again."

And even if there was someone there, it would be no use crying out for help. If Tissot was his enemy, where could he turn for a friend?

With a shock, the answer came and went. It had been Lucienne who had been standing there, silently, as he was led up to the top floor. Like a man going to the condemned cell. Were they going to hang him as a traitor, from a hook on the hoisting-beam in the roof?

Pierre neatly kicked his legs away. Justice dropped to his knees, then fell sideways, giving Tissot a chance to get a hitch round his ankles before he could kick.

They left him like that, doubled, with only a little room to stretch. All that Tissot had said as he backed down the ladder was a single cryptic word: *"Attendez."* Well, he had no choice. In the few moments before Tissot took the candle away, Justice had time to see that he was in a store-room, half-filled with sacks ranged across the little door that gave on to the platform at the top of the net-drop. Tied as he was, there could be no hope of shifting any of the sacks and trying to get out that way.

It would be equally futile to try to find the trap through which they had come up. As Tissot had slammed it shut, Justice had heard a bolt go home.

There was no way out. Probably no way in which a shout could attract attention, since Tissot had not bothered to gag him. In a building like this, a cry would be muffled by the wood and the sacks of stores which were obviously piled in every room.

Yet, distantly, he thought he could hear someone speaking.

No. It could be nothing but a trick of the wind he had felt coming in fresh from the north-east as they had walked from the inn. The wind that would keep Admiral Keith's patrolling squadron down Channel and leave the Straits clear. The wind that would let Boney send his slow-moving flotilla on a long tack that would take them straight to the beaches of Romney Marsh. And to Hook.

As JUSTICE rocked himself on the floor, trying to find some give in the rope which bound him, seeing how far he could move, he caught himself wondering what Hatherley or George Lilly would say now if he could see him waiting to confront the person who called himself Fielding. This was not a situation in which answers came easily to a man who had spent most of the years since his boyhood at sea.

Yet. He searched for the thought. In all this jumble of memories, an image was forming—a slowly sharpening picture like the one he had seen at a fair in Dover when, a schoolboy on a holiday, he had paid a penny to go into the darkened hut and see the town and harbour laid out before him by a marvel the showman called a magic lantern.

A grey sea, with half a gale flattening the wave-tops. That was it. Off Ushant. A war-brig, running up the Channel alone, hard-pressed by a French frigate which could outsail and out-shoot any brig that an English yard could build—a frigate which could stand off and pound the brig to pieces before the row of 12-pounders could make their broadside reach, before a depleted crew would have a chance to grapple and board . . . Drop the topmasts, slacken the rigging, tell the helmsman to let the head fall off in a succession of lurches, give the impression of a dragging bottom covered in barnacles and seaweed by trailing a jib-sail through the water on the quarter hidden from the frigate's lookouts—all these things had made that Frenchman believe he was dealing with a clapped-out mer-chantman beating a way to port after a long voyage, and brought him down with false confidence to the bitter fight that had given Justice his first prize to send into Plymouth.

And he had done it because of a simple piece of advice that Lieutenant Faulconer had given him, years before, on a quiet night watch on the *Welcome*. "If you're weak," Faulconer had said, "never run for it. Always make the enemy come to you."

It was still good advice. And apt.

The man he was about to meet wanted something from him, something that Justice must know without realising it. So let him come, searching for Justice's weakness and revealing his own as he did so. Let him come. Let him put the question that was so vital that Justice had been allowed to run all the way from Verdun to Boulogne in search of an answer.

Then Justice would know what Fielding had proposed to do. And whether it could still be done.

JUSTICE EASED himself up against the row of sacks as he came to it. He had rolled about the rough plank-floor without any effect, except to scratch and bruise himself as he turned awk-wardly, and if he was in for a long wait, even a hard-filled sack or two would make a more comfortable resting-place.

With a heave from his bound hands, a quick twist of his hips, his legs were round and he was lying on his side with his face against the far wall.

"We shall never have a better chance to finish him." Tissot's voice surprised him. It was low, but so close that he seemed to be speaking on the other side of the wooden partition. "Within a week. Dead—or in England as a prisoner." Tissot's words came through clearly as he pressed his point.

There was a murmur of dissent. Though Justice could not catch what the other speaker said, he was talking in a persuasive tone that suggested he was having an argument with Tissot. It was a familiar tone, too, if he could only place it. It was a man, anyway, and he could have sworn it was not a Frenchman. While the words were coming fluently enough, there was something in the pitch and pace of them that was wrong.

"It is what we had planned." Tissot was becoming vehement. "For months. Since your first message came."

Another mollifying mumble. Could it really be Fielding who was speaking? And what was Tissot saying about a message? If he had never seen Fielding before this week . . . if he had dealt with him only by couriers and codes, there could well have been misunderstandings . . . a French agent could well have impersonated him . . . but who . . . and when?

Justice strained to hear more. The men must be two floors down, for he would have noticed if anyone had climbed up to the room right beneath him. Yet, by some freak of sound, he could eavesdrop on their conversation. Or part of it. He guessed that Tissot must be very close to the dividing-wall that ran up through the middle of the net-house and that the wood itself was carrying his voice like a sounding-board.

But he was not picking up enough of what the other man said to understand it. He must be standing well away from that resonant partition, and unless he moved, his words would be lost—and there would be no way of telling who he was.

"I did what you asked." Tissot's irritation was evident, and Justice could tell that he was walking about, for the words came and went in snatches. ". . . at great risk . . . only a few of us left . . . spies and informers . . . the Valcourt swine who followed you . . . ready to act . . . waiting for weeks . . . the Corsican has been twice . . . losing one chance after another . . ."

He was talking about a plot to abduct or kill Bonaparte. He

must be. Another plot like Cadoudal's disastrous conspiracy. But surely Fielding would never have found money for a wild venture like that.

The other man's voice rose, as if he were simply repeating something to an obstinate child.

"I know. I know." Tissot was replying with angry emphasis. "The flotilla. The damned flotilla. All you English are the same. You think about nothing except those blasted boats creeping out of the Liane one dark night and heading for England. What about the man who gives them orders? That's where to strike, I tell you." He was speaking so loud that his voice rose right through the floors. "Is that why you promised . . ." The rest of the question was lost as the other man talked Tissot down.

Different motives, different ends. Lilly had been right to warn him that an English agent and a French conspirator could find themselves dangerously at odds when their lives—and a great deal of money—were at stake.

"It's the best solution for both of us." Tissot persisted, changing his tack. "Bonaparte will be back at the end of the week. His quarters at Pont de Briques are being kept ready for him, day and night. And the flotilla could sail on any favourable wind after he gets here. Stop one. Stop the other. That's the end of it."

Both men were silent again. Then Tissot burst out in frustration. "You English are impossible," he said, striking the wall so hard that the boards shook. "You send me messages I cannot understand. You get yourself caught, and I hear nothing for months. You escape. You come here, almost *en famille,* with no concern for anyone's safety. And you tell me nothing. You only ask questions, questions, all the time. You will not give me the money you promised. You will not tell me the names . . ." Tissot struck the boarding again, deadening his last words. "And you talk about destroying the flotilla. With what, I ask you. A dozen men? All that I have left that I can trust? You are crazy. Even the English fleet can do nothing until the ships sail clear of the line of batteries and gunboats that protect them. You'll see for yourself. Everyone says there'll be another attack in the next few days. And it will fail like all the others. Bonaparte's easy game by comparison, I tell you."

Tissot must have spent his fury, or moved farther from the wall, for Justice could hear nothing now except a blurred exchange of words.

Yet he had heard enough to realise that Fielding could never have told Tissot exactly what he was proposing to do. He would have been cautious, rightly cautious, at the start, and he had been seized and despatched to Verdun before he could get to Boulogne to see Tissot himself.

And it was clear that Tissot had jumped to the wrong conclusion. His fanatical wish to kill Bonaparte or carry him off had been father to the thought that Fielding was proposing to provide him with the money and the means to do it. For that was what he was now demanding from the man who had come from Paris claiming that he was Fielding.

The money and the means.

But the man had the money. The draft that M. Georges had given him in good faith. The draft that Tissot had mentioned as they left the inn. What else, then, did Tissot need to know that the man would not tell him? Or could not—because he was not Fielding?

The means. The means that could be used for more than one purpose. Means that could transport a new kind of weapon . . . or to carry off the despot who ruled France, dumped into a cask like a cargo.

New Wine in Old Barrels, Fielding had said.

Justice cursed as he stretched to ease the cramp in his thighs and the movement made him roll away from the wooden wall. As he wriggled back to place his head against the planks, he heard the last of Tissot's words. ". . . papers that Valcourt stole? Very well. Get it out of him. Or I will. Within the hour. This business must be settled tonight."

A few moments later the trapdoor was thrown back and Tissot came through, holding a lantern above his head. Pierre stood on the ladder with one arm across the edge of the floor to steady himself, and to hold the knife which guarded Tissot as he unlaced the rope round Justice's legs.

"He will see you." There was no trace of the feeling with which Tissot had just been arguing his case. "It would be wise to talk frankly. And quickly. Neither of us has any time to waste."

Justice stood up, feeling the blood prickle back into his numb limbs. "Nor have I," he said, as he moved towards the ladder. "I have still to do Fielding's work for him."

❧ 17 ❧

THE ROOM WAS LIT by a lantern hanging from a bracket-arm on the far wall, and it was bright enough for Justice to see the large print on one or two of the official proclamations which had been casually tacked to the timber—notices about shipping, levies of men for the army, and even a warning about English spies that must have been put there by someone with a sense of humour.

But there seemed to be no one in the room.

Until the door closed behind him and he felt a gun-barrel nudging him towards the bare table and three chairs in the middle of the room.

Before he sat down, he turned and spoke steadily to the man who faced him. "I never thought I'd see you point a pistol at me again, Mr Lovell," he said. "Except in an affair of honour. And by God's grace we shall have that before you and I are done with each other."

It was Lovell, after all.

Lovell. A renegade all the time. Wirion's man.

"Fielding," Justice spoke almost to himself. He looked up at Lovell, still standing, silent, obviously uneasy. At least the man had enough decency left to look embarrassed.

"Fielding." Justice said the name again. No. Lovell could not be Fielding, whatever he had pretended to Tissot. There were too many people in Verdun who knew them both. "Then he is dead?"

There was a curious scrabbling noise as the door opened again, as if a rat was running across the floor, and before Justice could turn, he felt a light thump on his shoulder and a bony clutch at his collar. "As I said the first time we met, Mr Justice, the little fellow seems to have a fancy for you."

O'Moira.

"Dr O'Moira." Justice kept his voice level to cover his consternation.

"Mr Fielding to you, sir." O'Moira kept his gentlemanly poise as he carefully crossed the room to feel for a chair and sit at the table. "And very much alive, you see." He rapped a knuckle on the wood, and the monkey sprang to his arm. "And Major Lovell assists me."

He waved vaguely in Lovell's direction. "Please sit between Mr Justice and the door, Major Lovell," he said. "I shall feel more contented in my mind." He spoke with such relaxed ease that they could all have been back in his room at Verdun.

Yet Justice felt there was something uncanny and unpleasant in that grim scene, as the blind man sat there with the renegade on one side of him and the monkey on the other.

The blind man.

O'Moira.

The voice that he had recognised but could not place.

The man Tissot believed was Fielding.

The French agent who proposed to discover Fielding's secret.

Within the hour.

"I DO NOT understand," Justice pretended, and he did not need much of an actor's art to sound dispirited. "You cannot be Fielding." The more broken he seemed, the sooner O'Moira might reveal what he was after.

"For present purposes, Mr Justice, I am." O'Moira was so sure of himself that he could afford his habitual courtesy. "Indeed, I have papers to prove it. Major Lovell, who is now at my service, will say that he helped me to escape from Verdun, can speak for me. So can Madame Lamotte."

The familiarity with which O'Moira had spoken of Lucienne made it clear that his betrayal was complete, and he winced inwardly, realising how that soft husky voice had cajoled and deceived him into the ruin of all he had hoped to do and all that Lilly had expected of him. She was simply an informer, making the most of her charms.

No wonder that she had been so urgent to go to Paris with him, and to desert him as soon as her task was done. What she had said that night in the Hôtel des Etrangers now seemed like a kind of epitaph, as if she had known that the sudden warmth there had been between them must cool as suddenly.

"You are all in it together," Justice said, in a tone of despair that would have thrilled the Tenterden audience in a melodrama. So they were, though he could not tell what secret tie bound Lucienne to O'Moira, or why Lovell had thrown in his lot with them. There had been no pretence about the struggle in the hut at Houdainville when Lucienne had rounded on him with such fury.

O'Moira spread his hands in a gesture of helplessness. "I am truly sorry, Mr Justice," he said pleasantly. "I rather took a liking to you. I certainly have no personal spite against you, unlike our friend Tissot, who is very keen to kill you to settle a grudge. Against a member of your family, I believe."

His manner was mild enough, but the hint of sarcasm confirmed what Justice had already suspected. Everything that Tissot had said to him in the inn an hour or so ago had come from the imperturbable Irish doctor. It was possible that O'Moira actually knew Luc de Valcourt, had even worked with him if his turncoat cousin really had become a confidential agent serving Fouché against his old royalist associates.

"But war is no respecter of persons, Mr Justice," O'Moira went on. "We must follow our luck where it leads us—and yours, I am afraid, has led you into very dangerous waters. To be precise, the waters of Boulogne Harbour in October 1804, where there is much more at hazard than your life or mine. For Bonaparte, the victory that will provide his crown as Emperor of France. For England, defeat and a republic. For Ireland—well, Mr Justice, liberty is the simple word for it. A whole nation rising like a phoenix out of misery and oppression."

Justice could see the colour in O'Moira's face as he spoke, and he noticed that the doctor's fingers were clenched with determination.

"That is what hinges upon our conversation." O'Moira leaned forward, almost as if he could see and was peering at Justice to gauge his reaction. "When that French flotilla sails it will be the final move in a game begun long ago. No, Mr Justice, I do not mean Bonaparte's ambition to crush England, the only power which lies between him and a mastery of the world as complete as his mastery of Europe. I do not even mean the old rivalry between England and France, which goes back far beyond these present wars. I mean the struggle of the people of Ireland for their faith and their freedom."

"An Irish traitor." Justice said the words acidly.

"Not at all." O'Moira seemed unruffled by the gibe. "An Irish patriot, Mr Justice. It depends upon your point of view." He paused. "I think you might understand better than some of your countrymen. Like an Irishman in England, a man who is half-English and half-French lives between two worlds. You may well have discovered that for yourself in these last few weeks."

It was a telling point. And Lucienne had known very well how to turn that double-mindedness to advantage.

"I say these things . . ." O'Moira hesitated, as though to emphasise what he was about to say. "I say all this, Mr Justice, for all time presses, so that you shall not mistake my purpose, or my will to achieve it by any means. I would do anything to ensure that those ships play their part in carrying freedom to my country. *Anything.*"

When O'Moira had first come into the room, Justice had itched to put a score of unanswered questions. But the desire for explanations had now been replaced by a burning need to know what O'Moira had meant by those last, earnest words.

They might be nothing more than rhetoric. The man had the Irish gift for a fine phrase. Or they might mean that in his fervour O'Moira had let slip a great secret. That the flotilla itself was only a vast scheme of bluff—a standing threat which forced England to keep ill-spared ships in the Channel and to tie down soldiers in Kent and Sussex who would never get a glimpse of a French grenadier's bonnet. That all those vessels herded into Boulogne and the other ports, that all those divisions encamped behind them—that all these preparations were simply part of a grand design in which the main blow would be struck at Cork, almost defenceless, or at Dublin Bay.

If that was so, then at all costs the news must be got back to George Lilly and the anxious overburdened men who sat with him on the Board of Admiralty.

But O'Moira might be deceiving himself, or be deceived by the French who made use of his services. A dupe. Or a conscious traitor.

Justice turned to Lovell. A distraction of his own would give him a little time to think, goad O'Moira into saying more. "In the name of the King, Major Lovell," he said formally, "I charge you to do your duty and arrest that man. And fail not, at your peril." The words sounded incongruous enough in the circumstances, yet they could one day echo in a court-room if Lovell or O'Moira was ever brought to stand his trial.

And Justice thought they might have gone home to Lovell. After twenty years of army service, a time-honoured ritual like that might strike some chord in him.

But not in O'Moira, who had seen the incongruity and laughed it away. "We are not in Dublin Castle now, if I might remind you, Mr Justice. And there's no English gallows in the yard, with the hangman waiting to turn me off. You'll not frighten me with such bogies. Be good enough to be quiet, will you, and let me finish, or Tissot will be taking care of you before I've had my say."

Justice had no wish to halt the flow of words. What O'Moira was saying of his own free will was far more important than some fragment wrung out of him by argument.

"I said I would do *anything*, Mr Justice. As any true Irishman would give his life, or watch his house burned over his head, or live like a hunted animal in the bogs, or see his children beg from one village to the next, dear creatures, and all for the freedom that's been denied him for so long. We're a proud people, Mr Justice, and you shouldn't forget it, for pride'll keep a man going when he knows he's beaten and he's got nothing left but a memory and a hope."

O'Moira paused, touched by his own words, and then the prophetic phrases rang out again. "When an Englishman looks at an Irishman," he said, "he sees only a pathetic, broken-down fool. And I'll tell you why. It's been an English wind that's blown over Ireland these past two centuries, Mr Justice, and my people have bent their backs to it. But they've not been blown over, for their roots are too deep in their own country. And now they are standing up again like men, with the feel of liberty to stiffen them, and they'll stand in the fields of Ireland and die there, if need be, until that English wind has blown itself out, and all you can hear will be the keening of the poor souls who watered the tree of liberty with their blood and their tears."

There was nothing Justice could say, for he realised that such ideas were beyond argument, and O'Moira himself came back briskly to their confrontation.

"So much for my feelings," he said. "Now for the facts."

O'Moira tapped the table, hesitating, and then continued. "As Major Lovell can tell you, I know a great deal—too much for his comfort, and for yours. Shall I talk about Lloyd's of London, Mr Justice, and the strange things that are sometimes done in its name? Shall I tell you what news M. Chappe's telegraph brought me soon after you landed at Etaples? What Saint-Haouen reported to Paris, and to me at Verdun? Shall I explain why Madame Lamotte sought you out in Balbi's? Why Charvet's men did not pursue you? Give me credit, Mr Justice. I may be blind, but I can see as far or further than most men when it comes to scheming, and up to this moment I could not afford to have you fail for want of a helping hand."

Justice knew that O'Moira's telling gibes were a preparation for something else. It was a far more effective way of getting under a man's guard than the repetitive questioning that Fayol had used in the headquarters that were only a few hundred yards away along the quay.

But before O'Moira started to speak again he cocked his head as if he had caught a stray noise, and gestured towards Lovell. "If you please, Major," he said. "At the door. Outside it."

As Lovell went out to stand guard, O'Moira made a wry face at his back, and as soon as the door was shut, he laid his hand on the table, palm upwards, as though he were making an offer. "What I have to say is better said between us, Mr Justice. You have something I want—very quickly. Within the hour. I want it so much that I can only buy it from you. I am a realist, you see. It is quite easy to kill you. If Lovell shrinks from it, Tissot will have no scruples, I am sure. But it would be far from easy to make you tell me what I want to know, even under the pressures which some of my French . . . er . . . colleagues could put upon you—pressures that a doctor who has taken the Hippocratic oath could not of course employ himself. You are young, and strong; and I must have an answer before Tissot returns to this room. And a promise of silence from you as well."

O'Moira was silent for a moment. "There," he said. "All my cards are on the table."

"I cannot play if they are face downwards," Justice replied.

"Of course. You must forgive a blind man his mistakes."

O'Moira could be jovial even when the stake was a life—or an empire. "Let me turn up the first." He went through the motion of picking up a playing card. "The ace of spades."

"That means a death," Justice said.

"Bravo." O'Moira took him up on it. "I like a man of spirit." His voice hardened. "Death, Mr Justice. Tonight, Mr Justice. Unless we can find a different omen for you."

He picked up another imaginary card from the table and pretended to hold it up in front of the monkey. "And what does the little fellow make of that? Ah. The king of hearts. For stubborn loyalty, shall we say? But that will always be trumped by the ace of spades, you know. Not so good, Mr Justice."

At the third try he waited a moment, and his voice sounded more crafty. "And the knave? That's better now. A troublesome character. Always getting into scrapes. But he looks both ways, you know. And he can run for his life. What's the rhyme, Mr Justice? 'He who fights and runs away lives to fight another day.' There's a lot in that, when you come to think of it. Now, which shall it be . . . the ace . . . the king . . . or the knave?"

"It is a neat game we are playing," Justice said. "But there is no point to it. I have no idea what you want me to tell you. Or the price for it."

His remark seemed to encourage O'Moira. "There's a reasonable man," he said. "I'll come to my question fast enough. But the price . . . Well, that depends on what you can tell me." The soft brogue went out of his voice and there was steel in its place. "And how quickly. At the least I undertake to save your life, though you may spend the rest of the war in Bitche or Briançon or some other uncomfortable fortress. If you were lucky, and behaved well, you might even work your way back to Verdun. At the best, you could be settled in France, which is half your home in any case, with a French wife . . ."

"A renegade." Justice could not conceal his contempt.

O'Moira ignored his interjection. "Or, if you insist," he added, "you could be exchanged, or sent home to England in a smuggler's boat, with no one any the wiser."

"Hard choices." Justice knew that he had to keep the dialogue alive, for O'Moira must be coming to the point of showing his last card. "I have your tariff now. In what coin must I pay?"

"Tell me what Fielding planned." O'Moira's impatience showed as he leaned forward.

"You know more than I do." Justice was convinced of that.

"I know that Fielding was the paymaster for a host of English spies and royalist agents," O'Moira said, settling back on his chair as though beginning a catechism. "Some are dead. Some have fled. Some are in prison. And we shall soon have all the rest." He closed his hand and struck the table with his fist. "But Fielding was more than that. I know that last winter he began to plan an attack on the flotilla that will carry the French army to . . ." He caught himself on the verge of a slip. "Across the Channel. Yes, Mr Justice, your friends in London would like to know where."

"Perhaps."

"No. Certainly, Mr Justice. This much I do know. For the safety of these ships is my special concern. I and . . . I and my friends in Paris watched Fielding for months. When the French finally arrested him, I followed him to Verdun. Then that fool Wirion bungled the whole business—just trying to line his own pockets . . ." O'Moira's anger flared again before he got control of himself and smiled at Justice. "Then you came, and I was back on the trail."

For the first time Justice began to see the true pattern behind everything that had happened since he landed in France.

"If it's a comfort to you," O'Moira went on, "Fielding gave away nothing before he died. It was you who led me to his money."

Another gibe, another hint. Did O'Moira think him both foolish and venal?

"I also know about Tissot, thanks to you." O'Moira was turning the knife. "All that would make a sad story if it was told the wrong way in England, wouldn't it, now?"

As O'Moira spoke, Justice was remembering Hatherley's words at Richmond Terrace. "There's more than one man who's gone out of that door thinking himself cleverer than Boney himself, Mr Justice, believing that in the pinch he could get what he wanted by pretending to turn his coat or by talking a little too much. Maybe he has got it. Maybe he has come back with what he was sent to find. But nobody ever trusts him again, sir. It gets known in the service, sir, though never a word

is said. Don't ask me how, sir, but it's ruin when it happens."
Had he now gone too far? Could O'Moira so twist the facts that
he would be discredited even if he survived?

"As you have helped me so much, Mr Justice, may we go a
little further?" O'Moira's voice was persuasive again. "I am sure
that Fielding planned to use some device that floated. Why else
should his friends in London send a naval officer to complete
his work?"

It was a logical question, but wide of the mark. Justice wryly
recalled how little Lilly had been able to tell him of Fielding's
scheme. If only O'Moira knew . . . But he saw he had to be
careful. O'Moira's line of thought was coming very close to his
own. "I was merely sent to find the money," he said. There
could be no harm in admitting what O'Moira already knew.

But the Irishman ignored his answer, coming back with questions he could not understand. "Have you heard of Robert Fulton?"

"No." That could be a forthright reply.

"Not as Mr Francis, the name he uses in England?"

As Justice shook his head, he remembered the flash of conversation with Lilly about infernal machines. "No," he repeated. "Who is he?"

"A clever American." O'Moira spoke as though he had met
the man. "Who makes bombs that explode under water, and
mines that are moored to the bottom of the sea. And talks of
using steam instead of wind in the sails to drive a ship."

"These are all novelties to me," Justice said. "I'm a sailor, not
a shipwright or a manufacturer."

O'Moira appeared to believe him. "Perhaps so," he replied.
"Perhaps so." He pushed the monkey to one side and leaned
forward on the table, speaking urgently. "I will tell you two
things, Mr Justice, and then I will put you some simple ques-
tions. If you answer them, you shall go free—in France, or in
England, as you choose; and be sure I shall keep that promise.
But if you do not answer . . . even if you cannot answer . . .
I must call in Major Lovell and tell him to shoot you. One way
or the other, it must be settled before that Frenchman returns.
Do you understand me?"

"I do indeed," said Justice. If he betrayed Fielding's secret,
so that O'Moira could lead Tissot and his men into a trap, he

could save his life and perhaps his liberty. If not, O'Moira would have to silence him for ever and try to bluff Tissot into revealing his part in the plot.

The devil of it, Justice thought ruefully, was that he did not know Fielding's secret. No doubt the key to it was in that first cryptic message he had seen in Edward Holland's house, but until he solved that puzzle, he could no more tell the Irishman what he needed to know than he could explain to Tissot exactly how Fielding had proposed to attack the flotilla.

"My first point is a matter of fact." O'Moira spoke like a judge beginning to sum up. "Months ago, Fielding asked Tissot to find some trustworthy men who could manage a ship in this harbour. Several ships, perhaps."

"Tissot told you that!" Justice was astonished.

"Not Tissot himself." O'Moira was unwilling to say much more. "I heard from a man who was less discreet," he said. "And I could infer a good deal from the questions that Tissot has put to me since I came to Boulogne."

"And the second point?" Justice was as anxious as O'Moira to get on.

"There can be no doubt that Fielding found some means of placing ships in Boulogne Harbour—ships that would carry a new weapon, possibly, or use an old weapon in a new way."

Justice's pulse began to beat faster. O'Moira had come very close to Fielding's own words. *New Wine in Old Barrels*. "There are a great many vessels in the harbour," he said, "They could not all be destroyed."

"That is true." O'Moira accepted the idea. "But they could all be prevented from leaving if the harbour were blocked—and that is something the English have never been able to do in their futile attacks from the sea." O'Moira let the point sink in. "I am convinced that Fielding intended to do something much more clever—with Tissot's help."

Thus far, Justice thought, thus far we have come to the same conclusions.

"And the question?" he asked as lightly as he could.

They were coming to the crisis, and whichever way things came out, he must be ready to move. To overpower O'Moira. Or Lovell. Or to find some way of convincing Tissot that he had been tricked.

He looked round the room carefully, wondering what might

216

serve as a weapon and seeing nothing but the chairs and the table, looking closely at the walls to see if there could be a window behind one of the large printed proclamations that adorned them.

As he did so, he was aware that he had noticed something important, and missed it again.

"Now the questions are just as simple, if you can put your mind to them," O'Moira ran on. "Three simple questions."

"Yes?" Justice, distracted, had almost lost the thread of what O'Moira was saying.

"What kind of ships did Fielding plan to use? And how many? And when?"

O'Moira was right. It was quite simple in the end. The number 3 had been running in his head ever since he had seen Hunt's portrait of Lucienne. Three birds. Three ships. Why a line of three ships under a cliff?

"I have no idea," Justice said. "Have you not searched?" The query might win a little more time to turn his racing thoughts in the right direction.

"Of course. But as you say, Mr Justice, there are a great many ships . . . and to be honest, without your help, we do not know what we are looking for."

Even at this critical moment, Justice caught the change of pronoun. *We.* He wondered how many men Admiral Bruix had set to work searching, probing, turning over sacks and stores, all down the quays, in the basin, on the lines of ships moored together in the stream. Fielding must have hidden his weapons well.

If they were there. They could still be in Bordeaux. Where they were built. And paid for.

"Fire-ships." Justice had to say it, or seem stupid.

"Naturally. But where are they? What do they look like? They are no ordinary fire-ships, I can tell you, or they would have been found." O'Moira was becoming more insistent. "And how was Tissot to recognise them?"

It was odd, Justice thought, if one of the harbour-masters was at a loss. A man who could go anywhere, look at anything he chose. Who saw the daily lists of ships in port.

"Come, Mr Justice. You are not a stupid man. Your liberty or your life. Which is it to be?"

Had O'Moira also caught that sound outside the door, as if

Lovell were becoming restless? Perhaps Tissot had already returned and was waiting below with Pierre.

"I . . . I . . . I cannot tell . . ." Justice stammered as he looked hard to see what had caught his eye, and slipped away again.

"But you must, Mr Justice." O'Moira was on his feet, with the monkey scrambling to keep a grip on his coat. "You have only minutes, even seconds." As he rapped on the table with irritation—or was it a signal to Lovell?—the little ape jumped onto it and sat gibbering and grimacing in the corner. "Come, Mr Justice. The names . . . The names . . ."

Justice was speechless. As the time ran out, he was not seeing O'Moira at all. He could only see the proclamation which hung a little crazily from a single tack on the wall over O'Moira's shoulder.

The proclamation which echoed the words the farmer had used. The words that Fielding had also used.

A proclamation—now out of date, with Bonaparte waiting to be crowned—which was headed RÉPUBLIQUE FRANÇAISE. With three more words printed in large type underneath.

Liberté. Egalité. Fraternité.

"*La Liberté,*" he said. "*L'Egalité. La Fraternité.*" Now, at last, Justice had it. The three words that had haunted him ever since Holland had shown him Fielding's note in London.

"A poor time for jokes, Mr Justice." The blind man, tense with anxiety, could not have known with what fixity Justice was staring past him at the printed proclamation, or caught the full meaning of the names he had uttered.

Three ships, and they were somewhere out in that forest of masts, ready to wreak havoc among Boney's flotilla as it lay under the great cliffs of Boulogne.

There was a moment's silence, in which he heard the first creak of the door.

O'Moira had also heard it, and took the noise to herald an impatient Lovell. "I warn you, Mr Justice. Time is very short. Tell me." He pounded the table in his frustration. "Or it will be the end of you."

"I think not." Tissot was in the room now, and Pierre at the door, and both were holding pistols. As Justice rose and turned in surprise, he caught Tissot's eye, and his heart leapt, for what he saw there was recognition.

"Take them away." Tissot motioned to Pierre, who came into the room prodding Lovell before him with the pistol, and when Justice glanced at the major, he saw only a disconsolate and bewildered gambler who had placed his last wager.

O'Moira was also puzzled, unable to tell what was happening but realising that things had gone wrong for him, and when Tissot went over and poked him with the pistol barrel, he put his hand down and fingered it in evident disbelief. "I order you . . ." He began to protest.

"You give no orders here, Dr O'Moira," Justice said tersely. "Matthew Fielding is dead, and we all know it."

The simple statement seemed to deflate O'Moira, and he made no attempt to resist as Pierre bundled him and Lovell off to the loft where Justice had spent such an uncomfortable and revealing hour.

And then Tissot turned to Justice. "So now we know what we are looking for, my friend," he said in a satisfied voice. "Three ships in this harbour. Three ships with the names that only Fielding knew."

⇜ 18 ⇝

"IT IS STRANGE," Tissot said, holding out a comradely hand. "We have fought each other, but we have not yet been introduced. I am Paul . . . well, Tissot is the name that you know me by, and that will do as well as any other for tonight. After all, it is the name that Fielding used for me."

"And Jean will do for me," Justice replied, taking the hand that Tissot offered. For the first time since he landed on the beach at Etaples, he had found a man he could truly trust.

"Good." Tissot apparently felt the same.

And when Justice said nothing, waiting for him to make the next move, Tissot also seemed at a loss to begin. "There is so much . . ." He stopped, uncertainly.

"I know." Justice was aware that there was some urgency in Tissot's mind that he had not yet understood—the same need for haste that had driven O'Moira to overplay his hand. "The ships. Fielding's ships. But before we come to them, there are still questions . . ."

"Why did I treat you so badly, my friend?" Tissot cut in, and Justice nodded. "What is it you English say—to be on the safe side? I am a Breton, you know, and like all my people I have a rather suspicious mentality." He put his hand up to his neck. "It has helped me to keep my head on my shoulders in these hard times. And last night, when Pierre came to say that two strangers were asking for me at the Chapeau Rouge, I was very doubtful. Very doubtful, in fact. I have escaped too many *agents de police* to be caught like a hungry young fox running after the first chickens he sees."

"Two?"

"The red-faced buffoon who looks like an Englishman in a farce. And the woman—I've seen that type working as a spy before. Sly. Butter wouldn't melt in her mouth. But just wait. Give her half a chance . . ." Tissot rolled his eyes up to the ceiling above which Lucienne sat, silent, and Justice wondered how much he had guessed. "Would Fielding travel with such people, I asked myself? Unlikely. But it was so unlikely that it might be true. But how could they have reached Boulogne? Through so many patrols and picket-lines? It is very difficult."

Not quite so difficult, Justice thought, remembering his own journey. Such things could be done. "But they had papers?"

"Good ones. So had the man who called himself Fielding when they brought him to me this morning." Tissot stopped. "They have been here ever since," he added, as though to assure Justice that he had not been careless. "I think his papers were genuine," Tissot said, as if to excuse himself.

"They were." Justice guessed that O'Moira must have got them after Fielding died.

"The others were good, you know," Tissot went on. "Old papers . . . that looked as though they had been hidden in a boot, or the hem of a coat . . ." Tissot slapped the table edge with his closed fingers. "I tell you, Jean. In these last years I have come to know about such things. One of Fouché's forgers in the Ministry of Police must have been proud of his work. They were not quite right, you see. That was clever. Good enough, but not too good. And done in a hurry. You could tell that. They had all been smudged, folded before they were quite dry."

There would have been a hurry, for Lovell could not have

joined O'Moira and Lucienne until after Justice had seen him in the Place des Vosges.

Tissot reached into his pocket, found the money-belt, took out the bank draft, and compared it with another paper he brought out of his pocket. "I thought these might be forgeries, too."

"They are both genuine."

"As I see. But that was another reason why I suspected him."

"The money?"

"Naturally. For one thing, a man so experienced as Fielding would never carry a draft for so much money himself. The risk of being compromised . . ." Tissot left the sentence to make its own point. "For another . . . well, when I asked him to sign the draft, he refused. He said he would cash it when the bank opened in the morning. I think he feared that I might have seen Fielding's signature."

"Had you?"

"As a matter of fact . . . No. The only messages I ever had from Fielding were brought by a courier, who merely repeated what he was told. That was the Irishman's mistake, you see. He said that he had written to me. More than once, though he was vague about it."

"And me?" Justice could tell that he was not dealing with a humble harbour-master but with a man with an acute mind, who might have been an attorney. Perhaps he had been, before the revolution had turned so many things inside out. He was also a born storyteller, with an ear for the effect he could achieve by waiting to be prompted. Even when he was pressed for time, and in danger.

The same thought seemed to have occurred to Tissot at that moment, for he reached into his fob to find a fine and good-sized watch. "I have fifteen minutes more," he said calmly, as though he had spent the last three hours gossiping in a café before a supper appointment. "I go on duty at midnight." Then he apparently felt that the excuse was too abrupt, for he extended it. "We keep ship's hours," he said.

Justice wanted to protest, to urge Tissot to act at once, but he could tell that he was dealing with a man who went at his own pace, and that patience was essential.

"Anyway, there is nothing that we can do at once," Tissot

went on, as though he had guessed what Justice was thinking. "The papers will be somewhere in my office, and I cannot get to them until I go on duty. And I shall need to make other arrangements. Besides . . ." He stopped, fearing perhaps that he had said too much already. "Coming back to your question," he said after a pause. "I admit it worried me. Especially when he warned me that you were Luc de Valcourt . . ."

"My cousin." Justice broke in quickly, and Tissot peered sharply at him. It was better said, and Tissot appeared to think so, too.

"It could have been true. Something was said about it at the time."

"At the time?" Justice was puzzled. "When?"

"When you first came to Boulogne. In July. In Saint-Haouen's office. That was what really worried me. You could easily have been working for Fouché, for Decrés, the Minister of Marine."

"I don't understand. In Saint-Haouen's office?"

"I was there. I'd just finished going over some papers when that greasy swine Fayol came in and talked quietly to Saint-Haouen. I just caught the name Valcourt. But that was enough for me." Tissot sounded as grim as he looked. "I knew a great deal about Luc Valcourt, though I'd never met him—and very little to his credit, if you'll forgive my plain-speaking about your cousin. So I assumed that the whole business was some villainous scheme that was being cooked up by Saint-Haouen. Or Fayol. I was better out of it."

"You thought I was a French agent? Setting out to impersonate an English officer?" Justice now understood why O'Moira's falsehood might have made some impression on Tissot.

"It's an old game," Tissot replied. "Pretending to be an emissary from England, or an English prisoner on the run." He rose and went across to a rough cupboard on the wall to fetch a brandy bottle and a couple of pewter mugs. "You'll join me?"

Justice nodded, taking the drink, but saying nothing.

"So he might have persuaded me despite my doubts," Tissot went on. "You can never be sure about papers, anyway, and he might simply have been careless about the money draft. These things happen, you know. But when he could not tell me what I wanted to know—what Fielding himself would certainly have told me at once . . ."

"The names of the ships?"

"That, or something like it," Tissot said. "Of course, he made excuses. He talks well, that Irishman, but not quite well enough to deceive me." Tissot stopped and gave Justice a shrewd look. "Since I didn't know what to think, whom to trust . . ."

"You put the two of us together," Justice broke in.

"Exactly. You might both have been Fouché's men." Tissot's hard face cracked in a sudden grin. "There you were, like two fighting-cocks. And the more you crowed at each other, the more I learned. It's a good thing that Pierre speaks better English than I do. I would have missed too much."

"You were listening, no doubt," Justice said. "I thought so. I certainly hoped so, with that swine Lovell sitting outside with a cocked pistol in his hand." As Justice pictured Pierre and Tissot in the loft, straining to hear what he said to O'Moira, he recalled the conversation he had himself overheard. "But the plot to seize Bonaparte?" The argument between Tissot and O'Moira had sounded so convincing that Justice had expected to have a hard time changing Tissot's mind—persuading him that Fielding's target must always have been those rows of ships tied up along the quays and huddled in the great new dock across the river.

"That confused you, eh?" Tissot was obviously pleased that he had laid his false scent so well. "What was I to tell him when I began to suspect that he had come to trap me? I had to spin some sort of tale that came close to the truth without giving anything away, and that one was easy, for I had toyed with the idea after Cadoudal was taken, and I was left, wild for revenge. But nothing came of it, and Bonaparte is now too well guarded for us to have any chance. Fouché sees to that, all right." Tissot shrugged his shoulders. "So I was ready to help Fielding when he asked."

"What did he want from you?" It was easier now that there was trust between them.

"Men. But it wasn't easy to find them. We had lost a lot of our best people in the *ratissage,* and others had gone to ground or were too frightened to help any more." Tissot's anger echoed in his words. "A dozen men at least he wanted, and I could scarcely scrape up half that number."

"That was all?"

"No. He wanted information as well, and he was ready to pay

well for it. That was the main reason I needed so much money. The lives of honest men come cheap. It is only the rogues who come expensive."

"And for bribes?" Justice remembered the chests of coins he had seen carried ashore in Brittany.

"Naturally. There are always men who can be more easily tempted by the sight of gold than the prospect of freedom. A lieutenant here who loses his copy of the next set of recognition signals. A captain there who can steer the wrong course." Tissot raised his head. "I wonder if the blind man knows why General Hoche never arrived when he set out to invade Ireland in '96? Even men close to Bonaparte himself." Tissot put his bent knuckles on the table and stood up. "As you see, I am cynical," he said heavily, and Justice could tell that he would say no more that night.

"Pierre will stay." The summary was like a set of orders, making it clear that the decisions still lay with him. That Justice must be content to accept that fact. "He will be relieved in the morning. And the men below."

"The woman?" Justice asked without expression.

"There is a lock to that door." Tissot's reply was equally flat. "And I keep the key." He laid his hand amiably on Justice's shoulder as he passed. "*A bientôt, mon ami.*" He jerked a thumb upwards. "We shall settle that business tomorrow," he said. "And our own. Never fear."

He was a rung or two down the ladder when he spoke his last word. "Sleep peacefully, Jean, even if you have no bed." Another of his slow smiles crumpled his weather-creased face. "And no supper."

IT WAS ALMOST light when Tissot returned. Justice heard him talking to someone below, and then he came up with bread, cheese, and a pot of wine.

"Rough fare." Tissot laid the food on the table. "But this isn't a hotel, even if it seems like it." For all the humour in his voice, he was plainly excited.

"The ships?" Justice could not conceal his eagerness.

"Hold on, Jean. I'll let you see for yourself." Tissot led the way down to the bottom floor, where Justice was startled to see a man in the uniform of the National Guard sitting on one of the tar barrels. Tissot waved a hand towards him as they passed through to the high space in the front part of the building, where nets and ropes dropped from the roof. "For the sake of appearances," he said. "If a patrol looks in."

Justice was beginning to see how Tissot had managed to survive so many man-hunts. He was careful. There was safety in his steady way of doing things. Even small things, for Tissot had tossed him a blue working-smock before he donned one himself.

"For appearances, too," he said as he started to climb the wooden pegs which reached up a side wall to form a crude ladder, and by the time Justice joined him on the small platform at the top, Tissot had the doors unlatched and was busy with ropes and blocks.

All the sounds of a busy quayside came up through the open hatchway, and Justice could tell what was going on—barrow-wheels trundling over cobblestones, horses snuffling as they were held while their owners talked, a set of barrels making a dull thump as a hoist dumped them clumsily on a deck. It was all so familiar that he might have been back in Portsmouth. But he could see very little, for the half-swung doors blocked his view, and as he moved to crane out, Tissot restrained him. "That's far enough," he said.

Upstream, Justice could only see as far as the edge of the Arsenal wall. "Powder-vessels," he heard Tissot say quietly. "But there's no hope of getting at them. Guards everywhere."

Downstream, Justice found himself looking through a tangle of spars and yards that obscured almost everything except the high cliff and the grey-green band of the sea beyond it.

Tissot knew where he wanted him to look. "Where the neck of the basin opens into the channel," he said quietly, and Justice turned to see what he meant, leaning out as he casually looped a fold of net over the sill. "There are several brigs, moored in pairs fore-and-aft," Tissot added, "so they cannot swing with the tide."

"Well?"

"The pair that lie closest to the basin."

Justice saw them at a second glance. They were less than three cables away—not much more than five hundred yards, he guessed.

"The *Liberté?*"

"And the *Fraternité*. The *Egalité* is not here. It may be in one of the other ports. I had no time to find out." Tissot lifted the length of net back through the hatch and closed the door before they climbed down. "It's better not to stay too long. There are eyes everywhere."

"Are the ships manned? Guarded? Loaded?" The questions came tumbling out.

"No." Tissot answered the first of them. "It appears that the crews were paid off when they came about three weeks ago. The captains had the money to pay them before they went back to Bordeaux. It was all arranged from there, apparently."

"And the crews?"

Tissot shrugged. "You know how things are. Taken on to ships that were short-handed, as soon as they had drunk their pay."

"As for guards . . ." Justice waited for him to finish. "They row patrols in the harbour, of course, and there are sentries along the quays. But they think ships moored out there are safe enough. There are many with no one on board." Tissot seemed about to say something more on this point, then he changed his mind. "As for cargo," he went on, "I'm not sure. I looked quickly at the papers in the office last night, when there was no one by. As I said, they came from Bordeaux. With wine for the army. That's all. And there they stay for the present, waiting for the flotilla to sail, so the *pochards* can be sure of their usual drink when they get to England!"

"In old barrels," Justice said, half to himself.

Tissot was quick to catch the words, though plainly they puzzled him. "In old barrels."

"A phrase that Fielding used. *New Wine in Old Barrels.* I never understood what he meant."

"And now?"

Justice laughed. "I'm no wiser." Why should Fielding ship wine to Boulogne? And draw attention to what he had done?

"Paul!" A man whom Justice had never seen before was at the door. He must have replaced Pierre in the loft, for he spoke at once of Lovell.

"The Englishman," he said. "He asks to talk." He looked at Justice. "To this other."

"Later," said Justice. It would do Lovell no harm to go on

cooling his heels on that hard floor. He turned again to Tissot. "Could they be fire-ships? O'Moira thinks so."

"How can I tell? It seems unlikely. Wine will not burn. Maybe there is something else."

"But what? Tar? Powder? Old sails? You know how much is needed to make a ship burn well—and fast. And O'Moira said last night that every ship had been searched."

"I think Fielding was a clever man," Tissot said slowly, "and that his secret was well hidden." He rose and paced thoughtfully about the room. "But perhaps you and I might find what Bruix's men missed, Jean . . ."

"We can only try." Justice was eager to start. "When can we go?"

"Not before dark." Tissot replied firmly. "It would not be safe. But then we must hurry. We may have very little time."

"Time?" Justice spoke sharply, in alarm and annoyance. "Is the flotilla to sail, then?"

"Not that." Tissot was quick to reassure him. "Bonaparte needs at least one more week before he can be ready. Perhaps two. I think he means to go about the middle of October." He stopped pacing and turned to Justice. "No, my dear Jean, it is your countrymen who are calling the tune."

"Keith?" From what O'Moira and Tissot had said when they were arguing the night before, Justice had suspected that another attack on Boulogne might be in the wind.

Before Tissot could answer him, however, he heard the tramp of feet behind a drum.

"You hear that?" Tissot nodded towards the quay outside. "Everyone is on the alert. Soldiers everywhere. Guards doubled. Bruix is convinced that Keith will make an attack, tonight, or early tomorrow, on the tide."

"Why is he so sure?"

"Word from smugglers, perhaps. Or spies. And a report came down from the telegraph station on the cliff last night. More ships have joined the English squadron, it sees. One great one. The *Monarch*."

"Keith's flagship," Justice said crisply. "What else?"

"Two fishermen came in early this morning to report that the English were making fire-ships." Tissot seemed unsure. "And another thing that I do not understand. That . . . it was a kind of trick, possibly . . . they said that the English were busy with something low in the water . . . like a small boat that had sunk . . ."

"If there is a serious attack, it will be our chance," Justice broke in excitedly. "Everyone will be watching the sea." He ripped the proclamation off the wall and found a stub of charcoal to draw a half-circle on the back. "Look, Paul," he said, speaking quickly as the idea came to him. "Here. Here. Here and here." He cut the smudgy line with his finger in four places. "Keith will send in fire-ships. Small boats to cut gaps in the ropes and chains and timber of the booms." He made a grim face. "And to pick up the fire-ship crews, if they can."

"That's been tried before," Tissot said. "It never works. The bigger English ships can't get in close enough to do any damage. The smaller ones are too weak to silence the French batteries."

"It has to be tried again. Perhaps Keith has a new idea, a new device. Who knows? But one thing is certain." Justice saw the whole scene clearly in his mind. "There'll be a great deal of noise and excitement out there. Nobody in Boulogne will have eyes or ears for anything else tonight. And we'll back here." Justice picked up the piece of charcoal again and drew a crude line to show where the Liane ran past the entrance to the basin where the invasion flotilla lay, out of reach of Keith's guns and fire-ships.

What would be a foolishly dangerous venture on a normal night could be unexpectedly easy once the attack began.

"Easy," he said out loud.

"To do what?" Tissot was puzzled. "To search the ships? Of course, but . . ."

"No." Justice spoke with assurance. "To use them. As I think Fielding intended."

❦ 19 ❦

AFTER TISSOT had gone, Justice climbed once more to the loading hatch for a quick glance through a half-open door to mark how the two ships lay to the channel, how the tide set through it, and how much room there would be as he sensed his way downstream in the darkness.

And as he ran his eye along the harbour wall, he saw why Tissot had warned him not to show himself too long and too inquisitively. There were as many guards as mooring bollards.

It could be done, he decided, coming back to sit at the table, where he began to move bits of wood and string about to make a crude model of what he had just seen. But it could be done only if they could count on an hour aboard the two ships before they cut them loose, and if there was a little wind—sufficient to give them steerage-way, to provide a draught to pull whatever fires they started, but not so much that they would be carried along out of control, bumping and scraping past the bigger vessels in the moored flotilla without doing any serious damage to them.

If they had enough men to do what had to be done.

"There's always more barrels than hands to lift 'em," Fred Scorcher was fond of saying, and the motto could never have been more apt. He would have Tissot, Pierre, himself, perhaps a couple of Tissot's men, and that would be a small crew for a smack loaded with tar and powder, with plenty of seamen to get it off to a good start by placing the combustibles and setting the sails. But tonight the five of them would have to get one brig moving swiftly enough to tow the other, with watchful enemies all round them. It would be very close . . . If anything went wrong . . . if it came to any kind of fight . . . And in any case, running a ship of that size in a narrow tidal-stream was always a tricky business in the dark . . .

They would need every man. And someone to watch the prisoners, unless Tissot dragged them along, a hindrance at best, a danger at worst; or unless Tissot cold-bloodedly dispatched them. The rules of clandestine war were far more brutal than the codes of honour which bound an English officer, and here he was on Tissot's ground.

A blind man. A strong-spirited woman. A renegade. They were a strong trio.

It was only as Justice thought about Lovell that he recalled that the man had asked to see him, and when the major had been fetched down, to stand before him in a wretched and dishevelled state, Justice felt no more anger against him. Only a deep contempt.

229

"I'm done for, you know," Lovell said, in a voice flat with despair. Justice, who had expected bluster, or whining, was so surprised that he waited for Lovell to go on and unfold his meaning.

"If I should ever get to England again . . ." Lovell faltered, and as his sentence failed, Justice nodded.

"I do know," he replied firmly. "And you may be sure that I should be the first to give evidence against you." It seemed possible that his peremptory demand that Lovell should arrest O'Moira had affected the disconsolate major, and that a stern demeanour might now have even more influence on him.

"Here as well, I mean . . ." Lovell found it difficult to go on.

"I think you had better tell it all quickly," Justice said. He suspected that Lovell must have spent the night awake, staring through the darkness at a bleak future, and that his nerve was ready to break.

"Went to live in France . . . avoid creditors . . . picked up with the rest last year . . . Lille . . . on to Verdun . . . Christmas . . ." Lovell mumbled brokenly through his fingers. Justice had guessed as much. He had seen enough seedy officers living on the debtor's fringe of disgrace to recognise that Lovell was one of a type that was far too common—men driven to live far beyond their means, and going to pieces under the strain.

At Verdun, it seemed, things had gone badly from the start for Lovell. He had been forced to borrow as soon as he arrived, and he soon lost what he borrowed. Some of it went on private wagers, where he had plunged heavily in the vain hope of restoring his fortunes; most of it trickled away at Balbi's; and long before Justice arrived in Verdun, he had come to the point where no one would take his name to a bill or accept his note of hand.

"Couldn't even cut and run for it," Lovell said miserably. "Prisoner be damned. A fellow can't leave that blasted place while he owes. Whole town's like a sponging-house. Fellow did, last year, you know. Got back to England, too. And what do you think they did? Packed him back again, back to Verdun!"

Balbi had twice sent his runners to give Lovell a rough reminder of his debts. When Lovell spoke of the drubbing they had given him, Justice ruefully recalled the painful welcome he had received on his first night in Verdun. It was a bad business, being mistaken for a bilking gambler. And then Balbi had called Lovell in to see him. He had a proposition, he said, combining bribes and threats to induce Lovell to accept it. For a little help, there could be a little credit, even a little cash. All Lovell had to do was to bring other men to the club, encourage them to drink, engage in some cautious cheating, swear the game was honest if a dupe claimed he was being swindled.

He had gone on like that for some weeks when Wirion summoned him. Lovell had gone to the Citadel fearfully, expecting a reprimand, thinking that someone had given him away; and he had been astounded to discover that Wirion was the man behind Balbi—taking a commission on all the money that passed across the tables of the gambling-rooms, and receiving all the chits that men wrote for their debts at Balbi's. "At a discount, naturally. He even squeezed Balbi."

"He was worse than people said, then." Justice realised that he had been lucky to escape the close attention of the prison commandant.

"He was a devil." Lovell was so fierce that he struck his fist bruisingly on the table. "I tell you, Justice, he was worse than all the money-lenders and duns in London. He sat there in his great room, gloating, a turnkey with the heart of a miser. 'Pay,' he hissed at you. 'Pay. Or earn your keep.' Pay? Twenty percent a month on your money was what he took. Or else you ran errands and told tales to him, and if you did what he wanted, he would give you some of your paper back. Not much, of course. Just enough to keep you keen to answer all the questions he and that little rat Charvet fired at you."

"What did he want to know?"

"You can imagine. Who had money in England. Or rich relatives. Who was in someone else's bed. Who was talking about escape. Any kind of gossip. Squeeze. Squeeze. Squeeze." Lovell obviously found self-pity the only compensation for the plight into which debts and drink had pitched him. "If you came empty-handed—well, you could expect a week of double *appels* to prick your interest. If that didn't work, he would give you a few days in the *souterrains*. And there was always a spell at Bitche or Sarrelibre if you were difficult."

"And Fielding?"

"I wish I'd kept out of that," Lovell said. "Look where it's got me." He jerked a thumb at Justice. "You, too." He paused, and when Justice did not react to the gibe, he started to speak again. "I met him a few times. Someone said he had been the Lloyd's man in Paris." There was a flicker of greed in his face. "That's money, in anyone's coin, and Wirion knew it as soon as I told him about Fielding."

"There was trouble at Balbi's." Justice was not going to let him minimise his part in Fielding's tragedy. "A trumped-up quarrel. They tried the same thing on me the first night I was there." He looked harshly at Lovell. "As you may remember."

"That was nothing to do with me," Lovell said hastily. "Wirion, perhaps. Even that damned Irishman. It was Lucienne who asked me to introduce her that night, you know."

"But you knew what was going to happen to Fielding?"

"It was only Wirion's usual blackmail, I thought."

Lovell's excuse might be true, Justice decided, but like all weak characters, he was always trying to shift the blame.

"I had no idea he would get himself killed trying to get out of Bitche," Lovell added. "I simply thought the fellow had a good deal of money tucked away somewhere, or coming to him, and hoped that Wirion might make enough out of it to wipe my slate clean."

"Then O'Moira had nothing to do with Fielding's arrest?" If the Irishman was working for Fouché, or for Saint-Haouen, he would probably have concealed his secret role in Verdun from Wirion—possibly from Charvet as well, though Justice was less sure of that.

"O'Moira says he was furious. Wanted Fielding left free, to watch him. And Wirion queered the Irishman's pitch, apparently, by packing Fielding off to Bitche. But I can't say more than that. First I knew about it was when he and the girl collared me in Paris."

"Collared you?" Justice was incredulous. He remembered Lovell at the hut outside Verdun, skulking near the coach stop, watching Duhamel's bookshop . . . No. Lovell must have known more than he was admitting.

"Collared me, yes. You didn't think I was in it with the girl, did you?" Lovell gave a hard laugh. "No such luck," he said, with coarse gesture. "Didn't you see how she clawed at me in the hut? Afraid I was going to spoil things for them again. At least, that's what she told me, coming up here on the coach."

"But . . . but you knew about her . . . ?" Justice found the question so disagreeable that he almost stammered it at Lovell.

"I wasn't sure whether she was on the game at Balbi's. You know, like me—only it's a different thing with a woman. And Balbi wouldn't have told me, anyway. He kept things like that to himself, so you never knew who was keeping an eye on you. But she might have been working Fielding from the other side, for she was always about with him. So when I heard he was dead I thought she might know something about the money." Lovell paused. "I saw a good deal of her at the time. I think she and the doctor fancied I might have been on to them, and they kept an eye on me just in case. As it happened, I was skulking about on Wirion's business, not my own, worse luck." He seemed full of disgust with himself and the mess he had made of things. "Then you came," he said. "I tell you frankly, Justice, I couldn't make head or tail of you. Still can't, for that matter."

"And then?" Justice prompted.

"I saw my chance." Lovell sounded bitter and disappointed. "Or I thought I did. If you were going to pass yourself off as Fielding, and get hold of his money, I would beat you to it."

"But why . . . ?" Justice hesitated, because there were so many things he wanted to ask Lovell. Why was the man so obsessed with the idea that Fielding had money hidden, and how did he expect to lay hands on any of it? Why did he suddenly ride away from the hut at Houdainville? Why was he skulking about the coach station in the rue du Boilou? How did he find his way to the bookseller's in the Place des Vosges, and what did he hope to find there? Justice stopped himself, and let the questions fade away. Lovell was not an accomplished plotter, working to a plan. He was such a bundle of fears and impulses that he was more like a cornered rat, darting backwards and forwards in a desperate attempt to save himself.

As Justice paused, he heard Pierre's voice below, speaking urgently, and he wondered if there was a message from Tissot. It was well past noon, and the day was beginning to ebb with the tide.

"There is very little time," he said to Lovell in a sharper tone. "Tell me about O'Moira."

"I was staggered when I saw him at the hotel," Lovell said rapidly, as if he were glad to get past some turn in a talk that made him feel very uneasy. "I followed you in Paris, you know. Then lost you. So I went back to the hotel to see what I could

233

get out of . . . of the girl, who might have known what you were up to."

"You went to threaten her?" Justice could see the blustering rogue standing over Lucienne.

Lovell was silent.

"And O'Moira was there?" Justice had to press him.

"Yes. In her room."

"And he persuaded you to come on here with him? To trap me? To work for Boney?" The scorn that Justice felt made him rasp the words. "And you hold the King's commission!"

Lovell looked ashamed. "No," he said, grasping at the digression to temper Justice's wrath. "No commission. I'd already sold out of the regiment before I came to France last year. But no one at Verdun seemed to know. Except Wirion, of course."

His explanation tailed away as Justice brought him back to O'Moira. "He offered you money?"

"A little. Enough. Papers, too. And a passage to Philadelphia. If I did what he wanted."

"Was that all?" Justice could tell that there was something left unsaid.

"I told you I was done, finished." Lovell was speaking again in the tone of black despair with which he had begun his story. "I couldn't get away to England. And I couldn't go back to Verdun. He knew it."

"Because of Wirion?" Justice could understand how the threat of Wirion's revenge might drive a cowardly man to treachery as the easiest way out of his troubles. "Bitche?"

"Worse." Lovell rose, clasping his arms to hug himself in dejection as he paced about the room. Justice watched him warily, but he could tell that there was no fight left in the man. "America was the only safe place for me."

Justice thought he had caught the drift of Lovell's cryptic self-pity. "You would face the gallows in England," he said bluntly. "Or a firing squad here. As a spy . . ."

"No. No." Lovell's desperation made him interrupt, and he grasped Justice by the arm. "Not a firing squad," he said so slowly that each word came out like the grunt of a tortured man. "The knife!" He released his grip on Justice, and put a hand to his cheek, pulling nervously at the skin where he once had whiskers. "In Verdun.

"I did not mean to kill him." Lovell gasped out the phrase.

"Hunt?" Justice had seen him struggling towards that confession.

Lovell nodded. "He knew I was on to you," he admitted. "He saw me that day when I followed you to the hut."

"Was that reason to murder him?" Justice felt like a cross-examining counsel.

"He was painting by the river," Lovell went on. "He stopped me as I went back to Verdun, and mentioned Fielding." Lovell looked back at Justice. "That took spunk, you know. He just sat there, with his brush in his hand, and calmly told me that I had sent Fielding to his death—and that he would not see me turn you over to Wirion. Just like that, when I could so easily have tipped him into the river."

"But you didn't?"

"No. I threatened him. I told him that he was making trouble for himself, yes. But that was all. I had no desire to kill him. I was simply afraid that he might try to make money out of me if I argued the point."

"You shouldn't judge others by your own standards."

Lovell missed the sarcasm in Justice's voice.

"No," he conceded. "I wouldn't have been in this mess if I had let well alone. But I began to worry. I was thinking of going to Hahn's to have it out with him that night—when you saw me at the club . . ."

"When I told you I was looking for him?" Justice broke in. "The night he stayed in the country?"

"So I had to wait another day. I was in a stew by then, because of the trouble at Balbi's." Lovell gave Justice a frank look. "I was in earnest about escaping with you," he said. "It wasn't a trap."

"You saw Hunt come back?"

"I was hanging about," Lovell replied. "I followed him up to his room to make sure that he didn't get to you first." Lovell's face whitened at the recollection. "He panicked as soon as I went into the room. I picked up a knife from the table . . ."

"You killed him in cold blood?"

Lovell shook his head. "He just ran at me. Straight onto the knife."

It was the kind of story that Justice had heard seamen tell

235

after a deadly scuffle, and it must have been tried often enough as a defence to a charge of murder. And rarely was it true. "And you left him to die."

"What could I do? I heard you moving about upstairs, and I ran for it."

"Sending a gendarme to find me with Hunt's body?"

Lovell said nothing to that last indictment, and Justice felt as if he were about to pass sentence.

But Lovell anticipated him, bracing himself now the sorry tale was told. "If I were still in the regiment—" he started to say.

"I would lay a pistol on the table." Justice finished the sentence for him.

"I would not use it for any other purpose." Lovell was pleading, but his voice was firmer now that he came to his request. "I would give my word."

Justice was silent for a moment, and Lovell took his silence as a contemptuous comment. "I *was* an officer and a gentleman," he said defensively.

"I know." Justice accepted his point. "But there may be another way. It would be no easier. Only more honourable."

✁ 20 ✎

THE SOLDIERS were at the door before Pierre had time to do more than pass Justice a primed pistol and, with evident anxiety, warn him that a military patrol was calling at every building in the lane.

Justice had at once hurried Lovell back into the loft, to lie beside O'Moira again, and as he crouched beside his two prisoners, he used the muzzle of the gun to make clear what he would do if either of them cried out for help.

But there was no need for drastic measures. Lovell was too cowed to make trouble; and though the doctor had guessed that something was wrong when Justice and Lovell scuffled up the ladder, he was taking no risks.

"You shouldn't excite yourself too much, now, Mr Justice," he had whispered in his most engaging brogue. "Even an Irishman knows he's beat when he's blind, his hands are tied, his legs are numb, and there's an ounce of lead only an inch from his brains."

Justice heard the voices rumble beneath him and die away as the patrol moved on. Then, as O'Moira gently asked if he could have his bonds loosened to ease his discomfort, Justice realised that the irony of the gibe had been calculated to win his sympathy.

And to distract him. While he was busy securing the wrists and ankles of the grouchy Lovell, he had a sense that something was missing in the loft. Something he should have noticed.

He shook off the uneasy feeling. Perhaps it was simply his dislike of leaving the two men together without anyone to watch them or to stop them talking. But there was no one to do it. Nor was there any way in which they could be kept apart—unless he put O'Moira or Lovell in the same room with Lucienne . . . And that . . .

"They said they were searching for an English spy." Pierre spoke coolly for a man who had just survived some uncomfortable questions. "They had his description—and his name."

"Fielding?"

"Exactly."

"But that makes no sense." Justice was puzzled. O'Moira had certainly carried Fielding's papers to use at the bank in Paris and to impress Tissot. Would he have dared to use Fielding's name elsewhere in Boulogne? At the bank, perhaps, or at an inn? To provide support for his story if Tissot enquired after him?

"Paul heard the name dropped this morning, and sent to tell me." Pierre's remark explained why he had hurriedly returned to the net-house while Justice was talking to Lovell. "Paul thinks that some people here—maybe someone in Saint-Haouen's office—knew what the Irishman was doing and the name he would use. And once he disappeared, the easiest way for them to find him would be to say they were looking for a spy." Pierre made a sour face. "Everyone in Boulogne likes hunting for spies, you know. There's money in it. And promotion, if you're lucky. And quite often a chance of paying off old scores. You can create a lot of trouble for a man before he can prove that he's a true patriot."

"Yet you got rid of them easily enough." Justice could not understand why the soldiers had gone away without searching the place.

"Huh!" Pierre was scornful. "Soldiers don't ask too many questions when they see a man in National Guard uniform and they're told that he's taking care of the mayor's personal property—not in Boulogne, at any rate. In this town you can find almost as much government wine and corn and sail-cloth in private stores as in the naval warehouses. And a mere sergeant doesn't like to be found prying into such things."

Despite Pierre's confident sarcasm, Justice felt that the visit of the patrol had been too close a call for comfort, and he knew that he would feel a lot easier in his mind when the afternoon had slipped safely away and all the waiting was over. "I'll stand a watch for you," he said to Pierre, knowing that the man had scarcely slept the previous night. "There'll be no rest for any of us when the fireworks start!"

EVERYONE SEEMED to be asleep as the gathering dusk made the ill-lit building seem darker than ever. Justice had gone up to look at the prisoners and found Lovell snoring and O'Moira breathing as steadily as if he were stretched on his own feather-bed at home; he had gone down to make sure that the door was barred, and seen Pierre dead to the world on a pile of old nets.

He had already decided about Lovell. He would be so short of men that night that even a pair of hands soiled with treachery would be welcome; and Lovell, a trained soldier who knew about fuses and explosives, could at least be offered the chance to make himself useful and die decently. It would have to be that for Lovell. That, or the single pistol-ball for which the broken man had asked.

O'Moira's case was much more difficult. He genuinely liked the affable and intelligent Irishman, had found him good company, had almost respected him. In another time, another place, they might have become good friends, and Justice felt more grudging admiration than a grudge for the clever way in which the blind man had deceived him.

He also knew enough of the tragedy of Ireland to understand how a man like O'Moira could throw everything to the winds for the sake of his wretched countrymen and their passionate religion. But O'Moira had chosen the French for his allies, hoping no doubt that they would do better for Ireland this time than they had done with their half-hearted expeditions in '96 and '98. Only the hangman had done well out of these failures.

What was it O'Moira had said last night? "I would do anything to ensure that these ships play their part in carrying freedom to my country. *Anything*." And he had meant it. He was like . . . like . . . Justice reached in his memory for the character of a king in an old Greek play he had read at Cranbrook, and had the fleeting sense that someone had recently reminded him of it. Yet for the life of him he could not recall the name of the king or tell why O'Moira had brought that classical text to mind. All he could remember was that it had something to do with ships . . . ships . . . and a favourable wind.

Lucienne? How had O'Moira driven her to such things? And why had she done them with such convincing ease? As he steeled himself to deal with O'Moira, he realised that he had been avoiding those devastating questions in the few hours since he had learned that she was the Irishman's loyal servant— avoiding them because he could neither understand nor answer them.

Had O'Moira gained some hold over her, as he had over Lovell? Did some French prison hold her father, or a brother, as hostage for her compliance? Justice recalled her evasions when he had asked about her family. Was she one of Fouché's conniving creatures, as Tissot had hinted? Or was she simply bought for her pay and perquisites?

The questions tumbled over in his mind, exciting and troubling him, for none of the images they conjured up seemed to fit the warm-hearted woman who had saved his life in the fight with Lovell and travelled with him from Verdun to Paris.

But there was no time to answer them now. It was already dark and Tissot would soon be back.

STANDING THERE in a motley of costumes, with the nets trailing up into the loft like curtains, the seven men seemed so much like a troupe of players dressing for a military farce that Justice laughed freely for the first time in weeks.

239

"I don't see what's so funny about it." Tissot sounded aggrieved. The risks he was running had made him too tense to share the joke.

"Never mind." Justice looked round at the men he was about to lead in this desperate venture. The odds against them were so great, he thought, that humour was probably the best way of keeping up their spirits.

Tissot was solemn enough, stocky and impressive in the harbour-master's coat that would pass unquestioned anywhere in Boulogne. With him to answer for the rest of them with passwords and explanations at the ready, they had a fair chance of reaching the *Liberté* and the *Fraternité*. Without him, as Fielding must have known when he sought Tissot's help, their prospects of success would be very slim indeed.

"We're an odd crew, all the same." Justice waved his hand airily round the little group as though counting men at a muster. "Or no crew at all," he said to himself as he summed them up, for the gangling Pierre was the only one of them who was wearing the working clothes of a sailor, and the rest of them were having to make do with what Tissot had somehow scrounged up to fit them. How would they move across the narrow but dangerously well-guarded stretch of quay to the small rowboat which Tissot had tied up at the foot of the nearest steps?

Tissot must go first, naturally, for he knew where they were going and what to expect of the patrols; and in any case he must be in command until they were all safely aboard the brigs. Next, as his escort, would go the two men who had slipped along like shadows when Pierre had led Justice through the lanes from the Chapeau Rouge. They were a silent twosome, so coy with their names that Justice had decided to call them Gog and Magog, and they seemed quite satisfied to be named after the biblical giants. Kitted out as marines of the Guard, in dark-blue coats and pantaloons smart with orange trimmings, they certainly looked impressive, although the ludicrously long red plumes which sprouted from their shakos made Justice feel that he was setting out for a regatta rather than a raid.

Pierre, of course, would be the fourth man to go, close on the heels of the two marines, wheeling the barrow in which a small sail and some carelessly laid oars would cover their tiny armoury. If Pierre was stopped and the barrow searched, he would have a hard time explaining why he was carrying pistols, knives, and boarding-axes, to say nothing of four lanterns, a set of candles, a basket of fuses and slow-match, two kegs of good powder, tinder, and the flints they would need to give them the vital spark.

The only innocent supplies in the whole lading were a few bottles of wine, a couple of loaves, and a decent piece of cheese. Tissot had been very thorough in his preparations. He had also been very plain that neither he nor the other Frenchmen could be expected to meet their fate supperless.

While Justice had been seeing this little procession build up in his mind's eye, Pierre had come across with a fragment of mirror. From what Justice could see by lantern-light in the cracked glass, it seemed that a captain in the National Guard might shame a post-captain in the Royal Navy about to appear before my Lords of Admiralty. Shopkeepers turned soldier always liked to dress up to the part. There were grey facings on his blue cutaway coat, red bands at his collar and cuffs, silver epaulettes at his shoulders. White breeches and hose ran down to his buckled shoes, and a silver cord and tricolour cockade gleamed in his black cocked hat. Tissot had done him proud.

Then there was Lovell, standing a little apart, uncertain how matters stood with him after he had gratefully accepted Justice's offer to redeem himself by joining the boarding-party. Justice gave the poor devil an encouraging wave as he changed his clothes. Since Tissot was unaware that he had broken with O'Moira, and had not provided any disguise for him, it was lucky that the major was much of a size with the man in the National Guard uniform who had been keeping watch all day.

That suited well. It would be a risk to leave Lovell to bring up the rear, walking a respectful pace or two behind like an orderly attending his officer, for he could easily run off or give a shout of alarm that would bring a patrol down on them in a matter of seconds. Yet he had to trust Lovell now the man had given his word. They could not manage without him. There were only seven of them.

Six were to go. That had been settled after Tissot returned. The seventh, Henri the watchman, was to stay with the prisoners.

"Hostages," Tissot had said grudgingly at last, after Justice had argued with him for ten minutes, insisting that they be dealt with according to the normal rules of war, not the barbarous habits of civil war.

"A blind man and a woman," Justice said repeatedly, as an obdurate Tissot reminded him that Fouché's men would have no such scruples.

"There will be no pity for us if we are taken," Tissot had said. "For you, perhaps, a firing squad. For the rest of us . . ." He stopped. "You should know, Jean, that we should not die while we could still be made to speak."

"I owe a life," Justice said flatly, when all other arguments had failed.

Tissot had looked hard at him. "Hostages, then. Perhaps we could try. He sounded very doubtful. "If we left Henri to guard them . . . we could try to bargain if we are taken . . . and if we succeed . . ." Tissot quite suddenly made up his mind, shrugging as if the fate of O'Moira and Lucienne were no longer of interest to him. "What's it matter? One way or another, we shan't be coming back, and there must be someone to start again at the beginning. Why not let Henri stay?"

Tissot was probably right in thinking that none of them would be coming back. It was that kind of venture, and nothing would be gained by pretending otherwise.

Lovell must have come to the same conclusion. He gave a last tug to straighten his uniform, brushed the back of his hand dismissively over the tricolour cockade in his hat before he placed it carefully on his head, and drew himself up to give an ironical salute. "Ready for duty, sir," he said, with a bravado that revealed his embarrassment. Then his face softened into the sad grin of a gambler who had seen the wrong card come up once too often, and he looked down at his long blue coat with the white cross-belts. "Damn queer rags for a fellow to go dancin' in, Justice, ain't they." He spoke in English, mocking himself. "But I don't suppose the doorman will be choosey where we're going, d'you?"

It was striking nine when Justice blew out the lantern, and as they waited in the dark for the order to move out into the lane, Tissot came up and drew him to one side. "Before we go," Tissot said very quietly, "there is one more thing. Here. In my pocket."

Justice put his hand to Tissot's coat and felt the stiffness of a folded piece of oilskin. "A will?"

Tissot seemed to be making some kind of mystery out of a gesture that men commonly made before an action at sea.

"No." Tissot was urgent. "A letter. Two of them, in fact. One for you. One for your friends . . . in England . . . if anything should happen. "You follow me?"

"I follow you."

"I hope so." Tissot spoke like a man who might never get another chance to speak his mind. "It is very important."

"Can you say . . . ?"

"Not now." Tissot gave Justice a quick embrace. *"Bonne chance, mon ami,"* he said, and turned to take his place in front of the two marines.

And as the door was eased open and the party slipped out into the fresh night-air, Justice wondered what secrets the dead Fielding and the living Tissot might yet spring on him before dawn.

If he should ever see it.

✎ 21 ✎

THEY HAD JUST reached the quayside when the challenge came, firmly enough to stop them, but not so loud that the next sentry in the line would hear it.

"Who goes?" The guard must have seen Tissot as soon as he led the way out of the lane, carrying a lantern in his hand; and as the unruffled harbour-master satisfied the man with a password, and a quip of approval for being so alert, Justice realised how sensible he had been to draw attention to himself deliberately.

"It seems very quiet." Lovell, at his heels, spoke nervously, prompting Justice to share his concern as he looked down the harbour towards the sea. Beyond the lines of moored boats that were nearest to him, he could see little except for the yellow lights which flickered from windows and among the tangle of masts. The defenders of Boulogne could well be in their beds— and they could equally well be crouched, invisible, behind their embrasures, slow-match and flintlock to hand, waiting for the signal that would send a searing hail of iron out through the night towards Keith's oncoming squadron.

"It's early yet," Justice replied, without breaking his step or turning to look at Lovell. "And the better for us. We've work to do before the dancing starts." He had picked up Lovell's phrase as he tried to sound reassuring. But Lovell was right. It was very quiet. He could see the tide running, eddying round bow cables and lapping at the harbour wall, and there was still no sign of an attack.

"Have we come on a fool's errand, then?"

Lovell's edginess annoyed Justice. "Keep your mouth shut." He was harsh to hide his own doubts.

Suppose Tissot had been wrong? Suppose the gossip from Admiral Bruix's office had misled him? Unless Keith's frigates and sloops drove in towards Boulogne well before midnight, they would be too late for the high water they would need to get into the mouth of the harbour, and too late for Justice as well. Without that assault from the sea, the attempt to save something of Fielding's original plan would end in a fiasco. Justice would be lucky if he could get even one of the brigs into the channel before the French boarded it and overwhelmed his tiny crew.

And suppose there was no way of firing the *Liberté* or the *Fraternité,* or of making a small blaze catch hold so fast that the French sailors would be unable to put it out?

Justice shrugged as he came up to the edge of the quay and looked down the steep stone steps at Tissot, who was already seated in the stern of the boat.

"Come along, we haven't got all night!" Tissot called loudly to Pierre and the two marines, knowing that they were only safe if they avoided any action that gave a furtive impression. "Look lively, and get all that stuff down and stowed." Tissot harried the three men while they stripped the barrow clean, handing the contents from one to another down the steps as though they had nothing to conceal. Pierre even took advantage of the sentry who had sauntered over to break the boredom of his duty, distracting the man's interest in the barrow by asking him to hold the end of the sail while he pulled it straight and rolled it up again.

Justice took no part in this skilful operation. He and Lovell simply stood at the top of the steps as if they were watching the cutter's crew out of idle curiosity. And then Justice called down to Tissot as casually as though the idea had that moment come to him. "Are you crossing to the Arsenal?"

Tissot took the cue, raising his arm in acknowledgement and dropping it to wave Justice to a place in the boat beside him. Even if the sentry went on watching them as they rowed away, they would be lost in the darkness long before he could tell whether they were really heading for the other side of the water or out to one of the moored vessels which almost filled the channel of the Liane.

When Justice was seated, he looked for Lovell, seeing with a shock that the major had disappeared, hearing Tissot draw a sharp breath as he also realised that Lovell had not followed the rest of them into the boat.

"Pierre." Tissot had hardly spoken before Pierre was out of the boat and splashing for a foothold where the water licked at the lowest step. "Busy yourself with the line. And be ready."

Justice was trying to decide whether to go after Lovell or to cut and row for it, when Tissot spoke again. "There," he said, nudging Justice gently. "Along the quay." Justice caught a glimpse of Lovell's hat bobbing along and guessed from the motion that he was wheeling the barrow away.

Lovell was soon back, scurrying down into the bow of the boat, pushing it away from the wall with a boat-hook, as though such menial tasks were all in the night's work for him. "No point in leaving our callin' cards all over the bloody harbour," he muttered caustically, settling himself beside the basket of fuses and tinder to make sure that the folds of the sail protected it from the splashing of the oars.

Pierre, too, was bothered about spray coming into the boat, for he was bending protectively over their little armoury, priming the pistols, wiping the handles of the knives and boarding-axes so that each man would have a dry grip as they came to the brigs.

At least they all seemed to know their business well. Even the taciturn Gog and Magog pulled steadily with the tide like men who were used to an oar. Tissot. Pierre. Gog and Magog. Lovell. Even if all went well, and each man did what he was asked, there were still far too few for a task which Justice would have considered a pretty desperate venture for a whole boat's crew of seasoned seamen.

As the boat moved easily across the harbour, Justice thought again about the scene in the net-house when he had given the little band their instructions. "It's really a very simple scheme," he had said as he showed them his wood-and-rope model of the harbour. "It has to be. We have no choice."

He held two pieces of wood. "The *Liberté* and the *Fraternité*," he said as he placed them a little above the horseshoe twist of fishing-line which he had used to indicate the great inner basin. "The *Liberté* is on the starboard side as you face down the harbour." He looked at Lovell and corrected himself. "On the right," he said, making sure that there was no misunderstanding, and glanced at Tissot for confirmation.

When Tissot nodded, Justice continued. "We shall board the *Liberté*," he said crisply, "for that's the brig we shall stay on to the end. But we shall try to move both boats. My idea is to turn the *Fraternité* loose at or near the entrance to the basin, and to take the *Liberté* right into the channel, where there are large vessels tied up along both banks."

"Very simple indeed!" Lovell seemed to be regaining his confidence, for he spoke sarcastically as he broke in with the obvious question. "Since I am neither a sailor nor a man who believes in miracles, can you tell me how you propose to move two brigs with only six men?" He spread his hands enquiringly. "Or four, if you and I are playing with the fireworks?"

"Like this." Justice tapped the two pieces of wood. "Paul says that they are moored fore-and-aft, and that they are also lashed alongside each other to stop them bumping and grinding. In a crude sense, that is, they are one ship until they are cut apart. Too clumsy to sail, of course, but if we are lucky, they will drift in the right direction . . ."

"Can we be sure of that?" Lovell was sharp with his queries.

"Not sure. But given the shape of the harbour and the set of the wind, we can't go far wrong. From what I could see today, it seems that there's so much shipping tied up that there's not much room for mistakes. Anything that comes down on the ebb would have to cross the piece of open water where the

246

basin opens into the channel, and the scour of the current should be enough to pull us into the channel itself."

"The tide is vital." As Tissot spoke, he drew out his watch and peered at it in the poor light. "We cannot hope to move before eleven." He carefully replaced his watch in his fob. "Perhaps a little later. With the wind in this quarter, the ebb is bound to start slowly."

"Then at eleven we shall start the fires. I will deal with the *Liberté*. And Lovell with the *Fraternité*." Justice spoke decisively to conceal his uncertainty. How could he judge in advance how Fielding's ships would burn? Or whether they would burn at all. Or whether they would contain hidden stores of powder that would blow them all to glory before they had drifted more than a few yards.

He looked at Tissot. "I leave it to Paul to tell us when the ebb is strong enough to carry us down into the channel."

Gog spoke for the first time, in the plaintive tone of a boy who feared that he was being left out of the fun. "And us?"

Justice gave him a friendly grin, but he remained as dour as ever. "Three tasks. First, you must act as lookouts while we are searching below, and if necessary defend us if we are surprised. Secondly, loosen the ties and sheets on the large foresail. It will droop, but no one is likely to notice in the dark. Thirdly, as we drift down towards the entrance of the basin, Paul will take the wheel of the *Liberté*, while Pierre and Lovell will cut the lashings that bind the brigs together. At that moment I want the foresail set as best you can."

He saw a flicker of protest in their faces, and in that second grasped from the similarity of their reactions that the men were twins. "I know. It can't be done with two men. But do what you can to make it draw enough to pull us off the *Fraternité*, and the rest of us will give you a hand if we can."

Justice separated his two pieces of wood, leaving one by the basin and pushing the other away from it.

"You can't steer one of those brigs with a slack foresail." Tissot sounded so horrified that Justice realised that the proposition had offended his professional sense as a sailor.

"You speak like a true harbour-master, Paul," Justice said jovially. "You're afraid of a collision. Or of us blocking the channel. But, for once, that's exactly what we want." And as Tissot gave a hint of a smile to show that he had taken the point,

Justice went on with his explanation. "We've got a light wind, west of south," he said, tracing the direction across his model with a forefinger. "With the helm hard over, and a sagging foresail turning the head just enough to bring us across the current, we should go down slowly, crabwise." He rotated his remaining piece of wood. "Thus. And, with luck, we should collide and sink about here." He picked a position about half-way down the channel, between the basin and the point where the long jetty began to run out over the sandbanks on the southern side of the harbour entrance.

It would be a good end to the affair, he thought with grim satisfaction. So far as he could tell, the place he had chosen would be almost abreast of Saint-Haouen's office in the naval headquarters. Saint-Haouen, indeed, was the kind of man who might see the joke.

"You have very little water there. Even at high tide." Tissot spoke like a man who knew every sounding in the harbour. "Less than three fathoms. And on some days there's not even a full fathom at slack water."

Sixteen feet, perhaps a little less at the edges of the channel. And these brigs could draw almost ten feet when loaded. "So we sink there . . ."

". . . and block the channel completely." Tissot knew the answer he wanted. "Nothing but light craft could pass."

"For how long?"

"For a week, certainly." Tissot, it was clear, had seen more than one wreck cleared from the Liane. "Maybe more. It depends on the weather. The cargo. How much damage the fire has done to the hull."

It was Lovell who put the sensible question again. "Why fireships, then? Why not blow a hole in the bottom and sink the damn thing in one solid piece?" For all the impression he gave of being a braggart and something of a fool, Justice was coming to realise, Lovell had a head on his shoulders.

"I don't know," he answered frankly. "I've only been guessing at Fielding's purpose." He thought for a moment. "Of course, if he had planned to attack the flotilla as it began to crowd out of the harbour, with troops and supplies on board, fire would be the best weapon."

"But a chancey one, all the same." Lovell was persistent. "All that trouble for three fire-ships! Among five hundred vessels—or twice as many, so far as I know. I don't see it, Justice. Not as a betting man." He shook his head sceptically.

"We shall soon find out." Justice could see the force of Lovell's argument, but there was no point in pursuing it now. "In any case, our target must be the channel. With so few of us, and only one ship, fire can be nothing but a means to our end."

He was so absorbed in his own problems, it suddenly struck him that he had forgotten the men out beyond the line of the Boulogne defences who would soon be climbing down into ship's boats and pinnaces, setting the sails on their own fire-ships . . . "And as a means to help Keith's squadron," he added. "Any disturbance we can create within the harbour could increase their chances of breaking through."

And then it crossed his mind that possibly Fielding had never intended to do anything more ambitious than that. Perhaps it was only George Lilly, with his mind on infernal machines, who had endowed Fielding with an undeserved reputation for ingenuity . . . or O'Moira, equally obsessed by the idea of balloons or new-fangled plunging-boats . . . or Mr Francis, or Mr Fulton, or whatever the American was called, who had bamboozled them all . . .

Pierre brought them to the point which Justice had deliberately left to the last, because he could think of nothing useful to say. "Then we all swim for England, I suppose, and live happily ever after."

Pierre had finished the sentence before Justice reacted to the fact that he was speaking in English, and using the old ending to a fairy tale to satiric effect. Whatever else Pierre might have been before he turned conspirator, he had certainly not begun life as a sailor.

"We shall trail the boat," Justice said lamely. "And if Keith's men get over the booms, we might be picked up."

"Or slaughtered by them." Lovell's sardonic interjection was too likely to be true for Justice to dispute it. No boat's crew in a fight would wait for explanations from men in French uniforms.

"Make for the south bank," Tissot said. "It will be far easier to get away. Not easy, but easier than the harbour wall and the town."

He spoke directly to Pierre, and then he faced the two men dressed as marines, who stood holding their comical plumed hats under their arms as if they were waiting for an official audience. "And you two as well. You know how to take care of yourselves." He turned his head in an aside to Justice. "Gog and Magog," he said. "What names!"

"And you?" Justice had come to see that Tissot himself had very little chance of escape even if he survived the hazardous trip down into the centre of the harbour. He was too compromised.

"We'll have to take our chances as they come, Jean." Tissot spoke steadily. "As they come," he repeated. "For you and me." He looked at Lovell disparagingly. "And for the major, of course."

It was a grim conclusion that stayed in Justice's mind as they moved farther out into the harbour.

Suddenly the danger was on them, and Tissot leaned forward urgently. "Pierre," he said. "Pierre."

He must have caught the regular beat of the oars in the guard-boat before he saw it, for Justice only glimpsed it looming low and black ahead of them after Tissot had spoken and he had heard Pierre cock a pistol. "All well?" Tissot called out loud and clear, and Justice marvelled at the cheerful edge to his voice, and the calm way in which he had taken exactly the right initiative to settle any doubts the patrol might have.

The guard-boat was barely out of sight when Tissot tapped Justice on the knee and pointed. They had come round to face down the stream, for the tide had carried them a little too far, and Gog and Magog were now rowing them carefully under the square sterns of a pair of brigs. "We shall go between them," Tissot said, "and no one will see our boat."

As they slipped into the space left by the tumblehome of the curving hulls, Justice could just make out the names painted over the transoms.

Liberté. On the right.

Fraternité. To the left.

He reached out to steady the rocking boat, and touched the damp and slippery hull of the *Liberté.*

It was hard to believe it was true, but Fielding's strange legacy was at last at arm's length from him.

THERE WAS something odd about both the brigs. While Pierre was casting up the boat's anchor to catch like a grapnel in the shrouds, Justice peered at the bulk of them, rising in the darkness on either side of him. They lay squat and heavy, there was no doubt about that, so deep in the water that there would be damn little free-board in any kind of sea. That could explain what had happened to the *Egalité*, if the third brig really had been lost.

But it was not only that. Justice looked up at the yards of both vessels towering above him, and they seemed almost motionless against the night sky. It was not natural for ships to lie so stiff in moving water and a breeze, even if they were moored fore-and-aft, unless they were so heavily loaded that they would go down like a stone in anything more than a moderate sea.

"How much water do we have?" Justice threw the question at Tissot, who was holding the end of the rope while Gog and Magog followed Pierre up the side of the brig, and watching keenly for any sign of trouble on board.

"Two fathoms," he answered without dropping his eyes from the line of the ship's bulwarks. "Over three at the flood." His reply was so precise that Justice knew that he must have been poring over his chart that very afternoon.

Justice absently watched Pierre hauling up the kegs of powder and their other supplies, but his thoughts ran on in a series of simple sums. So there was very little water under the keels. He had the impression that these brigs must be drawing over nine feet, for they were sizeable vessels. And if his guess was right, they would so far have lifted no more than a foot or two from the sludge onto which they must have settled at low tide. That was fine. What would be a serious problem for Admiral Bruix, if he ever tried to move a string of such ships out of this harbour in a tide or two, was an advantage tonight. The deeper they rode, the better. As Fielding must have known when he gave his order to the Bordeaux shipwrights.

They had certainly built Fielding's brigs well for him. As Justice pulled himself up and swung round the shrouds to drop lightly to the deck, the *Liberté* had the look and the feel of a fine piece of shipbuilding. He had often wished that the English boatyards could make vessels so sound and true—and just as often he had been glad for the sake of his country's safety that the French could never find crews to match the ships they sailed in.

Habit took him across to his customary stance on the starboard side of the quarter-deck, where he could see the length of the brig fading off into the darkness, before he realised that he had just captured the vessel. It was his prize, and though he was unlikely ever to see a penny of prize-money for it, he might one day have to account to the Board of Admiralty for taking and losing it. He looked across to his left. And the *Fraternité* as well.

It was the first time that he had set foot on a French deck without the blood and tangled ruin of a sea-fight all about him, and the empty silence of the deck made a ghostly impression on him. Pierre was up forward, helping Gog and Magog make out the sheets and bunt-lines they would use to release the foremast royal, and the halyard they would have to cut to drop the sail on an instant when the *Liberté* had to be stopped plumb in the channel. Behind him, wheezing from his short climb up the side, Lovell was sorting through his flints and fuses, and a light clink of metal told him that Tissot was setting out the lanterns they would need for their search.

With a word to Lovell and Tissot that set them to find and force the hatch to the upper deck, Justice went forward to the waist, noting what he saw like a clerk taking an inventory. It all seemed quite normal. Good standing rigging. Clean enough for a merchant ship that had tied up at the end of a voyage. Four guns a side. Well, if they could fight those 12-pounders properly, a crew could hold off a sloop or a privateer. Not much more. But guns might mean powder somewhere below. Two chests. Axes, perhaps, spare belaying-pins, some ends of rope, the usual oddments that were useful on deck. Two pumps by the foremast. That was a little unusual in a merchantman, and sensible, too, for a ship that was built to work the heavy seas off the rock-bound coasts of Brittany. Especially if it was loaded so heavily that it would wallow awkwardly through the long rollers coming in from the Atlantic.

Fielding, like a good Lloyd's man, would have tried to protect his vessels against any foreseeable risks.

Pierre came towards him as he stood by the pumps thinking about Fielding, and held out a thumb and forefinger to indicate the size of the bow cable he would have to cut. "Not too bad," he said. "Three or four minutes with the boarding-axe, I should say."

"It might be too long." Justice pointed to the deck lockers. "See if you can force those and find a proper axe."

Justice had his hand on one of the pumps, wondering about the bilges. That was where Fielding's secret might have been hidden. If he had packed powder or other combustibles in the bottom of the ship, he would be very anxious to keep it pumped dry.

So, two pumps instead of one.

He tried the lever where his hand lay, the iron curving down in a strong swan's-neck, just like the handle of the pump in the stable-yard at Hook. It moved quite easily when he lifted it to begin a stroke, although a dry rasp from the shaft told him that it needed priming.

Six feet away, there was a splintering noise as Pierre forced the locker, and then cursed at himself for his carelessness.

"Never mind," Justice said. "It won't carry." The wind in the rigging and the creaking of the hulls would be enough to cover the sound.

It was simply a fidgety thoroughness that made him grasp the handle of the other pump, and find that it seemed to be jammed. He tried it a couple of times. It gave a fraction of an inch if he pushed it down, but as it came back, he could feel it check against some metal obstacle near the joint at the top of the plunger. It was locked in some way.

Pierre was beside him with a gleaming axe in his hand. "And two more," he said with satisfaction as he strained to see what Justice was doing.

"There's a large pin here," Justice said, running his fingers round a stout iron collar that prevented the pump-handle from moving. "I saw something like it once on a water-butt tap in the tropics. But it's an odd thing to see on a pump. Who would want to stop a pump working?"

"Shall I knock the pin out?" Pierre raised the axe.

"No. Leave it." There was no need to run the risk that someone would catch the chink of metal. And if this had not been Fielding's ship, where anything out of the ordinary might be important, Justice would not have thought twice about the matter.

He walked back with Pierre to the mainmast, and saw that Lovell and Tissot had disappeared. "Take Gog or Magog across to the *Fraternité*, force the hatch, and search," he said. "Set the other to watch." It was a necessary precaution, although the harbour seemed as quiet as though a storm were coming.

And then, as Pierre left, he saw that there were two more pumps. Two more, behind the mainmast, where many ships of this size would not even have one.

One normal pump. He ran his hand over the top of the second. The other with the same strong collar and pin.

What was the point? Did those special pumps lead somewhere else than the bilges? To huge casks of spirits, perhaps—spirits which could be pumped up to feed a fire? The image of Gog and Magog labouring to spray cognac over the deck was so comic that Justice smiled.

Where then? he asked himself as he went down to join Lovell and Tissot. They had gone forward, tactfully leaving a lantern outside the captain's cabin so that he could search it, and he saw at once that it was almost as bare as the net-loft. A table, three simple chairs, a straw palliasse on the bed, an empty cupboard. Not even a scrap of paper or a drinking-mug. The only thing that was of any use was the lantern, half-full of oil, which he lifted down from its hook above the table. Before the search was over, they would need all the light they could get.

Tissot came back while Justice was still looking closely at the cabin timbers. "Still green," he said with disappointment, driving a thumb-nail into the soft wood.

"The same everywhere." Tissot was also disconsolate. "It would smoke well enough," he said, "but there's no flame in it."

Justice's hope that Fielding had left him a pair of ships that would burn like set-pieces in a firework display had been fading all day, and Lovell's scepticism had almost convinced him. Now there could be no doubt. Unless the hold was stuffed with barrels of tar and turpentine, and there was enough powder on board to turn the *Liberté* into a fire-bomb, they would find it hard to melt a bowl of galleyman's slush.

"And the cargo?" Justice saw that Tissot had found something.

"We can't reach the hold this way," Tissot said, as he led him past the small cabins which must have been used by the mates, and into a narrow companion-way which seemed to run through the centre of the ship. "Racks," he said, striking the plank walls on either side with his boarding-axe. "Barrel after barrel of them. Look."

They came to the place where Lovell had levered out a few of the boards, and he raised his lantern to show them what lay behind. All that Justice could see was the top of a large cask, lying on its side as it would in a wine cellar, with the name of a Bordeaux shipper crudely stencilled on the wood.

"It's quite usual in the wine trade." Tissot was so cool that he could have been a man explaining how he earned his living. "They fill the hold up to the level of the deck, and then they roll more barrels along these racks to trim the ship." Tissot paused, and there was an ironic flatness in his next sentence. "The plank facing is there to save the crews from temptation."

"On both decks?" Justice was beginning to understand why the two brigs lay so low in the water. The weight of these barrels could be enough to capsize them unless the holds were crammed tight.

"I would expect it."

"And can you reach the holds?"

"We could." Tissot was obviously reluctant to try. "We would have to take off the large hatch covers. Or cut through solid timber." He turned his hand palm upwards to emphasise his doubt. "I don't think we've the time or the men or the tools to do it."

While they had been talking, Lovell had been prowling restlessly in the passage ahead of them. He sniffed hard. "D'you smell anything?" He put his nose close to the cask, sniffed again, and shook his head.

"Not much," Justice said. Coming back onto a ship for the first time in months, he had noticed only the familiar and pleasing smell of timber, tar, and cordage.

"That's the point," Lovell exclaimed as though he had made a clever remark. "Believe me. If those barrels were full of wine, I should have smelt it."

"*Eau de vie?*" Tissot suggested, sniffing in his turn.

"That would burn."

"It would indeed," said Lovell. "And what a waste it would

be. But there's no brandy here, either. If this brig was full of wine or cognac, it would reek like a tavern on Saturday night." He ran a finger along the cooper's seams. "It's dry, I tell you. Bone-dry."

"Dry!" Justice heard his own voice, thin and incredulous, as he echoed Lovell. Then what the devil had Fielding's message meant? *New Wine in Old Barrels?* Or No Wine . . . ? Could they all have misread that scribbled note . . . Lilly, Hatherley, Holland . . . ? It was scarcely credible. But in either case Fielding was drawing their attention to the barrels . . .

"Dry!" He said it again as Lovell took the sharp axe that Pierre had found and struck at the flat face of the cask. "But the ship was searched! O'Moira said so."

"Perhaps only the top barrels in the hold," Tissot said. "They would be too lazy to look farther if they were full of wine." He rapped his knuckles on the cask. "And they broached one to sample it." He nodded to Lovell. "Strike again."

"Get it open," Justice said decisively. "More than one if you have to. Paul and I will search below."

But, as Tissot had expected, the lower deck was much the same. More racks. And while Tissot stripped away a few planks to make sure, Justice made his way to the space amidships where the mainmast thrust up through the decks. Even in the guttering light of his lantern, he could see the shafting for the pumps run down it, stapled against the massive trunk of wood to keep it rigid. There was nothing unusual about that—if you were going to have pumps by the mainmast.

As he rejoined Tissot, they heard Lovell call, and they reached the upper deck to find Pierre was there too, back from the *Fraternité*.

"Nothing," he said in a dispirited voice that made Justice even more depressed. "Barrels. Nothing but barrels."

"Empty barrels?"

"No." Lovell had caught the question, although he was standing a few feet along the passageway. "No fear. Full barrels." He raised his lantern so that Justice could see past the splintered wood at the grey and brown powder that had come trickling down as the axe struck into it. "See." He gave the cracked laugh of a bewildered man.

"Sand," he said. "Pebbles. And bloody great pieces of rock!"

He hacked high and hard at the cask and they could all hear the ring of metal on stone. "I'll try another."

"No," Justice said, restraining him. "It's Fielding's ship all right. If that's any comfort to us." He was sure that not even a thieving contractor would deliver a cargo of rocks to Boulogne when the Emperor's commissaries were paying for wine.

And these large and heavy barrels went a long way to explain why the brigs lay so burdened in the water. But why should Fielding go to so much trouble to ship sand and rock to Boulogne?

Unless he wanted the brigs to go down like a stone.

Before Justice could follow that thought, the flames in all their lanterns flickered at once, and the shock of a 32-pounder battery rolled up the harbour and beat against the timbers of the *Liberté* as though they were stretched as tight as a drum-skin.

"It seems that Admiral Keith is about his business, gentlemen." Justice spoke lightly as the rumbling gunfire put an end to his anxiety. "We must make haste if we are to finish our own in time to join him."

❦ 22 ❧

As JUSTICE reached the deck, he saw that the Boulogne defences were a line of fire, the yellow and orange flashes of the guns lighting the town so sharply that he could see the cliffs, houses, and all the mass of shipping as sharply as though they had been painted on a vast canvas. He had never been in a full-scale fleet action, yet the shaking power of this bombardment gave him a sense of what it must have been like as Hood hammered Toulon or as Nelson went in at Copenhagen.

For Keith's squadron was hammering back. Thick smoke was already beginning to roll across the mouth of the harbour, but he could see the sudden bars of red light as the larger ships fired their disciplined broadsides, and moments later the sound followed, as if someone were slamming great doors in an attempt to silence the irregular thumping of the French batteries.

257

With the tolling of the church bells, and the steady crackle of musketry soon adding to it, there was pandemonium in the town. It was bright enough when several guns fired in sequence for Justice to see figures scurrying along the quayside towards the firing line; and the movement of lanterns on many of the moored vessels showed that their crews or their guards had been roused by the uproar.

"You'd think *we* were invading *them*," Lovell shouted, and Justice was less astonished by his words than he would have been earlier that evening. Ever since they had all walked out onto the harbour wall, Lovell had behaved as impeccably as though he were back with his regiment—instead of being a twice-turncoat who had been given the option of making away with himself or taking part in this forlorn hope. Danger seemed to be making him grow back into the man he must once have been.

Justice shook his head. "More row than damage," he yelled back, waving his hand towards the guns. From all he knew of Boulogne Harbour, he doubted whether frigates or the big 60's and 74's could stand in any closer than half a mile from the jetties, and at that range they would be very lucky to do any substantial damage in the harbour. They must simply be giving covering fire to the smaller boats as they came in, and creating as much confusion as possible: it was always encouraging for the men to hear their own shot screaming over, even if it found few targets. But to a man such as Lovell, a soldier who was accustomed to seeing guns rip squares of infantry at close quarters, all this discharge of powder must suggest destruction of a fearsome kind.

And the futility of the attack made the seaman in Justice understand why Lilly and his friends at the Admiralty had backed Fielding's attempt to get at the invasion flotilla in some other way; why Lilly talked so hopefully of new methods and new weapons.

He looked at his companions. They were all caught by the magic of this vast fireworks display, and it was time to break the spell before someone on a nearby vessel began to ask why there was a little cluster of men by the mainmast of the supposedly deserted *Liberté*.

He pulled Tissot and Lovell close enough for them to hear him speak. "Paul," he said. "I want you to search the bottom

258

deck and bilges. Look for false floors or partitions—anything that could conceal barrels or boxes.

"You, Mr Lovell," he went on, slipping back into the formal speech he would have used on his own quarter-deck, "could also be about your business, if you please. Take Magog to help you and set your powder kegs on both brigs. Low, and as far aft as possible. If I can't do anything else, I want to blow the sterns off these beauties and let Admiral Bruix worry about raising them again."

"Fuses?" Lovell asked crisply.

"Ten minutes, or as near as you can. Not more, or the Frenchies may get on board in time to blow them out. And not less, Mr Lovell, or you may blow us out of this world."

Pierre and Gog stood waiting for their instructions.

"A long rope," Justice said carefully, "and weighted so that we can pass it under the bow and draw it back towards the middle of the ship. Cut part of the running rigging if you can find nothing to suit."

Pierre's hesitation was as good as a direct question.

"Do you know what the English word 'keel-hauling' means?" For the moment he could not think of the French equivalent, and he tried a simple way to make Pierre and Gog grasp the point. "To pass a man under the bottom of the ship," he said, as he began to strip and felt the October air chill on his skin.

It would be very cold in the water.

THE ROPE SNAGGED, came free, and snagged again, about ten feet from the foremast.

"We can pull it to and fro between us," Pierre said, showing him how it ran clear round the keel, "but we can't drag it any farther back."

"Fine." Justice surprised Pierre by his reaction. "So I could be right."

It had seemed a very foolish idea when it first came to him, and he knew that he would be risking his life in an attempt to prove it. But it was possible, and Captain Cochrane had once tried something of the kind with a fire-ship. It was the only way to make sense of those pumps—those damned peculiar pumps, so firmly clamped that they must be resisting a great strain.

"One tug," he reminded Pierre as he swung over the side,

"and Gog pulls. Two tugs, stop pulling. Three tugs, you pull me up. As fast as you can, or I'll be blue in the face before you see me." Then he was lowering himself cautiously into the gurgling and eddying water, so bitingly chill that it took his breath away. He would be doing well if he could spend much more than a minute at a time below the surface.

The line ran taut to a hitch in his belt. It would drag him sideways under the water, and if he was not careful how it tipped him, it would cut painfully into his crotch or even strangle him. But he had to leave his hands and legs free, so that he could push away from the bottom and the barnacles that could tear his skin to ribbons.

He took a twist of the rope round his left hand, looked up at Pierre gazing anxiously down from the deck, and gave the sharp tug that told Gog to start pulling.

Down. The rope snatched at him in great jerks, as Gog dragged it hand-over-hand. Down. Slowly. As if he were crawling across the slimy bottom of the hull like a great clumsy crab.

Down. At five feet he could see more than he expected, as the continuous flashes in the sky filtered through the clear water, but at ten feet, as he came under the curve to the keel, it was quite black.

Down. His lungs were already under pressure, and he knew that in a few more seconds he must make a break for the surface. But Gog was still heaving at his end of the line.

Two tugs, and the rope still pulled his belt hard under his ribs. Then it eased, and he gave three tugs, scrabbling hard for the air before Pierre had time to take the strain on the rope.

He gasped, getting as much spray as air into his mouth, and then called softly to Pierre to lower him a boarding-axe. He had realised that there was no way of getting deep enough if he had to rely on the rope and his bare hands, slipping on the seaweed and sore with slashes from the encrusting shells. The pick on the back of the axe might give him a better hold.

And he could try to swing himself round and feel with his feet, for that could give him a longer reach. It wasn't the depth that was beating him, but the width of the vessel. He would need to crawl ten or twelve feet under it to reach the centre line . . . the line of the pumps.

So down again. Bumping and slithering, and the harder Gog pulled to help him down, the more the twisting belt threatened to squeeze the air out of his lungs. His eyes were smarting now, as the salt washed at them, and he bunched his eyelids tight. It didn't matter. There was no light down there by which he could see anything, anyway.

He got a purchase with the axe, though the water so deadened the movement of his arm that he made more of a dab than a strike, and it was enough to let him pull himself round, and down again.

Now he was face upwards, pressed hard against the bottom of the hull, feeling that within seconds he would gasp out the stale breath that was beginning to feel like a great stone within his chest. Then die there. Miserably. Kicking and flailing against the unyielding timbers.

It was the first convulsive kick, at the onset of panic, that touched the chain. He felt the links slip past his toes, and then the feel of the chain was gone, for he had pushed it away as he struck out and up, tugging in a frenzy for Pierre to haul him back to the surface.

That method would not work. He must try another.

Up on the deck, dripping and bent double as he gulped in huge breaths of air, he heard Pierre trying to dissuade him from a third attempt.

"It can't be done, Jean," he said, and even as Justice clutched at his aching ribs, he was warmed by the way in which Pierre had used his name for the first time.

"It can," he answered fiercely, standing straight in his determination. "Fetch the boat-hook." The long wooden pole with the curving spike was the only thing he could think of that would give him sufficient reach; and if it was fastened to the line and pulled down ahead of him . . . if he could find it, fumbling for the line in the dark and the cold, while his blood thumped in his veins.

"It can," he said defiantly as he climbed across to the *Fraternité* and up into the shrouds to judge his aim and distance. "It must be."

He had done something like it before, in the clear waters of English Harbour, when he had watched the Antiguan slave-children dive right under a sloop and had decided that he could do the same.

But could he do it again here in this patchwork of blackness and glaring gun-fire that lay on the rippling water? Too high, and he would go into the mud at the harbour bottom. Too low, and he would not have the speed and the depth. And if he missed the yard or so of water at which he was aiming, he would crack his head on the timbers of one brig or the other.

Pierre and Gog pulled the boat-hook into place, and then Pierre came across to the rail and called across to Justice as he took his balance on the rat-lines. "Three tugs," he said, "and I come for you."

Then Justice was arcing down between the two hulls like a porpoise at the end of a great leap, swimming downwards and under as the water slowed his dive, and suddenly catching the rope well enough to feel his way to the boat-hook and grab it. He had thirty seconds, or a few more, before he would have to break free.

One. Two. Three. Four. He was counting as he swung the long pole clumsily in the water. *Five. Six. Seven.* It caught, slid loose. *Eight. Nine.* As Justice twisted the hook, it tripped into the chain, and he dragged himself through the trailing seaweed until he could touch the links with his hand. *Fifteen. Sixteen.* He had already brought himself round to face aft and follow the line of sagging links as they looped gently upwards. *Twenty. Twenty-one.* He could feel a large shackle, and a thick metal pin which was set in a plate and ran down through the eye of a shaft. *Twenty-four. Twenty-five.* The feeling of relief was so great that he almost let his breath go in a fatal gasp. *Twenty-six.* He felt farther. Only a large and sloping wooden box, a kind of kennel, fixed to the hull. *Twenty-seven.* His left hand clutching at the shackle to give him leverage, he made a last convulsive lunge and found his fingers running up a slit in the bottom of the box, and at the far end he could touch the fluke of a small anchor.

Twenty-nine. Thirty. Thirty-one. He caught himself just in time as he began the rhythmic counting that would have raced on and on until his mouth ripped open in the last despairing gasp.

Downwards again. It was the only way to be sure of clearing the hull. Still downwards, as his arms seemed to pull from his shoulders and his legs failed, and the water seemed to grip his chest like a cold iron jacket. Downwards and outwards, and the lightning of the guns was turning the water into scarlet glass as he used his last strength to kick himself away from the side of the brig.

The effort was too much, forcing the dead air out of him as he broke the surface and felt himself spinning into a whirl that seemed like a nightmare in the middle of sleep.

He slumped in the water and the tide was bumping him against the timbers of the *Liberté* before Pierre reached him, getting a rope under his armpits. It was all that Pierre and Gog could do to hoist him up to the rail and hold him there until Tissot came to help them topple him over onto the deck.

The drumming in his ears faded back into the thunder of the guns and he heard Tissot's anxious voice. "Is he dead?"

Justice forced his chest out to pull in a gasp of air that gave Tissot his answer; he opened his eyes, saw the spars sway and then steady themselves above him, sat up, and found Tissot offering him one of the bottles they had brought from the net-house.

"*Eau de vie*, Jean," he said for the second time that night. This time he spoke truly, and Justice gulped gratefully at the harsh spirit, washing the salt and mud from his mouth, feeling its raw warmth coursing into his chilled and shivery body.

His hands and his knees, his face, his back and buttocks were all smarting with a score of deep scratches, and as Pierre rubbed the water from him with a fragment of sail-cloth from the locker, it was turning black and carmine from the gun-flashes—and from the blood that was oozing everywhere.

Tissot gasped as Justice stood up, seeing the great stitched scar on his chest for the first time, and thinking it a new one; but Pierre shook his head to reassure him.

"He's a strong one," he said admiringly, as they helped Justice below. "One of us, aren't you, Jean?" And Justice knew that he meant the remark as the greatest of compliments.

THEY WERE ALL in the captain's cabin, where the guns were muted enough for normal speech, and Justice had hunched the straw-and-canvas palliasse about him to keep himself warm and to take up the blood that was still red and wet on his back.

"It's very simple, really," he said, as he started to tell what he had found.

They all laughed, with the nervous cordiality of relief at his survival.

"Each of these brigs has been given two extra, and hidden,

anchors." Justice took the cognac bottle, soon emptied when they stood by the table, to serve as a model of the hull. "One that lies under the foremast." He pointed to the bottom of the bottle, then moved his finger towards the neck. "That one must be bolted to the hull just behind the bow." He pointed back. "The other is held under the mainmast, and it must be bolted just forward of the stern."

"But why?" It was Lovell again, always curious about details.

"That really is simple. Lord Cochrane tried it once. That was how I guessed." Justice laid the bottle on the table, made as if to move it, and left it where it was. "If you get a fire-ship into position, there is a good chance that once you abandon it, the enemy will be able to drag it away, or cut the anchor cable to let it drift on somewhere where it will do no harm."

"Well?" Lovell pressed him.

"Suppose the enemy tries to move the vessel and fails . . . suppose he can't find what holds it where it is . . . before it burns, or explodes, or sinks . . . Look . . ." Justice now held two short pieces of rope so that they seemed to dangle from the bottle. "Two small anchors and two short chains. Nothing more is needed. They weren't ever intended for use in heavy winds or a strong sea. Fielding knew that they would only be used in a harbour—this harbour—against the run of the tide through the channel."

"Two would be enough." Tissot saw at once how it would be worked.

"You are sure of the second?" Pierre was as sceptical as Lovell.

"Not certain, but sure enough. There must be two. There are two pumps—one behind each mast."

"The pumps?" It was Tissot's turn to be puzzled, for he had not been with Justice and Pierre when they had examined the curious pumps with a locking collar, and he listened carefully while Justice described them.

"I see." He looked thoughtful. "You think the anchors are fastened to them in some way."

"In some way, yes. But not directly, because the combined weight of the chain and the anchor would tear away from any fastening if they hung full on that collar and pin."

How could he make them see something which he had never seen himself, and had only fleetingly touched with his fingers?

"I believe the pumps are like triggers," he said. "Release the handles and you let the anchors fall."

"But how?" Pierre was fascinated.

"So far as I can tell, the anchors lie in those sloping boxes like a chute, with a slit along the bottom to let the third fluke slide out. Until the anchor is released, the box takes the strain."

"But why doesn't the weight of the chain pull them out?" Tissot had obviously been drawing a diagram in his head, seeing the sag of the chain just as definitely as Justice had felt it.

"Because they are secured by a bolt that goes into the eye of the anchor—the other end of the trigger, so to speak."

"And those bolts rise to the pump-handles?" Tissot sounded impressed.

"I don't think so. They seem to be part of a metal plate that's set flush to the hull. I think it is that plate which is secured to the pump-handle—perhaps by a smaller chain rising to the shaft of the pump just below the leather washer."

"I see." Lovell had grasped at once how it would work, and he was pleased with himself. "Strike the pin out, up flies the handle, the chain drops, the plate falls out of the bottom of the boat, and the weight of the chain then hauls the anchor out of the . . . er . . . whatsit, the kennel . . . like a dog! You're right, Justice. It is simple. Damned simple. Damn clever, too."

"But the plates?" Tissot was thorough.

"Scuttle-plates," Justice said with a finishing flourish, throwing off the palliasse and reaching for his clothes. "Not much over a foot square, I should say. But drop them off the bottom, with all this weight in the boat, and you'll have water spraying up in unstoppable fountains."

Lovell was right. Fielding's idea had been damned simple, like all good ideas. And damned clever, as Lovell had said. Fielding had built a weapon so innocent in appearance that it could be sailed right into Boulogne Harbour, and searched, without raising any suspicions at all.

Now it was up to him to use it, and well.

"Jean." In the stress and the excitement, he had forgotten that Tissot had also been grubbing around the bottom of the ship, on the other side of the timbers. "You found nothing?" He knew there was nothing more to find, because he had at last solved the mystery of Fielding's ships.

"Oh yes." Tissot surprised him. "A great deal . . ."

". . . of what?" Justice had not expected anything more after the discovery of those rows of rock-filled barrels.

"Water. I suspect those pumps were never touched on the voyage. The captain wouldn't have wanted anyone looking too closely at them—or making mistakes, and sending the brig to the bottom. And new ships leak a good deal until the timbers swell, Jean."

"And what else?" Justice saw that Tissot was at his usual game of eking out surprises to get the best effect from them. "Rocks, again."

"Not rocks, in fact. Stones. Large stones, flat stones, cut like masonry, and laid between a false deck and the bottom timbers. It was hard to see, but I got up enough planking to get the idea."

"Masonry?" It was Justice who now had to guess at something he had not seen. "Ballast, surely?"

"No. Masonry." Tissot was definite. "Like stones locked in a pavement, or at the base of a harbour wall. Or a dam."

"That's what it is!" Justice was now as pleasurably excited as Lovell had been a few minutes earlier. "A dam. The whole brig has been built as a dam. The base. The frame. The barrels of rock. Not a fire-ship at all. But a dam." He looked at Lovell. "Good for you, Mr Lovell," he said. "You were nearer than any of us."

A floating dam. A dam that could be moved without anyone noticing, and dropped precisely where it would cause the most trouble.

Three dams, in fact, were what Fielding had intended. One for the entrance to the basin. One for each end of the channel to the sea. As the pieces of the puzzle at last fitted into place, he marvelled at the simplicity of the scheme.

If the plan was carried out as the flotilla began to move down from the basin and through the harbour, it would ruin everything for Bonaparte.

Even now, tonight, he could block the basin and the channel for long enough to keep the flotilla in Boulogne for a week or more, and then the westerlies would roar up the coasts of Sussex and Kent and make any kind of invasion impossible before the end of the winter.

The five men stood looking at him expectantly, waiting to be told how they would now finish what Fielding had begun so many months ago.

"Matthew Fielding!" Justice picked up the bottle and threw it into a corner to crash like a glass tossed into a fire after a toast. "May God save his soul."

"And ours." For once there was no irony in Lovell's voice.

⤙ 23 ⤚

PIERRE AND TISSOT had already gone forward and cut the bow mooring-cables when Lovell, carrying a length of smouldering slow-match, hauled himself up on the mainmast shrouds to cross into the *Fraternité*. "I'll say this for you, Justice," he said, linking an elbow through the ropes so that he could hold out his right hand. "You're as straight as your name." As Justice took his hand, he nodded confidingly. "Don't worry about me. I'll do my part all right."

In the light of a salvo from the Boulogne batteries, glaring through the drifting smoke, Justice saw him pause at the hatchway of the *Fraternité*, give a wave, and go down to find Magog and his keg of powder.

"On the next swing," Tissot said as Justice went aft to join him at the stern, lifting his axe so that Pierre on the *Fraternité* could clearly see what he was about. Both brigs had begun to pull hard on their stern moorings as the tide and the wind pushed at them, and Justice was trying to calculate how fast they would move when they rode free. It could be fifty yards a minute, give or take a little.

"The Irishman! The Irishman!" Gog was running back through the waist of the *Liberté*, shouting at the top of his voice, and Justice was so surprised that he could barely grasp what the man was saying.

"Cut as you're ready," he called to Tissot, going forwards again with Gog. All the more reason for speed if O'Moira had somehow got himself free and was on his way in a last desperate attempt to stop them.

As he was.

But before Justice could reach the bow, the two brigs shuddered and lifted as first Tissot and then Pierre cut the stern cables, forcing the bows round to get the best effect from the breeze and the water that was now flowing back down the Liane; and they came round so far that Justice had to cross to the *Fraternité* to see what Gog was trying to tell him.

About thirty yards away, and coming on like a water-beetle, was an eight-oared guard-boat, with a mounted swivel gun and four or five soldiers in the bow. Gog was right. The bulky figure standing like a statue in the stern, urging the rowers to speed, was unmistakably O'Moira. The light was erratic, but it was good enough for that.

"Put your hats on," Justice said quickly to Gog, and to Magog, who had come up to join them with a pair of pistols in his hands. Perhaps those foolish plumes might be just enough to cause confusion. "And challenge them when they come within hail."

He knew as he spoke that the subterfuge would gain him little, except to make O'Moira more cautious if he tried to board the brig, and hesitant about firing the swivel; and any delay would help while the brigs were slowly beginning to move through the water. The time he would need to get to the basin entrance, and then on to the channel of the Liane, had already begun to pass as inexorably as Lovell's fuses would burn once the slow-match touched them off. He saw the whole harbour before him, like the model he had toyed with in the net-house, and his mind had fallen easily into its old ways of calculating angles and speeds like a problem in Euclid. If no one interfered, he was sure he could get both brigs near enough to where he wanted to place them.

But the sums he was doing in his head also told him that O'Moira might very well interfere: that guard-boat would be alongside in a matter of a minute or so, and they could not prevent it. There was no way in which these drifting brigs could evade a well-rowed boat that was already so close—and no powder or ball to hand with which to try even a warning shot with a gun.

Justice looked again, as Gog and Magog came up and displayed themselves clearly, their plumes swaying in the breeze, and what he saw dismayed him.

Lucienne was also in the boat. The small figure wrapped in a boat-cloak, sitting with her hand up to steady O'Moira as he stood, could be nobody else.

Had the clever-witted Irishman brought her with him to make sure that no one fired into his boat? Or had she come of her own free will, guiding and helping the blind man to the last?

And how had they managed to escape?

"Challenge. Argue if you can. But hold your fire." It was doubtful whether O'Moira would hear a hail until he was under the brig's quarter, but there was nothing that Gog and Magog could do with a pair of pistols.

Justice hurried back to the *Liberté,* passing Pierre by the mainmast and telling him to cut the first set of lashings where they came through the ship's side and were looped round a pair of bitts. And to make sure that Lovell knew what was happening.

O'Moira's oarsmen must have brought his boat on faster than Justice had expected, or else the current had brought the brigs down on it, for O'Moira seemed already to have passed and ignored Gog and Magog. They threw away their useless shakos and jumped back into the *Liberté,* ready to drop the forecourse as Pierre cut the last of the ties linking her to the *Fraternité.*

There was nothing Justice could do until Lovell came up and Pierre could finish his task. Behind him, he could tell, Tissot was wrestling with the wheel, making sure that the rudder was hard over as soon as the sail began to draw. And then he realised that he must go back to the *Fraternité* to join Lovell in knocking out the pins that would release the hidden anchors and flood the brig. It was too soon, really, for they were still two hundred yards from the basin entrance, but the grapnels were bound to drag a little. In any case, the sooner they caught, the better, for they would drag the *Fraternité* away and leave O'Moira to board an empty ship.

There was a wink of red light near the stern of the *Fraternité* and the whine of a pistol ball across the deck. One of O'Moira's men had been quick to clamber up, and in a few moments there would be several of them, with muskets being passed up from the guard-boat.

Justice could not tell whether the man had aimed at him, or Tissot, or Pierre, or whether the shot was simply a challenge.

Pierre put his axe down and reached for his own pistol.

"No." Justice shouted, doubting whether his voice would carry. "We may want them later." Once fired, there would be no chance to reload, and they might well need all four pistols to hold off the guards until there was an unjumpable gap between the two brigs.

He looked at the last set of lashings, straining and creaking. They dared not cut them until Lovell came.

What was the man doing?

Justice peered hard at the hatchway of the *Fraternité*, but there was no sign of him. Farther aft, however, there were several men clustered together on the deck: the guard-boat must carry a rope-ladder if so many could reach the deck so quickly.

And among them, O'Moira.

He was walking forward, feeling his way along the ship's side, carrying a large white kerchief in his free hand, waving it backwards and forwards above his head. A flag of truce.

Justice let him come on until they were opposite each other.

"Very well, O'Moira," he called. "State your business."

Each step, each sentence, took them a yard closer to the basin. If only Lovell would come.

"A safe-conduct, Mr Justice." The soft polite voice carried astonishingly well under the noise of the guns. "Surrender the ships and you go free. Back to England." It was not clear whether the blind O'Moira could tell that the brigs were already moving.

"No." Justice could think of nothing more to say than the curt reply.

"And Major Lovell, of course." The afterthought confirmed what Justice was already thinking. The offer was not a trap— for him. O'Moira was offering nothing to the four Frenchmen.

"You're too late," Justice called to O'Moira, putting the uncomfortable thought away from him. "Get back. *Get back!*" His voice cracked into hoarseness with the ferocity of his cry. "Lovell has lit the fuses."

"You are trying to fool me," O'Moira said. "It was a last chance. Now take the consequences."

He began to move backwards, still holding up the kerchief like a talisman of safety, and as he did so, the last of the lashings began to snap under the growing strain. Justice, up on the rail, reached for the shrouds of the *Fraternité*, touched them

270

with his finger-tips, and knew that he had no hope of holding the brigs for a second more. He was still looking at O'Moira when out of the corner of his eye he saw Lovell move in the shadows.

Lovell took in the situation at a glance. O'Moira was only a yard or two from the hatchway when he stepped out and put a pistol to the Irishman's side.

At the same time, and before it was clear that Lovell was holding O'Moira hostage as they walked together towards the mainmast, the guards standing on the poop fired a ragged volley which whistled over the *Liberté*. But in that poor light, with so few targets, Justice decided, they were doing it more to impress O'Moira than in the hope of hitting anyone or doing any damage to the ship.

For the gap was widening. It was a yard. It doubled, and there was clear water, as Gog and Magog let the large forecourse fall to flap and shiver as it began to catch the wind. It was not much, but it was more than enough.

Justice stood still, while Tissot went back to join Pierre at the wheel, for he could not take his eyes off Lovell and O'Moira. They had reached the first of the pumps when he saw that Lovell had raised his right hand, swinging a boarding-axe wide and flat to bring it in sharp against the pin in the pump collar.

It was dark for a few moments, and then, like another tableau lit by the gun-flashes, Justice saw that they had reached the foremast.

So he had been right. Lovell must have seen the handle fly up on the first pump before he moved on to the second.

He never saw Lovell strike the second blow, for the *Liberté* was turning and pulling away; and he had not even begun to think what would happen to Lovell before he realised that the major must have lit his fuses before he came on deck and saw the *Liberté* moving away so fast that it would seem that Justice had abandoned him.

But he had done his duty.

With O'Moira on board.

And Lucienne in the guard-boat alongside.

Justice felt sick at heart, and he walked back to join Pierre and Tissot, knowing there was nothing he could now do.

Except count the minutes.

IT WAS NO WAY to sail a ship, with the large foresail hanging slack and sloppy, but it was giving Tissot just enough steerage-way to bring the head round as the *Liberté* cleared the entrance to the basin and drifted towards the narrowing channel.

But not enough to take the brig clear of the first row of the *prames*, troop-carrying vessels almost as big as the brigs, which were tied up in groups of three all down the south side of the Liane. The *Liberté* might be setting across the stream as she went down on them, but the impact was bound to twist her even if her rigging did not become entangled in the yards of the *prames*.

"Jean!" Tissot shouted at Justice, who was still watching to see what was happening to the *Fraternité*. "*Jean!*" His voice carried, and Justice looked along the line of his pointing arm. The sterns of the *prames* were little more than fifty yards away.

Pierre was already hurrying forward, his figure seeming to move in a succession of jerks like a puppet as the gun-flashes lit his movements, and as he reached Gog and Magog he took his place on the line as they struggled to tauten the flapping canvas. Justice was about to run after him when he saw a cluster of sparks on the deck of the *Fraternité*. The thought that they were caused by Lovell's fuse came and went so quickly that he knew they were musket shots before the popping sound carried over the water.

O'Moira must be desperate if he thought they could hit anyone at this distance.

They must be shooting at Lovell, of course. They would have cut him down if he still had the pistol in his hand.

And then he knew, as Tissot groaned and lurched and his body spun down the spokes of the wheel, that by the wildest chance a stray ball from that volley had found a dreadful mark.

Justice was beside Tissot at once, ready to take the wheel, while Pierre did his best with the sail.

But Tissot was on his knees, his right hand still firmly grasping a spoke, and Justice thought that he was trying to lever himself to his feet. "No, Paul. I have it." He put his hand to Tissot's left shoulder and found the torn cloth wet and sticky.

"No. No." Tissot was grunting, holding the wheel hard down with his uninjured arm, and Justice could see that he might have strength enough to keep the helm hard over for the few vital minutes it would take to get the *Liberté* across the stream.

In any case, there was no choice. Unless they could catch more wind, their short voyage would come to a futile end, with the *Liberté* causing no more trouble than any other ship that became snarled along the side of the harbour—and with so many vessels huddled together, that could easily happen two or three times a week.

If the brig were on fire, that would have been a different matter.

Justice faced the fact that he had never before tried to handle a vessel of this size with so few men. They might as well have been in a dismasted hulk drifting onto a lee shore.

Then there were only images, and quick responses.

Gog and Magog, scrambling up the foremast rat-lines . . . Pierre pointing up at another sail they might cut free . . . Pierre making room for him on the end of the foresail sheet, which they were hauling as if they were trying to wear the ship round by the force of their bare hands . . . twenty yards . . . figures on the poop of one of the *prames* waving lanterns . . . beyond the bow, in the surges of light from the battle, a church steeple slowly crossing his line of vision like a steering mark in a channel . . . the line of the harbour, stretching away now on both sides of the brig . . . the curious deadening of noise, as though someone had thrown a great blanket over the guns . . .

And then he felt the shock before the noise came roaring and thumping again, and the *Liberté* seemed to be painted in a deep red glow.

Thirty yards away, Lovell's powder keg had blown out the stern of the *Fraternité,* and as Justice and Pierre swung instinctively to face the explosion, they could see that the brig was settling fast.

Lovell. O'Moira. Lucienne.

Had all three of them perished in that blast?

Or had Lucienne at least been rowed clear in the guard-boat?

Lucienne. Lovell. O'Moira.

The names beat in his head as he saw that they were no more than ten yards from the outermost *prame* and that men were leaning along the rail with rope fenders and poles.

It was close. Closer. Justice could see the men clearly enough to mark their anxious expressions, and then he saw them pointing up. High up the mast, part of the topsail hung loose at a crazy angle.

Gog and Magog had done their best. It had been just good enough. There was a bump. Another bump, sending a shudder down the brig and setting the masts swaying. But they were clear.

Pierre thumped his arm and pointed. Justice followed his gaze. Gog and Magog had done their best, but they were gone. The shock of the explosion on the *Fraternité* must have shaken them loose from the yard. Or surprised them into losing their grip. Even experienced seamen sometimes lost their hold in the excitement of a battle. Or the shudder as they hit the *prame* could have shaken them off.

But in that case they would have come hurtling down to the deck . . . As the *Liberté* slid crabwise into the channel, Justice saw the men on the *prame* were cheering as if they had just seen a feat of seamanship . . . Gog and Magog . . . Justice was hoping that Pierre would remember to cut the foresail halyard . . . Gog and Magog had gone . . . and Tissot's words came back to him . . . They know how to take care of themselves . . . With their task done, they must have slipped quietly over the side . . . Good luck to them . . . Tissot . . . Now there were only Pierre and himself to do the work of six men . . . If Tissot could keep the helm locked over . . . Tissot . . . An axe . . . an axe to drive out the locking pin on °the pump-handle . . . There was too much . . . Slower, think . . . Lovell's powder train . . . Could he light it, with Tissot lying there . . . ?

There was a wrenching, flapping sound, and the foresail was sagging all over the deck . . . While Justice tried to piece his thoughts together, he realised that Pierre had not waited for the order to cut the halyard. And that he was already at the foremast pump, looking for the signal to strike.

And Justice had no axe. It came to him that he was exhausted and that everything was slowing to a state where he neither felt nor cared what was happening to him.

No axe. Useless to scrabble on the deck, searching.

They were lying fully across the channel, with the tide pulling them exactly as he had hoped. And Tissot had put them there. Exactly.

Then he saw, on the locker, the pistol he had laid down when he ran to help Pierre haul on the sheet.

He had already taken it by the muzzle and raised it to shoulder height to use the butt as a club when he saw Pierre take his cue and knock the pin out of the foremast pump. There was something wrong, and he could not force his mind to note it. Then he saw the lock of the pistol.

It was loaded. It was primed. It was cocked.

If he hit the butt against the pin the shock would fire it. With the muzzle pointing straight at his chest.

He checked the blow, reversed the gun, and blew the pin out of the collar in a continuous movement, standing so close that he could feel the swish of the handle as it came free and flew upwards with such force that Justice knew for certain that his guess had been right.

Pierre was at his side before the first grapnel snatched at the bottom of the stream, and for a second Justice feared that the *Liberté* would swing on it and lie fore-and-aft in the channel. That would be better than nothing, but . . . It snatched again, and held, just as the anchor dropping from behind the mainmast dragged through the mud and bit into the sand and gravel beneath.

The *Liberté* stopped. Not suddenly, but with a slowing jerk that made the masts tip, lurch, and pull the hull so far over that water splashed over the larboard gunwales, and Justice and Pierre grabbed at each other to keep their feet on the inclined deck.

It was done now. Justice felt the lethargy of relief sweep over him as Pierre, still holding his arm, put the anxious question. "Paul?"

As Justice waved him towards the slumped figure at the wheel, it came to him that one thing had still to be done. Boats were already putting out from the quayside, where there were gaps between the tied-up ships, and a guard-boat was rowing fast down channel towards them.

Could it be O'Moira? Again? And Lucienne?

He steeled himself against such thoughts. He had to light Lovell's powder-train.

Even if he had to stay with Tissot, waiting while the fuse hissed and spluttered away the last minutes of their lives.

He fumbled his way through the hatch, chiding himself for

failing to look where Lovell had placed his powder, and saw a lighted lantern on the floor of the captain's cabin.

As he ducked in through the doorway to fetch it, he realised what Lovell had done, and he was mystified, and dismayed.

There would be no explosion here. Nothing powerful, at any rate. For the keg had been forced and powder scattered over the remains of the splintered chairs and table; and the brandy bottles, uncorked, had been carefully placed next to the half-empty keg in the makings of the bonfire.

Justice felt a stir of breeze, and saw that two of the stern windows had been smashed open to create a draught.

So Lovell had been a fool, after all! But the angry thought faded as Justice understood that Lovell had known very well what he was doing. In a green ship, without other combustibles, there would have been no fire after an explosion—he had stored that fact in his mind as he had watched the *Fraternité* going down without any sign of flames. With no fire to deter them, therefore, the French would be on board in a trice, trying to find and stop the holes where the water was pouring into the *Liberté*.

But if there was a fire, no one would take the risk of climbing on board, in case the *Liberté* blew up like the other brig; and while the fire burned, the ship would be settling, settling, and once she lay on the bottom, the French would never be able to get at the holes where the plates had been and the water was now gushing in as though the bottom had been ripped on a rock. For those holes would lie beneath the layer of stone that Tissot had found, and . . . never . . . until the casks and the hull timbers and the stones were all shifted . . . never would be at least a week, and in war a week could make the difference between victory and defeat.

The reasoning had brought his thoughts down to a steadier pace again, and his hand was firm as he smashed the glass of the lantern and pitched it on the fuse that led to Lovell's pyre.

It was the same gesture of farewell that he had made to Fielding in this cabin less than an hour ago.

"Poor devil," he said. "And thanks."

THE SMOKE was already curling up to make a natural chimney of the hatchway as Justice reached the wheel to find Pierre supporting Tissot, who was scrabbling feebly at his coat buttons.

"He is trying to reach his wound," Pierre said. "But it is useless." The dark stain that was seeping through the cloth and onto the deck told Justice that Pierre was right. The musketball must have smashed into Tissot's shoulder and cut the artery far too high for any tourniquet to be of use.

Justice saw Tissot's eyes open as he began to unfasten the gilt buttons on the harbour-master's coat.

"Jean." Justice saw rather than heard Tissot's lips frame his name. "Jean." Tissot made another effort, and Justice thought he was saying *cher ami* . . . Then his fingers were slipping through the blood that was soaking across Tissot's body.

As Justice took the packet, he felt Tissot's body shudder and knew that he had gone.

Pierre was weeping as he stood up. "Such a heart," he said. "Such a man." He waited while Justice straightened Tissot's limbs and stood to salute him.

"He would have liked that." Pierre bent his head for a moment, and then looked at the packet which Justice was putting into his pocket. "There is something more?" he asked, but he did not press the question.

Justice was already at the downstream side of the brig, watching the fire begin to curl out of the stern and up through the hatchway, and he realised that the boat on which they had rowed out to the *Liberté* was still tied to the mainmast shrouds and lying out of sight of the guard-boat, which must have backed off higher up the channel at the sight of the fire. "We have a chance," he called to Pierre, pulling the boat alongside.

"You first." Pierre was urgent, and as Justice went over the side, he saw Pierre go back and stoop low to pick something off the deck.

He was in the boat and unshipping the oars when Pierre came up to the rail and tossed two objects down to him. One of them he caught, soft and floppy. It was his hat. The other flopped softly onto one of the thwarts.

"You must look like an officer," Pierre said, "if you and I are to have any hope of getting out of this alive." He cut the rope and took the oars from Justice. "Sit upright, in the stern."

It seemed odd to Justice, before he remembered that no one except O'Moira and Lucienne had any idea what they looked like. Pierre was right. Once they were clear of the *Liberté,* they might be safe. He shifted his seat, found something soft to his hand.

It was the cheese that Tissot had brought on board.

Pierre looked at him. "Hungry men don't run far," he said, with the wry common sense that Justice had come to like and respect in him. It was the kind of remark that Fred Scorcher would have made in such perilous circumstances.

"What the devil!" Justice exclaimed as Pierre suddenly swung the boat round to head towards the brig again, now with water half up the hull and flames rising all around the poop. It seemed an extraordinary thing for Pierre to stop to watch it go down.

"Stand up and point and shout," Pierre said. "That's what you would be doing if you really were a captain in the National Guard." Justice could hear the sarcasm in his voice. "And keeping clear of any danger, of course."

Justice did what he suggested, as other boats came up and lay on the water all about them, waiting and watching, and he thought how well Pierre had learned Tissot's lessons. Draw attention to yourself. Be what people expect you to be. Look busy, not furtive. If he survived this night, he would long remember those maxims.

All the time, while Justice went through his pantomime of excitement, Pierre was letting the boat drift a little with the current. Never enough to make a show of it, but enough to let other boats come up past them and lie nearer the brig; enough to move with the current, and always edging gradually towards the south bank of the Liane.

"It is no use going towards the sea," Pierre said, guessing his thoughts. "The attack is failing."

Justice had been so preoccupied that he had not noticed that the gun-fire was becoming more sporadic, that there were no more flares, and only scattered musket-shots.

There had been four or five big explosions, somewhere among that forest of masts, but that was all, and he could now see a couple of Keith's fire-ships drifting ineffectively past the harbour mouth, the trailing flames dying away as they burned to the water. So the wind had been wrong. Or the booms had been too much for Keith's ships. Or the French batteries had been too powerful.

He looked back. At least something had been done that night. It was too dark to see what had happened to the *Fraternité*, but the *Liberté* was across the channel, and her deck was awash.

Nothing of any size would pass in or out of the inner harbour for a week or more. They would have to tear Fielding's legacy to pieces timber by timber, stone by stone.

Perhaps that was enough. Perhaps that was all Fielding would have expected of him.

Of them all.

"Come on," he said to Pierre. "Let's make a run for it."

He must get back to England. With Tissot's packet.

And he had not the slightest idea how he would do it.

⤙ 24 ⤚

THERE WAS so much confusion around the harbour that night that Justice and Pierre found it surprisingly easy to make their way to the line of hills that lay south of the Liane valley. The English attack had been so spectacular, though little damage seemed to have been done, that patrols and pickets all round the edge of the port were more eager to know what had been going on than to ask uncomfortable questions—especially from a wounded captain in the National Guard, who had obviously been in the thick of the fight. With lacerations on his face and hands, blood on his shirt, tears in his uniform, mud on his shoes and stockings, Justice could look the part to the life without any effort, and Pierre's rough and unshaven appearance was all that was needed to create the impression that Justice was bravely making his way home to Montreuil with the help of a friendly sailor.

Justice got far more salutes than doubtful glances, and the pair of them were offered so many fortifying tots of wine and spirit that Justice had to tip them aside in the dark to avoid giving offence or taking too much.

The dawn was breaking in great bars of grey and yellow cloud, and washed patches of pale green sky, when they passed

Pont de Briques lying in the valley below them and saw the first light touch the turrets of the little square château which Bonaparte had made his headquarters.

"Do you think he's there now?" Justice nudged Pierre, cocking his head down the hill, wondering whether Boney was sleeping behind one of the shuttered windows that made the building look like a neat doll's house.

"He was here last week, they say." It might have been Pierre's business, for all Justice knew, to keep Tissot informed about the comings and goings of the man who had just made himself Emperor of France. "And there's to be a ball at the end of the month for all the officers and their wives." Pierre was speaking with sardonic bite. "To celebrate his royal coronation!" He made a disdainful gesture with his hand. "A Corsican," he said. "A Corsican king in the Tuileries!" He yawned, stretched his arms, and led the way into the edge of a thicket where they could lie concealed yet watch the sweeping grassland that ran down to the road.

"We'll be safe enough here for a while," Pierre said, though Justice noticed that he took his knife from his belt and kept it close to hand.

They sat there for a while without speaking. They had both been too distraught and too tired to think of anything but getting away from the port, where there would now be a hue-and-cry for the wreckers who had blocked the channel.

In their silence there was also a shared grief for Tissot.

"You should leave me." Justice lay back against the trunk of a tree and watched the morning clouds forming into great fleets of fluffy white sails. He had come through the night, against all his expectations, but it was doubtful whether he would survive another—except to see the sun come up as a shaft of light through a cell window. Pierre would be much safer without him.

Pierre, indeed, took the point straightforwardly, without any false show of protest. "You're right," he conceded, giving Justice an appraising look. "Our work is done. Well done, too." He paused, then put his question so apologetically that Justice could tell that he was torn between curiosity and caution. "If I might ask . . . ?"

"I shall go to Valcourt." The answer came so pat that it surprised him, and then he knew that the feeling of going home had been stirring within him through all the weeks since he had been washed ashore at the mouth of the Canche.

"A good choice," Pierre said, glancing sharply at him, and letting his words hang in the air for a moment. "If you are to hide, the farther from Boulogne you are tonight, the better." He seemed about to put a further question, yet hesitated as if the new thought were none of his business. "And to get to England?" He spoke as if to himself, so that the point could lie if there were some indiscretion in it.

Justice could tell that he was wondering whether this Englishman, who had come so unexpectedly out of the night at Boulogne, might have his own way of disappearing back into it. "No," he said, as though Pierre had said exactly what must be in his mind. "I have no means of escape. I had no idea where or when my journey would come to its end."

"There are always smugglers," Pierre said, in a way that reminded Justice of what Saint-Haouen had said about the covert Channel traffic that seemed so useful to both sides that they let it continue. Or perhaps because they could not stop it. "They come up to the beaches when the tides and moon are right, even into the estuaries, and they have friends in all the little valleys that lead to the sea."

As he spoke, Justice caught at the memory of something that Fred Scorcher had said in an unguarded moment when he had been telling him about Valcourt and the river running down to Montreuil. "Not a bad lot," Fred had grunted, as though it hurt him to speak well of a Frenchman. "Much about the same as the Rye people, really. Which is not surprising-like, considering the goings-on, there being fathers in common among 'em, no doubt."

And then he had added a phrase that sounded exactly like the words Pierre had just used. "Run the trade like a packet-service, they does," Fred had added, with a note of pride that showed he was speaking of some of his cousins and friends. "Which, considering its importance, is as how it should be."

At Valcourt, where he too might find old friends, there might be someone who could be trusted to take a message to the coast, or know a farmer who knew a man . . . "I shall find a way," he said confidently to Pierre. "I must."

As he spoke, Justice took out the oilskin-wrapped packet that Tissot had given him. Gently cracking the crust of blackened blood around it and lifting out two pieces of folded paper.

Then Pierre spoke. "May I know?" he asked softly.

"Naturally." Justice unfolded the first, written in Tissot's sprawling hand, reading aloud as he scanned it. "The other letter is a copy, but you may rely upon it. The copy was made in the château itself." Justice looked inquiringly at Pierre, who nodded down the hillside, and Justice squinted against the morning sun to follow the gesture. Then it came from behind those grey walls. But how had a letter from Boney's own headquarters come into the hands of Tissot?

The next sentence gave him his answer. It had been sold to him. Cash down. "You will see that the money you brought was well spent," Tissot had scribbled. "I have no time to write more, but I embrace you, my new friend, and my last friend, if you are reading this."

Justice passed the note to Pierre, knowing that he would share the memory of Tissot in his last moments of life reaching for these pieces of paper like a testament. Then he unfolded the second paper, covered in a large and chasing hand as though the writer were pressed by time or danger.

The superscription startled him so much that he broke off as he read it. "Bonaparte . . . Bonaparte to . . . Berthier 27 September."

Pierre raised a hand to his cheek in surprise. "To the Marshal?" He might well be astonished, Justice felt. A letter from Boney to the man who had been his Chief of Staff for the past six years, and was now his Minister of War? It was incredible.

"Paul knew many people," Pierre said firmly, vouching for the text that Justice held with such excitement that he could scarcely bring himself to go on reading it.

Only the night before, Tissot had hinted that there were enough men in Boulogne who would do anything for money— enough money: even men who were on Boney's own staff. And here was the proof of it. A letter from the Emperor himself, only five days old! What a legacy for Tissot to leave at the last, and without even a suggestion of what he had bought as he handed it over. He had been such a close man that Justice could understand how he had survived so long in the murderous world of plot and counter-plot.

A letter that would turn his mission into a triumph if he

could get it back to England . . . that would mean more to Lilly and St Vincent than the scuttling of a dozen ships in the channel of the Liane . . . Justice stopped, for his hopes were running away with him, and the paper was still unread.

"The expedition to Ireland is settled," he began.

"Ireland?" Pierre broke in, making sure that he had heard aright. "Then the Irishman . . ."

"O'Moira." Justice nodded. "It makes sense." He tapped the papers, and read on. "General Marmont is ready with 25,000 men. He will attempt to land in Ireland . . ."

"As a diversion?" It struck Justice that Pierre was very knowledgeable about such things, and it occurred to him that this man dressed like a common sailor might once have held a commission in the French navy.

"Perhaps," he said, as the thought passed, and he went back to the letter. "The Grand Army at Boulogne will embark at the same time to effect a landing in Kent."

"The same time?" Pierre echoed the phrase. "But when?"

"In three weeks," Justice said in an even voice, realising the implications of the final words scribbled on the page before him. "The navy holds out hope of being ready by October 22; the land forces will also be ready by that date."

On the road below, Justice could see a column of infantry filing over the bridge towards Boulogne, and the sight seemed an ominous confirmation of the message he had just been reading.

"Not three weeks any more," Pierre said with a surge of cheerfulness. "Not after last night. Your English ships will have scared them. And . . ." He gave a small laugh. "Our two French ships will have upset the Corsican's calendar enough to annoy him, eh, my friend?" He rolled over on an elbow and looked hard at Justice for a few seconds; and then he pulled himself to his feet, before the tone of his voice changed. "You must get that letter to England, at any cost." He gripped Justice's arm as he reached down and drew him to his feet. "Paul gave his life for it, and more men will yet die because of it."

As he spoke, Justice saw, in his mind's eye, a French line of battle drawing away to sea, all sails set, picking the moment to slip past the blockading fleet, deceiving Calder or Nelson by heading west, as if for the Caribbean, then doubling back to strike . . . at Ireland . . . at defenceless Cork . . . while Boney drew every regiment in England into the fight to save London.

"It will be different if we are ready for them," Justice said, almost as if he were home again, and speaking to Lilly. "We could take them at sea and ruin them for ever." He drove his fist into the other palm with a force that revealed his feelings.

"It may be so," Pierre said. "But that is not the question for you, Jean, or for me." He gave the grimace of a man who had seen his hopes dashed more than once. "We are not yet admirals, you and I. We can only do the duty that falls to us." He clapped Justice on the shoulder. "Come, we must be moving. I shall go a little way with you, through the woods, until you are safely across the road."

Justice thought of the horse he had left with the farmer, barely two miles away as the crow flew. He could not go back for it. Even if the farmer had no cause to love Bonaparte, he would find it odd if Justice returned in the guise of a battle-stained French officer. And he would certainly talk to a search party. For the same reason, the animal would be useless to Pierre. So let the farmer keep it, as payment for his sons.

"Lead on," he said to Pierre, searching across the valley for landmarks that might recall the hill-top tracks that would bring him to Valcourt, and realising as he walked that in his exhaustion his feet were moving to the beat of four words, like the taps of a drum. Bonaparte . . . Berthier . . . left right. . . . Ireland . . . October . . . left right . . . Bonaparte . . .

Pierre waited for the gap between two troops of cavalry before he hustled Justice over the highway and up another hillside to a line of beeches along the ridge. "You should stay until the light begins to fail," he said as Justice stretched his weary legs on a bank of golden leaves. "And now I will leave you, my dear Jean." He reached under his sailor's smock and then held out his open hand, where Tissot's fine watch lay glinting gold and crystal in the filtering sunlight.

"It is for you," he said, insisting as Justice shook his head. "Believe me. It was his last wish. What is it you call it in England? A keepsake, is it? To remind you." He stopped, searching for the words that would express his feelings. "To remind you that you will come back among us, where you truly belong, Jean de Valcourt!"

And with a smile and a wave he was gone through the trees like a shadow.

IT WAS a dozen miles over the rolling chalk-land and Justice had taken the risk of walking most of it before the autumn afternoon faded. He had slept, he was impatient, and he had decided that there was less risk of losing himself while he could see where he was going. He knew the farm folk were few and far between, and none of them were likely to go chasing after an officer in uniform; and though he once saw a group of men on horseback a mile or so away, there was no sign that the army was out scouring the woods like beaters trying to flush quail or partridge.

And once he was down in the valley, the footpaths along the tumbling Course came back to him as though he were walking in a dream. Here was a length of meadow where the whole family had once come for a local *fête champêtre* . . . There, running up the hill from the river, where the windows of Valcourt looked over the valley, was the cornfield where he and his cousin Luc had once spent the day setting their dogs to chase hares and rabbits . . . Luc . . . Justice had a curious sense that Luc had been somewhere in the wings all these weeks he had been in France . . . like a movement just caught at the edge of one's sight . . . and the feeling led him back to the last time he had been at Valcourt, and he and Luc had spent their time fishing and swimming in the pool above the water-mill at Recques.

The water-mill. The miller, too, teaching them how to tie a fly and cast it, and to lie quietly by the reeds and reach out to tickle a trout into the hand. Tisserand, that was it. René Tisserand. As the name of that patient and good-natured man came back to him, Justice saw again the small croft below the great wheel where a boy, or a man, might hide. Where local legend said that the head of the Valcourt family had once hidden, for the Valcourts had been Protestants at the time when Henry IV was trying to make up his mind whether to cultivate or crush them, and there had been times when a wise man kept his head down in order to keep it on his shoulders.

He knew it was safer, too, on the track that led down the left bank of the river, for the little villages were strung down the other side, and no one in the farms that verged on the track took any notice when a dog barked at a passing stranger. Justice came out of the trees, crossed the lower end of the pool on the top of the sluice-gate, steadied himself in the shadow of the wheel, and listened. For a moment he thought there was a man standing in the croft below, watching him, and in the same vein of fancy that had run through his thoughts as he came down the river, he thought it might be Luc.

But it was only a fancy. He paused, listened. There was no one there—not a sign of a guard or anything else to make him suspect a trap. Feeling his way down the steps, which were slippery with spray on the moss, he reached the dark space, and froze again. But it was nothing, only a low murmur of voices that seemed to come from somewhere within the mill, and he swung into the familiar opening with too much confidence, forgetting that the man was twice the boy and cracking his head on the stone lintel as a reminder.

If you turned and reached up, there was a loose stone above that lintel, and a space behind it, which would be the best place to put Tissot's precious packet until he found a way of getting it over to England—or of taking it himself; and there was something oddly comforting in the feel of his fingers closing round that damp piece of rock, and finding that it moved as freely as it did when he and Luc were boys playing Huguenots and Catholics.

The low light coming from the window was comforting, too, though the small panes were too thick and dim for him to see anything but the flame of a candle and the flicker of redder light from the wood fire which he had smelt on the night air as he came to the mill.

Go in boldly. He could almost hear Pierre's voice, prompting him. Give the impression that you have a right to be where you are. Especially if your middle name is Valcourt, and the graveyard by the little church at the cross-roads is full of stones carved with that name.

The latch lifted easily, with a firm click, and he was into the snug little room he remembered as if it were yesterday and the figure sitting at the table were the miller twisting wisps of horsehair round a barbed hook to tempt the gullible fish.

"MAY I SAY welcome home, M. Valcourt? Or do you prefer your English name? It might make the difference between the guillotine and the firing squad."

O'Moira spoke in English, rising from the table to come across to touch Justice, who was standing by the door amazed at the sight of a man he believed dead. "Ah. In French uniform. That rather settles the matter, doesn't it?" O'Moira was standing close, holding Justice by a button hooked between his fingers; his voice was hard beneath the banter, and Justice guessed that it would be foolish to strike at him and run for it. O'Moira would not be caught again as Tissot had caught him at Boulogne. There would surely be men within call, men who must have let him pass unchallenged as he walked into this trap like an innocent sleepwalker.

O'Moira was so confident, moreover, that he slipped his hand away from the button and turned his back on Justice while he returned to his seat. "I am glad my hurried journey from Boulogne was worth it," he said conversationally, as if they were merchants meeting in an inn. "My, er, colleague Saint-Haouen tried to persuade me that it would be a waste of time. When his men did not find your body on that brig, he was convinced that you would be picked up in the town, or dead in the water. Or even that you must have scooted with your countrymen."

The boyish word broke the spell of astonishment which had gripped Justice from the moment he set eyes on O'Moira. "And . . . Lovell?" he exclaimed.

"Dead." O'Moira was curt. "I would speak worse of him if he were living, for you owe your success to him. If he had not seized me while I was carrying a flag of truce . . ."

". . . and after your guards had fired a volley," Justice interjected in cold anger. "Let us at least have no fairy-tale excuses, Dr O'Moira."

"All the same, in fairness . . ." O'Moira blandly ignored the interruption. "We owe our lives to him."

We. Justice caught the point but said nothing. He guessed that it was the thought of Lucienne in the guard-boat alongside which had induced Lovell to warn O'Moira that the deck on which he was standing was about to be blown to splinters.

"It was a fair bargain," O'Moira said. "That we should leave him there to meet his end like a gentleman."

More than that, Justice thought, knowing that Lovell would have stayed to make sure that his work was done when O'Moira and the guards had hustled back to the boat in a rush to save their skins; to make sure that the *Fraternité* was really sinking, to light the fuse again if it had sputtered out. And then paid his debts in full.

"Amen," said Justice.

"As you say. And as I am afraid, Mr Justice, I shall be saying for you before the sun rises."

"You have threatened me before." Justice could not resist the reminder.

"So I have. So I have." O'Moira seemed to like putting a jovial tone to his macabre intentions. "But this time I am not threatening you, Mr Justice. You are wrong about that. You no longer have anything I want. Time was when you did, so that I had to flush you out of Verdun like a fox from a covert—and then chase you half across France, as it turned out." O'Moira spoke equably, confident that he was in control. "Now there are no friends at hand. There is no one living here but the old miller and the simpleton who helps him, and I have sent them for a sergeant's guard to take care of you."

"A sergeant's guard?"

"From the Château de Recques, of course. Known to you in the past, no doubt, as the home of your mother's cousins, the Comtes de Dixmude. Known to me as the headquarters of General Ney, whose gallantry as a cavalryman has made him a hero to every patriot."

Justice made a quick movement and O'Moira caught the scuff of his boot on the flagstone. "Until they arrive," he said, in a tone that bordered on a sardonic apology, "there is another constraint upon you." He lifted his hand, beckoning. "You may step forward, Lucienne."

There was a change in the shadows, where neither the guttering candle nor the flicker of the fire had reached, and the unmistakable snap of a pistol lock as the hammer was pulled back. Lucienne was still wearing the dark boat-cloak and Justice saw her face float out of the darkness like a mask.

She was holding a small pistol in her hand, and even as Justice took the shock of her appearance, he realised that she must have brought the weapon all the way from Verdun.

"So we three are met alone at last." O'Moira sat back like a man who had bet on the last race of the day and seen his horse come home at long odds. "I should say your game is over, Mr Justice, if game were the word for it. But it's a good deal more than that. You'll be a great loss to your country, I'll say that."

"As you may be to yours." Justice could not resist the gibe.

"As God will have it." A shadow seemed to pass over O'Moira's face, and Justice was suddenly aware that the man facing him was carrying the burden of great weariness. He had never thought before what the strain of the chase from Verdun must have cost the blind doctor. "But I think you will never see the Thames again, Mr Justice, while in a few weeks I shall be back beside the Liffey. Who knows, I might be sitting in some Englishman's chair in Dublin Castle. And if I am, I shall think of you sometimes, and think of you quite kindly. As Lucienne will, too, I'm sure."

Justice could not be sure from the way O'Moira spoke whether there was sarcasm or a peculiar hardness in his voice, and he noticed that Lucienne stood, impassive, not speaking a word, and the pistol stayed aimed at his chest.

"Come, Mr Justice, no questions? If I were in your position, I should be most curious."

"If you were in my position," Justice said coolly, "you would soon be standing your trial and you would be wise to keep silent." If O'Moira found pleasure in this cat-and-mouse game, it might temper his sense of triumph if he was reminded how matters would stand with him in England. Justice walked across to the fire. If he was soon to be dragged off to a damp cell, or stand shivering with the dawn chill as he faced a firing squad, he might as well enjoy a last chance to be warm.

"For instance?" He looked away from O'Moira to Lucienne as he spoke. Somewhere in all this talk there might be something to be turned to advantage.

"For instance." O'Moira's habit of echoing what one said could be very irritating. "How did we get away from that wretched warehouse in Boulogne? The smell reminded me of the Dublin wharves, you know. And how do we come to be here?"

"It's easy to guess." Justice thought the conversation was like the fanciful card-game that O'Moira had played with him two nights before. Was it only two nights? It seemed an age. "You would like me to say that your monkey played one of his clever tricks? Cutting you free with your scalpel as easily as I saw him peel an apple in Verdun? But I think not. If he had, he would have been here with you."

"Well done." O'Moira gave a brief smile. "He reasons well, Lucienne, as you said." Then there was bitterness in his voice. "The little fellow was dead. The man Pierre killed him, with his knife I think, for it was quick. I think he feared a monkey would be too clever for him, and run off with a message for the gendarmes." O'Moira never spoke for more than a sentence or two before the Irish irony came back to soften what he said.

"No. Not the monkey. It was Henri," Justice said. "It must have been. As soon as I saw you on the *Fraternité*, I remembered what you said about one of Tissot's less discreet men."

"And how right you were." O'Moira turned aside to speak again to Lucienne, as if he were on a stage. "Never underestimate an Englishman, Lucienne, m'dear," he said. "They're never so stupid as they appear to be—if Mr Justice will forgive the compliment."

Justice ignored the gibe, wondering why O'Moira always procrastinated, like an actor waiting for a man who had forgotten his cue. "As for Valcourt, well, that was easy, once you knew the family connection. If I was nowhere else, I would be here."

"Spoken like an Irishman," O'Moira said with a mocking laugh. "You and I would have got on famously if fate had been kinder to us both. It makes bonds between enemies as well as friends, you know."

"As Madame Lamotte can testify." Justice felt the words fling out unbidden, with a ring that told him they came truly from some mint of feeling. He could not imagine why he had said that—a need to probe and worry at a wound, a cry for help? "As she once told me, the truth of the heart is the same, whatever the language in which one tells it."

While he spoke, he knew his words had gone home as certainly as a huntsman knows when his bullet finds its mark. For a moment he thought she would lower the pistol and give him a chance to spring for it. But though the muzzle wavered, it still aimed straight at him.

"I think there are many kinds of truth." Her voice was soft, yet it came like a shock from the shadows. "Truths of lovers. Truths of loyalty. Truths that are ties of blood. And what I told you in the night was true, Jean, for if a woman loves a man she cannot lie to him, even if she may have to kill him." She broke off, her voice trembling with emotion, and he knew that if he survived, it would be months before her voice ceased to catch at his memory.

"She is right." Despite the fervor of Lucienne's words, O'Moira still seemed impassive, and when he spoke, he sounded more like an oracle than a conspirator who knew that three lives, and more, were at stake in the little room. "For in a queer sense we are children of the night. I am, I know, and so is Lucienne, and so are you, Mr Justice. We go our ways, as mysterious as owls and porcupines in the dark forest . . ." As O'Moira made these comparisons, Justice realised that he had chosen the nicknames for the royalist rebels and the secret agents who served Fouché and Bonaparte, and that the pause was designed to let him take the point. "But we are guided by our dreams, Mr Justice, as they are guided by their instincts. The dreams of lovers, as Lucienne said, the dreams of loyalty, the dream that we may in some way leave this sad world a little better than we found it when the Good Lord sent us sinners into it . . ."

He stopped in the middle of a sentence, and Justice thought that he had been distracted by the change of mood; and then he realised that O'Moira, even when he was speaking, had very sharp ears. For the doctor's voice had fallen quite away before Justice heard the sound of crunching boots on the gravel, and a rapped order.

The door was flung back with a crash, and a sergeant and two troopers came in at a rush. As they stopped, hands to sword-hilts, Justice caught sight of two figures in the darkness behind them. These would be the miller and his man; but Justice had no eyes for them.

Only for Lucienne. For at the moment that O'Moira had stopped speaking, she had lowered the pistol, and as Justice looked directly at her, he saw that the candle-light was glinting from the tears on her face.

He knew that he had only one, and that the briefest of chances. All the odds in the world must be against her allowing him to take it.

Standing with his back to the fire, and apparently in charge of the situation, for O'Moira was still seated at the table, Justice raised his hand and spoke in his most martial voice. "Sergeant! There is your prisoner."

O'Moira, unable to see what was happening, seemed stupefied. Lucienne moved a half-step towards Justice, and again their eyes met. Would she keep silent for the few moments he needed?

Justice pointed again at O'Moira. "Arrest him," he ordered the sergeant. "He is the English spy Fielding, for whom everyone in Boulogne is searching."

O'Moira was taken unaware as the guards gripped his shoulders, and he spluttered in the English he had been speaking only a moment before. "It's ridiculous . . . a mistake . . . preposterous."

Lucienne said nothing, letting him rant, and it seemed to Justice that it had been O'Moira's words as much as his own that had touched her.

"Hurry." Justice's rapped command had the desired effect on the sergeant, who had clearly been puzzled to find the three of them in the room, with the woman holding the pistol. He stepped over to O'Moira and dragged him to his feet, rummaging in his pockets while the Irishman stormed at him and struggled to break free from the grip of the troopers.

"Here's his papers, anyway," the sergeant cried, waving them, after such a cursory look at the documents that Justice wondered whether the man was able to read much of what was written on them. "Shut up, you son of a pig!" he shouted, striking O'Moira full on the chest. The more the Irishman babbled out accusations and counter-charges, the louder the three soldiers yelled obscenities.

"Ask him who he is, then!" O'Moira finally got out a phrase that was coherent enough to make the sergeant pause, and Justice realised that the balance could still tip against him.

He had only one more card to play. Standing in the doorway, watching the scene in the room with amazement, was a greyed and bent man of more than seventy harvests. Tisserand, the miller. But could he, in the shock of the moment, recall a Valcourt face from the past? Justice's resolve faltered as the old man shuffled into the room, leaning on the arm of the crouched and grimacing figure that must be his idiot assistant.

But his luck had held until now, and this last chance must be tried. He took up the candle and held it close to his face, and the room fell quiet as if a jury were coming back in an assize court.

"René." He spoke in a kindly voice, using the accent of the valley as he had learnt it from René as a boy. "Do you know who I am?"

The miller put up a faltering hand and ran it gently down Justice's face, and Justice was near enough to see his eyes glisten.

"Why," he said, in a tone of amazement. "It's young M. Luc come back again." He reached to the silver epaulette on the left side of Justice's coat, where the tassels glittered. "And a captain too, I'll be bound. M. Luc," he repeated, and the name sent the fool into a cackle of laughter which so affected Justice that he almost lost control of himself.

It was the oddest thing. The first time he had been mistaken for his cousin, it had nearly been the death of him. And now the miller was saving his life by making the same mistake Tissot had made.

"Ask the woman," O'Moira said, anxious and urgent. "Ask her. She knows that man."

"I do indeed," Lucienne said, speaking clearly as she crossed the room to stand by Justice. "I am his wife. Before God, and in my own heart, I am Captain Valcourt's wife."

This passionate declaration was enough for the sergeant. Unaware that O'Moira was blind, he gave the Irishman a push which sent him stumbling past the troopers and into Lucienne's outstretched hands, which saved him from a fall. While she steadied him, in the moment before the troopers came to grasp and pinion him, it seemed to Justice that she had whispered some word in his ear. For O'Moira's expression changed, and the cry of protest with which he had responded to the sergeant's show of violence died away on his lips.

"Take your prisoner, Sergeant, I shall follow," Justice said in a clipped voice which hid the turmoil of his own feelings, and his growing desire to bring the scene to an end before he was trapped by yet another change of fortune.

Justice looked for the last time at O'Moira, standing between the soldiers with his face as grim as a mask in the candlelight, wondering why the doctor had again reminded him of the old Greek king in a play; and why the memory had come back to him for a second time since yesterday.

"Agamemnon," he said, feeling that the name was one of the final pieces in the puzzle that Fielding had left him to solve.

O'Moira had turned to go, but he stopped and gave Justice an ironic smile. "It had occurred to me as well," he said. "But remember, when you come to quote your Aeschylus, that the play is not yet over."

As the footsteps of the escort died away, Justice held out his hand to Lucienne and smiled. "Thank you, with all my heart," he said, more moved than he had ever been as he realised that her action had been as spontaneous as his own.

Then he embraced the miller with both arms, feeling the warmth of the man's hug, and deciding that the less he knew of the night's events, the better it would be for him in the morning. "And you, old friend," he said, affected by so many boyhood memories that his words betrayed his sense of long-lost and innocent happiness.

But to the simpleton, now standing erect with a smug smile on his face, he said nothing, while he ran an eye over his torn and flour-spattered shirt and apron. "You almost overplayed the part, Fred," he said with delight, trying to puzzle what strange chain of circumstance had brought Scorcher to Recques. "We'll have you as Bottom the Weaver, next."

"*Agamemnon.*" Scorcher spoke severely, in the way he had of coming slantwise to an intimacy. "And what the devil has Lord Nelson's 64 got to do with it, begging your and the lady's pardon, sir?" And he put on such a look of mock-puzzlement that Lucienne joined in their laughter.

SCORCHER HAD HURRIED them from the mill, leading them so quickly down into the punt tied up by the wheel-race that there was no time for explanations; and Justice, pausing to hold Lucienne close to him before he handed her into the boat, almost forgot to go back for the packet he had hidden when he arrived at the mill.

He was careful, however, to say nothing about it as he joined

Scorcher and Lucienne with Marshal Berthier's letter safe in his pocket again. While there was no doubt that her help in deceiving the soldiers had been genuine, O'Moira's last cryptic remark made him cautious.

The play was certainly not over yet.

And though Scorcher was talking confidently enough as they paddled the flat-bottomed craft down the fast-running stream, Justice knew him well enough to be sure that he, too, was concealing some anxiety that was more than a desire to get clear of Recques before the troopers came back to find them gone.

He told his story quickly, in a series of sentences so short that Justice felt they could have been put in a run of signal flags. "Day afore you left, sir," he said after he told Justice how he had tired of waiting for news and as his leg healed had determined to find his way back to his captain's side. "My mind kept a-going back to that." Scorcher smiled and bobbed at Lucienne as he spoke, uncertain whether she knew enough English to follow him, and Justice was glad that he ran on and that she sat listening to him in silence. What had so recently happened between them could only be smothered by hasty questions and answers.

"You was a-talking about this place," Scorcher said, "an' your family . . . Came to me . . . said to Mrs Roundly, I said . . . if the Cap'n's in trouble, well, it stands to reason . . . he's run for there." Scorcher eased one knee, and Justice saw that there was pain in the old wound yet. Then he spoke in the embarrassed voice he always used when he mentioned his friends in Rye and their nocturnal affairs along the beaches of the Marsh. "It's not so difficult, you see, if you're in the right way of business, to come a-looking, if a man's got a mind to it."

Justice did see, and was more than glad that Scorcher had put his mind to it, but he knew that he would never be told the details if he asked. And no man who lived in a house along the Marsh would ever be so foolish or indelicate as to ask.

"At the mill, sir." Scorcher seemed to be searching for a marker of some kind on the bank, and Justice was amazed that he knew the run of the river so well. "Me and the old bloke, well, him being short-handed and agreeable, well . . . three weeks I been there, off 'n on . . . and nobody minds a simple fellow, sir . . . Over there, sir, if you please."

Justice swung the punt against the bank, cutting off

Scorcher's tale, knowing that the rest of it would have to wait upon some calmer time, and yet marvelling at the easy way in which Fred had insinuated himself into France, living almost in the shadow of Valcourt and only ten minutes from Ney's headquarters.

Scorcher gave the punt a push and sent it spinning down the stream, the gesture reminding Justice of the way he had abandoned the boat when he got away from Verdun; and of the part that such little boats had played in this mission since he had come ashore in the dinghy at Etaples.

Before Scorcher could say anything, Lucienne came up to Justice and stood facing him, holding both his hands. "Jean," she said very softly. "It is finished now."

They were the words he had so feared to hear her say that he had not spoken to her since that hasty embrace as they left the mill.

"Will you not come?" He put the question before he realised that he had no idea where Scorcher was taking him, or how he might carry Lucienne to England.

"No." Her voice was firm beyond argument. "You must travel fast. And I must stay."

"But you will suffer for it. When they discover that we have gone. And O'Moira . . ."

She put her finger to his lips to stop the flow of his pleading. "He will do nothing," she said with complete confidence. "He can do nothing, for he needs me." She held Justice close, hiding the tears that were soft on his cheek. "I love you. No matter what language we speak." She gave a little laugh at her remembrance of the phrase. "But I have my duty, and it lies with him."

"I don't understand," he said wonderingly, drawing back to see her face under the soft light from the sky.

"Agamemnon," she said, and her voice took him back to the schoolroom in Cranbrook and the text of the Greek play. *"He sacrificed his daughter for the winds that would carry his fleet to Troy."* She clung to Justice as she said a few words more. "He would have done that, you know. And yet I cannot leave him."

Agamemnon and Iphigenia. Of course. The last of all the pieces had been fitted into the puzzle. Lucienne was O'Moira's daughter, and she would always know her duty.

It was an obligation that Justice understood completely, and one that he knew was beyond all persuasion. For people like himself and Lucienne, divided in their birthright and in their feelings, it was the only star they could follow as they made their way through the dark forest. O'Moira had got as close to the truth as a poet. They were all creatures of the night, and when the dreams faded, there was nothing left but duty to sustain them and make life bearable.

Justice put his hands to Lucienne's face and kissed her lightly, as in a casual farewell between lovers who knew they would meet again on the morrow.

"*A bientôt*," he said, and then, like Pierre, she walked away into the trees and became nothing more than a shadow.

◄❧ 25 ❧►

THEY CROSSED the Canche above Montreuil, using a ferry that Scorcher found so easily that Justice knew they were following a route that had been carefully chosen for such a flight. Then south for a mile or two, on a track Justice could never have found for himself in the dark, moving fast, silently, saving their breath.

"Even a bad penny's better than none," Scorcher had said as they floated away from the mill, and Justice felt cheered by hearing this proverbial turn of humour again. Without Fred, he was sure, it would have been almost impossible to find his way back to England. Once he left the familiar paths around Recques and Valcourt, he would have floundered for an hour or so, and then dulling wits, hunger, and exhaustion would have driven him into the arms of one of Ney's patrols.

But Fred was making the dangerous journey seem as simple as a walk across the Marsh from Appledore to Camber; and as the thought of Camber beach came into his mind, he noticed that Fred had turned west towards the miles of sand that lay between the estuaries of the Canche and the Authie. Sandy beaches, like Camber, too long to guard easily, where a boat could come in and ride just beyond the breaking and shallowing waves at any state of the tide.

"It'll float you or sink you."

They had stopped at the edge of a cluster of farm buildings, and Fred had gone forward so confidently to make enquiries that Justice could tell he had been there before—more than once, he would venture; and he had come back with a bottle of Calvados, urging Justice to drink before they set off again. "Nother hour, or thereabouts," he said, and Justice heard relief in his voice as he looked back at the eastern sky, already beginning to pale. "Nother day, you'd 've been 'ere a week or more."

Justice had always realised, from the way men came and went in the Marsh villages, that some of the smugglers ran cobs and luggers and smacks across to France as regularly as the packet-boats used to run to Calais and Boulogne; and from Scorcher's manner, it struck him that this farm could very well be the other end of a run which began in St Mary's or a farmhouse behind Dymchurch, or even in Appledore. He gave Scorcher a hard stare. Even, yes, possibly even in Hook.

Scorcher looked at the sky again. "Best be off," he grunted, putting the half-empty bottle down beside the gate-post with the sureness of a man who was aware that someone would later pick it up, and then stomping on with only the slightest of limps to remind Justice of the wound that had crippled him for half a year.

Twice more they stopped, once at a farm again, once when they were coming to a road, and Scorcher spoke to a man who came out of a clump of trees. Justice hung back, knowing that this was yet another of the wraith-like people of the night who came and went through this part of France on their particular and peculiar affairs.

Then the air freshened, and the trees fell away, and they were sliding and scrambling in the coarse grass of the sand dunes.

Scorcher had started to pull him down before Justice, falling, saw the two figures, dark shapes against the sky, and caught the gleam of starlight on a short sword and what could well be a deadly two-headed axe.

But Scorcher whistled like a curlew, and had his answer, before the men were upon them.

"William Bonnycastle, sir," Scorcher said in a formal way as the largest of the men clapped him on the shoulder, "and not minding his name tonight, as how he's on the King's business—for once."

Justice was well aware that in this kind of company names were so rarely used that he was being specially honoured.

"A Rye man, sir," Bonnycastle added agreeably, "as was the friend of that there dead 'un as you called Albert."

The second man came forward, almost sheepishly, to take his hand.

"Joe Towton, from Peasemarsh." Scorcher was urging them through the dunes while he spoke. "And you'll mind Harry Truelock, too, nevvy to him as keeps the Woolpack." Justice looked round for the third man before Scorcher added, so definitely that he might just have come up off the beach, "he'll be keeping the boat, yonder." And then the four of them were staggering like tipsy men as they hurried through the deep loose sand.

He heard Scorcher say something to Bonnycastle in a low voice, and then the reply, coarse and hearty as between shipmates—"Not for another wet arse and no fish!"—told Justice that for his sake, and only on Scorcher's word, these men must have made several fruitless crossings to this rendezvous in the hope that one night Fred would bring him staggering out of the darkness.

It was a small cob-boat they had come over in, with sturdy curving strakes, a good sea-boat, with a great lug-sail that could slant it well across the westerlies that streamed regularly up the English Channel.

"Cap'n! Cap'n!" The man from Peasemarsh was pulling at his sleeve, and in the wind he caught a clink of harness and the muffled drumming of hooves on hardened sand.

They were back at the risky and familiar game that he and Scorcher had played so often on the lonely beaches of Brittany—a group of figures waiting by a boat, the surf running cold up the thigh, the squat shape of a boat heaving and twisting in the hands of a man holding the stern to keep it head on to the waves.

Habit sent Justice's hand searching for a pistol at his belt, and Bonnycastle caught the movement, touching his arm. "There's no shooting, Cap'n," he said. "Runners we are, runners we stay, and there's livings to be made after this."

In their trade, Justice saw in a flash, there had to be understandings, and money changing hands, or their profitable traffic would be ruined in a matter of weeks: and a casual killing, in fright or frenzy, could easily be the end of them.

They were smart about times and tides, too, never wanting to be caught by daylight on the wrong shore, and now they were splashing into the water ahead of Justice, anxious to be away, swinging up into their boat and holding out a hand to pull him panting over the stern.

"Scorcher?" he gasped, sensing that Fred was not with them, suddenly remembering the night last autumn when he had gone back for him—to find Fred lying with his leg sliced, to cut down the man standing over him, to turn and find a pike ripping at his own chest, to cut down a second man and somehow drag Fred back to the cutter . . . It was a set of memories that were suddenly compellingly real.

"Half a mo', sir." Truelock spoke as he might to an impatient child. "Got to settle the account, Fred 'as. 'Tis usual, like, the Frenchies being strong for ready money."

Justice peered at the knot of horsemen by the sea's edge, and saw them wheel away, Scorcher coming on hastily through the white froth on the shallows.

The horsemen had gone no more than thirty yards when one of them looked out to the boat and pulled his horse round to ride at Scorcher. Impulsively, without thinking that there might be a choice between saving Scorcher and carrying Tissot's packet to England, Justice slipped over the side, forcing his way through the water towards his man.

The horseman already had Scorcher by the collar as Justice reached him, coming up on the other side, catching at a boot, clawing up his leg to get a purchase. Justice heard the man curse, felt the change in weight as he let Scorcher go and swung in the saddle, drawing his sabre, so that Justice could see the blade like a shaft of silver against the sky. With a desperate tug he pulled the cavalryman sideways, and over him, so that the blade of the sabre spun out wide, and the hilt came down hard on the side of his head as the dragoon's falling body crushed him into the water.

Justice felt the horse tear the man free, one foot still tangled in a stirrup, and as he sprawled breathless and uncaring in the hissing water, he knew that Scorcher had him by the arm . . .

was reaching for a hold . . . was shouting . . . and then it was dark . . . the flashes came again as Keith's gunfire . . . and the pounding . . . the hammering in the darkness.

It was all over at last.

ADMIRAL KEITH sat in the great stern cabin of the *Monarch*, sifting through the neatly-engrossed papers spread before him on the table and feeling depressed at the tale they told of bravery and failure.

One thing was certain. The attack had been beaten off. He had sent in a dozen fire-ships, and there was really nothing to show for the effort.

He picked up a sheet. From Captain Edmonds, whose men had taken in the fire-ship *Devonshire*—blown up without any visible effect.

And another. From Captain Macleod, who had seen the *Amity* explode, and was regretfully unable to report any result.

Lieutenant Tucker, who had been in charge of one of the infernal machines provided by that damned American fellow, had the honour . . . Carcasses! Catamarans! Torpedoes! Whatever he called them, they were no way to wage war—cowardly, and useless into the bargain. Keith looked at Tucker's report again, and threw it down in irritation. So Tucker had the honour to report that the blasted object had been in a good position when it blew up! But what good, or harm, had it done?

The only compensation Keith could find in the reports was the fact that the men who had taken the fire-ships and catamarans into Boulogne had all come off without casualties. But even that news, when it reached some of the die-hards at the Admiralty, could be taken to mean that his men had not pressed the attack with sufficient purpose to come close to the enemy. Casualties sometimes counted.

It was a thankless task trying to get at the flotilla, as he told Secretary Marsden and Lord Barham again and again. There was only one thing his squadron could do.

Act as a stopper in the bottle. As long as the wind held, and he could keep his ships on station.

Keith swept the papers to one side and began to read over his own report for the last time before he sealed it ready for despatch. As soon as they came into the Downs and he could get a boat ashore, a courier would be riding hard for Whitehall.

Hm. He had put a good face on it. Stressed the difficulties. Hm. Praise all round. Heavy firing. Hm. A cautious word about the newfangled devices, because the American was said to have the ear of Mr Pitt himself. Then the nub of it: "No very extensive injury seems to have been sustained." True enough. And then the puzzling fact, which none of the reports before him had explained. "It is evident that there has been considerable confusion and that two of the brigs and several of the smaller craft appear to be missing." He shrugged his shoulders. Perhaps a couple of those infernal devices had got through, after all. Perhaps this, perhaps that. It was all supposing. Not like a straight sea-fight where you could see what you hit and watch it go down.

He had just folded and sealed the paper when there was a knock on the door and a young lieutenant was shown in. "From *Harpy,* sir. Captain Haywood's compliments." He was all freshness and uncertainty in the Admiral's presence.

"Well?" Keith was not in the mood to be troubled by the routine business of an 18-gun sloop.

"We picked up a boat off the French coast, sir." The lieutenant found it hard to get his story out, with his Lordship glaring at him.

"Yes, man. Go on. Go on."

"Four smugglers, sir, and a French captain. Been knocked cold, Captain Haywood says."

"Press 'em then," Keith said coldly. "Even if they carry protections. They're all forgeries, anyway."

"But the captain, sir . . ."

"Send him to the surgeon, if he's still breathing. Or put him in irons. I don't care. That's Captain Haywood's affair."

"Sir." The lieutenant was uneasy.

"*Sir.*" The growl showed that Keith did not like to be challenged by his subordinates, especially one so junior as this pink-faced young man.

"Sir, Captain Haywood . . ." the lieutenant began again, gabbling on before Keith could heckle him again. "Captain Haywood says the Frenchman was carrying a letter . . ." He dared to hold out a restraining hand as Keith began to rise wrathfully from his chair. "A letter from Boney, er, from Bonaparte, sir, to Berthier . . ."

"Boney? Berthier? Where is it? What is it?" Keith dropped back into his seat, thrusting out his hand impatiently.

"One of the smugglers is outside with it, sir. Says he's been told to give it to no one but you, sir. Captain's orders, he says."

"Captain's orders!" Keith's anger blazed again.

"Yes, sir. His captain, he says. A Captain Justice . . ."

HISTORICAL NOTE

THERE WAS ONCE a British naval officer named Thomas Wall Justice who served on *H.M.S. Bellerophon* and played a part in the capture of Napoleon in 1815. John Valcourt Justice, of Appledore in Kent, is an entirely fictional cousin of that honourable and gallant gentleman, and claims an equally fictional relationship—on his mother's side—with the Comtes de Dixmude. Dr O'Moira is also a figure of fiction, as are Lucienne Lamotte, Major Lovell, Caroline Chiltington, Montague Moon, Edward Holland, Paul Tissot, and Fred Scorcher.

But some of those who appear in this story really lived and played much the same parts as described in these pages. The name of George Lilly, for instance, only thinly disguises the real and remarkable George Rose, the friend and backer of William Pitt. And Captain Saint-Haouen, Wirion, and other French officers, like Admiral Lord Keith, actually held the posts in which the imaginary Captain Justice knew them.

The settings and situations of this story are also based on the truth, bizarre though it sometimes seems.

Appledore in Kent may be found as easily on the map as the village of Recques, just north of Montreuil, and the water-mill stands by the clear waters of the river Course.

Lloyd's of London was not only the centre of marine insurance. It was also a prime source of marine and other intelligence, and Lloyd's underwriters gave great assistance to the Admiralty. The banking system, moreover, maintained its links across warring frontiers and was used to pay funds for confidential agents, for bribes and other clandestine purposes. Smugglers played a considerable role in carrying news, newspapers, secret messages, and secret agents between the English and French coasts. In all cases, simple codes were used, and a later attempt to abduct Napoleon was indeed reported in the imagery of wine shipments.

Secret agents of various kinds and qualities were employed by governments on both sides of the Channel, by individual ministers, particular commanders, and curious agencies which resemble those which proliferated in the field of special operations during the Second World War. The royalist conspiracy for which Georges Cadoudal was executed was helped by Captain John Wright of the Royal Navy, whose covert activities were not unlike those of Captain John Justice, and who died mysteriously in the Temple prison in Paris soon after Admiral Keith's attack on Boulogne. The Irish rebels and patriots, for whom Dr O'Moira speaks in this story, were deeply involved in successive French invasion plans, and many of them paid for their support in prison cells and on the gallows.

There was a great storm at Boulogne on the 19th and 20th of July, when Napoleon was reviewing his flotilla, and on that occasion he almost shared the fate of the two hundred men who were drowned and washed ashore on the beaches between Boulogne and Etaples a day or so before Captain Justice drifted into the estuary of the river Canche.

The story of the British prisoners at Verdun is based upon historical records of the decade. In this French fortress town, they tried to re-create the pleasure-seeking world of an English watering-place such as Leamington or Tunbridge Wells. The references to the punishment fortress at Bitche show why it may fairly be described as the Colditz of the Napoleonic Wars.

In the summer of 1804, when invasion seemed probable, the Admiralty was supporting conventional—and some very un-conventional—means of attacking Bonaparte's huge collection of vessels in the Channel ports; fire-ships, stone-ships, and Robert Fulton's explosive inventions were all deployed against Boulogne. Admiral Keith did attack Boulogne on the night of October 2, 1804, and though this assault seemed at the time to be a failure, the *Naval Chronicle* said afterwards that it marked the turning of the tide in the struggle against Napoleon.

Admiral Keith's report on the Boulogne raid is accurately quoted, and so is the letter which Napoleon wrote to Marshal Berthier on September 27, 1804. According to the Keith Papers, Napoleon went ahead with his plan to invade Ireland and

Kent simultaneously, "until he found that copies had either been lost or intercepted in October," and from the moment of that discovery all idea of the invasion of England was abandoned. Some unknown counterpart of Captain John Justice had obviously done his duty well.